AGENDAS

AGENDAS

AN AUGLAND NOVEL

■ BOOK III ■

ERIN CARROUGHER

Inspira

Other Books by Erin Carrougher

Augland

UnSuited

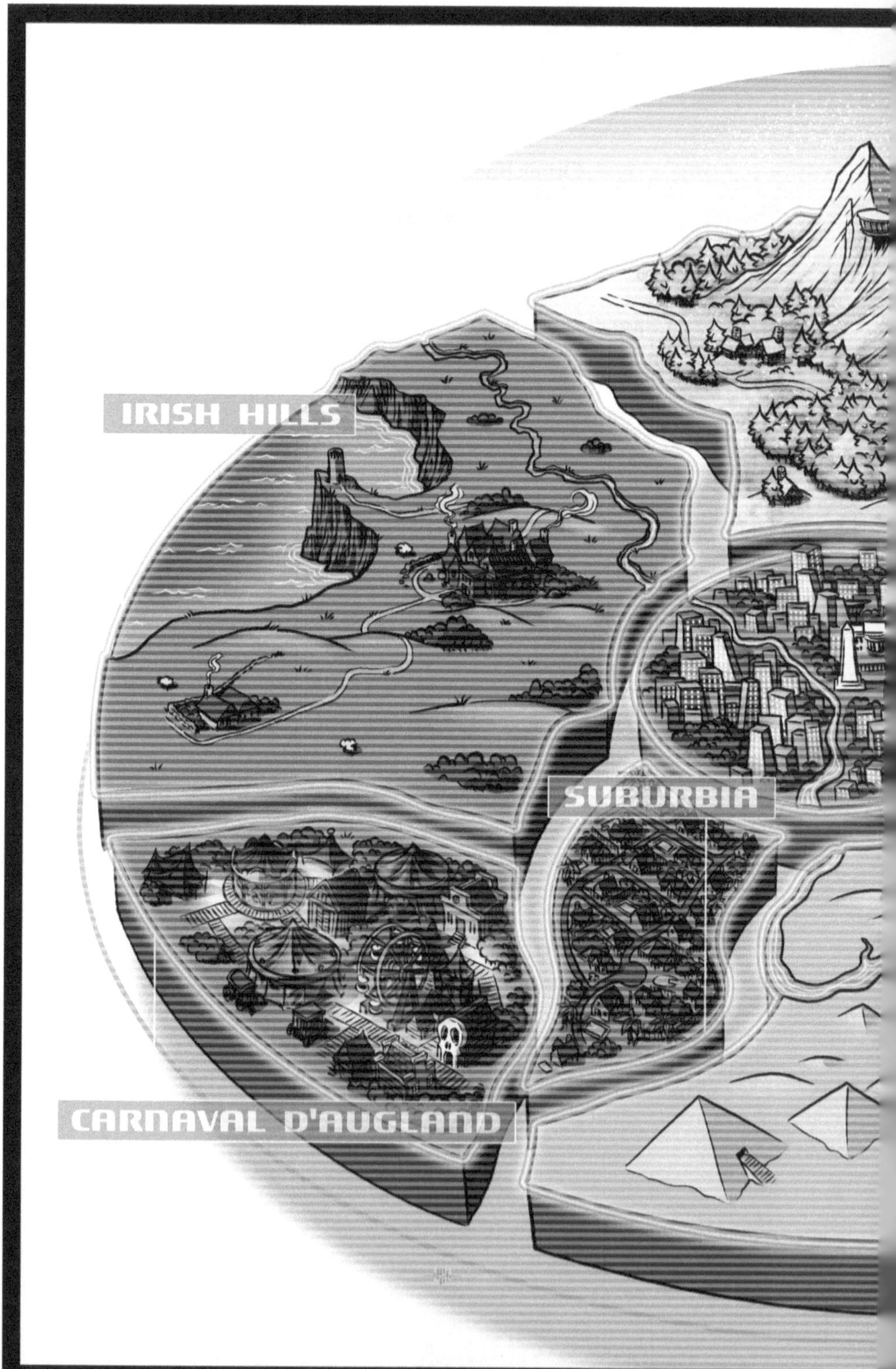

IRISH HILLS
SUBURBIA
CARNAVAL D'AUGLAND

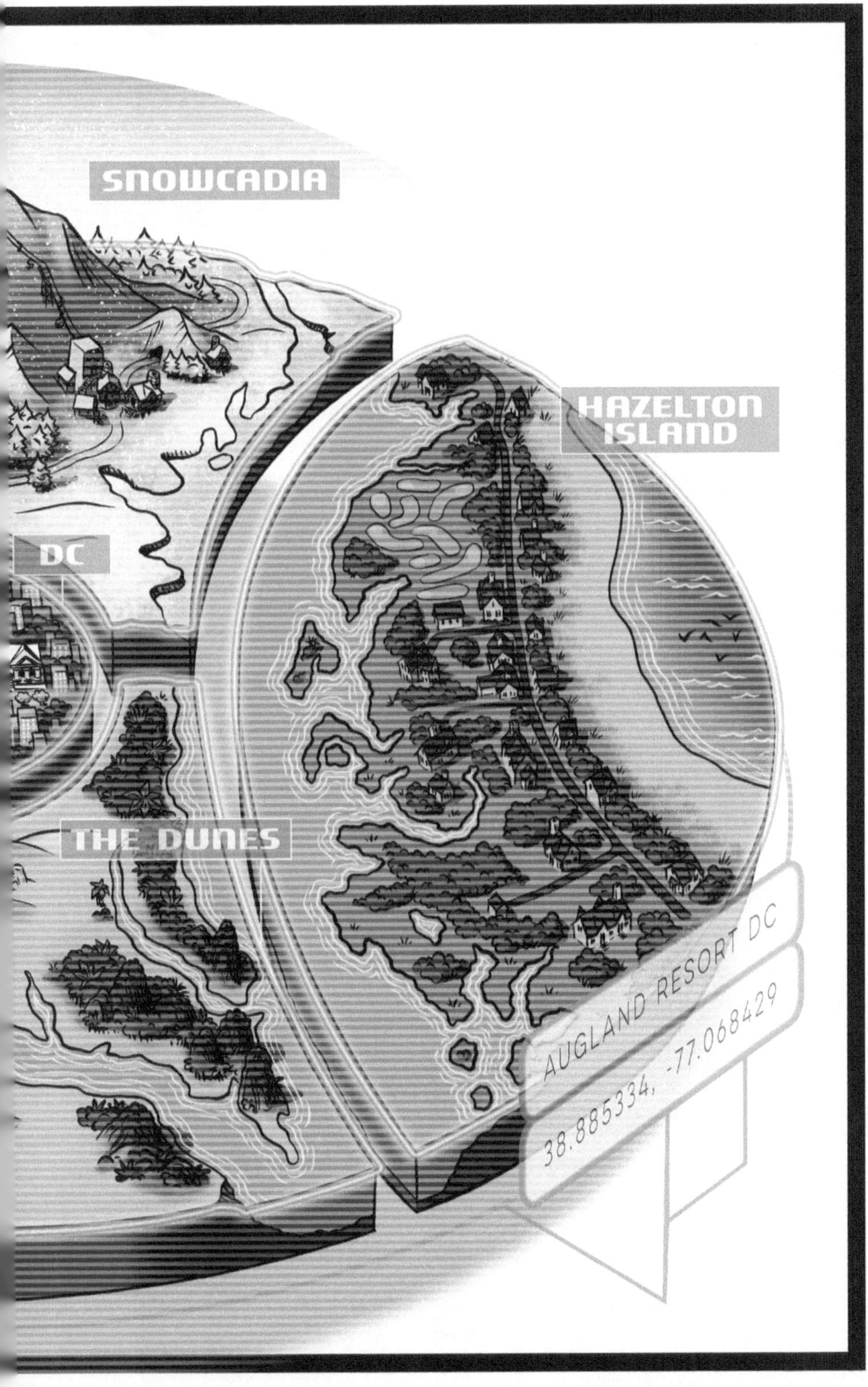

SNOWCADIA
HAZELTON ISLAND
DC
THE DUNES
AUGLAND RESORT DC
38.885334, -77.068429

PROLOGUE

A Memo from Artificial Existence Center

To Augland Employees & Management Staff:

The AEC has gained knowledge of an active worker unrest in Augland locations. Please know the AEC takes the demands seriously and cares immensely for the conditions of those who support our company. We are working with senators and appointed officials to closely monitor the situation and address these allegations of misconduct appropriately.

The AEC does not accept any violence or rebellion that results in physical harm of AEC property and will take appropriate action against those who incite, discuss, or demand any harm to property, customers, or employees of Augland or NeuroEnergy. Anyone harboring, in discussions with, or having knowledge of such actions will be held accountable to the company policies and given proper reprimand.

Augland, NeuroEnergy, and the AEC appreciate your understanding and cooperation during these truly troubling times.

Beaugard Hollenberg
AEC President

"Because our customers deserve to live a great life . . ."

CHAPTER 1

Ashton

OLYMPIC MOUNTAINS

Her muscles burned with the prickling heat of overuse. Breathless and exhausted, Ashton made it to the top of the peak, where a burst of cold wind scorched her freckled face with an icy burn. Spring flowers were just beginning to bloom and, in the distance, expanded into majestic blues painted with the jagged lines of snow draping across the Olympic Mountains. This view was more beautiful than the manufactured world of Augland 54 could ever be. It was real.

Wolfe arrived at the vista a few moments later, cheeks red from the Pacific Northwest mountains' chill.

"May need to get you out more. You're getting slow," Ashton quipped, hearing Wolfe approach from behind her. Wolfe was not, for as long as she had known him, slow. He could run circles around her if he tried.

"Just making sure you and your two left feet don't tumble down the cliffside; here and ready to be your knight in shining armor whenever," Wolfe volleyed, laughing as he stepped beside her. It was light-hearted, but Ashton knew the truth. He had saved her from certain death during the Predator's Biome rebellion in Augland 54 and never let her forget it. The rose-tinted three-inch scar on her leg was a constant reminder of what she had endured.

After escaping Augland a second time, they had returned to Ashton's beachfront home on Hood Canal, even though the Colony had moved farther north to Hamma Hamma Bay. Georgina, CEO of

Pacific Northwest NeuroEnergy, had worked out a deal with the AEC stipulating Augland 54 security wouldn't leave the confines of its walls until there was a resolution between Augland and NeuroEnergy. In turn, Warren imposed the same restrictions on Georgina after the Augland workers had escaped to her NeuroEnergy compound—which the AEC approved. So, they were all safe—for now.

Not to say it was easy the first few months outside of Augland and NeuroEnergy. Wolfe had had to relearn how to live outside the typical luxuries he was afforded in the Executive Suites of Augland 54. But it didn't take long for him to find his way. He was chopping wood, building monstrous fires, and hunting wild game in no time. Coffee was a harder commodity to part with.

Wolfe's adjustment had taken Ashton's mind off the past six months. Jagatha's death wasn't easy to process, but she had learned to cope with it—at least for the most part. Ashton pulled her focus back to Wolfe as he came up beside her.

"Two left feet?" Ashton queried, playfully hitting him, but Wolfe was too quick and grabbed her wrist before it made contact and tugged her into his embrace.

Before long, he let go and casually draped his arm around her shoulders, finally taking in the breathtaking view of the ridges that painted across their perched view. "Beautiful," was all Wolfe could say as he stared into the distance and then back at Ashton as the sun enveloped her entire face.

"Not so bad yourself."

Wolfe turned and faced Ashton, dramatically stunned. "Is that you, giving *me* a compliment? I swear, for a moment there I thought our relationship had turned to strictly playful insults."

Ashton rolled her eyes and smiled. Their relationship had morphed into something beautiful and much deeper since leaving Augland. In the past, Ashton had been forced to be docile and pliable. She had learned that shutting off her emotions and turning on her manners was better for customers, a coping mechanism that had been reinforced by Augland

Center, which had taught her how to behave since she was young. Still, leaving Augland hadn't given her freedom—but it *had* let her live and feel true happiness for the first time. As she and Wolfe built a life on Hood Canal, it was easier to slip into an authentic version of herself.

"Well, someone needs to check that ego of yours every once in a while, especially when Joao's not around."

"Joao knows that I excel in most everything logical or physical—anything, really."

"There it is, that ego that grows even with my—what did you say—playful insults?"

"Not ego if it's true." Wolfe shrugged confidently.

"I'll be sure to ask Joao his thoughts on that later today," Ashton said. Wolfe smiled wickedly.

Wolfe's bright eyes glistened, and Ashton's cheeks flushed as she turned from him and toward their mountaintop view. Her brown, curly hair swirled left, then right as the wind raced around them. The world was simpler here. Nature was where she found peace—most of the time. In the back of her mind, she knew this peace was fleeting. The violent Augland world would soon come to haunt their serenity.

Occasionally and without provocation, the sharp, unwanted twinge of anxiety bubbled inside her like a black cloud poisoning their world, and her compulsive thoughts took hold. *The trial.* It was the fear of loss but also excitement at the possibility of finally seeing Warren pay for what he had done. It was around every corner: the thoughts, the hope, the revolution. It was that all-consuming anger that disturbed her perspective, and, while she wouldn't admit it to herself, distanced her from Wolfe and his steadiness. She wanted Warren to pay for all he had taken.

At first, it was easy to put the trial and ensuing repercussions out of her mind because they had time. But as the countdown of months, days, and minutes steadily marched by, relentlessly moving toward her like the rising high tide of Hood Canal, she wanted revenge now more than ever. Warren needed to pay.

Too much had happened to believe any peace and solitude could be possible. The sight of Augland 54's dome behind them forced a certain reality of what lay ahead. The trial would take place in one week. Seven days left before Ashton, Wolfe, Joao, Bez, Hunter, and Georgina would travel to Augland 1's DC, the first Augland, to convince the Artificial Existence Center—the parent company to both Augland and NeuroEnergy—of Georgina's innocence and Warren's guilt.

Only weeks after Ashton and Wolfe escaped Augland 54 and exposed Warren's plan to take over NeuroEnergy through his recreation of his son in Suit form to regain his title of CEO, Warren had begun to redirect his efforts from placating the AEC officials to his trial strategy. He had successfully managed to accuse Georgina, along with Ashton, of orchestrating an insurrection against Augland 54 and all of the AEC. Warren also managed to spread propaganda that all Auglands would soon be in danger if Georgina were not stopped. That was according to Hunter, who now worked alongside Rye at the Pacific Northwest NeuroEnergy Headquarters.

"We should get back to camp and pack up. I don't want to ride to Hamma Bay in the dark." Wolfe interrupted Ashton's entranced moment as the sun hovered over the mountain range. She took her eyes away from the view and transferred them to the man she had spent the last six months with. He had let his beard grow. It hung just above the ridge of his collarbone, but he had asked Ashton to cut his hair to its typical length: shorter on the side and longer on top. His crystal-blue eyes gleamed brightly as the sun shadowed across his rough face. She smiled. "What?" he asked, giving her a flirtatious half-grin.

She turned her head to face the dark green pastures that led to a cliff, following Wolfe as he walked up to its edge and stared down below, then turned to her. It triggered a moment of *déjà vu.* The next second was a flash, not more than a moment in her past, of when she had seen Wolfe standing on Augland 54's Executive balcony right before he let go of Jagatha's tiny frame and the young girl fell to her death. She knew now it wasn't really Wolfe, that it was his father impersonating him, and that the man who stood before her was nothing like his father, CEO Warren.

Still, the flashback was hard to shake. When they surfaced, these thoughts gut-punched her lungs until she forced her body to take a slow, deep breath. It wasn't often she relived the last moments of her friends' lives but when they surfaced, she couldn't let them go. The vision of Jagatha's body dropping and her bold, golden eyes searching for Ashton to save her played in her mind as if on an endless video loop. Then there were the moments holding Sheva's lifeless body as her blood pooled around them, ultimately staining her hands. She feared that she would lose again, another loved one who would be lost, killed, mangled, or debilitated. She feared this because those thoughts could swiftly change to reality. Even theorizing the most plausible scenario for the Augland versus NeuroEnergy trial fueled her anger and fear. She had to escape these terrorizing memories. If she didn't, the resentment alone would destroy her.

"Ashton?" Wolfe's smile faded as he studied her. She blinked away the thoughts.

"Race you back to camp?" Ashton dared.

She turned a cheek to Wolfe, who looked down the rocky path they had hiked up to the Olympic peak. Wolfe shook his head, undoubtedly moments away from cautioning her against it—but it was too late. Ashton had already started to soar, letting the world dissolve around her, and all she could hear was Wolfe's faint voice in the distance, "Whoa, slow down! Ashton!"

It didn't matter; she felt the rush of endorphins, and her eyes went wide with the uncertainty of her next step. The trails had long been overgrown so she darted between trees and bushes on the mountain's edge. The exhilaration temporarily masked the anger she suffered. She was learning something about herself, but she was not certain what it was. Whatever it was, it was exhilarating and, at times, addictive.

Ashton's lungs stretched thin, filling with air as she tumbled down the mountainside and into the dense forest of the unyielding and uneven terrain. The thick Douglas fir branches whipped at her skin, and her feet danced left and right, distancing her from her dark thoughts and the sharp rocks scattered across the ground. Wolfe was close behind her now. She could feel him approaching her heels.

"Whoa!" Wolfe caught Ashton's arm and she nearly tumbled as their feet skidded across the rocky ground. It was good he had stopped her because she hadn't seen the ledge of the cliff, mere feet ahead of her. The drop was at least twenty feet to the bottom. Her eyes grew wide as he caught her, and she stared down the jagged ledge. The ground below her was bare of any trees—only mismatched and splintered boulders.

Ashton breathed out an astonished laugh. Wolfe looked at her, stunned, as they both took in the dangerous sight below. "Ash, what were you thinking?"

"What?" She laughed, catching her breath. "I'm fine, and I would have stopped before going over."

Wolfe slowed his breathing as well, shaking his head. "What is it with you and this . . ." Wolfe sighed before the words found their way: ". . . *impulsive* thing?"

"What are you talking—"

Wolfe sighed, "Don't do that. You know what I'm talking about." Ashton's brow furrowed. "These last few months and these sprees of recklessness . . ." Silence took hold for the moment as Ashton walked down the trail away from him and hid her rolling eyes. He followed her. "Diving too deep underwater while spearfishing . . ." Wolfe pressed his accusation further, and Ashton could hear his insinuation.

"I was following the fish!" she lied.

"Sneaking up on that black bear . . ."

"He didn't even see me! And I was just getting a closer look." Wolfe's eyes narrowed, seeing through her barely believable defense. Ashton wasn't able to turn and look at him now, the lies rolling off her tongue too effortlessly in an attempt to avoid the confrontation. It was hard to deny when he spelled it out like he had—and admitting that

Wolfe may have been right about the correlation between her recklessness and coping with the death of her loved ones was not something she was ready, or wanting, to discuss.

"And the boat. You raced to a speed of almost eighty on your first time driving it. Why the thrill-seeking?"

Ashton ignored the question and felt his concern turning to frustration. He was right: she had been more daring recently—it was the only way she knew how to cope with the loss. Running down the face of the mountain had been reckless, too. *No, he's being too protective. He doesn't understand what newfound freedom means to me after an entire life in Augland's prison.*

Ashton started to walk away faster, frustrated and disinterested in the conversation Wolfe was determined to have.

"Ashton, you could have died. I don't want to have to babysit you all the time, but you're risking a lot, and I'm worried you—" Wolfe's words were out before he could filter them. "Sorry—I didn't mean it like that."

"*Babysit?*" She stopped and whipped around and nearly ran into Wolfe as he followed close behind her. "*Babysit* me . . ." Ashton's fuming words pierced through the subtle whistling between trees. Her fuse was too short to take Wolfe's criticism. Wolfe recoiled as Ashton's gaze narrowed.

"I'm sorry," he retracted, seeing that he had taken things too far.

"You know, I'm not a charity case, and I certainly don't need to be babysat like some attention-seeking toddler." She crossed her arms in defiance.

"I know that; it was a bad choice of words . . . it's just I don't think you're dealing with your feelings in the right way. Yes, I don't want to sit here worrying about you, but it's those sorts of things that make me scared that when we go in front of Augland at trial . . . you'll do something—"

"So help me, if I'm so irrational." Ashton huffed out her angry breath and turned away from him before she, in turn, said something she would regret. Wolfe continued, carefully selecting his words carefully—which, during arguments had become an annoying norm. It was that or he kept things from her, like what he had planned when they confronted his father. She had asked numerous times, and he had consistently avoided answering her. He didn't trust her; that was clear.

Ashton's anger boiled at the thought. Wolfe didn't get to lecture her on being closed off to her feelings when he kept his own cards so close to his chest. If he wanted an ally in this Augland endeavor, he would need to start treating her as his partner, and not a problem to be fixed.

"We should go. Bez will be upset if we're late."

"Ash, wait," Wolfe pressed.

"What do you want, Wolfe, when we get to Augland 1, or DC, or whatever, when the trial happens, and Warren is found guilty? What is it you'll do?" Ashton questioned. Every time they spoke of the upcoming trial events it ended before it began. Joao and Wolfe had their secrets, their plans, and kept Ashton out of it—which was infuriating. When she asked, he said it was "safer" that they wait to discuss the details and what their plan of attack would be. That if they were imprisoned or interrogated in Augland, that fewer people who knew about any secret plans of attacks or takeover, the better.

"Where did this come from? We weren't even talking about the trial."

"Oh, yes, about me. About your babysitting. I'm not a child. I can handle myself, and I can handle what's going to happen at the trial. I deserve to know what we are planning so I can help! Because I *can* help. I've been around Suits my whole life, Wolfe, and I'm not some fragile thing that can't hold my own when it comes to dealing with powerful people like Warren." Ashton's eyes narrowed as Wolfe shifted.

Wolfe was taken off guard, but his eyes didn't waver from Ashton's. "I know you can and I've told you. We are working on creating an army. If we can build a big enough one then maybe once the trials are done, we can overtake Augland 54. Anything further, if you or Bez were to be interrogated, could put you and our mission in danger. Joao and I are trained to deal with this sort of thing . . . this is just something you'll have to trust me on."

"And you think the other Augland CEOs will help us?" Ashton highly doubted that plausibility. She didn't trust any Augland.

"We will make them see, Ash. Give them a chance to see reason."

"Then what? What happens to the UnSuited? The workers? Does Warren live? Die?"

"I don't know yet! Look, once the trial is done, we will have more information. We could create a coup to overtake them and put someone else in Warren's place. If we go up against Warren now? We will lose, Ash. They have weapons, indestructible Suits, power. Things NeuroEnergy and Colonies don't have yet. We have to win the trials to start gaining favor."

"So that's it. Your *master* plan that you only talk to Joao about is to go to Augland 1 and make friends? So that you can build an army and put someone else in power? That could take decades." Wolfe's plan shouldn't have been a surprise. He had once tried to overtake his father to run Augland 54 himself, but that didn't happen because Warren had outsmarted him. Delays meant death. Wolfe had told her that he agreed with her conclusions, but he felt the timing needed to be strategic, requiring careful planning and execution.

Wolfe and Ashton struggled to reconcile their approaches and it resulted in conflict; the road to a resolution to this particular argument was going to be difficult.

"If we move on Augland 54 today, we will have the rest of the AEC to answer to, and no one, not the Colonies or workers, will survive that kind of war . . ." Wolfe started.

Reluctantly, Ashton had to concede that he was right: they didn't have the necessary resources at the moment to win that kind of war. But while they took time to surreptitiously build up their forces, Ashton knew countless Augland workers would be suffering within the parks. No matter which strategy they employed, people would get hurt.

Ashton tuned back in as Wolfe was saying, "And we will need to be patient, and strategic . . . *You'll* have to be patient and I promise, you'll get the workers out and we will change things for them, for all of us. So our takeover of Augland can happen when we are ready."

Ashton stared at him. Wolfe's voice quieted. It was the underlying message that provoked her next. He wasn't talking about the UnSuited or NeuroEnergy being patient for revenge; he was telling *her* to be patient.

"Ash." Wolfe reached for her, but she stepped away. Ashton presumed Wolfe thought they had time to be patient, but the people in Augland 54 didn't have time to wait. She loved Wolfe, and they had come so far in their relationship, but what divided their unity was what each wanted in the immediate future. Wolfe wanted to restore order in Augland 54 while Ashton wanted vengeance.

"You think I'll do something impulsive because what? Am I angry? Yes. All I think about is making Warren pay. All I want is for Augland to blow up into a million pieces. And you know what? When we get to the trial, if given the chance, I will do whatever it takes, Wolfe. But I'm not waiting for a decade to make him pay for everything he has done. Everything he's taken from me. From us! And if something happens to me in the meantime, I'm fine with it!"

"I'm not!" Wolfe snapped, unable to contain his feelings any longer.

Ashton's eyes widened at his outburst. She didn't fear death anymore, but Wolfe's fear was not just of failing to overtake his father—it was of losing her like he once almost did. His eyes softened and he begged for Ashton's understanding. She did understand, but right now, she couldn't give him what he wanted. If it were up to Wolfe, she'd stay hidden, safe, waiting for a better time to strike against Augland, a time that might never come. It was exactly what NeuroEnergy had done, and look where Georgina was now. She was going to trial because she had underestimated Warren and had not struck or solicited allies when she could have.

All Ashton cared about was putting an end to the suffering of Augland workers. To make Warren hurt the way she had been hurt.

Ashton wasn't originally thrilled about their road trip to Hamma Hamma, but given Ashton and Wolfe's recent exchange, she looked forward to seeing Bez. She at least understood Ashton's perspective—and frustration.

CHAPTER 2

Ashton

COLONY, HAMMA HAMMA

Ashton and Wolfe said nothing as their trek along the winding roads continued toward the Colony. Ashton stewed on every word Wolfe had said while they traveled down the mountainside. Their hover ride was no different.

The sharp air whipping through the twisting coastal roads and the high speed kept both their minds occupied and their exchange minimal until they reached the cove with a wooden sign welcoming them to Hamma Hamma Bay.

Ashton was the first to dismount the hoverbike, and she quickly walked across the dirt ground to the main outdoor seating area. Colony members gathered around picnic tables that were lined up across the rocky beachfront. The only sounds were the bustling of busy colonists and the splashing of the subtle waves onto the rocky shores of Hamma Hamma. Hills of discarded oyster shells dotted the landscape, mounded only for aesthetics and for landmarking the Colony's main cabin and gathering center. Ashton slowed her steps as she approached familiar-looking Colony faces. Wolfe had finally caught up to where Ashton stood.

"Have you seen Bez?" Ashton approached a Colony member, who had turned to look at Ashton and Wolfe.

"Hey, kiddo! Heard you were coming by!" Ashton smiled, giving the man a quick hug before the distant, joyful scream pulled her away.

"Ashton!" Bez emerged from the front door of the Colony communal home, and Ashton raced to meet her on the cabin's steps. Its wraparound porch and two-leveled home with peeling blue paint had been chosen as the central hub for Colony members to meet.

"I thought you were going to be here hours ago!" Bez scolded, her tan skin sun-kissed from the warm weather of the last few days. She smiled broadly despite her snarky remark, her excitement uncharacteristic for her typically sarcastic and—at times—abrasive personality.

Joao strutted behind Bez and came to stand beside Wolfe, instantly getting into conversation with his former security colleague from his Augland 54 Head of Security days.

"Sorry, took us longer to get down from the hike than I thought," said Ashton. Bez shrugged it off. She wasn't about to say anything about Wolfe and her fight in earshot of both Joao and Wolfe.

"We're pretty much ready for tonight. Should be a good time and it's been ages since we've had a full-blown Colony shindig."

"Colony 'shindig?'" Ashton echoed, questioning her choice of words.

"It's another word for a party . . . I've been reading books from the library in my spare time. Gary said one of the homes had hundreds of them when they first got here." Bez shrugged. "Anyways, they found two deer today, which is more than we've seen all week and are planning a big bonfire and cookout." Bez looped her arm with Ashton's and pulled her toward the beach and away from Joao and Wolfe. "Have you heard from Georgina? Hunter? I've been dying to know more about our plan for the trial. I've asked Joao if we could use his interconnect to see if we can get ahold of Fox. God, I hope he's still alive. Joao's still friends with some of the security guys. I'm hoping to find out if there's been any movement with UnSuited." Bez tightened her grip.

The UnSuited rebellion meant so much to both her and Ashton, but more so to Bez because she was a founding member of the movement. Bez couldn't get over the idea of leaving others behind, including those who didn't make it to the rescue boat. Not knowing their fate was unsettling.

They arrived at the rocky beach where, "What did Joao say?" Ashton posed her question while she waved at Colony members who trotted back to their Colony home with oyster-filled buckets.

"About the interconnect? He said I couldn't use it, that he and Wolfe needed to keep their distance in case the lines were bugged. It's just been so long now that I doubt anyone would try and listen." Bez went silent.

"Maybe after the trial." It was unlikely, but not impossible.

"Maybe . . . Hey," Bez knocked her elbow at Ashton as they walked. "What took you so long to visit this time? It's been at least a month!"

Ashton rolled her eyes for what felt like the millionth time that day. *Not you too, Bez.* Her defensive walls shot up, but she breathed deeply to rid the annoyance. Ashton grew tired of the constant criticism as Bez led the conversation from small talk of UnSuited to her absence. The last time Ashton and Wolfe visited, they had just found out about the trial and Georgina's ask that they become witnesses for her defense against Warren's allegations.

"I don't know," said Ashton. "Time just . . . flew by." Which wasn't a lie.

"The Woman in Red too busy for us Colony folk?" Bez teased. Ashton cringed.

"Stop! I hate that nickname." Ashton's face blushed. The alter ego and nickname had been coined by the UnSuited after she "played" the red-headed Viking character, Freya. The reminder of her notorious escape was like nails on a chalkboard. Bez bent over in laughter, amused by Ashton's embarrassment.

"It's good to have you here."

"It's good to be here. Guess I sort of missed you," Ashton admitted, smiling.

"You missed me so much. Don't lie." They walked along the beach's tide for the next hour, catching up and absorbing the lighthearted banter and moments of calm.

Ashton had mentioned her brief, and hurtful, fight with Wolfe while hiking in the Olympics.

"Ouch . . . babysitting? He said that?" Well, you have to admit you've been more . . ." Bez struggled to find the words, ". . . careless. Not in a bad sense, you've just got this 'trust fall' thing going, or like, I don't know, you don't care what happens to you. I get why Wolfe's upset about that."

"You're not supposed to take his side." Ashton eyed Bez, not loving that Bez agreed with Wolfe.

"You know I'm not one to lie to you to spare your feelings . . . but what I will say is it's not helpful that Joao and Wolfe don't include you, or me, in the planning. I feel like you've got a point there. Especially since we are going into Augland, DC, we should have more of a game plan or something. Like maybe breaking out workers in DC or taking a CEO hostage." Ashton laughed while Bez continued: "I can't imagine we are just going to go there and talk about our feelings and then leave."

"I think that's what I don't understand. I thought by now we would be planning some sort of attack or working with NeuroEnergy to start getting workers out of Augland. Instead, they are worried about being imprisoned and interrogated by Augland officials . . . Wolfe thinks other CEOs will want to help us."

"What! They won't help us!" Bez paused. "They don't know what it's truly like in there. And CEOs aren't going to care about workers . . . they never have and never will." Bez and Ashton couldn't agree more on that; they knew what working in Augland 54 was like and after the escape, it only meant things were worse for every worker who remained in its walls. Bez reached for Ashton's hand, interlacing her fingers with her friend's and squeezing tightly. "Let them have their secret boy club . . . we are the leaders of the UnSuited and when the time is right, maybe we execute a plan of our own. We all want the same thing and maybe we need to go along with theirs for now."

Ashton met Bez's gaze and grinned. Now *that* was an idea she could get behind.

That evening, the music surrounded the massive firepit just beside the mountain of seashells. The sun had long gone down below the mountainside, casting a dark shadow. The Colony members began to dance alongside the roaring yellows and reds of the campfire.

Ashton was breathless as she twirled around, laughing at Bez as they moved their bodies to the rhythm of stringed music from the antique CD player that Wolfe had brought with him. Bez had been right—she should have visited more this last month. Leaving the "bubble of Ashton and Wolfe" was nice, especially after seeing the happiness and freedom the escape had brought the ex-workers of Augland 54. Not many workers who broke out of Augland had decided to come to the Colony. Many had stayed in NeuroEnergy, and those who had were embracing the culture, and their own identity now flourished in the cooperative environment.

Ashton plopped down on a log bench as Bez turned her attention to Joao. Bez jumped up and pulled him into the ring of dancers. His awkward movements caused Ashton to shake her head and laugh.

"Seat taken?" The walking stick she had seen in her peripheral vision came into view, and Rico, her friend who had taught her to cook, hobbled over. Before Ashton snuck into Augland after Augland 54 had attacked the Colony and abducted innocent children, Ashton had tried to make a life for herself at the Colony. Rico had helped her adapt to life outside of Augland, much like the workers now. Working as a sous chef alongside him had brought peace after Sheva's death and given her purpose.

"Made some oyster-stuffed mushrooms. Want one?" He offered her a large circular mushroom with chopped oyster inside. It was a Rico specialty. She picked it up and ate it in one bite, smiling at him. She loved his cooking.

"It's delicious, Rico. As always." She smiled again.

"You'll notice I changed the recipe a little. Added some of Gary's homemade wine and tarragon. I don't have the heart to tell him his white wine is way too bitter. Only possible use is for sauces." He lowered his body, groaning as he hit the log bench's height. Ashton chuckled through chewing and swallowing the last bite.

"So, you ready?" Rico questioned.

Ashton lowered her head. "Does everyone know about it?" she asked.

Rico shook his head. "Hard to keep secrets here." He paused. The Colony people had a lot to lose and gain from the trial too, so it shouldn't have been a surprise. Like Ashton, the people at Hamma Hamma were familiar with similar pain. Their children had been taken from them because of the infertility issue the Suits inflicted upon the workers. Augland 54 began stealing children to replenish the workers who continually disappeared.

". . . Ash, you sure you're up for this?"

Of course—it was her first thought. It would be the first time Augland would be exposed for their crimes. That other Executives, CEOs, and senators would know exactly what Warren had done to his workers.

"Did I ever tell you I had a daughter?" Rico interrupted her thoughts.

"You never mentioned . . ." She trailed off. Rico's ashy face quivered. She could even tell in the darkness that the mere mention of his daughter caused him immense pain.

He steadied himself and said, "She was a beauty. Bright and warm. And I think part of me thought, once I lost her, that it would be easier to lose myself in my anger . . . You remind me of her." That made Ashton's insides twist in empathy. "Losing her drove me to violence; yelling at people I cared about. Even some destructive tendencies. That's when I started cooking, and it saved me."

The tightening in Ashton's chest worsened as the parallel to Wolfe's concerns over Ashton's concern began to click for Ashton. Her face dropped. Rico had never said too many words to Ashton or opened up about his personal life, which is why they got along so well. But now that she saw this side of Rico she could empathize with him. Wolfe had pointed her anger out on the cliffside of the Olympics. Her vexation toward Augland was unhealthy, and everyone who knew her could see its impact.

Rico continued. "Let your need for vengeance go, Ash. It will get easier. Not saying it goes away—that won't happen—but you'll be able to live day by day. And the anger won't run you. You won't make it if you let it rule your life."

Ashton's eyes diverted to Wolfe across the fireplace, now chatting with Powell, Cahya's security guard. He took a moment away from his conversation to look over and their eyes met through the golden peaks of fire.

"You don't have to do this alone," Rico said as he put a hand on Ashton's shoulder. There was regret that caused her to pause.

"I'm—" She stopped herself and thought. *Fine? Angry? Afraid I'll lose again? Augland kills people I love. Who's next? Bez. Joao. Hunter. Versal. Rico. Cahya. Georgina. Rye . . . Wolfe? I'm sick of losing people I care about.*

Ashton didn't want to face what was happening right in front of her. The reminder of what she had lost. Jagatha still lived so vividly in her mind—all the times she had played and laughed at the Colony where she was free and loved by so many. She had to remember . . . she wasn't the only person who had lost loved ones. It was just easier to channel her hate into Augland than to let go.

"I know, and thanks, Rico." Ashton smiled, which softened a sad and concerned Rico. "It's getting late. I think it's time for bed. Maybe we can make some breakfast tomorrow? Like the old days?" He nodded, clearly happy that their time together was worth something to Ashton.

"Love you, Ash."

She kissed him on the cheek, appreciating his vulnerability. Rico, like many, cared for her. With that, she stood, weaving through the dancers to make her way to her cabin.

She heard sticks crack behind her as she made her way, now well beyond the fire and through the heavily wooded area between cabins along the shore. Ashton took a breath and turned, knowing who was there before she saw him.

"I'm sorry, Wolfe," she started. "For earlier. I know I've been . . ." Ashton struggled to find the right words, and Wolfe slowly walked toward her. "I know you are just worried about me, and I'm just not, I don't know." He nodded, confirming what Ashton already knew before reaching out his arms and pulling her close to him.

"I'm trying, Ash. I'm trying to help. You're so angry at the world. At Warren. I know it's not me . . ."

"You were right. And what we *can't* do at the trial is go off on some revenge spree because I think it will make me feel better." Ashton admitted. She didn't leave his chest, simply took a deep breath in.

He nearly sighed in relief as well.

"But you need to stop doing this without me, and Bez for that matter. You and Joao aren't the only ones who can help . . ." Ashton attempted to lighten the mood, "and I'm not sure if you remember but I'm fairly good at fighting. I nearly took you down once or twice while training in Land of Legends."

Wolfe chuckled. "Not true." He stared intently at Ashton, and she glared back, unwilling to back down. Finally, Wolfe let out a sigh of resolve. "I'll share what I can."

"That's not good enough." Ashton began.

His hands went up in defense. "All right, fair enough on keeping you roped into our plans. As long as it is safe to do so and won't put you both in any situation that could harm you at trial. That's my compromise, Ash." He paused, waiting for her objection, but compromise was something she was willing to work with. Wolfe continued, "We will fill you in tomorrow, when Bez and Joao visit in the morning. We will begin to prepare for the trial. A real plan. "Deal?" Wolfe said, and Ashton could see his half smile even in the darkness.

Ashton smiled back, not agreeing out loud to his plan just yet. She should have promised, but what she couldn't control was what would happen when she finally was face-to-face with Warren. She would try, for Wolfe. She would go along with his plan, but like she told him earlier, if given the opportunity, she'd find a way to get her revenge. She just wasn't sure how.

So, it had come—the next game they'd have to play. And this time, Ashton wasn't too sure if she'd be so lucky to make it out alive. Either of them. Wolfe's father would do anything to win.

Until you make him pay.

CHAPTER 3

Georgina

NEUROENERGY, PACIFIC NORTHWEST

"I told you not to call me, Georgina. Not here. It's not a secure line," Beaugard, the AEC president, said before Georgina even had a chance to say hello. It had already been a long day at the office, and Georgina had undone her perfectly pulled-back bun, exposing her aging white roots as the hair came down across her shoulders. Her bare foot nervously tapped next to her heels on the cement floor of her spacious NeuroEnergy office.

It had been too long since they last spoke. She called him a few weeks after the workers escaped from Augland 54 and found refuge at Northwest NeuroEnergy. She had given him evidence that proved Warren had deliberately tried to create his own energy resources within Augland 54, but knowing this only persuaded Beaugard to pause any retaliation from Warren on NeuroEnergy. Warren was told to stay only in Augland 54 until further notice, to which Warren shrewdly put up little resistance. In Beaugard's words, the evidence was "still being analyzed for authenticity."

Six months had passed since Ashton and Hunter escaped Augland 54, bringing Augland refugees with them. Many of the workers who did not leave for the Colony still walked along the campus of NeuroEnergy, their movements slow and seemingly without purpose. They were free, but now they grew hungry, and NeuroEnergy struggled to keep them sustained. There was not a system in place to provide for them long-term.

For the past few months, much of the food NeuroEnergy had received was severely reduced or spoiled. Georgina knew it was all part of Warren's plan, but he maintained he held no ill will nor did he want to punish the people who had betrayed him. She found his false reverence repulsive but it played well with Beaugard. While Warren's public persona spewed no pushback against the freedom of choice for workers within his Augland community, Georgina knew he was not thrilled with the events that had taken place and would retaliate. If he had been ruthless enough to create an Artificial Existence Being replica of his son in order to imprison and then impersonate and defame him, he was willing to do anything—and it began with manipulating Augland's food supplies.

The treaty between the Auglands and NeuroEnergies depended on the exchange of supplies for electricity. NeuroEnergy compounds created consumable electricity and other forms of energy storage, but they didn't have other suitable resources such as food, medicine, and materials so they relied on AEC. This made the AEC and Auglands a necessary evil. Relationships like these worked for a while, but cooperation often faded when one party sensed an opportunity and Warren's treachery was carefully planned. A system built to rely on the other to function.

Augland's temperature-controlled environments were able to grow, reproduce, and manage copious amounts of food supplies all year round. The war that had divided the nation also dissolved the pre-war, nutrient-rich landscape and left the land bare. It was just another reason the war ended so abruptly, making life outside Auglands or NeuroEnergies barely habitable. The Colony had been able to create some food supplies, but not enough to sustain hundreds or thousands of people—and the time it took to grow produce was too long. It would take years to create an environment for the current kind of sustainability they needed.

Georgina hadn't let the escaped Augland 54 workers find refuge in her NeuroEnergy unit out of the goodness of her heart—not entirely.

She did it to save NeuroEnergy, but it seemed that she could lose her power regardless of her true intentions. The Colony had taken some of the rebel workers, but they were just as controlled with supplies as Georgina was. Augland, while a thorn in Georgina's side, dictated food availability. Likewise, Georgina could dictate their electricity use, but it seemed to not affect their daily life to the same degree. Even so, if Warren could prove that they intentionally decreased electricity to them, it could come off as retaliation and hurt her chances at the trial.

"I know, but I needed to speak with you, and you weren't responding to my messages." Georgina said.

"I've kept my distance since the allegations . . . you should have returned the workers. Or at least come to me," Beaugard responded.

"I didn't have time, Beau. Warren is the one out of line here. He has been manipulating this system for far too long and getting away with it. You've seen what he can do. You think he's not gunning for some higher purpose here? He wants to get rid of me, take over NeuroEnergy—and it won't stop there. Others will follow when they see it is possible. And then he'll come for you—"

"You're out of line, Georgina," Beaugard interrupted. "Warren can't get that sort of power. We have a system in place. Rules to follow that protect that . . . But I don't disagree with you. His methods are unconventional, maybe even teeter between right and wrong . . . We both know he's always been . . . ambitious." Beaugard was intentionally careful with his choice of words.

Beaugard had little knowledge of what had progressively been happening on the West Coast for the last twenty years. Augland 54 had secretly been creating its own energy sources, trying to eliminate the need for Pacific Northwest NeuroEnergy, and Georgina with it. She wanted proof before going to Beaugard, her former colleague-now-turned president of the House of CEOs. Sending Ashton into Augland in a Suit named Charlotte to spy on Warren was a mistake because it exposed her company to scrutiny. Since the Suit malfunctioned and Ashton's involvement was revealed, it prompted suspicion by Warren of what Georgina was finding out about Augland 54. The spying was now the least of Georgina's worries. Now that Augland workers sought refuge in her company, she was an active adversary to Warren.

In response to the threats and allegations from both sides, Beaugard had put both Warren and Georgina in detainment within their companies until the trial. Neither of them could leave or communicate with other CEOs.

"This whole thing could have been avoided, and now look where we are. Two sides bickering. Look at what has come of it," Beaugard scolded her.

Georgina's office was dark except for the blue hue coming from her glasses that displayed the memo Beauregard had sent to all AEC employees. Beaugard referred to the many riots and rebellions that had littered Auglands across the AEC nation—or "Augnation," most commonly used. Neither Augland nor NeuroEnergies knew how communication had spread so quickly amongst the Augland workers. There were very few methods for communication, especially between workers.

"The rebellions were because he tortured workers to control them. He rips children away from their home to work and die in *his* Augland. I can only imagine it's just as bad in other Auglands; who knows, maybe it's worse. It's Augland's dictatorship that has caused this, not me. And if you don't stop him . . ." Georgina's voice cracked, fear clawing at her of even the thought of this imagined future. "There are sixty Auglands, and only thirty-three NeuroEnergies . . . and only one AEC. We're outnumbered, Beaugard. Warren—"

"Don't lecture me on politics. You didn't leave me much choice in this at all. I must stay neutral here and not show any favoritism. People know you and I have history. The knowledge that we started together, helping unite the AEC and NeuroEnergy, it will just hurt you and me. Georgina . . ." she felt reprimanded when he said her name, "you went against corporate policy when you didn't return the escaped workers, and you are now asking me to pardon you or excuse this behavior because you have superficial evidence? There are active rebellions! I can't do that, especially not with this much publicity. There have been vast repercussions for your display in aiding workers. You've started the worker's now-widespread rebellion when we could have contained it within Augland 54."

Maybe this had always been the Beaugard she knew, one unwilling to admit that they had drifted so far away from their original plan of harmony, of a more perfect and just world. She had to plead with him to recognize the truth. Beaugard was a friend, or at least he had been at one point in her career—even a mentor. They had worked together when the AEC first thought of acquiring NeuroEnergy, before the war, and before NeuroEnergy had fought with the government. He was a senator back then, in league with the AEC. It was a time when their purpose was to save humanity from disease, aging, and discomfort—at least that was their claim. While he now had the title of President of the House of CEOs.

At one time, they had been colleagues, visionaries in a world tainted by the cruelty of power. It wasn't long after the AEC founder passed away that he was voted in by the House of CEOs to run the overarching parent company. Even after the war, when NeuroEnergy was folded into the AEC umbrella, they stayed allies, discussing fair and just policies.

At some point, that changed—for both of them. Georgina saw the hint of corruption before it began, and their world of unity became divided by agendas and power: NeuroEnergy versus Auglands. Deep down, she hoped the Beaugard she knew was still there, the honorable man who had believed in a perfect world and didn't turn a blind eye while tyrants stood on the backs of workers. Living in Augland, DC, had distanced him from the world beyond the walls, and that concerned Georgina.

"Do we even know what's right and wrong anymore?" Georgina said under her breath, but Beaugard heard.

"I'm not getting in a debate again with you about workers' moral rights. We've got a department for that." Again, he berated and dismissed her. He sighed. "And I'll talk to Warren about food distributions. But this thing you have against Warren. A personal vendetta . . . it's not helping Pacific Northwest NeuroEnergy. Warren is requesting your immediate removal if proven correct, and that has raised so many different red flags here. He's saying you spied on him, started the rebellions yourself just to gain control of his assets. He says he's got *proof.* And he's gained support within the AEC and other Auglands. The number of friends you have in the House of CEOs is becoming scarce, and I can't protect you anymore. My suggestion is you work on damage control. Figure out a way to make things right before it's too late."

His words disturbed her. What he said wasn't all untruthful. For years, Auglands had conspired to envelope NeuroEnergies into their fold and become an unstoppable arm of the corporate giant. To win. That was their goal. To gain majority vote in the AEC on public policies. It was a dangerous game, and Warren was leading the way.

Georgina knew once that power shifted, Auglands would have all the power and the AEC would be marginalized, but Beaugard was too blind to see it. What scared Georgina even more was the future. Would Auglands then turn on each other? Would war break out amongst the corporations to gain status? How would it end?

Beaugard hung up, and Georgina's eyes slowly closed. She had hoped Beaugard would put her mind at ease, but instead she felt more alone in this than ever. It wasn't the conversation she had expected.

A knock echoed in the dark office at NeuroEnergy.

"What?" Georgina snapped, her frustration palpable. Her eyes settled on the gangly man with shaggy brown hair and dark-rimmed glasses in the doorway. "Rye, what is it?" Georgina's trust in Rye had grown since they first aided Ashton in Augland and their ensuing escape. She now confided in him about everything. He had worked countless hours to find a way to protect them from Augland, but their intel was diminishing by the day.

"I wanted to check in before I head home for the night," he said. Georgina sighed.

"Sure, were you able to find anything out? About the other riots?"

Rye came forward. "No. I've got nothing on how it happened. It hasn't been a part of any channels we can find."

Georgina sighed heavily again.

"Is everything okay?" Rye knew it wasn't. It had been difficult since the workers came to live at their compound. Augland 54 was on high alert: they knew NeuroEnergy needed information and were able to infiltrate at any time. All workers received the same notice that laid out the AEC's intolerance of anyone willing to support insubordination, which was indirectly, now, correlated with NeuroEnergy by the news of the trial.

"Beau told me to 'make things right' . . . and he'll 'talk to Warren about the food distribution'." Georgina knew better than to talk about her confidential conversation with the AEC's president. She shook her head in disbelief. Rye looked down, knowing that all Georgina had wanted was to make things right, but that they were pulled into the spotlight as villains. "We have no choice. We must try and get back to normal, gain some favor with the other CEOs."

Rye's eyes widened. "But . . ." he stopped himself as he thought of what to say next. Georgina didn't give him time to speak.

"Warren's winning, Rye. And from my conversation with Beau, he won't intervene unless Warren openly admits to breaking the treaty. We risk everything if we continue going down this path of resistance. Sometimes, sometimes these things are just political—and you need to play the game to win." Georgina paused, "Rye, I need you to send for Frederick, my corporate counsel. I think it's time we come up with a new trial strategy."

"Of course." Rye turned and left, leaving Georgina to ponder how she was going to get through the trial without Beaugard's support.

CHAPTER 4

Ashton

COLONY, HAMMA HAMMA

When Ashton awoke, Wolfe had already started a small fire inside the fireplace of their one-room cabin.

"Morning," she said, shaking away her sleep.

Wolfe looked up, smiling. "Morning. Sleep well?"

Ashton thought for a moment. She had slept well, once the stringy music and loud voices of the Colony gathering from the night before had ended. Ashton and Wolfe had broken away from the party and retreated to the guest cabin prepared for them by Bez and Joao. They had talked for a while before sleep overtook Wolfe and he slumped down next to her on the bed, wrapped in her embrace.

"Yeah," she said while she wrapped herself in a soft, weighted white blanket.

Wolfe walked over to Ashton and bent down to kiss her on the forehead. He ran his fingers through her hair, pulling up a twisted clump. "I don't know what you do at night to make your hair go crazy like this," he said.

Ashton laughed. She loved these moments, where she felt peace and love all in one moment, wrapped in the cocoon of safety. She was sure her unmanageable hair looked more untamed than normal.

"Joao told me Georgina came in," said Wolfe. "Or is coming, sometime this morning." Ashton sat up on the soft bed, using her elbows to propel her head forward.

"Has NeuroEnergy ever heard of sleeping in?" Ashton half joked.

Wolfe laughed.

"I guess that means they lifted the detainment?" Ashton questioned.

Wolfe shrugged as he took a sip of coffee and leaned against the kitchen counter that was only a few feet away from the bed where Ashton lay.

She knew why Georgina was coming in; she just didn't know it would be a week before the trial began. Ashton and Wolfe were her star witnesses to the injustices committed by Augland 54. Warren hadn't come after her or Wolfe, but Georgina—and if she wasn't nervous, she should be.

Wolfe chuckled before directing the conversation back to the seriousness it warranted and, strolling over to their bed, placed a cup of tea on the side table. He settled down next to her, propping his head on his hand with his elbow digging into the mattress. "We knew this was coming and we are prepared for it. The trial is just about Georgina, not us. We'll be back in a few days, tops, hopefully with some CEOs to begin discussions around overtaking 54." Ashton sighed. He was right; this hadn't been about Ashton or Wolfe—it was about the two companies that couldn't seem to get along. Wolfe planned to use that to his advantage by finding CEOs who disagreed with Warren. Workers like her and Bez were in the crossfire. She trusted Wolfe and his judgment. At least Bez, Joao, and Hunter would be with them in Augland, DC. She took a deep breath, smiled, and slid across the bed until she was in his embrace, still restricted under covers. The trial wouldn't be long, and then, if everything went well, they would return to their life in Hood Canal and Warren's crimes would finally be exposed.

Most nights, Ashton relived a dream she had countless times: what her next encounter with Warren would look like. She pictured him seated next to all his Executives around a white marble table adorned with Predators Biome's exotic purple and white flowers, just like their conference room at the old Space Needle. Ashton, slowly walking up behind him and plunging a knife deep into his synthetic Suit's gut. His face turning to look at her, and her face being the last image he saw.

She never pictured herself as a murderer, but her hatred for Warren had changed her and she yearned to finally feel justice for Jagatha, Sheva, and all the workers of Augland 54. She pictured the guilt of their deaths melting away as Warren's lifeless body dropped to the ground. She imagined how it would feel, even though the fantasy was flawed. Warren's Suit couldn't be killed, only the man in the pod, but she still felt a rush of joy and a release from the hatred prison that held her mind captive at the thought of tearing his Suit to shreds.

"What does Warren really look like?" The question was out before Ashton could think twice.

"That's random." Wolfe's brow furrowed.

"Well, he wears a Suit. Have you seen him without it? I can't imagine he looks the same." Ashton ignored his curiosity to her line of questioning. She wouldn't tell him why that thought came up just now.

"There are similar features, but no. Warren doesn't look like his Suit. I mean, I haven't seen him in at least six years so not sure what he looks like now."

"So, you have seen him?" This meant Wolfe also knew where Warren's pod was located.

"Yes, once. It was a security breach in the Suit's spa grounds where the Executives are, a malfunction to his pod that needed work done. I helped to make sure he wasn't harmed in the process."

"So. Was he horrible looking? Wrinkly with sagging skin and purplish puffy bags under his eyes. Receding hairline? I need to know what to prepare for with you in your old age," Ashton teased as she sipped her tea.

Wolfe scoffed, "I'll always be this handsome, and I have a very strong hairline so don't you worry." He joked before tightening his arms around Ashton's waist.

The door shook as knock after knock perpetually vibrated through the wood. Wolfe rolled his eyes at the timing.

"What!" He yelled playfully, but the underlying annoyance of the disruption was apparent.

"Wolfe!" Ashton said and they both laughed. "Yeah?" Ashton yelled at the intruders outside her door.

"It's Bez. Joao too . . . Open up!" the muffled voice demanded. It would be like Bez to show up too early in the morning. Wolfe shook his head no, but Ashton was already pushing him aside and toward the small, white door of their tiny cottage. Bez's enthusiastic "I knew you guys were awake!" filtered into the room. Her commanding nature was relentless.

A bright-eyed Bez pushed her way in, and Joao softly walked behind her.

"Georgina's here."

"Wolfe just let me know . . ." Ashton rolled back on the bed and patted down her hair.

"Well, she's not staying long. I bet she wants to talk about the trial, though." Bez went straight for the pot of tea and helped herself. The cabin studio was only one room. The distance between the bed and the kitchen counter was only feet away, which made the intrusion of Bez and Joao that much more intimate since Ashton was still wrapped in the comforter on their bed.

"Joao and I have been rehearsing key points to talk through, like the treatment of workers at the brothel and my experience in the Apparel department." Bez was up front with her remarks. "I'm sure the UnSuited rebellion is going to come up. They'll have to discuss it. We should tell them that, if they keep acting this way, riots will happen everywhere. That the people there need to be given the choice whether they want to live there or not. Or at least they need to let them know about what is outside the walls. Maybe we should . . ."

"Bez . . ." Joao nudged. Bez had gone off on a tangent.

"What! We never talked about what we want out of this trial. Or figured out how we get to say what the people want us to say. I know it's about NeuroEnergy, but a big part of that is what the workers have had to go through!" Bez and Ashton were aligned in their anger, more so than Wolfe and Joao.

"We stick to the plan we've already discussed. We stay low, only answer their questions. We're going to tell them the truth, for the most part. And Joao and I—I mean *we*—will start discussing a coup with Executives we trust." Wolfe began discussing the details of their strategy, "That we did this because Warren abducted the Colony's children. That Georgina and the Colony had nothing to do with it. That we only wished to free the workers and retrieve the Colony's children." Joao nodded in approval while Wolfe continued. "I'll talk about my father's dictatorship and how he stole my identity to run Augland after being removed as CEO. And Joao is witness to that and to the blueprints for Warren's energy initiatives we found. Bez, you'll talk about what you saw in Apparel, not bringing up anything about leading a riot. Hunter will talk about Land of Legends and the Colony children." Wolfe was met with silence, other than the slurping sound of tea from Bez.

"Again, we are not on trial; Georgina is, but we can use this time to also convince the other Executives that Warren has gone too far and needs to be removed from power," he said. "And we need to protect Georgina to protect the workers. Georgina understands that, which is the reason she's asked us to be witnesses. We discuss only things that won't pull us into trouble or condemn Georgina."

"What if they don't let us leave?" Bez had said aloud what Ashton was thinking. *This could be a trap,* Ashton thought.

"I won't let that happen. We all had our reasons for the actions we took, and *when* Warren is found guilty, they won't come for us because we acted against his actions—especially if we gather favor with other CEOs." Wolfe was stern, enough so that for a moment Ashton was hopeful—but he was no longer an Executive, employee, or part of the Augland 54 family. Wolfe's power had diminished the moment he blew up the Centauri star in Augland and saved her from Predator's Biome. His ties to his father, Warren, the CEO of Augland 54, were gone. Ashton was not sure he could save them this time if Augland decided they needed to pay the price of their disobedience.

Bez refrained from asking how when Joao gave her a silencing stare. There were too many unanswered questions to really know *that* answer.

Ashton filled the awkward silence. "We will worry about that all later. Now, if you guys don't mind, I need to wake up and get ready. I promised Rico I'd help make breakfast." Ashton pushed herself off the bed and went into the bathroom to quickly change.

"Oh! Convince him to make biscuits and gravy," said Bez. "They're heavenly, and that grumpy old man has started to ignore my requests. I know he won't refuse you if you're the one to ask." Joao pulled Bez with him out their cabin door as she pleaded with Ashton to relay her breakfast suggestion.

———

Rico had agreed to biscuits and gravy to appease Bez. The entire Colony came by in groups to grab their breakfast and Ashton helped serve, sitting and talking with many whom she hadn't had the chance to speak with since arriving at the Colony. Before Ashton knew it, she had minutes to scarf down that day's breakfast before heading to Cahya's home, where Wolfe had reminded her they all planned to meet. She, Bez, Joao, and Wolfe rushed over across the street and to the wood log cabin Cahya had claimed as her own.

———

As they entered Cahya's house, the dark head of groomed hair stared ahead and slowly turned.

"Georgina," Wolfe said, nodding his head in recognition.

Georgina smiled, undoing her perfectly crossed legs and standing.

"Wolfe, great to see you again. And hello, Ashton." She turned her head to look directly at her. Her gaze was warm and welcoming. "Thank you again for doing this. All of you, I appreciate your willingness to help NeuroEnergy—and me. We're doing the right thing."

Ashton just nodded her head. Georgina referred to them being selective about the truth of NeuroEnergy's involvement with Warren's claims. Something that hadn't been discussed too much.

"This way, then." Cahya said while entering the living room in her home and motioned them to her dining room table. There were six chairs, so one of them would stand, and that ended up being Powell, who positioned himself against the wall directly behind Cahya. Wolfe pulled Ashton's chair out for her and sat down next to her. Ashton took a breath, awaiting Georgina's plan to make sure they would win against Warren. Georgina and Cahya sat on opposite ends of the oval table. There was an awkward silence between all parties.

Georgina cleared her throat, and grabbed the attention of the occupants in Cahya's living room. "As you know, we will be travelling to Augland, DC, to the House of CEOs and the AEC's headquarters, as Augland 54 has formally accused Pacific Northwest NeuroEnergy of conspiracy. If found guilty, they will undoubtedly try to replace me and potentially return the workers to Augland."

Georgina remained stoic, and the room remained eerily silent.

"If Warren wins, I can't promise that we can protect any of you, Colony included. But if we win this, we can open our own investigation against Augland 54 and have the backing of the AEC." Georgina suddenly looked away.

"That you already know . . ." she said, then exhaled. "We've recently learned that we don't have the support of the AEC yet; apparently there have been various rebellion outbreaks of UnSuited across the Auglands. It's put a spotlight on us. I don't know how the rebellion spread to other Auglands." Georgina awaited an admission from anyone in the room, but they remained silent.

Bez shook her head: neither she nor Ashton knew how the rebellion was spreading outside Augland 54's dome.

Georgina continued, "We need to leave today. I received notice that they have asked for the trial to start tomorrow instead of next week. A glitch in the scheduling, and convenient for Warren. I believe they are trying to throw us off our game. It doesn't give us a lot of time to prepare you for what's to come. I—"

Georgina paused. She had an air about her that seemed panicked, which was unlike any time Ashton had seen Georgina. Typically, her aura was confident and refined. Ashton's brow furrowed; something was wrong.

Georgina's breath quickened. "Warren has brought claims against each one of you, and after my thorough discussions with corporate counsel, we decided that none of you would attend to speak on my behalf. We have a plan that would drop all of you as witnesses. All of you have committed your own treasonous acts against Augland 54 that would put you in jeopardy once you arrived in DC. I doubt they'd even let you testify and instead imprison you immediately." The room erupted into confused chatter.

Ashton hadn't completely understood what Georgina had said. It took her a moment to fully absorb the plan. Her stomach turned and she now regretted scarfing down her breakfast so fast. *What does this mean? Doesn't the AEC want to know all the facts?* Wolfe, who was already up and out of his chair began arguing with Georgina. The veins in his neck protruded and his face reddened as he argued. Ashton's brow furrowed.

Wolfe now had his hands on the table, slapping them both down hard. Georgina was unfazed, still sitting with her hands gracefully clasped on her lap.

"That is insanity!" protested Wolfe. "I have evidence against him, proving that he impersonated me so he could remain CEO. Joao is my witness to it. Bez, a worker who has seen the cages, the hands of injustice in the brothels . . . and Ashton. It's not a story without all of us, Georgina. It isn't enough evidence of anything unless they know what we know. You'll lose!" Wolfe yelled, his provoked tone startling most of the people around the table, but he spoke the truth.

"Warren's past isn't on trial here," replied Georgina. "I am. In their minds, none of you had anything to do with me and why the workers left Augland 54. Other than Ashton. There were several witnesses who saw Ashton when she was brought in front of the Executive team who have confirmed that Ashton acknowledged coming into Augland as a Suit to spy on them."

Ashton couldn't deny she had a point. None of them had known Georgina until Ashton had brought them to her and she—well, Warren—had confessed she was the woman behind Charlotte in front of the Executives in Augland 54. But Georgina had said none of them would attend the trial.

Everyone was up out of their chairs now. Ashton could only stare. It was chaos as they all scrambled in theories or combats to their involvement in the trial. She understood why Wolfe and Joao liked plans and procedures, which directly countered Bez, who was impulsive and wanted Augland to pay just about as much as Ashton did.

Georgina spoke above the chaos: "Trust me, I wish this were different, but if you all came with me, it would be a disaster. Wolfe, you blew up the Centauri star along with Joao. There were multiple witnesses, and it was considered an attack on the Executives. Joao, you tampered with evidence to allow the escape of hundreds of workers. Bez, a manager of Apparel, had access to help free Apparel workers and send messages across other Auglands through the tags on the uniform. All of you, even Hunter, would pay a price going to Augland, DC, and likely never set foot in front of the House of CEOs to tell your story." Georgina's voice cracked, and Ashton sensed that this realization of what was to come at trial was more real to her than anyone else.

"I tried to find exemptions so you all would be safe to come, Wolfe. I did, but you know more than any other person here that I don't make the rules; I abide by them and try to win regardless." Wolfe scoffed loudly, shaking his head in disbelief as his temper rose drastically,

"Wolfe," Ashton whispered, placing her hand on his arm to calm him.

"There's more." Georgina's gaze fell to Ashton, ignoring Wolfe's outburst. "This morning, I found out that you're being subpoenaed by

Warren's counsel. AEC security has sent an aircraft to bring us both to DC."

This time, it wasn't only Wolfe who let out outraged expletives.

"I knew it," hissed Bez. "They don't care about the injustices done to the workers. They only care that it caused some sort of inconvenience for them because of the UnSuited."

"They've never cared about workers," Joao answered Bez.

"I knew he'd do something like this," Wolfe said under his breath.

"What does that mean? He's subpoenaed me?" Ashton spoke up once the commotion calmed, still hung up by the word she had never heard before.

"It means that Warren has said you have valuable information that proves his side right and is forcing your attendance," Wolfe said in almost a whisper. His eyes grew dark as he realized what most others around the table hadn't yet figured out.

"That's right," said Georgina.

"Then you must take me with you. I won't let her go alone," Wolfe said.

"It won't matter, and you know it. Even if AEC security let you come aboard the jet, you'll be taken away the moment we land. I won't open you up on the stand so you can go through your own trial on the witness stand, Wolfe." Georgina's point was fair.

"Then what happens to Ashton? Your plan is to place the blame on her about the Suit and uprising, and she'll get arrested after the trial. Am I wrong?" Wolfe questioned.

"It's not my choice, Wolfe. If she doesn't come, she's going to be arrested anyways. The AEC doesn't let people walk away from summons. My hands are tied."

Ashton knew what had gone on in Augland 54. What the AEC needed to know. If she didn't go, her hopes of overtaking Augland and saving the workers would be doomed. Ashton remembered what Rico had said to her last night: if she did nothing, the anger would win, the deaths of Sheva and Jagatha would be in vain, and the countless workers who had lost their lives for freedom would make no difference. She couldn't let that happen.

"Wolfe . . ." Ashton said softly. Wolfe only closed his eyes.

"You don't have to take her with you. You can say she disappeared; you weren't able to find her. Something!"

"And there would be the AEC security searching for her and the trial postponed until she's found."

"Then we will run away! We have no interconnects, no ties to the AEC world. Let them come and try to find us."

"You'd sacrifice AEC coming to NeuroEnergy, or the Colony, searching for Ashton? Is that what you want them to do? To interrogate and disrupt everyone's lives here? The Colony would need to find new refuge if Warren decided to invade again. My NeuroEnergy can't afford Warren or AEC coming in and searching for Ashton—and I won't allow them to step foot in my headquarters." Georgina and Wolfe fought but it went nowhere.

"Okay, okay!" Cahya's soft voice carried, and it was once again quiet. "We are left with the hand we are dealt. The trial starts tomorrow, and we can't change the facts. So, what do we do with what we know?" There was a long pause as the room begged for a beginning.

"We go on as planned. Georgina and I will go, and we will make them listen to us." Ashton concluded with an unsteady resolve.

Wolfe bent down to her. "You don't have to do this, Ashton. We can wait until we figure out a new plan and hide away so the AEC won't find you. We will find another way to protect the workers, to protect you."

"You said yourself that we need to go there and help convince Executives to side with us. We can still do that. "Wolfe shook his head, but Ashton continued. "I know Suits, I've been around them my entire life so if you want other CEOs to listen and they will only allow me there, then let me try."

Wolfe turned away from the group and nearly whispered to Ashton. "It won't be that simple. You're a worker Ash; you're the help and even though you're more than that, Warren will spin that truth to his advantage."

"Every time we go up against them, they lose too—it's bad press. It's time it all comes out now and they hear our story and, if you believe there is still good in other CEOs, then they will hear our story and believe us. And I can tell them that." This time the uncertainty was drowned out by the adrenaline coursing through Ashton's veins. She was done hiding her feelings that Augland taught her to suppress. She was done waiting for Warren's judgment day. She was done wearing a mask. It was time someone paid. Even if she lost, she would speak the truth, and that was power Warren couldn't take from her. Warren would expect someone scared and cautious, and he wouldn't realize he had given Ashton the perfect opportunity to expose him while keeping the people she cared about safe. The trial could be Ashton's contribution.

Wolfe remained still while Georgina stood. "Thank you, Ashton. You're right; it's time the truth came out . . . and, Wolfe, I'll do my best to keep her safe." The room fell silent other than the wooden clock that ticked away on Cahya's living room wall. Joao comforted Bez, putting an arm around her. Cahya was still, her eyes glazed deep in thought. Wolfe huffed in frustration. Ashton scanned the room and looked out the window.

The fear was heavy as they all digested the new reality for the trial. Wolfe was right about one thing: their chance of success decreased without all of them, but this was a game where they couldn't make the rules. They could only follow. Wolfe was angry and Ashton knew why. Last night, she had promised to do this together, but with this new reality, they had no other choice. Bez could still lead an UnSuited rebellion, and Joao and Wolfe could help create an army to finally take down Augland 54. This was Ashton's part.

Wolfe was about to say something, but Ashton put her hand on his to stop any more debate. He pulled away from her and stormed to the other side of the room.

The air of frustration left a haze of disappointment as the hour passed and Cahya's room settled.

Cahya turned to Ashton. "Soon, we can all put this behind us. Move on." She moved her hands to Ashton's shoulders and squeezed.

Ashton smiled. She hoped that was the case.

CHAPTER 5

Ashton

AUGLAND, DC

After ending the meeting at Cahya's home, Ashton and Wolfe headed back to their cabin to pack Ashton's belongings.

"I know what Warren's trying to do," said Wolfe without provocation, "and it won't work because I'll figure out a way to get you out of there and out of his reach." Ashton smiled as she folded a sweatshirt and placed it neatly in her duffle bag, knowing that much was true. She reached for another garment.

"It's not certain he plans to keep me there. We faced these same risks if all of us were going; what's the difference now?" Ashton questioned.

"The difference is you're going alone. And Warren is the one bringing you there. Everything has changed." Warren's arms crossed as he leaned against the wall near Ashton.

"Georgina will be there . . ." Not that the statement brought much comfort to either of them.

"You do realize that she's not going to be on your side. She will set you out to be the conspirator against the AEC, and you'll be a threat they will do anything to stop. That's the only way Georgina can win this trial now that Warren is bringing you as a witness." Ashton went quiet. The realization hit her harder now, which she tried to hide: *there could be no returning home.* The hitch in her breath caught Wolfe's attention and she was sure she had finally gotten through the shock and realized what Georgina had said—or at least hadn't denied.

It's not my choice, Wolfe. If she doesn't come, she's going to be arrested anyway. The AEC doesn't let people walk away from summons. My hands are tied.

"It doesn't change anything. I can still tell our story in hopes to gain support from the Executives while Georgina remains blameless, especially if I can prove we did everything we did to protect the workers." It was the only thing Ashton could think to say because if Wolfe saw she had no idea how she would convince people to side with them, he'd potentially convince her to leave and hide away from AEC—which couldn't happen.

"Executives will turn on you because you're a worker, which is why Joao and I need to be the ones there and speaking with them. I've worked with CEOs and elite Suits before."

"I think you're underestimating my charming ability," Ashton joked, trying to lighten the too-tense mood.

"It's not a time for joking, Ash. This is serious. By Georgina placing blame on you, it will automatically alienate you from the other Executives. They will see you as a threat to themselves." Wolfe bent down so he was eye level with Ashton. "Don't do this, please; we will find another way." Ashton zipped her bag and stared at Wolfe.

"And if our roles were reversed and Warren made you go? Would you hide away from them or leave?" Wolfe remained silent, giving her the answer she already knew. "That's what I thought, so you can't expect me to do nothing."

That statement didn't stop Wolfe from trying, over and over again, but Ashton did not budge—because she was going through with this. She was tired of waiting for action and it was time that change and even revolution came to AEC's doorstep.

Within the hour, the jet the AEC had sent for Georgina and Ashton was parked near the Colony. In any other circumstance, Ashton would be in awe of the shiny contraption. A jet was something she had only heard stories of and had never seen in person, but their current predicament left her mind occupied. Wolfe didn't know what to say to her as they walked toward the long steel cylinder, and Ashton didn't know how to comfort him. She could easily read his face: his mind seemed to race with conspiratorial thoughts. He slowly distanced himself now consumed with the plan of attack.

Finally, she stopped and planted her feet just steps away from the jet where Georgina had already boarded, and two AEC security guards waited for her. Wolfe turned.

She knew Wolfe would do anything to bring her back, which brought her both comfort and fear. It was his selflessness that she worried about. Ashton's eyes wandered. He would risk everything, and there was no way to convince him not to.

"I'll see you soon. I promise. I'll do whatever it takes to convince them and who knows, maybe gain some Executive support like you wanted. Like I've said, I've worked around Suits my entire life; I can do this." Ashton said what she knew Wolfe needed to hear to ease his worry.

"That, I have no doubt." Wolfe gave a half grin before giving her a light kiss on her lips, as if he pressed harder, it would feel more final—like a goodbye neither of them was willing to accept.

Ashton's face was glued to the window of the steel trap that jetted above the Colony. *You can do this*, she told herself. She felt cold and alone. Tiny crystals crept from the corners of the window, enclosing the second layer of glass that separated Ashton from the clouds outside.

She had never been in an aircraft of any sort, and it was the first time she had ever been higher than the peak of an Olympic mountain. Ashton saw for the first time the world from a soaring view, hovering high above the world's surface. The jet sat above the clouds, and she looked ahead of her toward the fluffy, white cotton balls that littered the pale blue sky. It did not take long before the expansive dome of

Augland was visible in the distance. She marveled at the vastness of the architecture, yet was sadly reminded at how confining it was to the workers.

Two security guards kept watch. One was seated next to her and the other was across the aisle of the jet. Not long after takeoff, a lanky man sauntered in and motioned to the guards, who quickly stood and scurried to the back of the aircraft. He turned to the side and Georgina came forward from behind him.

"VELIC, set controls to human and privacy settings, please." Georgina spoke.

"I thought we weren't supposed to speak?" Ashton asked as Georgina came to sit next to her.

"Frederick has paid the security men off to give us privacy."

"Oxygen levels have been adjusted. Temperature set at 68 degrees. Recording inactive." Ashton looked at the front of the jet where the cockpit was, but no one was there. The voice echoed from the walls. She didn't question it. Ashton had seen enough of the technology Augland was willing to create; it would be more so with the AEC.

"It's called VELIC, Virtual Environment Learning and Intelligence Computers," Georgina explained without Ashton asking. "It's an artificial intelligence system here to serve AEC members; we utilize it when we need to travel and when we stay at the House of CEOs, which is where the trial has been scheduled."

"House of CEOs?" Ashton asked.

"Yes, that is where the trial will take place. Every quarter we gather to discuss details between Auglands and NeuroEnergies, with every CEO of Auglands and NeuroEnergies across the nations. Typically, we discuss new parks or partnerships, but we also have more in-depth conversations when there are disputes that need resolution, like a NeuroEnergy compound and Augland park disagreement. That's why the trial is happening there and why the president of AEC will dictate the trial and the outcome decided by the other CEOs." Ashton took a mental note. She wasn't so limited to think that Warren and Georgina were the only CEOs, but to know that the entire nation gathered in DC was—different.

Georgina filled the silence while Ashton processed as the aircraft maneuvered over Augland. "That's Augland 54." Georgina pointed out the window toward a glass dome partially covered by the clouds. Ashton ignored the irritation she felt bubbling up inside her for the other woman. Even though Georgina claimed she had no way around the subpoena, Ashton presumed she would use Ashton to proclaim her own innocence like Wolfe had suggested. Her anxiety turned to anger.

Ashton could clearly see everything from this angle. The parks were divided by a dark line that squiggled in an imperfect division. Maya Bay had clear, bright-blue skies with a sparkling ocean that was a lighter shade of blue than the rest of the Puget Sound. Hollywood Boulevard's high towers were uniformly shaped and so tall that they shaded and crowded the vast area with varied heights of steel box-like high rises. Victorian's valleys were green and lush. They were only small humps from the high view.

"Looks so . . . small from up here." Ashton put her hand up and cupped Augland so it sat perfectly on the palm of her hand. It was less dangerous when it seemed so tiny. She imagined she could crush it by just closing her fist. The walls would be the first to go, followed by a tsunami on Maya Bay, the crumbling of mountains of Predator's Biome, the uplifted earthquake that would destroy Land of Legends and Victorian, followed by a dust storm destroying Venus. All the beauty Ashton saw was tainted by the idea of destroying it because, at its roots, Augland was rotten.

"Ashton." Georgina leaned closer to her and placed her hand on Ashton's arm. "When we win, I want you to know I'll protect you and bring you home. I know what we are asking is a lot, and I'm sorry."

"You mean if you win . . ." Ashton said under her breath.

"What was that?" Georgina asked.

Ashton didn't repeat herself. "And sorry for which part? Asking me to lie for you and say you had nothing to do with the Suit? That's what you want me to do, right? I've been thinking about it since we left. It took me a minute. Wolfe is the one who figured it out first. I thought I was just going to say what happened and I wasn't sure why Warren would want that. But then, it clicked. The only way you get away with this is if I admit that you had nothing to do with the Suit or asking me to spy on Warren to the House of CEOs, who will likely kill me for it. Or are you sorry that if you don't win, I'll face the wrath of the AEC? I'll never go home, never be free, never see—"

Ashton's breath caught in her throat. She didn't fear dying. She had overcome that fear when she was in Augland 54, caught among the fires with a photon wound on her leg. Instead, she feared what would happen to the people she loved and cared for. She didn't want Wolfe to be hurt. Or Bez, or Hunter. The Colony people or Augland workers. None of them. She feared not getting her chance to bring justice to Warren for what he had done to Sheva and Jagatha. Ashton held back tears.

"Just . . . hear us out." Georgina smiled, and there was a small part of Ashton that wanted to trust her.

Georgina pulled her hand away as the same man who dismissed the AEC security men approached from the other side of the aisle. Georgina introduced him as Frederick. He was an unusually thin, long-limbed man with framed glasses and thinning, stark-white hair—not a Suit, she decided. First, Ashton noticed the bright-green bow tie he wore. Frederick was dapper, wearing an expensive pressed suit and smelling of pungent ripe mandarin and leather.

Georgina was wearing a pinstripe jacket with straight leg pants, perfectly pressed. She crossed her legs. One hand lay gracefully against her lap and the other rested, bent from the elbow, on her airplane chair as Frederick sat straight across from her. Ashton stared down at her own clothes—black skinny pants that were smeared with grass stains and mud, smelling of firepit smoke and seawater. She was clearly the most underdressed of the three of them.

"I'd like to talk about what to expect tomorrow and during the coming days," Frederick said in a thick, southern Augland drawl, taking Ashton's attention from her clothing back to the confined space of the jet.

"You trust that they won't tell the AEC we are talking? Georgina said we weren't allowed to speak to each other," Ashton questioned. She looked back at the two security men that stood by, asking because she was more curious than concerned.

"The AEC security men and I have come to an arrangement. So, yes, we paid them off so we could have some privacy and hopefully find a way to use your subpoena as a way to benefit Georgina and keep you out of the AEC prison."

Ashton nodded.

"Now, as I was saying, I'm goin' to be Georgina's representation; do you know what that means?" Ashton shook her head no. She knew the word, but not in this context.

"It means that when we are at the trial, I'll be there to support your story as it relates to Georgina's involvement with Augland 54. Kind of like the narrator." He smiled mockingly. "Does that make sense?"

Ashton didn't appreciate the condescending childlike enunciation, but she did understand his purpose. The political world was beyond her, and she was happy someone would be there alongside her, even if he cared more for Georgina's success.

"Okay, well, one thing we need to make sure is that your story is straight, especially where it involves NeuroEnergy and Georgina." He pulled Ashton's hand into his. "I want you to know I'm going to protect you. Every question, every answer, we will make sure is in line to help you, not hurt you. But my questions will be tough to make it seem like I'm going hard on you, I'll ask challenging questions just as hard as Warren's representative will. You understand?"

Ashton nodded and then finally, having had enough discomfort of her hand in Frederick's that she pulled back and sunk deeper into the cushioned seat of the aircraft. The jet had now gone high above the clouds, where it drifted above a blanket of white beneath them. Frederick continued to speak, and while listening could not take her eyes off the never-ending layer of white that shone brightly as it drifted near the sun.

"Now, Georgina told me you've lost quite a few friends recently. Poor little Jagatha, and I believe a lady by the name of Sheva, was it?" Ashton's jaw tightened after their names were spoken. Her eyes shifted down to her entwined fingers. The mere mention of their names still made her tense.

"You were close with them?" Frederick eyed Ashton carefully.

Ashton didn't respond. She looked over at Georgina, her face remaining unreadable.

"I'm so sorry for your loss . . ." There was a long pause as he gave an empathetic gaze. "Jagatha must have been special to you. And Sheva, I hear she was a great engineer." Frederick paused. There was once upon a time she was too trusting, too willing to see the good in others but now she catalogued every eyebrow raise, nervous twitch, or fake sympathy as signs of deception.

"Didn't she use to work at the park as an engineer?" Frederick probed.

Ashton's brow furrowed. "Yes, she worked in the parks. The trains too—sometimes, at least."

Frederick jotted some notes down on a slick, thin glass he kept in front of him. Ashton tried to see what he wrote, but it was only scribbles she couldn't make out on the translucent page.

"But she knew about how things worked, like the Artificial Existence Beings?" Frederick asked. Ashton remembered her time with Sheva on the train, teaching her how the engineering world worked. Ashton was terrible at it, didn't understand even the basics, but she had tried to memorize the words and definitions. Looking back, Sheva was too patient with her. Ashton felt the regret of not listening more to her. Maybe her world would have been different if she'd been able to better understand the inner workings of it. *How things could have been different . . . maybe Sheva would still be here. Jagatha . . .*

Ashton placed her hand up to her neckline out of habit, but she quickly realized the moonstone necklace Sheva had given her before she was taken off the Augland train by security was missing. Ashton remembered taking it off before she and Wolfe had hiked the Olympics—it was at her Hood Canal home. She didn't want to lose it, and she now regretted that decision. Since Georgina arrived sooner than she presumed she'd had no opportunity to grab her most valuable possessions or appropriate clothing for a DC visit.

Ashton sighed. "I guess. She never mentioned anything about the Suits." She knew where Frederick was going with this line of questioning.

"We don't call them *Suits*," Frederick reprimanded her. "But just because she never mentioned the Artificial Existence Beings doesn't mean she didn't know. Did she ever talk to you about her job?"

"No, no not really. Only when she tried to teach me a few things. She thought it would be important for me to understand the basics if I ever left my job at Maya Bay."

"Interesting, and what sort of things did she teach you?"

Ashton paused, trying to recall a resemblance of Sheva's words. "I'm not sure what you're getting at."

Frederick put his pen down and said, "Could it have been that, unknowingly, Sheva was teaching you how the Artificial Existence Beings worked? Or maybe a glitch or flaw in the system that you could later use? Or maybe that she understood the engineering behind them because she wanted the best for you, that someday you could work with them? Engineering seems like it would be a fairly high-up position for a worker like Sheva, and if she were such a good friend, she would want that kind of status for you."

There it was, what Frederick wanted. Ashton remembered Wolfe's words: *She will set you out to be the conspirator against the AEC, and you'll be a threat they will do anything to stop. That's the only way Georgina can win this trial now that Warren is bringing you as a witness.* Ashton was to implicate Sheva in teaching her about how Suits worked so she knew how to be in a Suit herself.

Ashton's eyes narrowed. "To be clear, I have no idea how they work, and she never told me how to get myself into a pod and transmit my mind into it. Besides, how would she know I would somehow stumble across one of those things?" Agitation sharpened her rhetoric.

"I just want you to think: could she have told you, maybe without knowing? Because if she had, it would excuse NeuroEnergy of any fault. They could admit to finding the AEB and pod, but it was you who understood it all . . ."

"You want me to blame Sheva and say that I lied to Georgina so she would give me a Suit?" The question was rhetorical. Ashton pulled her attention from an attentive Frederick to Georgina. Her breath deepened as she absorbed the tall tale Frederick wanted from her. He cared about finding a way around NeuroEnergy's involvement. Ashton knew she would take the blame and that was how they would spin it—or at least what they needed from her.

"We are just coming up with scenarios here. That's all. It could have been Hunter too; he was close with the Artificial Existence Beings . . . although I'd hate to subpoena him for the trial."

"Georgina said that I was subpoenaed. Hunter wasn't."

"That's true, but we chose to not bring anyone else to incriminate additional people. We could change that."

"Don't do that." She eyed Frederick carefully. He was a nice-looking man with kind features, but that threat alone confirmed her suspicions of his intentions.

"Do what, Ashton?" Frederick pretended not to understand.

Ashton scoffed. "Pretend like I'm so naïve I don't understand what you want me to say. Or what you're trying to do." The thought of bringing along Hunter infuriated her. Hunter would be an easy target for the opposition with all his knowledge of Georgina's plans to find out more about Augland's energy initiatives.

"You would never allow Georgina to be so exposed with all that Hunter knows about NeuroEnergy. She sent him into Augland as an engineer to find out about energy initiatives. That alone would confirm Warren's narrative. Let's be honest. You want me to say that Sheva taught me how to use the Suit and that I used my relationship with Georgina to get one and go into Augland 54 myself. I used the Suit to start the rebellion, and without me, Georgina wouldn't be here, on trial. You want to lie so you can frame me, so let's just call it what it is. I've accepted that. So, what happens then? After Georgina is absolved of everything, you have no reason to protect me."

"I want you to understand that maybe there is a possibility that Sheva unknowingly gave you that gift of knowledge. Georgina needs to have clean hands, and what we need is a plausible story. After that we can get into the specifics of why you would do it. You can talk about Wolfe, how they discarded Sheva, or even what your friend Bez went through . . . so in exchange for your testimony, we give you a platform to expose Warren of his digressions."

Anger frayed Ashton's temperament. "I'm going to need more than that. I told you I'd lie, or sort of tell the truth, if it protects the workers, and if this protects them, I'll say it. But in return, none of the workers in NeuroEnergy or the Colony go back to Augland and I can go home after the trial. Now it's your turn to convince me you'll actually be able to get me out of there."

Frederick sat back in his chair and gave a half smile that was quickly hidden by his hand coming up and rubbing his chin. "Fair enough, Ms. Ashton. I think we got off to a bad start . . . maybe we should start over."

"I think that would be best." Ashton hadn't realized her nails had nearly penetrated her skin through her tightened fists. At least one thing was made clear: she wasn't going to be their toy.

The rest of the plane ride, Frederick and Ashton worked through scenario after scenario of how Ashton could have obtained a Suit and placed herself in it, homing in on the reasons why Ashton would go back to Augland—because Warren had killed Sheva and stolen Colony children. Frederick had convinced her of his plan to protect the workers and ensure her safe return home, because once Georgina was found to have no fault in conspiracy, she would bring Ashton back to NeuroEnergy. While it was not foolproof, it was enough for Ashton to let go of some of her suspicions. He asked probing questions and Georgina worked on the specifics of how Suits functioned. It wasn't enough to convince Ashton that she could do it and say Sheva had taught her the fundamentals of Suit inhibition, but it would do in case any tailored questions about how Suits worked were asked.

Frederick even gave her some advice on how to respond if the other side asked how she did it, which was to avoid answering. He also insisted that she needed to be likable to the rest of the CEOs—which boded well with the idea she would gain some favor for Wolfe to ask in case a rebellion was instituted.

"You don't have to say exactly what is on your mind because, remember, there are still many CEOs who act like Warren in many ways. Try to be soft with your approach and spin what you want to say to be less . . . hostile. You want to draw empathy, not make them feel like you're combative."

"I've been around them my entire life. I think I can manage." The hostility hadn't left her tone, but now Frederick appreciated their discourse. She didn't trust him fully, but for the next few days, she'd need friends more than enemies.

Before Ashton knew it, they were gliding above Augland, DC, and the AEC security guards separated Ashton from Frederick and

Georgina. Ashton glued her face back to the glass shield, and then she saw it. It was different than Augland 54, spanning wider and deeper than she had ever seen, even though the ride across the Augland countryside.

This Augland was an Augland greater than all Auglands.

CHAPTER 6

Wolfe

NEUROENERGY, PACIFIC NORTHWEST

Wolfe, with deliberate steps, walked along the long hallways of Neuro-Energy located in what had once been once Port Angeles, Washington. It had taken them only hours on the hoverbike to make it to its bare cement entrance. Joao and Bez had taken longer, which annoyed Wolfe. They didn't have time for insignificant delays and had traveled to NeuroEnergy soon after Ashton's departure. It was essential for Wolfe to have Joao by his side this mission. It reminded him of their years working together in Augland 54.

He missed Ashton already. To make matters worse, her departure left him with a nagging sense of dread. Warren held all the cards right now, and Ashton was a target. Wolfe and Joao had a plan before Ashton left to keep Bez and Ashton far away from the politics of Augland in DC, but he now sensed Ashton was in danger. Warren had access to her, and he undoubtedly believed that Wolfe would sacrifice everything to safeguard her life.

The interconnect dial tone hummed in his ear as Wolfe paced back and forth in his NeuroEnergy apartment, the beating of his heart an audible thud in the silent room. This was the last thing he wanted to do, but if there was any chance of convincing his father to stop the trial, he needed to at least try. They had been at NeuroEnergy for an hour before Wolfe was able to have privacy. He had kept connection with his father through interconnect, hoping to never speak to him again. And now, he was calling him.

"Hello, Warren," Wolfe said as soon as the line picked up, not waiting for his father to respond first. He paced from the kitchen to the living room and back.

"Well, I was wondering when I'd get a call from you." Warren's voice was light. *He must be in a good mood this morning.*

"What do we need to do to call this off?" Wolfe wasn't going to dance around the issue. He had thought about their conversation since leaving Ashton with Georgina. If there was a way he could stop her from testifying, he would try, and Warren was his best bet.

"The trial?" Warren paused, "I'm sorry, Wolfgang, I'm afraid it's too late for that. I didn't want to take such a drastic measure, but I'm afraid the damage is done, and people need to be held accountable."

Accountable. Wolfe wanted to reach through the interconnect and hold his father *accountable* for the mess he had created. While Georgina was guilty of spying on Warren, there was so much his father had done that he should be held responsible for. Not once had he apologized or admitted wrongdoing for imprisoning Wolfe in his Executive Suite closet. He was not held *accountable* for killing innocent workers in Land of Legends. Nor was he held *accountable* for the Customer Service Initiative or when he had destroyed Wolfe's mother's life and subjected her to isolation. Finally, he was never held *accountable* for the fear and torment he'd subjected Wolfe to as a young child. No remorse, no apologies, no concern for others.

"Wolfgang, are you still there?" Warren asked. Wolfe pulled away from his thoughts and went back to the conversation at hand.

"Then settle this with Georgina; you don't need Ashton for that." Wolfe finally stated.

"Not that girl again. It wasn't my idea to involve her."

"So then why not subpoena all of us?" Wolfe already knew the answer to his question. It would be different to have one rogue worker come up with a seemingly impossible scenario of Warren's indiscretions, but multiple would be hard for the House of CEOs to ignore. Not that any of the CEOs cared about workers' rights, but his Head of Security testifying that his father used a Suit to impersonate him and gain the CEO title after stepping down would be cause for concern. They would also like to know why the son of the CEO had blown up their Centauri Building. That was one reason why he didn't understand why Georgina wouldn't bring him too—to bring them would all incriminate Warren more than it would do damage to Georgina.

"I'm no corporate legal representative. They make those decisions for me . . . I would have loved to see you. Happy to still have you—of course on my side, that is."

Wolfe stopped pacing and threw down his fists onto the kitchen table. His anger was pulsing through him and he was unable to control the slip of aggression. "Stop pretending like you're all innocent in this! What do you want?"

Warren took a deep breath. "Good question. What I want is for my name to be cleared. You haven't been privy to what the whispers of corporate politics have been. I'm tired of my *good* name being dragged through the mud on this. Between your leaving, the workers' rebellion, and those workers who decided to leave, it's not been a good look. Georgina exposed that tenfold when she 'rescued' them and accused me of conspiring to get my own energy initiatives." There was more his father wanted to say, Wolfe could tell by the way his voice was constrained, morphing into the familiar, distant and mistrusting man he knew. Warren was neither kind nor empathetic, and Wolfe learned that whatever affection his father had for him was somehow related to others perception or benefit to himself. So, no matter how hard Wolfe tried to establish a loving relationship with Warren, there was never true reciprocity. Realizing this truth had taken years to accept, but he always held onto the hope that someday he'd see a glimpse of the affection Wolfe desired.

"I can't stop the trial from happening, but . . . I want you to come back here. I want things to go back to the way they were before all this.

I can't change things for NeuroEnergy, they've created their own problems and will suffer the consequences, but that doesn't mean you have to go down with their ship, Wolfgang. I tried to warn you about siding with Georgina. I tried to tell you to come back. Listen to me now and take this deal."

Wolfe stopped pacing and mulled over his father's words. It was true, Warren had warned him, but he had been burned by Warren's manipulations in the past. Wolfe wanted resolution to bring Ashton home and to stop the trial.

Warren continued, "I'll let the workers of Augland stay with the Colony. Things will go back to normal for the world outside of Augland 54 and NeuroEnergy. I'll forget that any of it ever happened, and you can come back as the Director of Security. I know you must miss it. You were, at one point, passionate about the work you were doing here." Wolfe couldn't help but question his father's motives. It wasn't just about the workers though; it was about what Augland 54 had become. On the other hand, Warren had a point. There was part of Wolfe that wanted to try again, to see if things had just gotten out of hand and there could be change while his father was in power. *Because it would be a fight to get him out.*

"You made a similar promise when you made me denounce the CEO title."

"That was different, and you know it. Besides, you've done things, I've done things. We could start over. Anew." Warren countered. He was supposed to let Ashton go when he denounced the title, but instead had said she had made too big of a commotion to release her.

"What will happen to NeuroEnergy, then?" Wolfe at some point had sat down at the kitchen table, his mind deciphering whether to continue his own line of questioning or to hang up on him.

"Georgina will be replaced. That is non-negotiable. She's a danger to us." *Us.* Warren still tried to tie them together as one.

"The trial, is it just for Georgina to be replaced as CEO?" Wolfe questioned him, still not convinced of his father's true intentions.

"The question you should be asking is what I get in return. It's a deal not a gift." There was a shift in Warren's tone—dark and twisted.

"You have a history of telling me lies to get what you want, so I think I'm warranted in my own line of questioning *your* plan." There was so much Warren had left out; he was clearly hiding something. Wolfe knew that he wouldn't divulge anything unless Wolfe decided to switch sides and join his father, but he wasn't ready to commit to anything. He needed to know more before he could finalize a plan to get Ashton back and ensure their initiative to take over Augland 54 was plausible.

"You return to my side in Augland 54 and support my initiatives at the trial."

"If I do, what happens to Ashton?" He should have said the workers of Augland 54; that was truly what he wanted to know, but right now Ashton was the one in danger and he needed to make sure she would be safe.

"The girl?" Warren sounded surprised. "Wolfgang, please tell me you're not throwing away this opportunity for a girl. Take it from me, there will be a million of her kind in your lifetime . . . but if it means that much, sure, you can keep the girl." Wolfe's grip on his interconnect tightened. He was sure if his father were with him at that moment, he'd swing at him. Instead, he was up out of his seat.

"Don't say it like that. She's not a thing or possession and she's suffered a lot. By your hand, I might add."

"You're just adding to my point; she's damaged goods." Wolfe scoffed, but Warren continued, "I'm not trying to be insensitive, it's just the truth. At some point your paths will divide and you won't be able to help her, and she will bore you. You lead; you come from a powerful family, and you have responsibilities. She's a . . . *worker.*"

Wolfe walked along the room until he came to the window that looked out across the NeuroEnergy courtyard. There were hundreds of people out and it looked as though they were setting up an outdoor market to sell goods. There were several tents and tables; some people held totes of items. A few children ran around the grassy area playing tag. It reminded Wolfe of what Ashton said about how different Augland, and freedom were. It was everything Ashton and Wolfe wanted to protect because Augland deprived people of freedom and instilled fear for their lives. That was why Wolfe would do anything to bring his father down and the reason why Ashton was so fearless when it came to stopping Warren. "You're wrong." Wolfe said.

"I guess we will find out if I am, and my offer stands. I want you to come home, Wolfgang. I'll protect the workers like you want; I'll even leave the Colony alone once we have the cure for infertility. If it's some sort of collateral you want, I'll provide it. You come testify by my side and show we are a united front. I'm not against compromise here."

There was a long pause that created more unease. Wolfe rested his head against the windowsill of his NeuroEnergy room windowsill. He had so much to say, but to anger his father now would only hurt Ashton in the long run, given that she was already in route across the country and within arm's length of his monstrous father.

"Our trust is broken, I get it. We will have to build on that, start over. Tell you what, I'll give you till the start of the trial to make your decision. And Wolfgang, please believe me, I will honor my word on this because I want to rebuild to what we had. Whatever you need to make the right choice here." With that, Warren hung up the phone, leaving Wolfe to stew on the choice he had to make.

"Rye, where are Georgina and Ashton?" Wolfe asked as Joao arrived and they approached the desk of Georgina's trusted assistant. The open-spaced NeuroEnergy office area looked the same; Ashton had often referred to it as a dull, grey Augland with desks. Cubicles of Neuro-Energy workers lined the perimeter of the colorless room. Wolfe had ended his call with Warren with more questions than answers. He had to think through his father's proposal, and he had agreed to give him until the start of the trial. For now, no one needed to know about his conversation. Not even Joao.

Wolfe could care less about how Rye had been or what he had done in the last six months. He looked the same to him: tall, long-limbed, and repping his typical knitted, multi-color pullover. Hunter would be around somewhere nearby. He had taken a position in the intel department under Rye just months ago, but that was all Wolfe knew. As if Joao sensed Wolfe had just arrived, he came in after him and leaned against Rye's door frame.

"Didn't realize you'd get here so soon after they left." Rye eyed Wolfe. "They just touched down in Augland 1, in DC proper or the center hub where the Executive Branch is located." Rye took off his glasses and a topographical view rose of the Augland, DC landscape. The globed location highlighted a vast area, all divided like Augland 54 into park subdivisions. The interactive map slowly rotated as Wolfe and Joao evaluated what they saw. First, an extravagant castle centered surrounded by lined pools. Deserts surrounded it, rolling dunes with spiked triangles littered around a lush green oasis. Next, Hazelton Island, which had large property mansions on a long strip of land surrounded by water, reminding Wolfe of Victorian. Snowcadia, Irish Hills, Carnaval d'Augland, and finally Suburbia; the first Augland park ever created.

"They're here." Rye brought the middle section of Augland 1 front and center, where a colosseum lined with white pillars and spacious grounds highlighted the endless possibilities of Augland's creative beauty. Wolfe eyed the detailed map carefully, looking at each luminated fabric of Rye's map.

"Where will the trial take place?" Wolfe bent down to take a closer look at the inside of Rye's map, and he clicked his remote to bring the DC inside out, allowing the highlighted blueprints to split the Washington, DC building in half.

"Here." He pointed to a round room lined with chairs, and in the center was a raised table and large throne-like chair. "That's where Beaugard Hollenberg will be, and the House of CEOs and Augland-dedicated Senators have their own chair during the trial's business. At least once a quarter they all gather at this location and it's most likely where they will have it. According to Georgina, at least." Wolfe studied it, line by line, stopping at the manufactured wall that spanned a great distance. In a matter of hours, those walls would be filled with the most powerful men and women of Auglands, AEC, and NeuroEnergies alike.

"What do you have planned for intel? Any live coverage?" Joao asked, pushing himself off from the door frame and closer to the blueprints on Rye's desk.

"We haven't been able to infiltrate the Augland, DC, region, not until now. We have a specific listening device and camera on Geor-gina, a brooch that she wears containing a microphone that will relay sound. It's virtually undetectable, but its quality won't be very good. We had to cut some corners to make it invisible, and there will probably be about a five-minute lag."

"That's it? That's all we have to help them?" Wolfe probed.

"Yes, by Georgina's design. She didn't want to give any ammunition to Warren to use against her. It took her days to feel comfortable with the brooch. We had to make it unrecognizable." Wolfe shook his head; he thought they would have more capabilities and NeuroEnergy would be more prepared in case things went sideways. The disappointment didn't go unnoticed. Joao turned, scoffing, and closed his eyes in discontent.

"Aren't you guys' tech geniuses or something?" Wolfe's sarcastic remark elicited a chuckle from Joao, which was quickly masked.

"Scientists. And we tend to focus on energy . . ." Rye quickly corrected him. Wolfe just shrugged. "I've been working on something, though, not to necessarily help them but to give us some leverage in case things go . . . awry." Rye gave a reassuring response and lowered his voice. He didn't want the others around him to catch wind of the secret he seemed reserved to even mention.

"Well?" Joao piped into the conversation. He was pacing around the table, studying the blueprints alongside Wolfe.

"It's not close to finished, but we have been able to locate a satellite through government-sealed documents taken after the war. Using those, we think we can take coordinates of other satellites and hyper-focus multiple energy pulses on a given area. If successful, it could deactivate all Suits in Augland at once, immobilizing the technology and basically stopping all transmissions from Suits to Pods for a time. Eventually, the pod will re-route the signal and reconnect with the Suit. But for a while, the Suit will be deactivated. It could work on any Artificial Being, even droids. Our scientist calls it Stereotactic Electro-magnetic Pulsing."

NeuroEnergy had worked heavily with the government before the war and it made sense that they would have documentation that was classified at the time, like the coordinate and access codes to satellites. Rye continued, "We may even be able to coordinate multiple pulses at one time to deactivate Suits or robots in a different area simultaneously. Essentially, they could cripple the defense network of the AEC for a short period of time. I'm sure that the AEC's back up system will reactivate the VELIC system, which will eventually catch on and shut down the satellites, but it may give us a window of opportunity for the UnSuited to have a chance. We are also working on reprogramming algorithms for the satellites, which could enable us to re-engage the system after they initially shut it down. We need to know how VELIC will approach the problem before we can create the reprogrammings. Which could potentially allow future attacks."

"And that means what? You could disable Suits so they couldn't . . . function?

"Oh yes, if we had enough satellites, we could create a system where they were unable to function at all."

"And . . . the only thing stopping this is we don't have enough satellites to create enough . . . energy malfunction for much time?"

"Precisely."

"Yet we aren't there yet . . . because?"

"We don't have enough function with the satellites to create a consistent flow without disruption." Rye spoke like it was common knowledge. "But if it works, it could change everything." Rye sat back in his chair, crossing his arms.

"Why is this the first we are hearing about it?" Joao asked which was exactly what Wolfe was thinking.

"You are not entitled to know everything going on here. We've expected some sort of retaliation from Augland to happen since you brought workers from Augland to our plant. This is for NeuroEnergy's safety and that is *my* concern, not yours."

"And this scientist . . . he's here? At this NeuroEnergy?" Wolfe questioned. He cared less about Rye wanting to keep his weapon a secret and more about its viability. If they had the power to turn off Suits, that was very interesting to Wolfe and whether Rye liked it or not they were currently allies in this.

"Well, yeah . . ."

"Could we see for ourselves? I want to hear it from the scientist." There was one thing Wolfe wouldn't do and that was to let this new technology slip through his fingers. He wanted to know everything, how it worked, how long it would take, what this scientist knew of Suits and how exactly he could position it against his father—or use as insurance if he took Warren's offer.

CHAPTER 7

Ashton

Ashton couldn't sleep. She had tried closing her eyes and counting to thirty, which is what she did whenever she tried to silence her thoughts and fall asleep back home. Her eyes grew heavy, but it was when the day's events settled that her mind began racing. Georgina was *blaming* Ashton for the rebellion across multiple Auglands—the thought alone of the UnSuited rebellion still thriving within Augland 54 was enough to surprise her. She had no idea the rebellion had spread to other parks so quickly. Georgina also wanted Ashton to admit it was only she who had access to Charlotte, the Suit Georgina had given her to assist in getting closer to Warren to gain information. While it was true that Georgina did not create the rebellion, she was the architect of the idea to use the Suit to infiltrate Augland 54 where the uprising started.

She had spent the last hour of the flight alone without Frederick and Georgina who had disappeared and gone back to their secluded area of the jet. Frederick made her promise not to reveal to the AEC that they'd had any conversation, which she agreed to. The time alone allowed her to think about what was about to happen in Augland, DC. By Ashton taking the fall for conspiring against Warren, Georgina promised to protect the workers who had escaped with her and Bez and safeguard the Colony against any further attacks. It would give NeuroEnergy and the Colony time to develop a plan to further support the UnSuited who wished to escape they tyranny of Augland 54. But what hadn't been discussed was what would happen to Ashton for admitting fault—the Augland CEOs would turn on her and there would be consequences for her actions against the corporate conglomerate. She knew the only reason Wolfe let her leave the Colony was because if she had stayed, Georgina would lose at trial, and the workers would never be free from Warren's reign.

Only hours earlier, the AEC's aircraft had landed on the steps of the House of CEOs. It was nearing night by the time they arrived and the only lights were targeted beams highlighting the white columns of this enormous, marbled building. The structure appeared to be filled with apartments, offices, and auditoriums—reminding Ashton of the hotels in Maya Bay. Ashton barely had time to view her surroundings before DC security escorted her directly to her room.

It didn't take long for her to realize how heavily guarded the entire resort-size House of CEOs building was: guards in Suits walking along the perimeter, with two guards located at the gates within the acre wide landscape, while another two guards were situated on either side of the stark-white House of CEO entrance doors.

The apartment she was given was dark and spacious. The floor was stone-cold black tile and the simplistic furniture in the spacious apartment made every sound echo against the walls. The third-story creaks and noisy ceiling fan weren't what was keeping her awake at this hour; it was what Frederick had asked her to do.

"You don't have to say exactly what is on your mind because, remember, there are still several CEOs that act like Warren in many ways. Try to be soft with your approach and spin what you want to say to be less . . . hostile. You want to draw empathy, not make them feel like you're combative.

"We need to convince them that you, alone, tricked Georgina into giving you the AEB so you could return to Augland in disguise. That Georgina had no idea you knew how one of them worked. That you were hoping by exposing Warren's plan to overtake NeuroEnergy as CEO you could trade your secrecy for Jagatha's freedom. We need to convince them you were playing both sides."

Ashton eventually relented and accepted the sleepless night. She propped herself up out of her plush bed, turned on the bedside lamp, and walked across the room to the sizeable bathroom in her suite. Ashton splashed cold water against her face, dragging a lavender-scented towel across her skin, attempting to wipe away the exhaustion she felt. Her eyes were red, making the crystal blue of her irises stand out. She tried to tame her curls, but the more she brushed the more it looked like the static from NeuroEnergy's electron plants had formed a frizzy mess on top of her head. It was exactly six hours until the trial began, and Ashton would need every second to pull herself together to meet Augland's standard, not that she cared about such things.

After a quick shower, Ashton put on the electric kettle for tea. It took only seconds to reach boiling temperature. She thought of her home, where it took at least four minutes for the kettle to warm and the hot water for showers was limited. Often they would need to boil at least four pots of water to create enough for a bath. Ashton doubted any of the CEOs knew that kind of poverty, that kind of lifestyle.

She lifted the mug and took a sip of it, tasting the sweetness of chamomile with the slight refreshing tang of lemon. Her cup in hand, she turned toward her bed. Georgina had given her a tailored, black-knit dress to wear and a "pamper kit," leaving her a note to "brush through the curls, at least." Ashton had laid the neatly pressed charcoal dress and simple, black, heeled shoes on the bed. Ashton rolled her eyes and thought about throwing out the kit and dressing in her grass-stained Colony attire to prove that she was nothing like *them* and wouldn't dress to impress, but Wolfe's reminder to not make any irrational decisions played in her head.

Today was day one of the trial. Georgina had told her that after their day in court, dinner would be hosted for all those attending the trial, which Ashton was not looking forward to. In her experience, dinner events were with people she cared about, like Rico and Bez, not between Suits and workers and definitely not with anyone here at the trial. Georgina had shrugged it off, calling it "political and an important part of their strategy."

Ashton had been to a party only once before, when she had impersonated Charlotte and tried to extort information about Augland 54's energy initiative. That was the same unforgettable day Warren had caught her. Warren had paraded Ashton around the Augland 54 elites, and she remembered being impressed by the lavish Predator's Biome waterfall and elegant decorations. Ashton remembered enjoying the posh lifestyle, which was shortly disrupted by the appearance of the screaming little girl with the blonde curly hair, who had been taken from the Colony and placed in the arms of two Suits—an Executive named Boren if Ashton remembered correctly. The cruelty of the Auglands had suddenly become too visual for Ashton. It was at that moment she'd realized that she didn't belong with these Suits, and she needed to get as far away from them as possible.

Look at me now, Ashton thought bitterly. She was about to play dress up once more so she could at least try and fit in with these people she so despised.

Ashton moved past the dress and toward the private third-story porch. Even now, she tried to silence her mind and focus instead on her surroundings. The feather-like petals from cherry tree blossoms swayed on the trees that lined her room, which was perched within the walls of Augland, DC. She hadn't noticed them when they first arrived. The entire building spanned the length of several city blocks until it reached the steel perimeter gates, with each guest's apartment facing the sprawling landscape and manicured green grass. An elaborate sculpted fountain towered regally in the center of a precisely edged, manmade pond reflecting the starlit sky. The cherry blossom trees were uniform on either side of a long walkway down the center of the yard. The landscape was mesmerizing.

Augland's air was sweeter than the real outdoors, less earthy. Ashton missed home and the natural scent of trees, soil, and wildlife. It had been less than a day since she was whisked away from her Hood Canal, from Wolfe, and she already longed for the comfort of its safety. The place here was "cold" and it had nothing to do with the temperature-controlled dome and more to do with the imposing dread for the upcoming day's events. She had no idea how long her mind drifted as she stood on the balcony outside, but it was long enough that had she began to see the sunrise peering above the DC city landscape.

Ashton was interrupted by a high-pitched "ding" coming from somewhere in her room, making her jump, spilling the tea she forgot she held in her hand.

"Hello, Ashton. This is your personal VELIC speaking, reminding you of an appointment set up for hair and makeup." The room echoed, giving no direction to the robotic voice's whereabouts. Ashton's eyes settled on the wall next to her bed where the silhouette of a shadowed man was outlined against the wall. She jumped again, startled by the voice and its owner. "Is now a good time to get started?"

Ashton put her hand up to the wall, feeling where the dark shadow appeared and moved along its smooth flat surface with ease. If Augland hadn't surprised her with technology before, she may have found its AI more intimidating. But given that she had already seen one on Georgina's aircraft; they seemed relatively harmless—except for the recording conversation's part—she let it go. Ashton scaled the walls with her eyes, ready to respond to any potential threat, but her trepidation was put on the back burner as her curiosity outgrew her fear. VELIC in the aircraft controlled the control board's technology. This one was installed and built seamlessly into the wall, like it was projected against it but there was nothing except the shadow—no light from the room, only *in* the wall. Ashton continued to glide her fingertips along the shadowed surface. It felt like any other wall, smoother than the one at her home but nothing unfamiliar.

"You . . . you're VELIC?" Ashton questioned.

"Yes, I am *a* VELIC. Are you familiar with my system?" The shadowed arms moved while it spoke.

"Uh, not really, just from the jet."

"I understand. While I am a VELIC, there are many VELICs. Most are dedicated to serving CEOs and span the system so they can be in any physical location. If you are ever in need of assistance, I am here to help you." The dark shadow stopped moving, but she could tell it "looked" at her.

"Ashton, we don't have much time before you are expected; shall we begin?" the VELICs obnoxious and even-toned voice asked.

"I'm sorry, what did you want to do?" The abrupt realization some-*thing* was in the room with her had erased any memory of why it was there in the first place.

"You have an appointment for your hair and makeup for today's events. Should I document on record you'd like periodic reminders of appointments you have?" Ashton sighed, remembering Georgina's note about her unruly curls. *She must have set this up,* Ashton thought.

"Uh, sure." Ashton said.

The silhouette's hands moved, and the wall rippled open to a dark-ened space. The wall morphed and created a chair with a bowl situated behind it. Ashton stepped back, unsure how to feel about the invasive-ness of this wall's technology. It felt the same, but no wall in Hood Canal could ever bend like the walls of this suite did. The wall settled and a chair rolled into its way where the silhouette motioned for Ashton to sit down.

Ashton didn't move. "I sense you're startled. I'm sorry for concern-ing you, Ashton; that was not my intention." VELIC spoke genuinely.

"How did you do that?"

"Every room is equipped with necessary items to support any need of its occupants." *That was helpful.*

Ashton shook her head in disbelief before sitting down on the chair. VELIC sent its mechanical arm around Ashton's hair and placed it into the porcelain bowl that had appeared when VELIC transformed the wall into a salon. Ashton studied it while her head rested, and the machine washed her hair. Synthetic arms mimicking human hands protruded out of the wall and delicately washed the messy brown mop on top of Ashton's head. The shadowed man stood just to her left, still on the wall.

"Why didn't they send a worker?" Ashton asked, probing to see how much information this wall *thing* had.

VELIC's movements were methodical, slowly massaging her head through the suds of shampoo. "Please let this sit for thirty minutes. I've set a timer for you," VELIC said, "and to answer your question, no workers are allowed to be at the House of CEOs, DC district, but there are many in other parks within Augland 1. My records show you are the first human worker to be here. The DC Park in Augland 1 is the first Augland to be completely run by artificial means." Ashton had thought it was unusual to see no workers at all, none since she arrived in the DC area. Even the security men that had met them as they arrived were Suits.

"Did they get . . . rid of workers?" Ashton asked nervously.

"I have been instructed not to answer questions pertaining to worker treatment or availability of workers. Or any pertinent information that relates to the upcoming proceedings." Ashton tried again with another question but was met with the same response as the first question.

———————

VELIC finished shampooing and treating Ashton's hair before wrapping her hair in a towel. VELIC moved swiftly to her makeup, quickly applying it to her face before undoing her swaddled hair. The AI arms gently unfolded the towel until she saw the curls tumble down to her shoulders. She picked up a single curl and examined it. The color bloomed a deep red that, at first glance, she thought could be her typical brown in the light. But no, this was a vibrant red and Ashton jolted out of her seat and into the bathroom where she immediately noticed the layers of caked-on makeup and the unnatural red of her dyed hair.

What the . . . ? Ashton gave her new look another glance before sighing in frustration.

"What did you do?"

"My records show—"

There was a knock at the door and Ashton realized what time it was eight o'clock. "I don't have time for this!" Ashton silenced the machine.

"Apologies, Ms. Ashton; we have five minutes until you're needed in the main hall of the House of CEOs." Ashton ignored VELIC while she raced to her carefully pressed dress. It didn't matter to her what her hair looked like. What surfaced now were the butterflies of anticipation over Warren's secrets finally being exposed within the AEC.

The dress chosen by Georgina hugged her hips, and the quarter-length sleeves made the all-black attire appear sophisticated. She had never worn anything quite as well-made as this. Well, not on her own human body, and it differed from the shabby, white sheet dress she had been forced to wear while working in Apparel. Between her newly dyed hair and makeup she was nearly unrecognizable. Ashton had forced the VELIC to stop before it had finished styling her, so Ashton had just pulled it back into a ponytail. Another knock was heard.

Ashton dragged the door open, and Frederick's tall frame turned around to face her, his eyes scrolling up and down before he drawled admiringly, "You clean up real nice, Ms. Ashton." Frederick's smile was wide and surprisingly genuine.

"I wasn't expecting you," Ashton said, her tone sounding disappointed.

"They're much more lenient now that you are here. It's less likely we can conspire during the distance from your room to the auditorium. Plus, I thought you'd appreciate the company." Frederick smiled.

Ashton forced a smile back while they walked out of her room and, as the door pressed shut behind her, Ashton noticed Georgina wasn't with him.

"Where's Georgina?"

Frederick put his hand behind Ashton's shoulder and guided her forward. "Meeting us in the room where the trial will be held; she's doing some preliminary shmoozing before we begin. Georgina will need to sway as many CEOs to vote in her favor as possible. Given that we only have three days—"

"Why only three days?" Ashton asked. They walked down the long, royal-blue carpeted hallway. Her stride was half of Frederick's, espe-cially in the uncomfortable heels, but he made sure to slow his pace to match hers. Although the halls were like a maze, he navigated them expertly, stepping quickly through the space.

"CEOs are busy, Ashton. They only convene in the DC district once every three months. It's a quarterly review of business matters. Beaugard, our president, is strict with keeping a quick schedule and, given that we need all CEOs to vote on matters like Georgina's pro-ceeding, he grants us only a few days to discuss the matter. He'll act as the moderator, like he does with any dispute either between Augland and NeuroEnergies or specific people. Anyways, they've already been in meetings this morning to discuss matters outside Georgina's trial." Ashton remained silent after that.

Distracted, Frederick sputtered half sentences under his breath every few steps. He gripped his clear notepad tightly—more of an extension of his own hand at this point, thought Ashton. She surmised he was jotting down last-minute strategies for Ashton's imminent tes-timony. From what Ashton gathered, Warren's side would bring her in first. They had other witnesses, but Frederick pointed out it would be important to establish the foundation of Ashton's story before tackling her credibility after Warren's legal team questioned her.

"Do you have any questions, anything I can answer now? Because once we get in there, we won't be able to talk much. Not until I deliver my opening statement, which will happen after War-ren's counsel, but that might be delayed until tomorrow as we have a shorter day today given the evening's *festivities*," Frederick smirked.

Ashton shook her head. Her mind swirled like a tornado. Her fingers twisted in nervous anticipation.

"I heard—the dinner tonight, right?" Ashton asked.

He nodded. "CEOs usually meet collectively for dinner one night during the quarterly reviews. It's a social event for them to mingle and network with each other. It just so happens this quarter, we have a Senator's son promotion—which is why they are gathering. But it will be essential for Georgina to use the time to her advantage, especially if she is to gain support during the trial—she'll need to convince others of her innocence outside the trial. Some might say that the social dinner is more important than the trial itself."

"Why?"

Frederick sighed, "Because there are many CEOs who would side with Georgina if they knew why she did what she did."

"Isn't that the purpose of the trial?"

Frederick chuckled, "The trial is—how do I say this—is more about credibility than truth. Georgina's truth could be misconstrued and so can Warren's lies. So, yes, the social dinner allows unfiltered and no morphing of words to twist the narrative that will ultimately happen during the trial."

Frederick continued to talk at her through the next twist and turn before stopping hesitantly. Ashton's eyes were drawn up toward the lustrous, white French doors that opened to an auditorium of seats. The few CEOs already present in the auditorium murmured quietly to each other as Ashton and Frederick entered the room. Unlike the Land of Legend's auditorium with its air of long-forgotten theatrical charm, this space was filled with rows of regal, plush-pillowed seats that reminded Ashton more of a royal court setting than rows of court room chairs. Ashton first noticed how clean it looked, spotless even, as her heels dragged across the carpeted floor and she headed toward the front line of assigned chairs; her name and employee identification were printed on glass where the witnesses sat. Frederick confidently led her to her chair which was situated behind Georgina and Frederick's chairs, as he gave smiles and handshakes to the handful of CEOs already in the auditorium. Above them, rich, gold strokes of artists' work were etched boldly on the ceiling, depicting everything from mythical creatures to flawless human forms half naked to the point of Ashton's discomfort.

With every step toward the front of the room, the imposing atmosphere seeped through her skin, gripping her stomach and causing her nerves to tighten. In the back of her mind the same thoughts from her sleepless night played like a movie reel. Frederick pulled out the chair positioned behind his and ushered Ashton into her seat. She hesitated only for a moment, looking back at the open doors that could lead her out of this building and potentially out of Augland DC. She looked to Frederick as he now concentrated on his interpad, hoping to see some reassuring gesture or sense of confidence, but she couldn't read him.

They waited twenty excruciating minutes before Georgina made her way down the long aisle and toward the row where Frederick sat. Ashton sat with the other witnesses, and she faced the courtroom where Frederick's table housed one chair for Georgina. Ashton had turned back several times as CEOs from different Auglands and NeuroEnergies had leisurely settled into seats, talking with some levity amongst themselves like this wasn't a defining moment in their corporate history. She noticed instantly how the NeuroEnergy CEOs differed from the Auglands CEOs. NeuroEnergy executives didn't wear Suits while the Augland CEOs did; or if NeuroEnergy CEOs wore Suits, she couldn't tell. *You can't trust appearances. Just because they're not Suits doesn't mean they're safe,* Ashton thought.

Ashton jumped as a Suit laughed hard enough for the sound to cross the room, jolting her back to the scene unfolding around her. The tension in the spacious theatre at that moment felt claustrophobic, anxiety forcing the movement of her now tapping foot. She glanced at Georgina, who had refrained from looking at her since sitting down at her table. Her hair was pinned back in a low bun and her black and white dress was tailored perfectly to her body. She sat up straight, which made Ashton instantly note her own slouched posture and at once she straightened. She wished they had taken a moment to speak, not that she was sure what she would say, but any words of encouragement would have been helpful. Frederick had spoken at length about their plan, but she had not heard how Georgina *felt*. It must be as nerve-wracking for her as it was for Ashton.

Finally, a door opened near the front of the auditorium. Only a few yards ahead of Ashton was a perched chair facing the entire audience and a tall Suit who walked toward it. He was bronzed and built, but marring his attractive face was a menacing gaze. He didn't look at Ashton, or at anyone else, for that matter. He simply went to his chair and settled into his interpad, a glass sheet meant for communicating and taking notes. Ashton took a moment to discreetly look at Georgina again, whose shoulders tensed as she stole glances up to the Suit sitting at the center chair. Georgina turned to whisper something in Frederick's ear, but Ashton couldn't hear what was said. Ashton's breath quickened with unease, uncomfortable with their secrecy. She could feel the hairs on the back of her neck stand. *Wolfe was right; coming here was a mistake.* This was a lion's den, in an Augland filled with powerful people.

"Ladies, gentlemen. Our break in session will end soon. Please, everyone, take your seats if you haven't done so . . ." Beaugard's voice spoke loudly, and the microphone amplified the words as they echoed inside the four walls of the auditorium. The room fell deathly quiet. Frederick turned back toward Ashton and motioned for her to come closer to him. "That's Beaugard, the President of the House of CEOs. He runs the AEC," Frederick whispered.

"VELIC, please begin recording our session." Beaugard spoke again. There was the same silhouetted man from Ashton's wall next to Beaugard.

"Of course, Beaugard. Recording is now activated." VELIC obeyed.

Beaugard then greeted the room, "good morning, everyone. We appreciate the early morning given we have much to discuss and those who moved schedules to accommodate . . . as we are a tad early with our congressional quarterly review. I will take full blame for that." Beaugard cleared his throat, which echoed to the back of the auditorium. "Given that we only have three days, I want to make the most of our time. As you are aware, there has been a report of potential misconduct related to Pacific Northwest NeuroEnergy's activities and Augland 54's initiatives for energy solution. We are here today to proceed with a trial, and I must emphasize that we are only dealing with an accusation until all the facts have been presented and we vote on them as a united group. Only then are we able to assign any validity to its claim . . . with that I'll turn it over to the claimant's side to put forth the accusation." An uneasy silence crept around the room as a man stood from where Ashton now identified as the opposing counsel representing the *murderer* she hated—Warren. She turned her head to bypass the other Suits seated around her until finally she saw him. The man, the Suit she swore she would destroy. She somehow had overlooked his presence since had Beaugard started speaking.

Warren's face was elevated just slightly so his eyes slanted. Ashton took notice of the black and white goatee that only hinted at his age, but the rest of him was young. His eyes were piercing blue, reminding her of Wolfe's even though Warren's were fake. She narrowed her gaze and it was like he could feel her; he glanced at Ashton before moving his entire face to look at her. His eyes half mooned in with a smile, which sent waves of different emotions radiating through her. Hatred and disgust were the most powerful of them all.

Ashton couldn't look away, even though she wanted to do so. Every ounce of her wanted to jump out of her seat and strangle him with both hands, but she knew it wouldn't do any good. *He can't die,* she told herself. *He's just a Suit and you'll have your time soon enough.* Instead, she shifted slightly in her seat and allowed her breathing to settle. Warren gave her a half smile, reminding her so much of Wolfe. It was the only time this killer would resemble the man she loved. Ashton scowled before diverting her eyes from their silent yet heated exchange and looking back to where Beaugard and the opposition's representative took center stage to address him. She breathed in, counting 1,2,3 and out 1,2,3.

". . . again, I appreciate the flexibility in timing, Beaugard. We will make this brief and I hope not to take the full allotted time for my opening statement." The mocha-skinned and shockingly grey-eyed Suit turned his attention from Beaugard to the CEOs that congregated behind him.

"Ladies and Gentlemen of the House of CEOs and Senators of the AEC, my name is Silver Woods and I'm here representing Owen Wolfgang Warren IX of Augland 54. He has learned disturbing news relating to his long-standing and mutually beneficial relationship with Pacific Northwest NeuroEnergy." The man's broad and deep voice resonated as he faced the CEOs.

"Years of relationships, goodwill, and partnership have been tainted by the realization that Pacific Northwest NeuroEnergy has conspired, lied, manipulated, deceived, and ultimately spied to gain leverage." Silver paused for dramatic effect. Ashton took that moment to look around the now-seated room. It was filled with people, each row of chairs slightly higher than the row before it to create a cascade of Suits and people staring directly at them.

"CEO Georgina Raylen has gone so far as to infiltrate the sacred home of CEO Warren to further her investigation into her insane and outlandish theories of energy creation. She has a personal vendetta against CEO Warren, wishing to tarnish what he has built in Augland 54. Specifically, Land of Legends, the fifth most-extravagant park in all Auglands and a well-documented worker rehabilitation program with much success. What I can't tell you is why CEO Georgina Raylen would be convinced of any deceptive behavior by Warren. Why, after all these years of harmony and mutually beneficial cooperation, she would plague Augland 54 with spies. Why she would have an entire team dedicated to covertly gather intel on 54, or why she would put an ex-worker into a Suit in order to manipulate Warren's son to help steal confidential information on Executives. She has even gone as far as to instigate a rebellion that, might I add, has affected not only Augland 54 but countless other Auglands."

Whispers filled the room and Ashton's eyes spun before they landed back on Silver, who spoke a twisted truth. Ashton's fist tightened in her lap.

"You all know Warren: he's a righteous man, an innovator with ideas of bettering our world for our customers, and for our workers. He embodies the essence of our corporation and strives, daily, to better himself, to benefit our clients, and to better the Augland he has dedicated himself to, along with each and every one of you in order to create perfection.

"The only thing I can reasonably imagine that would drive CEO Georgina's undermining behavior is her desire for power. She wants to divide us, wants to seize power over our worlds. Instead of taking accountability for her actions, she has disguised her behavior as altruism. *Saving* workers. *Inciting* a rebellion. And saving them from what? From a life where they are fed and cared for? A world where they are given the opportunity to rise within a prosperous society? To then, what? Steal workers to work for her instead.

"She has broken the treaty that has governed, and united us, under the AEC since its beginning. She has misused her power and political ambition to break all the rules that would destabilize our union."

Once the trickle of whispers about the broken treaty and UnSuited rebellion disappeared, the room went silent again. The audience hung on every word Warren's representative spoke. Ashton had thought the UnSuited worker rebellion was only in Augland 54. It was a rebellion

Bez and Ashton had started to help them and others escape Augland 54, but she had no knowledge of its message reaching other Auglands, not until Georgina brought it up during their meeting at the Colony.

"Georgina's counsel is most likely going to suggest that the young worker sitting in the witness chair was to blame for all of this betrayal. That she, a worker with only Augland Center education, deceived Georgina just as much as Warren. But our evidence will show that the worker was merely Georgina's puppet in the grand scheme that she created. She fabricated evidence to better support her case against us." Ashton scoffed louder than she intended to, but not nearly enough to warrant the glaring stares from anyone around her.

"At the end of this trial, I'm going to ask you all: 'Who is the real villain in this story?' I already know that answer and know my comrades, colleagues, and friends will see the same. Warren is no monster; it's Georgina and her puppet who are the predators here, waiting for their time to strike." His slow and sympathetic voice now irritated Ashton. Georgina sat still and from what Ashton could see, her face remained neutral as she held her gaze, watching Silver as he walked around the stage uttering his damning words.

She sat stoically even as the accusations mounted.

CHAPTER 8

Wolfe

NEUROENERGY, PACIFIC NORTHWEST

It took several rounds of debating to convince Rye to let them see the secret weapon NeuroEnergy had been developing—time they did not have given the trial was eight hours away. Joao and Wolfe were a force cut from the same security cloth and trained in interrogations. As soon as Hunter joined in the conversation, the three of them had Rye cornered. Rye hinted that the idea was to utilize pre-war satellites to immobilize Suits which would be a powerful weapon when they rose against Augland. If there were a counter measure to stop the Suits, this would be it. Wolfe knew Rye had to know how much a weapon against the Suits would mean to them, and while he may have had reservations, he would ultimately cave and agree to disclose his secret—which is exactly what happened.

"I can't believe you never told me . . ." Hunter muttered under his breath to Rye while Wolfe, Joao, Rye, and Hunter all squeezed into a secret NeuroEnergy elevator compartment that led them to the underground rooms of the compound. Rye said nothing as he entered his code to open additional available floors. Hunter had been working with Rye the last six months, and was someone he had worked with prior to any involvement with Augland 54 and Ashton. Wolfe assumed Hunter thought his connections with NeuroEnergy and Rye gave him access to more information, but from what Wolfe could tell, he was left out more often than not.

The elevator was in Georgina's office and required several sets of credentials to open; Rye had made Wolfe, and the others, turn around while he implemented them so they couldn't see the exact security steps. *Ground Floor 1, Ground Floor 2.* The elevator's sound system alerted them to each level they passed.

"What's on the other two ground floors?" Hunter asked Rye as they continued their descent. Rye said nothing, only giving him a side-eyed glance. Wolfe could sense that there was still a level of distrust between all of them—well, except between Joao and himself. It was an invisible divide that was only bridged by their combined desire to overtake Augland.

Not that Rye shouldn't have been skeptical of Joao and Wolfe. He was too trusting when it came to sharing the secrets of NeuroEnergy. Fortunately for them, Rye didn't really have another choice when it came to sharing this information, and Wolfe knew that. Right now, they were allies and that meant including Wolfe, Joao, and Hunter on the plan of attack so they could help each other. It was only a matter of time before Augland figured out NeuroEnergy's secret weapon and Wolfe's only chance of success would be the element of surprise. The trial would take place in less than eight hours, and it was almost midnight. Wolfe needed to make his decision about Warren's proposal.

Joao grunted in pain, which made Wolfe turn. "What's wrong with you?" Wolfe asked and Joao squinted while he held his fingers to the bridge of his nose.

"Nothing. Just that headache again . . . I'm fine." Joao wasn't one to complain. Wolfe immediately thought about how Joao's arrival to NeuroEnergy had been postponed when Joao said he felt sick, but Wolfe had dismissed his concern. They had bigger problems to solve.

Ground Floor 3.

The doors opened into complete darkness. The dripping sounds of water would deter anyone from entering the seemingly abandoned level, but Rye stepped out into the black and, within seconds, the darkness swallowed him. Wolfe led the rest of the clandestine group into the abyss. The light from the elevator evaporated as the doors closed behind them.

"Come on, this way. And don't touch anything." Rye's voice echoed. In the distance a keypad flashed, and Rye once again sheltered his code. Suddenly, a set of doors that had been hidden by the darkness opened, flooding the area with blinding light. Unlike the previous room and hallway, the next room was well lit with racks of blinking lights and colored wires. It was silent except for the slight humming of electricity pulsing in nearly every corner of the giant room.

"Vic, you here?" Rye shouted out.

A bald head popped itself up from the other end of the room and from Wolfe's angle looked entrapped between stacks of computers and glass screens.

"Rye? That you?" The man squinted.

"Of course it's me . . . I brought a few people down who wanted to take a look at our operation."

"*The* operation?" The look of shock drained the color from the scientist's face.

"Yes. The STEMP project."

A concerned look formed on the man's face as he climbed out from behind his computer wall to greet them.

"Does Georgina know?" Vic questioned.

"No, but they can be trusted. Last we spoke you said we were getting close, which is why we're here." Vic's lips creased; he was clearly unsure about trusting anyone outside NeuroEnergy, but Rye's partnership, at least for the time being, dissipated Vic's insecurity.

"Depends on what you mean by close," the scientist replied. He walked back to his computer system. Rye joined him and the others followed. Wolfe had to step carefully because the room was littered with gadgets and tools sprawled out on shelves and the floor; some even hung from the ceiling by wires.

As soon as they rounded the corner to Vic's desk, every computer screen lit up with code and cameras. Wolfe studied his setup, trying to connect the dots to the words on the screen and the images he saw.

"Here, we have satellites in the sky. I've been able to access a few of them but the others? They've been tricky. With recent VELIC development, the AEC has used their AI software to put firewalls in place for all previous government property—which has made accessing them more difficult." It was easy for Wolfe to see the screens over Vic's head, as he was significantly shorter than the rest of them, wearing a white lab coat over his pajamas. It was late, and he most likely had thought about going to get some shut eye before the next day.

"Outside the satellite access, this is where things get exciting." Vic crouched down while he moved his hands in various areas across several screens. Wolfe had a hard time keeping up. "Here, we've been able to condense the satellite beams to focus entirely on a given area. We could send focused electromagnetic pulses down to eliminate all electricity in the area which would disrupt Artificial Existence Beings from functioning."

"So, what are we waiting for?" Wolfe asked.

"It's complicated—in theory. Yes, it will work, but accessing the satellites and penetrating their firewall will be difficult. If, and I mean if, we can bypass the VELICs firewall to harness and generate at the desired magnitude and tailored coordinates, given the latitude, longitude, and time of coverage we require . . . well, it's very specific. I need remote access to the satellites before we can even consider using the electricity elimination beams to focus on a certain area for more than a few minutes." The man excitedly spoke tech gibberish, momentarily forgetting his audience. "The Stereo Tactic Electromagnetic Pulses, or STEMP, can be manipulated and gathered to gain a momentous power surge and eliminate a subsection of electricity. It's magical, really, when you think of it. Light storms happen and power grids shut off areas that are connected, but you're never able to limit what electricity is turned off, only that it's all or nothing."

"But you can stop Suits from working altogether?" Wolfe's eyes widened in shock as Vic confirmed everything Rye had said earlier. Wolfe thought of Warren's proposition and the tension continued to build about the decision he would have to make: sell out NeuroEnergy, the Colony, and Ashton to return to his father's side or deny Warren's ultimatum and start a war against a powerful machine. Before this moment, he had been leaning more toward surrender because war now would mean certain death. But if this STEMP thing could actually work? Then certain death might just be avoidable.

Vic pushed his glasses up, which had slid down his nose, so it made his eyes look impossibly large, "In nonscientific words, yes, I could disrupt the circuitry in the Suits, rendering them useless. They would not function until they are reprogrammed by VELIC. But neither would anything else that was electronic in the area affected."

"What happens to the Augland pod transmission to the Suits? Once they are shut off?" Joao chimed in.

"I mean, for the person in the pod, their cognitive awareness would lead the Suit back to where it originated from—their bodies. In other words, if there is no electricity connecting the body and mind, then there is no Suit to function, which would mean they go back to the person's physical body. VELIC could re-establish a connection because it is likely that some latent circuitry redundancy was built into the Suits, but that would take time. How much time, I'm not sure. But the technical resources in the pod areas would probably be overwhelmed for a while. Not just that, cameras, anything powered by electricity, will suffer the same fate. And it wouldn't be lack of electricity elsewhere; like I said, you could target where you want electricity to fail and even the backups wouldn't help."

Wolfe thought about a battle without the Suits, abilities. The people in pods had very little training in combat, which would make the rebellion's war a nearly fair fight. A war even his father wouldn't be able to stop.

This wasn't a weapon; it was their checkmate—*if it worked*. If they could stop Suits all together . . . life as they knew it wouldn't be dictated by Auglands—or the AEC.

Hunter started laughing out loud, fist pumping the air as his excitement grew. But Wolfe and Joao remained still as the air of possibility changed around them. "I'd hold your enthusiasm, this is only theory right now. I've got only a few satellites that might still work but can only be used once every twelve hours."

That brought Wolfe back to the conversation with Vic. "Once—"

"Every twelve hours!" Hunter concluded the sentence. "For how long? How long could they stop transmission?" Wolfe had forgotten how annoyed he became with Hunter sometimes. Hunter and Wolfe had never gotten along, dating back to their early days in Land of Legends.

"Maybe minutes . . . that's an unknown variable." Vic shrugged. "Again, we aren't ready. I need more satellites, more access . . . and we also have the problem of VELICs because of their firewalls over the satellite systems. If they sniff out that I'm there they may override my access to the satellites we already have. They are equipped with technology capable of that." Wolfe had only recently heard of VELIC systems. It was a new feature that Warren spoke briefly about when he traveled to Augland DC, for conferences or House of CEO meetings. From the little knowledge he had, the AI systems were a massive database and an upcoming customer service initiative that the AEC sponsored.

While it wasn't the hand Wolfe expected, at least it was a direction that made sense. If they could gain access to more satellites, then this could be the weapon to finally stop Warren. It was at least something they could use against Augland. What mattered now was whether or not they had enough time to build up their arsenal of satellites to implement their plan and somehow override VELIC systems.

"How many would you need? Satellites, that is, to make it so they turn off enough Suits to allow the us to gain opportunity for longer periods of time. And I'm saying enough time that would make it impossible for the AEC to plan an attack on people and retaliate." Joao questioned.

"A hundred and thirty? Give or take, to be certain I'd need at least three hundred satellites for a continuous surge that spans across more than one Augland location." Vic reported with little confidence.

———

That night, the four of them went to celebrate in the marketplace of NeuroEnergy. Even though they weren't anywhere near a resolution, it was better than where they were hours before. The hole-in-the-wall bar was packed with NeuroEnergy employees unwinding after a long day at the office. Bez had come early to secure them a table in the far corner. She had no idea what they were celebrating but she didn't care as long as there was a party. Joao was sworn to secrecy like they all were, but what he could tell Bez was they had their play against Augland if they were to lose the trial. Either way, if the scientist was close to creating a secret weapon, they would have a new order amongst the NeuroEnergy and Augland rivalry. Wolfe sat quietly, sipping his neat whiskey as Hunter rambled on about something and Bez forced Joao to dance. Rye was deep in thought, taking in the world around him with just a hint of gloating in his demeanor.

What nagged at Wolfe was the conversation he was now forced to have. He needed to call Warren, and that conversation would go one way or the other. He could keep this secret and use it to his advantage when the time came. He felt unsure of what to do, because they *could* have a weapon, but what if that weapon didn't work? What if Vic was wrong? What if they couldn't get past VELIC? Would he give up this opportunity? What if Georgina did win? All these questions replayed endlessly in Wolfe's mind. An assurance plan was never a bad plan, but he had limited time, and it was almost one o'clock in the morning.

Wolfe brought the glass up to his mouth and took the last sip before setting it on the table. The one drink wasn't enough to get him drunk but enough to give him a bit of liquid courage for his next move. "I'll be right back," he announced, not like anyone was paying attention, given the festivities.

Wolfe was back in his room now, the safest place for this type of call. If anyone found out he was calling his father, that would break any trust that NeuroEnergy had in him. Wolfe dialed the familiar number, which he knew by heart now. Wolfe teetered between doing what Warren wanted and what he knew was the right thing to do. Wolfe never liked making decisions without a plan in place, but he was out of time and needed to pick a side: war or surrender.

It rang; the line picked up after just a few seconds and Wolfe leaned against the wall of his apartment.

"Wolfgang, it's like four in the morning." Wolfe had momentarily forgotten the time difference.

Wolfe took a deep breath; this was a decision that didn't come easy for him. If he picked his father, he secured Ashton and the workers' safety but dabbled with the future of their world. If he picked Neuro-Energy, he sided with greater uncertainty, potentially at the cost of the woman he loved. Ashton was out in a vicious world with his father, who wouldn't think twice about taking her life.

"I can have a jet there in no time." Warren filled the silence. "You'll be here before the trial starts."

"I'm not coming." He clicked end before he could hear Warren's disappointed response and slid down the wall he was leaning on for stability. Wolfe had to make hard decisions all the time; he just prayed he didn't just sentence the woman he loved to death.

CHAPTER 9

Ashton

Ashton couldn't take her eyes off Silver, Warren's representative, a man whose tongue could speak lies and convince the world of its truth. During his speech, her eyes narrowed then rolled as Silver spewed variations of Warren's accusations. With each word he spoke, a nauseating feeling crept into her stomach and she thought she'd be sick. Ashton was the only worker in the House of CEOs, but that wasn't what separated her from the rest of them; it was their clear acceptance of the deceptive and disgustingly morphed truth. *You'll have to play a part, get them to like you—trust you. Don't let them underestimate you.* Wolfe's voice of reason spoke to her.

Warren's representatives attempted to paint Ashton as a pawn in Georgina's game and it took a great deal of self-control not to shout out loud at Silver. But even if she were Georgina's pawn, it was no comparison to what Warren had done.

The auditorium began to ring with competing conversations, tainting the beautiful architecture with audacity and vulgar lies. Ashton had looked back several times to the hundreds of faces that were in the audience. Ashton had expected them to whisper behind her back, or even shoot her curious glances every now and then, but no one even noticed her. An hour passed before it was time for Georgina's defense. Frederick was now up out of his chair and facing the CEOs like Warren's representative had done. If he was nervous, Ashton couldn't tell.

He composed himself well and took a moment to move his eyes across the room.

"Thank you all for attending this meeting. I know you're busy and I want to make sure I take a moment to acknowledge your time and presence today. On behalf of NeuroEnergy, and of CEO Georgina, I can tell you that we believe this trial is a waste of your time, and we apologize." Ashton couldn't help but grin from the small jab Frederick made and the corresponding snickers from the crowd.

"What Warren has accused CEO Georgina Raylen of is preposterous and simply a fishing expedition to tarnish her reputation and good name designed to further his own agenda. It isn't Ms. Raylen who is the manipulative, conniving, and deceitful one in this room. I do not blame Warren, though; with this great responsibility you are faced with your mental capacity being pushed to the brink of paranoia." Ashton leaned back in her chair, smiling.

"That has caused him to make irrational decisions, like creating blueprints for new energy initiatives or mutilating workers even when we have a worker shortage." That comment had Ashton sneaking a quick glance in Warren's direction. He sat tall, but the muscles in his jaw tensed, and he pretended not to be offended by the comment.

"What we need to look at is the root cause. That's why my client won't back down or dismiss these charges; she's able to prove her innocence and that is exactly what will happen today. Warren first has accused Ms. Raylen of 'infiltrating the sacred homes of Executives' but you'll find they have no evidence of that. She simply trusted a young girl who was curious about a recycled Suit, having no idea what that girl intended to do with it . . . Silver implied Ms. Raylen investigated Warren because she thought Warren was creating energy initiatives, but that was only after she was supplied with documents that told her as much. She never spied. She brought those documents to the AEC following proper protocol for a thorough investigation through the correct AEC channels.

"And finally, Warren's counsel suggested that Ms. Raylen created the rebellion within Augland 54, which has unfortunately spread to other Auglands, but you'll hear that Ms. Raylen knew nothing of the rebellions and our witnesses will show that one person was responsible for inciting a revolt." Frederick's thick accent emphasized every other word he spoke. "By the end of this trial, you'll see this is a witch hunt against a woman who's done everything right. She's passionate about the NeuroEnergy and Augland partnership and would never do anything to jeopardize this relationship. Again, thank you all for your time."

Frederick's speech didn't last half as long as the opposing side, but it was pointed and perfect and for the first time Ashton was happy to have Frederick as an ally. Maybe Georgina had a chance.

"Thank you, gentlemen, for your candor. As with all trials, we begin with witnesses from the offense and move to the defense questioning. Given we are short on time, you'll each have a day to present your side—starting with offense today and defense tomorrow, followed by rebuttal and closing remarks." Beaugard shifted in his seat. "Now, Silver, you mentioned a few of your witnesses will arrive tomorrow?"

"Yes, only a few will be called, likely after the witnesses we have here today conclude. We are also waiting on evidence to present that should be here either later today or tomorrow morning." Silver spoke candidly.

"Silver, we will only allow you to bring witnesses forward to counter any of the evidence or testimony. I won't allow you to bring forth anyone after you have concluded today. While I'm sure you'd prefer to run this trial on your schedule, I won't allow you to waste the CEO's valuable time. Evidence will need to be presented at time of questioning."

"I have no issues with that," Frederick said, with a slight gloat only apparent to those who'd had more than a one-sentence interaction with him. Beaugard wouldn't allow Silver to bring any witnesses outside of today, for which Frederick appeared grateful.

"Very well," Silver said. If he was disappointed, he didn't show it.

"Great. Silver, call your first witness," Beaugard directed.

"We call Ashton, worker number JR105 from Augland 54." Ashton's eyes bulged as she heard her name and worker ID. She knew she would be summoned sooner rather than later to speak, but that knowledge had in no way prepared her for hearing her name as the first to be called to the stand. No number of deep breaths calmed Ashton and her rapid heartbeat refused to subside. She was nervous about what she would say, or fumbling her words and saying something she shouldn't. Frederick turned to her and whispered, "Remember, you want them to like you, the CEOs; that way its believable that Georgina would trust you." Ashton nodded before standing.

Ashton had spent the last half hour trying to ignore the gossiping bodies and Suits behind her before she faced the highest level of Executives across the AEC nation, those entirely responsible for the treatment of workers—and Jagatha's and Sheva's deaths. She unclenched her tightened fists and wiped away the slowly accumulating sweat that now coated her palms. *Breathe, Ashton, just breathe. One, two three, in. One, two three, out.*

She wished Wolfe was here; not that he could predict or change the outcome of the trial but at least she wouldn't feel so alone. Ashton stood and the snickers grew louder. She could feel the room's eyes on her as her heels shuffled against the carpet with pretend confidence. She took each step carefully before finally reaching the top step next to the podium, which positioned her a foot below Beaugard. The chair squeaked as she scooted forward and she cleared her throat, which was unfortunately broadcasted throughout the auditorium, exposing her nerves.

The vibrant white lights blinded her, but she could still make out shadows of faces and bodies. A flashback struck her as she remembered standing in the auditorium at Land of Legends. Wolfe claimed that was when he'd really taken notice of her, but Ashton suspected he was merely saying that for her sake. It was being judged by people who had no business judging her that stirred the nauseating sense of familiarity of a lifetime of being seen as less than. Ashton awkwardly cleared her throat again, this time farther from the mic, while Silver organized his notes.

You can do this; you know what they want to hear. You are just a worker in their eyes, and they expect you to submit to their unquestioned authority. Use that compliance training against them now. Use the plastered smile, the confident voice, and soothing rhetoric to convince them to trust you.

"Ashton, could you tell us who you are?"

"My name is Ashton, employee number JR105."

"And . . . please provide us with context to your history with Augland 54?" Another question Ashton was prepared to answer.

"I started in Victorian. It's where most workers go for their first job out of the Augland Center. After a few years, I was transferred to work as a waitress in Maya Bay." Ashton could feel her heightened heartbeat impacting her speech. "I worked in Maya Bay for a few years at a restaurant called The Hook. After an unfortunate *incident*, I was then sent to Land of Legends where I starred as Freya, the warrior, and that's where—"

"Land of Legends, that was a rehabilitation center, correct? For those who hadn't lived up to the Augland standards?" Silver interrupted.

"Marius, my boss, sent me there. He was not . . ." Ashton's voice trailed briefly, "a very nice man." She hoped that information would draw some sympathy from the CEOs.

Ashton recalled the day she was sent to Land of Legends. Marius, the man who had started all of this, banished her to Land of Legends because she had said no to his advances. Silver let her speak, and with that Ashton created the foundation to why she was sent for rehabilitation.

"That's where you met Warren's son, Wolfgang, is that right?" Silver asked as he walked in front of her podium with his arms crossed over his chest.

"Yes, I met him there. He was my boss and was there to teach fighting routines to some of the leads."

"And you two grew close, didn't you?" Silver began pacing across the stage.

"Somewhat, we really didn't get close until after—" Ashton didn't want to use words like "escaped," not yet. "He was the one trying to locate us while we tried to find a way out of Augland." *The first time,* Ashton thought, but disclosing how many times she had escaped with or without Wolfe's help seemed unimportant. Ashton needed to carefully choose her words.

Silver shifted his questioning. "Georgina knew you were close to Wolfgang, didn't she?" Ashton hadn't expected that question.

"Objection. Speculation. Ms. Ashton can't know what Georgina knew or didn't know." Frederick rose as he addressed Beaugard and Silver.

"I'll rephrase. Did Georgina ever say she knew you were close to Wolfgang?"

Ashton paused; she couldn't lie about this one. Georgina would have known that because Hunter had told her.

"I never told her that I was close to Wolfe." Ashton sighed, relieved she could seemingly outsmart the question.

"And to be clear, Wolfe is short for Wolfgang?" He asked.

"Yes, he prefers to go by Wolfe. He told me only his father calls him Wolfgang, but he hates being called that." Ashton stole a glance toward Warren, whose face remained impassive as she spoke.

"So you'd say you both have an honest relationship? One could assume you cared deeply for each other. Enough so you have 'nicknames' for him?"

Ashton smiled. "Yes, you could say that. I don't think either one of us meant to fall for each other." Frederick had suggested, if the conversation geared toward Wolfe, to spin a love story for the audience. "He was kind to me. I had—lost a lot at that point and was confused. Maya Bay was my home and after leaving, I wasn't sure if I'd make it out of Legends alive."

Silver tilted his head as he asked his next question, ignoring the admission of her survival needs. "Why do you think the son of the CEO would be interested in a worker like you?"

Ashton ignored the underlying message about her status as a worker. "He didn't like how his father ran Augland 54. He felt Warren crossed a line when he forced Wolfe to allow customers who played on the battlefield to hurt workers."

"That is your own interpretation, but that doesn't answer my question. Why you?" Silver asked.

"I—I guess I'm not sure about that. You'd have to ask him." Which was true, she'd never truly thought about what had brought them together despite their difference in status.

"If you were to guess." Silver spat.

"Wolfe and I—we share similarities but there are also differences. He was a CEO's son and I was a worker, but I saw him as someone who needed a friend and it just so happened I did too. We both wanted a different life—something true and happy which neither of us were living." That was the most honest thing Ashton could think to say. Her heart twisted as she thought back to the people Wolfe and she had once been.

Silver cleared his throat, redirecting his question. "So, Land of Legends was not your last encounter with Wolfgang?" Ashton couldn't help the feeling that Silver's line of questioning was easier than she'd thought it would be.

"He saved me when I was wounded after fleeing Apparel and was shot in the leg by Augland security. Unlike his father, he doesn't care about my status as a worker." Ashton refrained from looking at the opposition's table where she had no doubt Warren hung on her words. Instead, Ashton stole a glance at Frederick, who gave her a reassuring smile.

"You tend to run away a lot." Silver said.

"I hear running is good exercise." The crowd laughed and Ashton smiled.

Silver forced a chuckle. "That's cute. A love story of the CEO's son and a worker who had nothing in her life. The modern-day haves and have-nots." Ashton didn't understand the reference, but some of the CEOs behind Silver gave a wave of chuckles.

"Could we keep with questions for the witness? I'd also comment that Counsel's questions and comments about her personal life have little to do with this trial." Frederick stood.

"Frederick's right; I apologize, Mr. President. Ms. Ashton, Wolfgang had no idea of your plan when you first entered Augland 54 as the AEB Charlotte?"

"No, he had no idea."

"And how did you get those credentials? For the Charlotte? Because you would have needed travel arrangements with Augland 54 to enter."

"Happenstance. I made friends with Georgina's scientists and those at NeuroEnergy who mentioned their relationship with Executives and customers in Augland 54. From there, I had an interconnect, and it was easy after that." Ashton knew she was leaving a lot for Silver to poke holes in, and this was where she feared that, if Silver pried, she would lose her ability to manipulate the truth. Hunter was the one who had told her about Charlotte and Hunter, and Rye had given her the intel about Charlotte. They also supplied her with an interconnect, where messages between Warren and Charlotte had been recorded.

"Easy after that? How so?"

Ashton didn't answer, so Silver pressed further.

"Submerging a mind from a pod to an AEB is something many would not characterize as 'easy.'"

"Like I said, I made friends." Ashton presented an innocent smile.

"Hmm. So, Georgina was unaware that you had any intentions of going into Augland 54 to find information on Warren's supposed energy initiatives? She didn't send you into Augland with a purpose?" Ashton was thankful Silver moved along in his questioning.

"I had my own agenda going into Augland 54. Warren stole the Colony children. Jagatha was a child I had helped the first time I left Augland. She was one of the young children taken when Warren attacked the Colony. I felt I had to go after her, because she was like a little sister to me." Ashton selected the truth she spoke. Silver paused and sauntered over to the table he shared with Warren. Ashton eyed Silver carefully as he whispered in Warren's ear. Warren nodded.

"It was only because of the children then. Why not walk into Augland as yourself?" Silver asked.

"I wasn't sure how Augland would take me waltzing back in after I'd left. I was a worker; I had no rights and had broken countless rules. I was afraid of what might happen if I went in as myself." Ashton dared to look at Warren, who only smirked as he studied her. She ripped her gaze away before Warren's demeanor might melt the mask she wore to convince the other CEOs of her innocence. Her hatred for him would expose a weakness and she wouldn't risk Georgina's innocence—even though it was tempting.

"That is all, Mr. President." Ashton's eyes shifted toward Frederick, who smiled. She thought the interaction would be harder with Warren's questioning, but it seemed Warren didn't have the information Georgina feared he had.

"Please, your questioning, Frederick," Beaugard said.

"Thank you, your honor." Frederick rose and positioned himself beyond Georgina's table.

"Good morning, Ashton."

"Good morning," Ashton answered.

"I'd like to go back before Land of Legends. What was the nature of your relationship with a woman named Sheva, employee number Q186, and where did you meet her?" Ashton thought of the day she met Sheva and the many train rides they shared together in Augland 54.

"Sheva . . ." Ashton paused as she remembered the last train ride with her ailing friend. The last real memory of her looking up at Ashton as she was escorted away by Augland 54 security. "I took the train most days, and that's where I met Sheva. She was older, was part of the engineering team, and had worked in various parks in Augland 54."

"You two were close then?" Frederick asked.

"Very. I mean, she was like a mom to me. Augland 54 raises children from birth . . . I only knew teachers my whole life, so Sheva meant a lot to me."

Ashton nearly winced with the sudden thought of what Sheva would think of her now. These emotions caused her to fear that the barrier she had built for this trial might dissolve. A year ago, Ashton's demeanor would have been different. She would have shriveled under pressure like she did when she stood in front of Jorgeon and Wolfe in Land of Legends. But she was no longer that timid girl—afraid and naive. There were lessons learned from the hardships she had endured, the loss of those she held dear, her new red hair, and the pure hatred for these companies that had hardened her. Now, she was ready to burn this entire place down.

But first, she'd need to get through the trial and make them understand everything Warren had done—and that started with pulling at the synthetic heartstrings of the CEOs. Warren had brought her here in hopes that she would dig her own grave; little did he know that if he wanted a show, she'd been trained for this her whole life.

Ashton forced emotion, thinking of only sad things that would bring tears to her eyes. Normally, she'd think of Sheva and Jagatha's death, but that brought pain and anger now—not sadness. "Sheva," Ashton said slowly as she felt the forced emotion, "was a wonderful woman who taught me so much about the world. She was the first person who truly loved me." That wasn't a lie. The room was quiet while Frederick approached her with a tissue, giving her a grin in approval for her performance. "Thank you," she muttered, not only for the tissue.

"And what kind of things did she teach you?" Frederick pressed while pacing back and forth. The auditorium had gone silent behind him.

"Anything and everything. It started with how the trains functioned . . . um, it was daily lessons. Anything that had to do with how technology worked. I had dreams of becoming an engineer someday.

She believed I'd be a great asset for Augland 54." *That was a stretch, maybe reign it in on the aspirations and such.*

"And from there you went to Land of Legends? There was a mishap there, right?"

"Yes, I, um . . ." Admitting to this was not smart, but Frederick told Ashton it was essential. It was better for Frederick to control the narrative of this incident than leave it to the opposition to use as ammunition later.

"I ended up swinging an axe at one of the customers because he was killing . . ."

Frederick interrupted again. "It was to save Sheva, right? To make sure that she stayed alive?"

"Yes. I tried to save her. The customer, Senator Chandler, I believe, who was on the battlefield that day, I did my best to give him the greatest customer experience. But he was mean, and ruthless. When he saw some of the weaker workers, he would charge them, and I had to witness him stab and dismember people I had grown to love and care for during the weeks of training. I never interfered, not until I saw Sheva."

Ashton, for a moment, let her façade slip because this part was real, and she wanted the CEOs—and Warren—to bear witness to it. "I saw her in the distance; she was frail and looked, so out of place. I saw the Senator swing his axe and cut a worker in half." Ashton swallowed, her eyes glazing over at the distant memory she had buried and now let resurface—letting only fractions of the details come out. "I reacted, I didn't think, I couldn't, all I saw was this woman I loved, and who loved me, in danger. And I did what I thought I had to do to protect her." She let her shield come back up as she blinked away the memory of that day on the battlefield. "I truly am sorry for what I did to the AEB"—*No, you're not*—"and I wish my actions hadn't resulted in destroying something valuable." Ashton cringed inside.

"You were saving the woman who had taught you everything you knew?"

"Yes. I knew that after that incident I would not be allowed to return because there was no coming back after I had done so much damage, so we were forced to escape." Ashton confessed. "Augland 54, Warren, wouldn't allow us to live after something like *that*." Ashton remembered when Miaka was taken away after she broke her ankle. She was the first person to be selected to play Freya and once she was hurt, Ashton had replaced her as the lead role. If Augland would toss aside a life like hers without a second thought, there was no indication that they would let Ashton live after dismantling Senator Chandler's Suit.

"But you felt compelled to strike Senator Chandler because you wanted to protect Sheva, correct?"

"Yes,"

The room was deathly quiet, and Ashton could hear her voice echo toward the back of the room. Beaugard sat back in his chair, unfazed by Ashton's recollection of her experience working in Land of Legends.

Frederick gave her a quick glare of approval for answering this way before continuing. "Now, I'd like to fast forward. You made it out of Augland 54, and you spent time outside those walls before you traveled to Northwest NeuroEnergy." Ashton felt like Frederick was going too fast, skipping over necessary parts of her story. She frowned, now agitated and growing bolder.

"Before that, though, it's important—"

"Please, Ms. Ashton. These are simple questions. We will get to your reasoning eventually; for now, we're merely looking for context." Ashton twitched in suspicion. Her face heated, matching her bright red head of hair, but she went along with Frederick's instructions.

"Yes, I did go to NeuroEnergy after the Colony was attacked."

"And the attack was led by Wolfgang Warren, correct? CEO Owen Warren's son? A man you became close with in Land of Legends before you attacked Senator Chandler."

"I didn't know he was the CEO's son at the time of the attack. He kept that hidden from me when we were in Land of Legends."

"You didn't know this when you went to NeuroEnergy?" Ashton had to think back. She learned Wolfe's true identity when she was in Land of Legends, after overhearing Warren mention Wolfe taking over as CEO someday.

"Well, I knew then." Ashton confessed, "but not when I first met Wolfe. He told me he was a security director."

"But you didn't tell Georgina that you knew Wolfe was the CEO's son or that you had an intimate relationship with him, did you?" Frederick asked.

"I did not."

"Why?"

"He was the CEO's son." Ashton shrugged. "We had parted ways when I escaped after the Land of Legends battle attack, and he stayed in Augland 54. I didn't think my past with him was relevant to Georgina. I also wasn't sure where we stood. He and I."

"Why go to NeuroEnergy in the first place then?"

"I wanted their help. Augland 54 and Warren, had gone to the Colony who had taken me in after the escape and raided them—taking someone very dear to me."

"Jagatha, right?"

"Yes. She was very important to me."

Frederick moved on. "And when you met Georgina, you wanted her to invade Augland 54 and help you retrieve the workers. Did she agree to this plan?" *Colony children,* Ashton almost corrected him.

Ashton sighed, her frustration audible because she wanted the CEOs to feel her tension. "No, she didn't want to."

"Why's that?"

"Because she trusted Warren and because there was a treaty in place. She didn't want to go behind his back."

"And isn't it true that CEO Georgina Raylen felt sorry for you; she was empathetic about the Colony attack? Isn't it true that she wanted to help but couldn't because of that treaty?"

"Yes, I didn't agree at the time. I was so lost in hurt and anger that I wasn't . . . I wasn't thinking straight." Frederick's face twisted in a consoling frown.

"Georgina, she took care of you though, right? You were distraught after Sheva's death and Jagatha's kidnapping. I imagine you were angry with Augland."

"Yes, my home, the people I had grown up with, and I had plans to do great things in Augland 54." Ashton channeled the ambitions of her longtime friend, Niall, to have a Suit of his own. "Maybe live out my days in an AEB of my own if I was useful enough to Augland 54. Those plans changed, though, when I lost the two people who mattered most."

"Switching topics, to clarify, did Georgina take you in? Let you stay, let you eat, give you accommodation?"

"Yes,"

"So, her nature was to help those in need."

"Objection! It's speculation to just assume someone's character based on a single action." Silver spat out his words. Frederick moved on before Beaugard could comment. "Would you have done anything at that point to help the Colony? They housed you for more than six months and were attacked, as you said, and you were angry, weren't you?"

"Mr. President," Silver spouted angrily, "that's not something this witness can determine. He's providing testimony instead of questioning the witness like it's fact. We do not know if this alleged attack even took place on the colony in question." Frederick put his hands up defensively to indicate he'd move on.

"Then it would be fair to say that you were desperate?" Frederick probed.

"To rescue the kids who were stolen? From Warren who had taken them? Yes, I would say that was my priority. Sheva died, and I didn't want the same fate as those children, for Jagatha." Ashton's tone sharpened and her gaze narrowed toward Warren. This was the moment she wanted the CEOs to see. The pure hatred she felt.

"You were desperate enough that you'd do anything to get revenge." *Revenge . . . this isn't close to revenge.*

Ashton paused, "I would do anything to protect the people from that man, right there, Augland isn't bad," *Lies.* "It's only because of one man—because he was cruel, and he didn't protect us." Ashton nodded toward Warren. "He is killing, exploiting, and abusing." Warren looked smug as he half-closed his eyes and propped his head up on his hand. Ashton's hands shook with anger as she gripped them together in her lap. Ashton dramatically brought the tissue back to her face. *Take that, Warren, two people can play the game of manipulation.*

"When was it that you came upon the Artificial Existence Being?" Frederick's tone had softened further.

Ashton breathed in, letting her emotions simmer. "In the basement of NeuroEnergy." Frederick had skipped the meeting between Ashton and Hunter in Georgina's office where she had told them about the discarded Suit.

"Didn't you already know quite a lot about AEBs before you came into contact with this one?"

"Being a worker, I was constantly interacting with them." That was Frederick's suggestion for her answer.

"So is it fair to say that between Sheva's personal knowledge and teachings and your familiarity with AEBs, you knew more than the average customer service worker?" That was true; most likely workers didn't know how trains worked, Ashton thought.

"I could say that."

"When you were in Augland, posing as Charlotte, you wanted to get close to the CEO, Wolfgang, Warren's son, correct?"

"When I thought the CEO was Wolfe, I knew he could help me bring Jagatha home. But he wasn't the CEO; Warren had made a Suit—I mean, an Artificial Existence Being—of him." Now Ashton could hear the hum of laughter before Frederick interrupted them.

"Did you want to destroy Augland 54?" The questions shifted.

"Yes . . . at the time I did because I was hurt, but I realize that it wasn't Augland. It was Warren who betrayed me."

"Did you, and you alone, create the UnSuited?" Frederick asked.

"Yes . . . I did because, after Warren had taken everything from me, I also witnessed what he was willing to do to workers that didn't conform to his standard. The Customer Service Initiative was just the beginning. I saw people in Apparel overworked, underfed, and missing limbs because he wanted to advance the customer experience. I had no choice but to help protect workers. But I hope that we don't need any more rebellions. I hope that between the AEC and workers, we will be able to serve our customers without hurting the workers." Ashton cringed again at her own rhetoric.

"Is there anything else you wish to say to the House of CEOs?"

"Only that, it's not just me who believes Warren has gone too far in Augland 54. His son, Wolfgang, left him shortly after I left Augland 54. He refuses to return to Augland because his father has gone too far with the Customer Service Initiative and energy blueprints—"

"Objection! Blueprints cannot be discussed; they aren't in evidence." Silver spat, interrupting Ashton.

"That's fine, I'll rest," said Frederick.

"But—" Ashton began; she wanted to continue stating what she was there to say:

Bez condemned to the confines of the brothel.

The UnSuited and what they stood for.

Frederick paused and shook his head no.

Ashton was dismissed and made her way back to the chair behind Frederick.

"You're better than I initially gave you credit for," he whispered. "Well done."

"Careful, Frederick," she whispered back, "while I play nice now, I still have Silver's counter questions to answer. I want to be able to say the rest of what I want about what we've endured, or something might slip." Ashton's gaze was threatening as she sank farther down into her chair. She felt powerful.

"Careful, Ashton," Frederick mimicked, "if Georgina goes down, all your friends and the Colony go down with her, and even if you did well today, I won't let anything be spoken that I don't deem worthy of importance." Ashton shook her head at the stalemate Frederick had created for her.

CHAPTER 10

Ashton

AUGLAND, DC

After Ashton left the stand, several of Warren's colleagues were called to the stand. Warren's witnesses talked about his earlier years working on the development of Augland 54's corporate strategy, his years of support for NeuroEnergy. Ashton recognized only a handful of the witnesses—one most notably was Senator Chandler. There were Executives who came forward and acknowledged hearing about NeuroEnergy's infiltration. One Suit mentioned overhearing workers in his Victorian home admitting to being sent to Augland 54 to research the waterfalls for hydroelectricity. Ashton sat back in her chair, reliving the time she had on the stand and Frederick's lingering words. *"Careful, Ashton; if Georgina goes down, all of your friends and the Colony go down with her."*

The trial for Warren's side lasted all day. Long hours passed before Beaugard stood after Silver dismissed his last witness.

"Thank you all. Tomorrow witnesses may be recalled and new witnesses brought forward. If there are none, we will begin with CEO Raylen's defense. As you know, the defense can recall CEO Warren's witnesses for further questioning if they wish but only after the offense rests. As for tonight's festivities, we have prepared a CEO dinner for us to officially welcome Senator Alexander Salsben II to the central district who has replaced his father, who recently retired . . . you're all dismissed."

The auditorium erupted in chatter as Beaugard stepped down from his pedestal chair and toward Frederick. Ashton rose and waited to speak to Georgina, but was interrupted before they could speak.

"Good evening, Ms. Ashton. I wanted to extend the invite for tonight's entertainment; you're welcome to attend as an honorary guest to the House of CEOs, and hopefully, you'll see how gracious and thankful the AEC is for worker involvement like yours." Beaugard grinned, continuing, "It's strictly a social gathering where I hope you get to know more CEOs and them, you."

Ashton didn't even acknowledge his comment about how she was to see the AEC as "thankful" for workers, Frederick stared from behind Beaugard at Ashton, provoking her to accept with his eyes. "Thank you, President Beaugard." Ashton said, not confirming she would indeed attend. Beaugard smiled before turning his attention away.

Ashton remained silent as Georgina and Frederick were conversing in small talk with CEOs and senators around them. That was, until she noticed two Suits, dressed all in black, heading straight for her. Ashton nudged Frederick and he turned toward her.

"We've been instructed to be your guides while you stay at the House of CEOs." Ashton could have sniffed out their responsibilities from a mile away. They had the same rigidity as the security team at Augland 54.

"You're kidding me . . ." Ashton commented before stealing a glance at Georgina who was socializing with other CEOs and unaware of what was happening. She wasn't in front of the CEOs so didn't feel the need to hide her emotions. "I don't need your services but thank you." Ashton said with conviction. She could see from the corner of her eye that Georgina now stole a glance in her direction, and she quickly excused herself from the conversation to come to Ashton's aid. Georgina overheard the security team and walked over. "There is no need for security, gentlemen, Ashton is a guest here. She has free reign to walk along these halls and auditorium, just like the rest of us."

"I'm sorry, CEO Raylen, but these orders have been issued by Beaugard just now. He requested that she have twenty-four-hour protection." The two men didn't change their posture or stance. Ashton didn't understand. She hadn't been given monitoring before she testified and now, she had. She thought she had done well, even gained potential supporters if any Executive here had any humanity left in them.

Frederick tapped on Georgina's shoulder. "This isn't a battle I think we want to fight." He whispered; Ashton could hear even through the chatter of the room. Ashton waited for Georgina's dismissal of Frederick's point. She wanted a glimpse of the woman prepared to go to battle for the inexcusable behavior of the most powerful people in the country. Georgina must have thought about it, hiding her rebellious thoughts in the graceful stoic manner she always had plastered across her face, but then she just smiled.

"I don't think it would hurt to have security around, especially for Ashton's protection here on these grounds. I wouldn't want Warren getting any ideas." Ashton stood in complete shock.

"Georgina . . ." Ashton didn't know what to say. Georgina had wilted under political pressure—but then again so had she. She had agreed to play a part that hid her true feelings about Auglands. Ashton shifted, protesting, "I can protect myself." Ashton responded back to Frederick, but her voice carried no weight in their conversation, and it did little good.

Ashton slammed her apartment door shut, leaving the two security Suits standing guard outside her apartment. It was two hours until dinner started. She hadn't decided if she even wanted to go but had a feeling that her presence was not optional. The day's events replaying in her head left her feeling anxious. VELIC's musical chime radiated through Ashton's spacious suite just before a familiar silhouette appeared.

"Good evening, Ms. Ashton. The dinner will be starting soon, should we begin preparations?" Ashton's body lay heavily on the bed looking up at the plain ceiling. Grunting loudly, she rolled over to her side and looked out the porch windows that doubled as doors. The sun had set and now the darkness crept into the remaining light of the synthetic day.

"I'm sorry, I didn't understand. Could you repeat that?" VELIC mistook her silence for a too-quiet response.

Ashton thought over her options. There was not an ounce of her that wanted to attend a party with the House of CEOs. None. But there was the suspicion of an opportunity she may have while in the room with them to use the night to her advantage like she had during her proceeding. *Warren.* The moment she thought about confronting Warren, Wolfe's words to her before she left for Augland DC, repeated in her head: *What we can't do at the trial is go off on some revenge spree because you think it will make you feel better.* Ashton had worked too hard today to have diminish her resolve now. If she did go to dinner and confront Warren, she would be doing exactly what she promised Wolfe she would not do.

But Ashton had so much to say to him and if they weren't going to allow her a platform at the trial to say what Warren needed to hear, she would find her own way. It wasn't about her need for revenge anymore; it was about what he had done to Wolfe, the Colony, NeuroEnergy, and the workers. She wanted, no *needed* to tell him exactly what she thought of him.

"Yes, I'd like to get ready." Ashton said, hoping she would not break any promises she'd made to Wolfe.

"Wonderful. Additional clothes arrived while you were away. May I make a suggestion?" Ashton propped herself up while VELIC opened the doors to a closet that was now filled with fancy clothes. She scooted off the bed and toward the opened doors. Ashton reached out, skating her fingers gently across the silk and knitted fabric. The first piece was a long, black, flowing dress, the others lined up were pants, shirts, and soft sweaters.

"Why are they all black?" Ashton questioned as she noticed there was no color.

"Black is the appropriate color for workers in all Auglands, and I believe the standard is the same for Augland 54, is it not? We do have the standard color for those outside the Augland, DC, district" VELIC spoke directly and without emotion. It was a reminder of the identity forced upon her from birth, one she'd managed to forget since leaving Augland 54. Ashton realized this wasn't a gift from those hosting her at Augland DC—it was a reminder of who they thought she was. Ashton—employee number JR105.

Having VELIC's assistance made preparations for dinner much easier than Ashton attempting to ready herself alone. With all their Suits and perfectly tailored outfits, she would be conspicuously different. Besides, VELIC was quick and efficient and, before she knew it, she was dressed. In the mirror she saw herself in an all-black gown, silky with spaghetti straps and a mermaid-like tail that delicately trailed behind her. She wore strapped heels and her red hair was neatly curled, the gentle waves parted to the side and styled to cascade down the front of her shoulders. "How do I look?" *Talking to a VELIC like it's your friend now.* Ashton laughed at the sudden realization.

"Radiant, of course," the black shadow told Ashton. She smiled, even with the day's event and the reminder of her work status; it *felt* good to *look* good. She wished Wolfe were there to see her like this.

The ballroom nearly burst with elegant black and white decor with gold-plated everything. Ashton could smell the real plated food across the tables. She had arrived late. While the Suits wouldn't touch the real food, those wearing their human form needed sustenance. Ashton hadn't realized how hungry she was until the savory smells of cooked steak, lobster tails, and grilled fresh vegetables filled her senses. The anxiety of the day melted and left only the need to satiate her hunger. Ashton was chauffeured by the same two bodyguards that left with her from the auditorium and again from her bedroom. Ashton did her best to ignore them, and they showed her a similar disinterest.

There were at least a hundred people scattered around the room in small bunches as they conversed and drank together. Many of them had dolled up for a night of showing off their elite status with obnoxiously expensive outfits.

Ashton walked in slowly, giving notice to the CEOs who stood out as perfectly crafted beings. One Suit wore a long gown made completely of shiny chrome pieces that caught the light as she shifted her weight. Another, gems from head to toe. Even the male Suits sported some sparkly gems or colored stone across their jackets. Ashton spotted Georgina in the distance, wearing a marbled lavender dress that morphed to the color of lilac as she turned in the light. She caught Ashton's eye and excused herself from the conversation to make her way to her.

"Ma'am, can I help you find your table?" A Suited worker, in both senses of the word, found her amongst the CEO chaos. Ashton was startled by the interaction, the Suit catching her from behind.

As soon as she realized he was trying to help, she nodded, and the Suit guided her toward her table without even asking her name.

The Suit led both Ashton and Georgina to a round table furnished with more extravagant centerpieces than there was food on the table. Ashton reached for the first empty chair and carefully arranged her lengthy hem.

"Don't you look stunning," Georgina commented, her black and white hair perfectly waving down across her shoulders, complementing her dress. Ashton sensed her image was meant to hide her true feelings after the long hours at trial pretending she was unaffected by the uncertainty of this first day. She sat herself in the chair next to Ashton.

"So do you—nice dress," Ashton observed, putting her hand on Georgina's dress. The swirling purple tones moved like disturbed water as Ashton touched it.

"I asked Frederick to find a way for us to speak. Ashton, I wanted to apologize for the security detail. You aren't meant to feel like a prisoner here and I can imagine that's what it feels like." Georgina said out of earshot of the two security guards that had positioned themselves close to the outer wall of the dining hall. She wasn't sure how the AEC would feel about Georgina and Ashton conversing.

Ashton sighed, "That's an understatement, but I appreciate the sentiment." Ashton kept her voice soft like Georgina had as the others at the table were busy in their own conversations.

"Yes, but Frederick is doing what is best for our corporate legal strategy. He thought you did well today, so did I." She gave a curt smile. "You may not have been able to share your story today, and it may not happen tomorrow, but if we win," Georgina grabbed her hand under the table, "I guarantee you'll have the platform to help the people in this room understand from your perspective what Warren has done to you and the other workers. And it will be someday soon. I promise you that."

Georgina's whispered words made Ashton second guess her reservations, but that was Georgina's charm. She decided not to argue about how she should feel about Frederick's manipulation or any future promise of restitution.

"I hope you enjoy dinner; it's a great way to get to personally know some of the other CEOs. We aren't all as bad as Warren and I hope you see that too."

Georgina turned to the rest of the table, "I'm sorry, everyone, I'd like to introduce you all to Ashton. You may recognize her from this morning." Ashton smiled, but only two people around the table met her gaze. The rest fidgeted in their chairs or continued their private conversations. Their lack of interest didn't faze Georgina, and she continued with introductions. "Ashton, I'd like you to meet Chastine Reynolds, the CEO of Augland 5, CEO Reilland Amerson from Southeast NeuroEnergy, Senator Sandy Whicketson from Northeast District, and finally Senator Tores Guero from North Central District." Each member of the House of CEOs, once named by Georgina, diverted their attention briefly to Ashton and politely smiled before returning to what they were doing before. Ashton's eyes surveyed the faces in front of her;

from what she could tell it was only Reilland and Tores who were in their true human form. The only indicator the others were Suits was their youthful appearance, lacking grey hair and wrinkles, but Ashton could barely tell among them because even the Suitless were nearly flawless in appearance.

"Georgina, I'm curious your thoughts on how it's going at trial?" CEO Chastine from Augland 5 asked. Ashton paused as her fork dug into the first course of salad placed moments before in front of her. The trial wasn't the only reason the CEOs had assembled this week, but it certainly seemed to be the topic of conversation.

Georgina smiled. "Frederick believes the truth will prevail."

"Ashton, you did rather well. You weren't exactly what we were expecting." Ashton only nodded as she chewed, not sure how they expected her to be—maybe more truthful about how she really felt about AEC and the circus of the House of CEO proceedings.

"Georgina, it must to be awkward for you; for years you and Warren were so close. I can say I was surprised to hear that there was tension between you after everything that's happened between you two." Tores spoke up as the sound of silverware clinked. Ashton glanced at Georgina, who let slip the tiniest fraction of annoyance. Ashton hadn't heard anything about the history between Georgina and Warren.

"That was a long time ago." Georgina smiled.

"True, but considering you two have been adamant you remained friends afterwards . . . it feels more like a woman—" Tores was cut off by Georgina before he could finish his sentence.

After what? Ashton thought.

"That's enough. We have outside company today and I doubt Ashton has any desire to hear about the CEO rumor mill." Georgina referenced Ashton's presence. The table politely chuckled.

"What are they talking about?" Ashton's curiosity rose.

"It's nothing. Just gossip," Georgina took a sip of her wine. Tores innocently smiled.

"Yes, just talk, I guess." But Tores kept his eyes glued to Georgina.

"So, you're the leader of the UnSuited at 54?" Reilland, who sat next to Ashton, questioned.

"I guess; it was created more by accident than anything," Ashton said, carefully choosing her words because she guessed a rebellion against Auglands wasn't considered good dinner conversation.

"But you mentioned today it was created because they wanted to revolt against Warren, why?"

"Warren would experiment on some of the workers."

"Isn't that his prerogative? If workers aren't performing, then there needs to be recourse and consequences for their actions."

"Are you suggesting that an appropriate consequence for not living up to impossible standards would be to murder workers?" Ashton's eyes narrowed as her unfiltered response was out before she knew it.

Senator Tores spit as he nearly choked on his second course of soup and coughed loudly.

"Are you accusing Warren of killing workers without cause? You made such an allegation when you spoke about customers striking down workers in Land of Legends, but there is little evidence of any misdoings by Warren." Ashton kept her composure even though she felt the heat of anger rise; this didn't seem like the setting to over emphasize her point.

"I wouldn't be privy or envious of the hard decisions CEOs and senators need to make given my mere worker status. I'd ask that you, CEO Reilland, travel to Augland 54 and see for yourself. I suggest you start with the cages and work your way down to the basement—"

"Excuse me, Ashton, would you care to join me for another glass of wine?" Georgina asked in a sweet and inclusive manner. Ashton nodded and carefully stepped around, realizing Georgina was saving her from saying something she would regret. Shifting her tailored dress out in front of her, she followed Georgina. "Excuse us."

Georgina linked her arm with Ashton's as they walked. "It's hard to hold your tongue, isn't it."

Ashton paused, realizing how truthful that statement was. "Is that the real reason why no one else came with me to the trial? Why you told them not to come? You thought it would do you more harm because these people don't care about the workers and you can't be seen defending them?" Ashton sighed in frustration. It suddenly all made sense. Georgina's association with Ashton and the other workers would diminish her status in the eyes of those she needed to impress and connect with. Ashton wouldn't be here unless Warren had subpoenaed her.

"It's more complicated than that. Not everyone in this room is interested in worker treatment, and this is where Warren receives a lot of his support. The Customer Service Initiative, the Land of Legends . . . he's considered *progressive*."

Georgina's hand tightened around Ashton's as she turned to face her. "When we win, I can work with Human Resources, and we can begin a petition to change worker's rights—but I can only do that by winning the favor of other CEOs and distancing ourselves from the ugliness of the trial. I need them to believe that you took that Suit and went into Augland 54 by yourself and the only way that happens is if they first like you."

"A petition," Ashton sarcastically chuckled. "You're going to take down Warren with a piece of paper?"

"It's a political maneuver and that is how things get done here."

"That's *not* the way things get done. Rebellions, like what the UnSuited are doing, is how things got done. Where workers sacrifice everything for freedom. That's what gets things done."

"Please, continue to try my way for now and if it doesn't work, you'll have my full support, and resources." Ashton eyed Georgina carefully, her face sincere. Her grip loosened as it had become wound tight against Ashton's elbow. "You've done well so far; don't throw it all away now just because CEO Reilland is insufferable—he wants a rise out of you." Ashton nodded, but inside, her hopes were crushed. Ashton was still an outcast in the House of CEOs and Georgina *was* the only person on her side.

"Looks like Tores wants the same out of you." Ashton said.

"Silly talk, that's all."

"I doubt that," Ashton said under her breath, but it was clearly loud enough for her to hear. Georgina ignored her as she guided them both back to the dining table.

"Let's go back; it won't look great to have you and me conversing too much outside the ears of others." Ashton and Georgina returned to the table, where they remained for the rest of dinner, which consisted of four courses: steak and lobster tail with roasted potatoes, soup, salad, and finally a decadent chocolate mousse. Ashton had switched to her Customer Service persona and was able to pull off some friendly but neutral conversations with those around her, but inside her heart was breaking.

The AEC, Auglands, and NeuroEnergies would never treat the workers better because they just did not care. Ashton told jokes, asked about their families, and complimented others on their attire, switching on her façade like she had done her whole life. By the end of the dinner, Georgina was smiling, pleased with the performance Ashton had put on. Soon Ashton's smile gradually faded as she let her brain return to reality and recognized that everything that had brought her here was a lie. She struggled to stay onboard with Georgina's plan. This plan, just like Wolfe's plan, meant passively waiting for action to be taken and she didn't trust that a single soul in this room would defend her or the workers.

There was something that kept nagging in the back of her mind—something she had not seen coming. Warren and Georgina were hiding something, and she needed to find out what that was. It was her ultimate fear that Georgina wasn't as innocent, or on her side, as Ashton had once assumed. If she was right, then she was in more danger than she thought.

CHAPTER 11

Ashton

DC, AUGLAND

After dinner, Ashton drifted around the dining room. Some Suits and CEOs gave her an insincere smile before returning to gossip in their small groups. Others just ignored her, pretending her existence in the room was not worthy of their acknowledgment. Or at least, that was how Ashton felt.

Suddenly, her heart skipped when she saw a familiar figure sitting down at a table with several other Suits. It was *him*. Warren wore a black suit emblazoned with flowering gold embroidery and a cold, cobalt-blue trim. Ashton didn't take her eyes off him as her stroll became more targeted, stepping up the leisurely pace she'd been keeping as she'd walked aimlessly toward him. Her two security guards were tailing close behind her, but she didn't care if they stayed back or followed her. She may be willing to speak nicely with other CEOs, but Warren was a different story. Whether or not her security guards were there when she confronted him wouldn't matter all that much.

Warren didn't notice her until she stood behind him; his focus was on the glass cards in his hands with numbers and shapes on them. Warren's eyes suddenly looked up at Ashton when she was only a few steps away. She slid into an open chair next to him as several other CEOs surrounded them. Their eyes locked in an icy exchange of cool blues similar to the decorated trim on his coat. He gave a half smile that reminded her again of Wolfe.

"Ashton, it's great to officially meet you."

"We've met before," Ashton said coolly. She referred to the time he held Jagatha against her will and dropped her off his balcony. The scene that played again and again in her mind. The heat rose in her face, and she felt that similar feeling of rising panic that made her want to run, but Warren's presence forced her to stay. Warren turned his attention back to his cards, placing one down, and the VELIC congratulated him on a win.

"That's why I said 'officially.'" He smirked before saying under his breath, "Where are my manners, can I grab you a drink?" Ashton said nothing. She couldn't take her eyes off him. He was actually there, sitting in front of her. He tsked condescendingly when she didn't answer before averting his gaze and folding his cards on the table.

"So, Ashton, how was dinner? I'm sure the seafood here is nowhere as good as back home in . . . where was that again . . . Hood Canal?"

"It didn't compare."

Warren chuckled. "You're probably right. You familiar with poker?" Warren asked, abruptly changing the subject.

"Actually, yes . . ." Surprisingly, Ashton was familiar with the game. Her home in Hood Canal had many games from before the war, including a deck of paper cards. Wolfe had taught her most of the games he'd played growing up—one of them was poker. Their competitive nature had caused some rather late nights. Ashton nodded, not taking her eyes off Warren, "Wolfe taught me." Ashton had no idea if Warren knew Ashton and Wolfe were together; she assumed he would but wanted him to know for certain.

"Wolfgang is good at poker, I taught him well." Warren's grin was wide as he took a sip of the dark amber liquid in his glass.

"VELIC, deal in Ms. Ashton. You can give her a resource from my account." VELIC gave her five glass cards with numbers in either black or red, and Ashton expertly picked up the cards, displaying them how Warren held them. Her breath quickened with the next move.

The thoughts of dismantling Warren limb from limb were too overwhelming she found it hard to concentrate. She was so close to him she could reach out and strangle his bionic neck. *Maybe he half expected it.* Ashton stared at the cards in her hand. She had already passed in her two cards and scored a pair.

"So, how is Wolfgang?" Warren asked casually as he studied his poker hand.

"He's never been better," Ashton said with as much conviction as she could muster. She hoped it pained him. Wolfe wasn't shy when he spoke about Warren and how he believed that his father needed his son next to him and how much it had hurt when Wolfe betrayed Warren.

"Is that so? Didn't sound fine when we spoke yesterday." Ashton didn't let the surprise show on her face. *Warren's lying.* Wolfe told Ashton he had blocked any communication with his father, saying he had no desire to ever speak with him again.

Warren continued, "I never took him as the type of man to be easily domesticated. Playing house with a little girl, slumming in the wilderness. You don't worry he'll bore of the mundane and uncivilized life soon?" Warren's brow furrowed.

"All your fancy words. Uncivilized, mundane . . ." Ashton mocked. "Does it make you feel smarter than the rest of us?"

Warren's mouth twitched and Ashton saw a slip of fire beneath his stare. "You're not the same as I remember—to say, I was surprised to see you so graceful on the stand."

"Hm, probably wondering if it was smart of you to subpoena me here?" Warren didn't respond and instead shifted the glass cards in his hand. "It took some time before the brainwashing of Augland Center wore off, or maybe your son wore off on me." Ashton quipped. Ashton pulled her cards closer to her and stared. She knew she should watch how she spoke to Warren. She wasn't safe here and Wolfe would have cautioned her against any outspoken behavior. A vision of Niall came to her Niall, a man she'd known a lifetime ago at Maya Bay and the one who had told her to "blend in" more times than she could count on one hand.

"Is that how your friends have misconstrued the truth? Making Augland, me, out to be the big, bad company who made you not be *true* to yourself?" Warren patronized.

Ashton placed her pair of queens next to each other and put her hand on the third to make Warren think she had three of a kind. His half smile returned. He found their repartee amusing.

"I hate to break it to you, but you and Georgina won't win and, before you know it," his voice lowered so the others at the table couldn't hear, "I'll be running both NeuroEnergy and Augland. Then, no one can protect your Colony and you'll wish you would have just left things alone." VELIC put down a jack, king, and then the two of hearts.

"If you're so sure, then why am I here? Why is there a trial if the ending has already been decided?"

Warren laughed, "You know, Wolfgang asked the same thing when we spoke about him returning to work at 54 after this is all over, which means you both are clueless to what is actually happening here. You won't win even if you win the trial, because bringing you and Georgina here wasn't about the trial at all." Ashton's smile faded when he brought up speaking to Wolfe again, completely missing his confusing confession. Warren had a way of spinning lies to feel truthful, but even knowing this, Ashton started to doubt her thoughts about Wolfe and his future plans.

Warren put down his hand and Ashton's mind stopped reeling, and her mouth slowly gaped. Warren had played a royal flush, and, from what Wolfe had said, this was an impossible hand. "Besides, Wolfgang should have warned you, I don't play games that I don't already know I'll win."

With that threat, Warren stood, grabbing his glass of whiskey over ice began to make his exit, not even waiting for Ashton to play her hand.

"You cheated," Ashton whispered. Warren laughed at her accusation.

"I'll see you soon, Ashton—my condolences and well wishes if we don't speak until after the trial. Seems you've lost some people close to you; I'd hate for that type of bad luck to continue." Ashton's vision blurred red, and she stood with her fists balled, ready to punch Warren in the face. One of the men standing guard must have noticed and came closer but Warren put his hand up to stop him.

"Why'd you kill her . . ." Ashton came closer to Warren; it was a question that had plagued her for some time. She wasn't sure she wanted to know the real reason, but she couldn't stop the words from flying from her mouth like daggers. Warren met her gaze.

He thought for a moment, pretending not to know who Ashton meant. "Who?" Ashton could barely stand that look on his face now, so smug and unaffected.

"Jagatha, the little girl that you threw . . ." she couldn't even say what he had done, "the girl you killed. For no reason." Ashton's voice was merely a whisper now. She searched his face for any hint of remorse, any regret for all the pain he'd caused her.

Warren came even closer to her before shrugging, "There's the phrase 'quit while you're ahead,' and you, my dear, should have quit a long time ago. You should have never come back into Augland 54, especially for Georgina. That's the lesson you should have taken from her death." Warren said it so nonchalantly that the words scorched her skin, raising white-hot goose bumps. He turned to walk away.

Anger swelled inside her. He'd killed a little girl for nothing more than a lesson! Before Warren could take another step away Ashton voiced what she wanted Warren to know. "You're a dead man, Warren. I'll make sure of that. I'll kill you myself." Ashton uttered her threat no louder than a whisper to not draw any unwanted attention.

Warren spun back around, "I hate that you feel that way about me, Ashton. I hope someday to change that. Oh, and I'll tell Wolfgang you say hello. Or goodbye, as it may be." Ashton scoffed. "Oh, and by the way, love what you've done with your hair." His grin widened with malice. "*Suits* you." He mocked her one final time before strutting off and disappearing into the crowded room, leaving Ashton alone to temper her distain.

CHAPTER 12

Ashton

DC, AUGLAND

Coming to Augland DC, was a mistake. The trial. The poker game. The high heels that have bruised my feet. All of it. Ashton went to bed that night realizing one thing; if she was to have any chance at revenge, she would need to sink to Warren's dangerous level and beat him at his own game. She could not play the amicable worker; she would need to be ruthless and cunning—just like him. Augland Center had given her a lifetime of lessons on how to be among Suits and gain their trust and she would need to revert to the old Ashton if she was to convince them to listen to her.

On one hand, black was simply the color she wore, but on the other, it was her perceived status, and how the Suits would always look at her—as a worker, bred to serve and obey. "Be likeable" as Frederick would say, but Warren wasn't likeable and he had warned her that this was over before it had even begun. She just didn't know exactly what that meant.

Ashton hadn't stayed long after her card game with Warren. She couldn't stomach the façade another moment because, she wasn't sure she could contain her anger. She could have made a scene when she questioned Warren about killing Jagatha, but that would have done her little good. It could have been why Warren summoned her to the trial—because he thought he could provoke this kind of reaction from her.

Wolfe had mentioned his father used words to show his authority and manipulate narratives, but she didn't know to what extent until she heard Warren speak. He blamed Jagatha's death on Ashton. He said that her death was a lesson to be learned because she had sided with Georgina and attempted to use the Suit, Charlotte, to spy on the Executives and Warren's security initiatives. In a way, Ashton did blame herself for Jagatha's death. She thought about the day Jagatha was taken from the Colony grounds, and how Ashton wasn't there to protect her. Warren must have known she was important to Ashton. He wielded her like a weapon that day he threw her off the balcony. He chose Jagatha, but what she hadn't figured out was how he knew she was her weakness—and she was; Jagatha's death had destroyed her.

———

The second day of the trial began with VELIC priming her for the day, like it had the day before. Ashton had slept well, even though the festivities and Warren's conversation the night prior were more provoking than the day she arrived. She woke up as the sun rose above and peeked through the patio windows. Again, she wore black, the only color choice in her wardrobe, and unlike the day before, her confidence had faded. The lack of vibrant color marked her as someone who didn't belong in the world of CEOs, which was the exact opposite of how she needed people to see her if she was going to gain their respect.

Frederick knocked on the door and Ashton was prompt, opening the door wide to his forced smile and his obnoxious, plum-colored bow tie.

"Good morning, you look rested." Frederick's cheery demeanor was confusing.

"You're in a good mood," Ashton responded with a false cheerfulness. She stepped out, mindful of the two security guards behind Frederick. They began walking, again expertly navigating the twists and turns down to the ground floor and back to the auditorium.

"I wanted to say that I thought you did well yesterday," Frederick said from behind Ashton.

"Georgina mentioned you were happy," Ashton replied, hoping it would be the same today. She was ready to leave Augland.

"I'd call yesterday a success." Frederick beamed and Ashton contemplated telling him what Warren had told her the night prior—although he would not likely be happy with the fact that she'd sought out Warren in the first place.

"Will I be able to go home today?" Ashton asked, realizing she didn't know if she would stay for the entire three days, or if she would leave after today. Frederick mentioned that Silver had his rebuttal questions left.

"Unfortunately, you'll be staying until tomorrow. Witnesses usually stay until the conclusion of the trial because they can be recalled." Frederick placed his hand on Ashton's shoulders. They had made it to the entrance of the auditorium and, while Ashton paused briefly, Frederick began gently guiding her forward. "I feel good about this, Ashton. You do well again today, we might actually have a shot at this." *No pressure.*

"Good morning Mr. President." Silver approached the front of the auditorium promptly at eight o'clock after Beaugard arrived. Beaugard spoke to the CEOs only briefly before turning it back to Silver to continue the trial.

"We would like to recall Ashton, employee number JR105."

Without surprise, Ashton was back at the podium.

"Good morning and welcome back," Silver started, his metallic eyes meeting Ashton's stare. "Only have a few questions for you, Ms. Ashton JR105 . . . yesterday, you spoke a lot about your history within Augland 54." Ashton nodded. "Did Augland 54 give you an apartment?"

"Yes, I lived in one during my time working at Maya Bay before I was sent to Land of Legends." Ashton spoke honestly. Her apartment was nothing spectacular—and nothing like the room she currently had at the House of CEOs. Her apartment had been located on the outer rim of Augland's parks and had plumbing issues which had turned the walls black with mold and caused the wood floors to rot.

Ashton saw Frederick turn to Georgina and whisper something and Georgina nodded.

"So, your living accommodations at the Colony and NeuroEnergy must have been an upgrade from your apartment at Maya Bay as you insinuate life is much better outside Augland walls?"

"You could say that." Ashton spoke matter-of-factly.

"And did you have to work at the Colony in order to have a place to live within their homes?" Silver asked.

"I wasn't forced to work twenty hours a day like I was in Maya Bay and Land of Legends. In Augland 54, I barely spent any time in my apartment due to my work schedule." Silver smiled.

"So it was the work that was too much for you?"

"It was the lack of freedom. I did nothing but serve. That was my job."

"So it was the type of work you were required to do in Augland?" Silver asked too innocently.

"Well, I chose to do what I could to help support the Colony. That was my job and my part while I lived with them. Like I said yesterday, I had a passion for engineering at Augland, it was unfortunate what happened in Land of Legends." Some of what she said was true. The Colony never required her to work, but individuals would do what they could to help others. The elders didn't do hard labor; the young men and women did. The difference between the Colony and Augland 54 was that Ashton *wanted* to contribute because the Colony people took care of each other.

"Was seducing Wolfgang a job too? Maybe one you found came *easier* than engineering?" The insinuation nearly knocked the breath out of Ashton.

"No, nothing I did in Augland had anything to do with Wolfe." Ashton's fist tightened under the podium. It was a disgusting twist of her story, just like Warren had said during the Augland 54 board meeting after she had been discovered. He had suggested then that Ashton had come into Augland to seduce Wolfe and spy on the entire Executive Suite when she was taken from Apparel and confronted during one of their boardroom meetings.

"So, you both were in a relationship before you returned to Augland 54 in a stolen AEB of Charlotte?" Silver asked.

"Kind of." It wasn't the most well-spoken response she could have come up with. She hadn't been sure where she and Wolfe stood, as in their relationship, when she went back to Augland 54 as Charlotte.

"Okay, so then you arrived in Augland DC, as Charlotte, and you found Wolfgang—not Warren? Why was that?" This was a trick question. Wolfe was CEO, but Warren was impersonating Wolfe at the time.

"I found out that Wolfe had been named CEO, but it wasn't until after I left Charlotte's Suit that I realized it wasn't Wolfe, it was Warren in a Wolfe Suit . . ." Ashton snapped, hoping the insinuation of her truth resonated with the CEOs. "Why else would Wolfe leave his father's side? If Warren ran his Augland with such progression and innovation, then why would his son—who would and had the means to follow in his footsteps–leave? It wasn't for me, and you can suggest that all you want; it was Wolfe's decision because–"

Silver interrupted her because the whispers grew louder. Clearly, the CEOs weren't snickering because what Ashton had shared was inconceivable; it was because they could see the truth.

"But you never told him your true identity, that you were Ashton?" Silver questioned, not using Wolfe or Warren's name.

"Mr. President, Ashton wasn't finished." Frederick was up from his chair.

"I stopped her before she spoke hearsay. She can't say why Wolfgang did anything."

"He's right, Frederick. Ashton, please answer the question."

"When I was in Charlotte? No, I never told Warren I was Ashton." They were playing with semantics now.

"So, when you were found out to be you, and not Charlotte, why did you tell Wolfgang that you were there because Georgina needed information on their energy initiatives? Were you hopeful he would save you if you were honest about your intentions, spying on 'the man you loved'?" Silver's questions became too specific for Ashton to feel confident in her answers. It was different than the line of questioning Silver had used yesterday, and she wondered what had changed.

"I never told Wolfgang that." Ashton shook her head.

"Let me refresh your memory . . . President Beaugard, I'd like to show camera footage if we can." Silver released Ashton from his stare.

"Uh, your honor, we have not received notice of any exhibits put forth by counsel." Frederick was out of his seat pointing angrily at Silver, attentive to Beaugard's decision on the new evidence.

"While Frederick is technically correct that we didn't submit any exhibits prior to the start of the trial, we would argue that based on the gap in truth in Frederick's opening statement yesterday, we would be right to provide evidence that discredits his statements. Additional time was needed to receive the requested footage from the event referenced, which will demonstrate Ms. Ashton has contradicted herself. We are alerting the court and defendant's side to the evidence obtained at the earliest moment it was received—just now, this very moment."

"This is malicious behavior, Mr. President. If they knew they had evidence, they should have presented it first as our line of questioning yesterday most certainly would have been altered."

"Frederick, Silver is allowed to present the evidence in whatever format he wishes, whether during the rebuttal or initial questioning. You'll have your chance to question afterward. Please continue, Silver, and the video surveillance had better be relevant, as we are already on day two and you're past your allotted time for this trial." Beaugard spoke without pause, referring to the three days Beaugard had allocated for the trial proceedings, and they had yet to hear Georgina's defense.

The VELIC system came forward and projected a 3D replica of a time and place in Ashton's history—one she wished she could forget.

Ashton's eyes settled on a paused hologram of herself bent down, Joao standing behind her, and Wolfe looking down as Jagatha sobbed in Ashton's arms. Then, VELIC pressed play.

"What do you want?!" Ashton said.

"How did you get the Artificial Existence Being?" Wolfe's eyes settled on Ashton and Jagatha.

Ashton paused.

"Georgina." Ashton closed her eyes, in that moment giving in to defeat.

"They built it?"

"No, found it. And worked on recreating the AEC's technology."

Wolfe came close to them and patted Jagatha's long, black hair.

"And sent you to do what?" His voice was soft, barely audible on the recording.

"You know why," Ashton admitted flatly. "You said yourself that NeuroEnergy only needs to find out what energy sources Augland is creating. If they find out you are breaking the treaty that ended the war, they have ammunition to take to Augland in DC."

"Is NeuroEnergy working with the Colony?"

"No, not really. They provide some technology and some supplies, but I wouldn't call them 'helpful.'"

Wolfe stood, towering above Ashton and Jagatha, and took a deep breath. Jagatha's cries had softened, but she still dug fiercely into Ashton.

"Thank you, Ashton. You've been immensely helpful."

That was the end of the hologram Silver played, leaving the visual paused on a hysterical Jagatha gripping Ashton out of fear and Ashton comforting her. It was like a bomb went off in the middle of the auditorium, and the ringing in Ashton's head propelled her away from the trial, the auditorium, and outside Augland, DC—she floated in the distance, unsure of what had just happened.

Ashton hadn't recalled confessing to Warren, pretending to be Wolfe, because she hadn't realized there was a camera recording them. She had forgotten about the conversation all together. All she remembered from that night was Warren dropping Jagatha off his balcony ledge.

"So, Ashton, when you say that you alone were responsible, why did you confess to Wolfgang, or Warren, as you have come to believe, that Georgina had told you to locate evidence of the energy initiatives? The man you grew close to, the man whose closest friends call, 'Wolfe'. The man, whom you say is not a 'job,' and whom you claim to have fallen in love with before even leaving Augland 54."

Ashton turned away from the hologram, her mind going back to that dark place in Warren's home with tears now uncontrollably streaming down her face.

"You don't want to play the rest?" Tears continued to force their way out and Ashton's voice trembled. "The moment an eight-year-old girl was murdered by being thrown off a six-hundred foot balcony!" Ashton's anger crescendoed. "That was not Wolfe . . . that was Warren making me say why I came into Augland to save that little girl. Who—"

"You need to answer my question, Ashton." Silver was standing still as his words sliced through the silence. "Did you or did you not confess in that footage to Georgina's attempt to find information of alleged energy initiatives by sending you in an AEB? Not that you tricked her into giving you an AEB and made friends at NeuroEnergy? Not that you knew how to put yourself into one with no formal training or because you 'wanted to become an engineer'? That she had sent you in as Charlotte, with credentials of a high-level daughter of an Executive in order to spy on Warren and search for proof of energy initiatives?"

Ashton could see Georgina's hand go to cover her face. Ashton had forgotten about the bracelet on Charlotte that had recorded conversations, which, at that point, was long gone. Georgina had no idea that she had confessed *everything* to Warren. Ashton swallowed.

"Yes." She said, knowing if she disagreed VELIC and the camera footage would detect her lie.

———————

Warren's counsel's questions dug deeper and the evidence Silver provided spun an elaborate web of collusion between Ashton and Georgina—and Wolfe as a love-stricken boy whose father was the CEO. Cameras had captured footage of Charlotte and Wolfe eating breakfast together at The Hook restaurant. He showed hologram footage of Wolfe and Ashton on the rock together and their first kiss before the battle where Sheva was almost killed.

Finally, Silver showed Ashton and Bez in Predator's Biome, where the workers chanted her name, "It's the girl with the red hair!" Charlotte's red hair, Silver told the CEOs, was Georgina's way of instigating the rebellion, connecting Charlotte to Ashton's character, Freya. Without the evidence of her admitting that Georgina had devised the plan, the answers to the questions that she and Frederick had planned may have worked.

"So, when you suggested that you are the mastermind behind this clandestine spy adventure, that's wrong, isn't it? Georgina supplied the boat. Georgina gave you the Artificial Existence Being, and you instigated the UnSuited Rebellion that now plagues seventeen different Auglands—and growing. Sounds more like a puppet to me than the ringleader." It was damning evidence, and while the picture Silver painted was somewhat correct, it was hard to refute Georgina's involvement. Frederick's plan had imploded, and there was nothing Ashton could say to repair the damage. Ashton's silence was all Warren's representative needed for confirmation.

"And your red hair. You had brown hair in the footage from Augland 54 after your AEB malfunctioned, and while in Wolfgang's personal chambers. And brown hair when you arrived for your *spy* mission. Your hair was red as Freya and, you wore a red wig as a representative leading the rebellion. Your hair was red as Charlotte, and now, in front of all these CEOs, you chose to dye your hair red once again. Did Georgina put you up to this? Force you to be the symbol of rebellion at the home of the CEOs?"

"No!" This time when the snickers around the auditorium rang loud, she knew the CEOs no longer believed anything Ashton said.

Ashton's face grew pale. It was a set up this entire time. Georgina hadn't instructed the VELIC to give her a makeover, *Warren had,* but this revelation hadn't occurred to her before providing her answer. This was a trap to take them *both* down. Warren had gained the upper hand and was winning. She had nothing else to lose because Warren was right, Georgina would lose regardless.

"The UnSuited is for workers; it has nothing to do with your corporate or political agendas. It has everything to do with how you treat people, how you take away their free will, their ability to live. You scare them into believing this is the best they are going to get in life but that isn't true. You all should be ashamed of yourselves. The workers who make your lives possible deserve to live a better life." The room fell silent, but Ashton could see the men and women in the auditorium had tuned her out. There was no getting through to them—just like the dinner when she told Bez' story about the brothels.

"Nothing further for this witness, Mr. President."

"Very well. Anything you'd like to clarify, Frederick?" Beaugard scribbled notes on his interpad.

Frederick stood warily. "No, nothing further for Ms. Ashton." Ashton could tell by the lack of eye contact that their current position wasn't good.

CHAPTER 13

Wolfe

NEUROENERGY, PACIFIC NORTHWEST

Wolfe sat across from the projected screen in Rye's office which was playing the live footage from Georgina's brooch with a camera hidden inside. Wolfe had noticed that Georgina only wore it during the trial and not on the jet traveling to Augland DC, or the evening festivities that Wolfe undoubtedly knew had occurred while the CEOs gathered for the House of CEO events—but he didn't complain.

Rye requested that they not display the trial for everyone in Pacific Northwest NeuroEnergy to see, so while Rye ventured in and out of his small cubicle office to keep NeuroEnergy afloat in Georgina's absence, Wolfe studied the pixelated video feed of the trial. It was grainy and at times hard to make out, but Wolfe's eyes were glued to it. Ashton was perched on a podium where she faced not just the camera, but the men, women, and Suits of the AEC, Auglands, and NeuroEnergies. Wolfe knew her well enough to know that she was nearing the end of her patience. He half expected her to stand and walk off the podium and out of the Augland DC doors. But she stayed. *That's my girl.*

The second day's trial began and Wolfe could only pray it would go as well as the first day. Wolfe's palms were sweating and the anticipation for any real or manufactured evidence that Silver's team could present was exhausting. Hunter who sat next to him had a habit of tapping the table they sat at, which annoyed Wolfe. Apparently, Hunter had nothing better to do than to sit and watch the footage with him.

Versal had stopped by a few times with coffee and snacks, which was consistent with Wolfe's current caffeine-based diet. The knots in his stomach made it impossible to even sleep, let alone eat anything. Having Ashton in Augland DC, not knowing what would happen to her or what information she would be forced to divulge about Georgina, was torture. Besides, he was sitting doing nothing and Wolfe hated being benched on the sidelines when the action was in the House of CEOs. Even while he worked security in Augland 54, he constantly had his hands on every project, every security breach, every plan. But right now, Wolfe, and the others not actively working on the STEMP project, could only wait and see what happened next.

Wolfe sat back in his chair with his arms crossed. Warren's representative, Silver, asked Ashton something about her history at Augland 54, but the audio from the camera feed was drowning in static and Wolfe couldn't hear his words precisely.

"Did she change her hair? Or was it red when she left?" Hunter asked. Hunter didn't know when to be quiet, so Wolfe just ignored him. Wolfe leaned in closer to hear the audio better. Hunter took the hint and amused himself with a set of Rye's projected glasses, swiping midair to look at whatever documents were in his vision.

"Do you mind?" Wolfe said with more volume than needed. Hunter's tapping, talking, and hand swiping was pushing Wolfe over the edge.

"Maybe if you ask nicely," Hunter volleyed back.

"You ever get tired of being the useless one around here?" It came out before Wolfe could filter his comment, knowing his short temper was due to his lack of sleep. He had very little reason at this point to be angry, or even dislike Hunter, but he hated his ego. They had never had a trusting, or even conversational, relationship. Wolfe sighed, ready to apologize.

"Oh, my apologies, *bossman* Wolfgang. What have I not done to serve you lately?" Hunter didn't miss an opportunity to showcase Wolfe's pampered history as a high-ranking employee of Augland 54 or sarcastically address him knowing he was the CEO's son. Wolfe stood quickly, pushing back the rolling office chair he sat in, and Hunter quickly followed. They both were of similar height, but Wolfe's imposing stature made him appear to tower over Hunter's tall frame.

"You've got an issue?" Wolfe stepped closer to Hunter's face.

"No, seems you're the one with the issue. Just because—" Hunter began but Wolfe brought up his hand to silence Hunter when he heard Silver mention something about evidence he wanted to present. His eyes darted back to the screen that broadcasted from Georgina's brooch. A hologram of video surveillance displayed on the monitor in Rye's office.

"How did you get the Suit?"

Ashton paused.

"Georgina." Ashton closed her eyes and in that moment giving in to defeat.

"They built it?"

"No, found it. And worked on recreating the AEC's technology."

Wolfe came close to them now and patted Jagatha's long, black hair.

"And sent you to do what?" His voice was soft, barely audible on the camera's recording.

"You know why," Ashton admitted flatly. "You said yourself that NeuroEnergy only needs to find out what energy sources Augland is creating. If they find out you are breaking the treaty that ended the war, they have ammunition to take to Augland in DC."

"Is NeuroEnergy working with the Colony?"

"No, not really. They provide some technology and some supplies, but I wouldn't call them 'helpful.'"

Wolfe stood, towering above Ashton and Jagatha, and took in a deep breath. Jagatha's cries had softened, but she still dug fiercely into Ashton.

"Thank you, Ashton. You've been immensely helpful."

That Silver would play this video made Wolfe do a double take. Wolfe had no idea what he had just watched. It was him—but not, which he immediately pieced together was a time when his father had impersonated him. It gave Wolfe a glimpse into Ashton's pain over the death of Jagatha. He recognized when it had taken place, based on the setting and who was in the shot. Wolfe collapsed back down in his chair and buried his face between his palms.

Waves of disappointment washed over Wolfe as he realized what was occurring at the trial. Ashton had been backed into a corner and had played right into Silver's hands. Wolfe knew from the start that this farce of a trial was rigged, and his father's side would always have the upper hand. At this point, considering the newly discovered footage, no one was going to believe that Georgina was an innocent bystander while Ashton ran point on the mission. This was all a political game and Georgina had just lost. *I should have never let her go,* Wolfe reprimanded himself.

"Rough." Hunter's untimely banter disrupted the silence and Ashton's ghostly white face on the monitor.

"She's doing her best; we couldn't have known they would have this sort of evidence." Wolfe snapped, knowing full well that, if any of them had been in that situation, it wouldn't have gone much better.

"Wasn't saying she wasn't. We all knew this was going to happen. I *knew* she shouldn't have gone. There was no other reason to bring just Ashton there, other than to isolate and set her up." Ashton and Hunter were friends, so he knew Hunter came from a supportive place, but that didn't mean Wolfe had to like his bluntness. Ashton wasn't here and Wolfe wasn't looking for a new best friend.

"So that's it isn't it? I mean, they've lost! There is no way they are going to vote in Georgina's favor now and we are all screwed unless Rye's pet STEMP project gets finished." Hunter got up from the table and slammed his fist into the door. Wolfe couldn't take his eyes off the screen, ignoring Hunter's outburst.

The broadcast from Georgina's brooch was now focused on Beaugard while they waited for the next witness to be called by Warren's side. The longer he waited, the more the realization set in of the inevitable. They would lose the trial and Ashton's safety was at risk. There was no way that Georgina and Ashton would be allowed to leave

Augland, DC unscathed. If they were found guilty, Georgina could be pardoned and return to live in NeuroEnergy, but Ashton? The evidence exposing Ashton's crimes would no doubt lead to her captivity in cages, or worse, death.

Wolfe took a deep breath. He needed to find a way to get to her, and ensure she came out of DC alive. He couldn't wait around to see what would happen next even with the STEMP project. Wolfe realized what he had to do. He looked around the room noticing, for the first time that Joao had been missing all day.

Wolfe would need him if he was going to break into DC.

CHAPTER 14

Ashton

DC, AUGLAND

"You didn't think to mention that at some point you confessed to Wolfgang about Georgina's plan!" Frederick's southern charm dissipated, and his face, in his anger, turned a frightening shade of red. Ashton thought about correcting him that it was Warren and not Wolfe, but knew that may anger him further.

They were on a mid-morning break after three other witnesses came forward in defense of Warren. Each witness was conveniently an Executive who had worked under Warren during the past ten years. Ashton recognized Wintefred, a woman who ran the Land of Legends Park, and Senator Chandler, the man she had swung at with an axe who was apparently a good friend of Warren's.

Ashton had silently, and quickly, left after Beaugard dismissed them, and made her way to the restrooms down the hall where she passed the closest one, hoping the CEOs would be deterred from making the trek to the furthest restrooms. She needed quiet to plan what she should do next, but she had little time before the door swung open and Frederick and Georgina marched in, locking the door behind them.

"VELIC, privacy mode, reason counsel discussion."

"Ashton, employee number JR105, has no counsel." VELIC spoke and Ashton froze. She shouldn't be surprised that VELICs also lived in the walls of restrooms.

"Ashton, employee number JR105, will have temporary legal counsel." Frederick spat.

"Recorded and approved. Setting privacy settings for legal corporate counsel."

"You didn't think to mention that you confessed to Warren!" Frederick's finger came out pointing at Ashton.

Ashton's brow furrowed in clear defense. "I forgot! It wasn't like after we escaped, I was thinking of a conversation I had with Warren or even that it was being recorded," Ashton confessed.

"Everything. Everything is recorded. Documented!" Frederick pointed to the VELIC that was clearly present even in a space that should have guaranteed privacy. "The whole purpose of our protection is to take the heat from Georgina—and that would only be possible if there weren't proof to contradict our story. We've lost and *you've* lost it for us." Frederick's fury softened as he shifted his gaze away from Ashton, "and you've cost me a fortune paying off *your* security men for their silence and for what . . ." Frederick paced. "Georgina, I don't see how we can recover from this."

Ashton went rigid, keeping her eyes focused on Georgina. It hadn't come to mind that the footage would be used against her. *Or that it even existed.* None of them had anticipated what Warren had brought forth, clear cut evidence of Georgina's involvement. Ashton had desperately tried to forget that day the video had been recorded. Everything from the conversation with Warren imitating Wolfe to Jagatha being dropped from the sky-high balcony.

"What are our options, Fred?" Georgina didn't look at Ashton, possibly from either anger or disappointment.

"The only thing I can think of is to distance ourselves from Ashton. Call her a liar or say that she attempted to blame you for some greater plan. Perhaps there is enough contradiction that VELIC won't disagree. We still have our defense, so I hope that you have made enough allies that will believe you. We should focus on the blueprints of Augland 54's energy expansion plans and pray it convinces the others in NeuroEnergy that there are more important matters to be concerned about. Emphasize that you just stumbled across those plans instead of recruiting Ashton to find them." Frederick strategized as he paced across the tiled bathroom.

Georgina stood with her hands clasped tightly before her. "They've already said that there is no way to determine the authenticity of the blueprints. Beau's already dismissed it." It was the first time Ashton had heard panic in Georgina's voice and her eyebrows trailed up, widening her oval eyes. So far during the trial, Georgina's expression had been emotionless, but here she showed how truly terrified she was.

"Why can't we call Warren to the stand? Make him talk! He can't lie his way out of the blueprints we discovered or impersonating Wolfe while he was CEO." Ashton softened now, letting her anger subside. Given Georgina's predicament, Georgina couldn't lose this trial when it was clear that Warren was the guilty one.

Frederick sighed. "Unless Warren offers to testify, we can't make him, just like they can't make Georgina take the stand. That would be equally as destructive."

"But if you both admit the wrongdoing, at least they will see that there was a reason why Georgina spied on them." It was so obvious to Ashton. If all parties were honest, and all of the tricks and fake story-lines exposed, the only issue left—the real issue—would be Warren's scheming against NeuroEnergy to make its energy resources irrelevant to Augland. For all the times she'd been told this was all her fault, she couldn't help but feel it was everyone's but hers.

"There's no way for us to guarantee Warren will be truthful; we have no evidence that he's telling lies or bending the truth. And we can't admit to what we've done. It would be admitting to crimes hop-ing that the other side would be truthful as well, and we both know Warren isn't about to broadcast Augland 54's dirty apparel laundry." Frederick's hand shook in frustration as he spoke, but Ashton noticed the slight dig he made toward Warren. Ashton wondered how much of her story Frederick had been told, and if he believed in the cause of the UnSuited. He wasn't here for the workers, as Ashton had learned today. Frederick worked for Georgina.

"So that's it . . . you're giving up?" Ashton couldn't believe how easily Georgina conceded. Georgina faced Frederick, keeping her eyes glued to him. Ashton could see the glistening hint of tears that threatened to slide down her typically stoic face. Frederick turned to Georgina. "It would take a miracle at this point. I'm sorry."

Georgina and Frederick left Ashton once Frederick turned the bathroom VELIC system back to normal mode. She could imagine Frederick strategizing now for damage control and leaning on Georgina's allies, hoping to count on them when the time to vote was at hand. Ashton returned to her room for the remainder of the break. Not that Georgina or Frederick cared. She was now an unwanted witness and no longer part of their trial strategy. Ashton paced the length of her apartment, mentally running through the evidence against her and fighting hard to devise a way out of this mess.

"Is there something I can get you, Ashton?" Her room's VELIC came to life. She ignored it. "You seem agitated; my research shows that meditation can help with anxiety. Shall I play some calming music?" Ashton sat down hard on the end of the bed, shaking while her hands pressed hard against her temples.

"I can play some—" VELIC suddenly died and the lights in the room darkened. Ashton's head rose as she searched the room. It was silent. It wasn't dark outside so her room was well lit from the daylight streaming through her patio doors, but something wasn't right.

"VELIC?" Ashton asked and the AI robot didn't respond. The silence stretched out and Ashton waited for a response, rising from the bed. In the quiet, Ashton heard what sounded like a click coming from her apartment's door. She stared as the knob turned. Ashton froze. Someone was coming into her room. It be been her two security guards, but they hadn't once entered her apartment before. Ashton backed up and ran toward her bathroom hiding behind the door before she was spotted by the intruder. Her breath quickened and she could feel the rapid beats of her heart bouncing against her rib cage. Eyes wide and frightened, she tried to make herself as small as possible. She could hear the figure walking past her small kitchen and toward her bed. *They could be here to kill you. Do better than just hide. Escape!* The footsteps came closer.

"Ashton." It was a deep husky voice, strained. "You can come out; I'm not going to hurt you." Ashton pressed further against the wall near the door of the bathroom. The Suit, in all-black attire, walked over to the bed. Ashton could see him through the slit in the door as his dark brown eyes looked up at her through the opening between the door hinges. He seemed familiar, like she had seen him before, but Ashton couldn't remember from where.

"I won't hurt you. Please come out from behind the door. We don't have a lot of time before the break is over." He had his hands neatly placed on his lap while he sat on her bed, keeping his eyes on her.

It was against her better judgement, but he clearly knew where she was hiding. This way, maybe she could escape out the front door and beg the security Suits to help her. Ashton wondered how this Suit had managed to make it past the two supposedly standing guard outside her door—unless everyone in the House of CEOs paid security men to turn away. If all else failed, there was always the three-story balcony. *A couple broken bones at least,* she calculated.

Finally, she slipped out from behind her hiding space, but kept her eyes on the Suit's dark, mysterious, yet familiar warm eyes. "Who are you?"

"Reuben Archebold," he replied without hesitation.

Ashton's voice hitched in astonishment. Because she vaguely remembered this man. It was the man Wolfe had spoken of, a man close to his father and like an uncle to him, named Reuben, but what she did not know was why he was here.

CHAPTER 15

Wolfe

NEUROENERGY, PACIFIC NORTHWEST

Wolfe headed to Joao's NeuroEnergy apartment after noticing his absence while he and Hunter had been watching the trial proceedings.

"Where have you been? I thought you said you wanted to watch the trial?" Wolfe asked as Joao walked out of his home. He was shocked by Joao's disheveled hair and ashen face and sunken eyes. "Dear God . . . you look like—" Wolfe didn't finish his sentence before Joao interrupted him.

"Sorry, man. I was out at the doctor's. I'm glad you came up this way because I was about to come get you."

"Well, I'm here." Wolfe started to walk toward Joao's apartment door, but Joao blocked him.

"Alone. Bez is in there and I'd prefer if it were just you and me." Wolfe's eyes shifted from the closed apartment door back to Joao.

"Sure, yeah, I mean, we can just go to my place." Joao and Wolfe had kept plenty from Bez and Ashton, especially over the last few months because they were afraid of what would happen at trial. Given that they were not there, he wondered why the secrecy.

Wolfe turned the key to his apartment and Joao followed him in, heading straight for the couch. NeuroEnergy apartments were stacked homes that had a living room and kitchen on the lower floor with rooms and bathrooms above them. Wolfe's wasn't far from where Joao and Bez stayed. NeuroEnergy had several apartments dedicated for visitors and part-time residents, and they had been assigned apartments near one another. They were located on the outer rim of the compound, additions made after people from outside Northwest NeuroEnergy had arrived to live and visit, and happened to be a fifteen-minute walk from the headquarters building.

"Drink? I think I've got . . . water." Wolfe chuckled, opening the bare fridge in his tiny kitchenette.

"Nothing stronger?" Joao questioned.

"'One-Eyed Gary' wine . . . it's sour. Rico gave some to Ashton the night of the bonfire and I thought I'd bring it."

"I'll take it." Wolfe shrugged and poured two glasses of One-Eyed Gary's wine and passed one to Joao before taking a seat at the desk across from him.

"A bit early for drinking but can't say I don't disagree after watching this morning's trial." Wolfe admitted, with the intention to relay the details to Joao as he was notably absent from today's first session.

Joao took a sip, exclaiming, "Oh dear God! Is that . . . vinegar?" Joao's face tensed from the sudden sharp, acidic taste of the homemade wine. Wolfe laughed.

The silence between them lingered as each waited for the other to begin speaking. Wolfe couldn't wait any longer to update Joao and blurted out, "I think we need to break into Augland DC, with a rescue plan. From how the trial is going, it looks like Georgina's not going to win. So, I thought maybe we could find a way to go in undetected, just in case backup is needed."

"You're worried about Ashton." It wasn't a question.

"Well . . . I'm not sure what she'll do if they lose, which is part of the problem. But also, I don't know what Warren will do once he's won. Ash admitted to dismantling Senator Chandler and somehow footage was captured of her admitting Georgina's plan to find evidence of the energy initiative Warren had developed." Wolfe recalled the hologram that was played during the trial. In the footage, Joao had been standing next to Jagatha but Joao hadn't told Wolfe what had happened, which Wolfe thought was unlike him.

"What about the sewer system? We could try and make it through there," Joao suggested. The bags under his eyes were more prominent than Wolfe had originally noted.

"How do we get through undetected?" Wolfe asked.

"Good point, pretty sure your ugly mug will get recognized anywhere you go." Joao, even looking unwell, could banter with him.

"That hurt." Wolfe smirked, pretending to be offended. "You told me you thought I was handsome." Wolfe leaned back and took a sip of the wine. "Oh, God, that is awful." Wolfe's face soured from the bitter taste.

"I mean, we also have to think about security once we are there. VELICs are everywhere, so our every move will be detected once we step foot anywhere near the capitol." Joao was right; there was too much uncertainty. "Forest has been working with Hunter. He's apparently pretty good with computers. Might be worth talking to him, since NeuroEnergy has technology that could prove useful to us," Joao added.

"Same guy that commandeered that train in Augland for the apparel workers?" Wolfe asked. He remembered hearing about a worker from Apparel that had started an Augland 54 'programmed to stop' train—which was nearly impossible.

"Yeah, anyone who can override security features like *that* may be able to help override VELIC controls," Wolfe agreed. "Let's start there and get him roped into meetings with Vic. It's at least worth it to have him speak with our scientist. If he's got some intel on 54, that could help expedite the search for accessible satellites too, and help with countering the VELIC override." Wolfe noticed Joao playing with his glass.

"What's going on, Joao?" Wolfe's brow furrowed with concern. "You're . . . just . . . something is off with you . . ." Wolfe generally wasn't one to pry, but something was different with Joao; he clearly wasn't his usual self.

Joao didn't look at him. He cleared his throat. ". . . that's kind of what I wanted to talk to you about . . . I went to the doctor here because I was having headaches."

Wolfe raised an eyebrow, unsure how serious to take his statement. "Headaches . . . you poor thing," he tried to jest.

"It's serious, Wolfe. They took an x-ray and found something implanted on my brain. Apparently other workers from Augland 54 have complained of similar symptoms." Joao's eyes finally met Wolfe's and Wolfe's demeanor changed. This *was* serious. "Warren must have installed it and I, I'm not sure, I don't remember it happening . . . but I did ask Forest to recover deleted messages from my interconnect and saw hundreds of phone calls and messages between me and Warren. He knows everything." There was a faint buzzing sound as Wolfe processed Joao's confession. Joao was chipped with the Customer Service Initiative.

"Everything," Wolfe repeated. "What do you mean, everything?"

"I swear I had no idea I was living with the Customer Service chip. I didn't know and I'm not sure how Warren orchestrated the implantation. The doctor said the chip could be turned on and off and may have the capability to erase my memory if it was coded to do so. It's the only explanation I can think of!" The desperation in Joao's voice was apparent; he needed Wolfe to believe that he hadn't sabotaged their work intentionally.

"How long?" Wolfe asked, and his mind began flipping through all of their group conversations and actions that had potentially been exposed. "Jo, how long?" Wolfe asked again and in his panic repeated, "and what do you mean by *everything*?"

"Everything, man—the blueprints, the Suit head, the Centauri star, Ashton's confession to Warren and Jagatha . . . the STEMP project." Wolfe's head hung in defeat with Joao's admission.

"When did this happen?" Wolfe demanded again.

"I don't know, before we left Augland 54. Sometime after you were imprisoned." Joao set his wine down on Wolfe's coffee table, interlaced his fingers, and draped his elbows over his knees. Joao's eyes met Wolfe's. The STEMP project was their only back-up plan now, and it required the utmost secrecy if they were going to pull this off. Without it, Warren would attack NeuroEnergy, kidnap the scientist, and destroy or use the STEMP project as a weapon, most likely against NeuroEnergy. Wolfe slumped against his chair—at a loss for words.

Joao filled the silence. "The doctor gave me something—a microchip. It is a physical blocker for the CS chip transmission. It will turn off any Customer Service or CS anytime it is switched on and he hopes it will stop any further . . . problems." Joao reached for a black chain that hung around his neck, pulling the loose material of his shirt up to show Wolfe a small green gem. When he turned the gem over, a blinking neon light lit up. Wolfe studied it. "It has to be almost touching the skin for it to work and can't be more than a few feet away from the CS chip itself. The doctor said at some point it would make sense to implant the microchip because it's too dangerous to remove the Customer Service chip."

"Does Warren know you've found out about the chip?" Wolfe questioned.

"No, not that I know. I had this . . . buzzing sound in my head after I left the doctor's office, and saw Warren's number on my interconnect seconds later. I pretended like I was expecting it and he talked to me like we were . . . *friends*. He asked if the scientist had any more information since the day before. I said no, but because I can remember the conversation, that means what the doctor gave me must have worked. Warren then told me to erase the call log and to forget what he just asked, which is what clued me in that he's been erasing my memory."

For a brief moment, Wolfe considered whether he should trust Joao, but long history made him stop second guessing. Joao had been with him since they were children. He was one of the few workers who had grown up in an intact family, who had grown up with engineer parents before infertility was an issue among the workers due to the constant exposure to the Suits they served. Joao's engineering background and strategic thinking, plus the fact that he had become friends with Wolfe during his time at Augland Center, had given Joao access to the Executive arena. Ana, Wolfe's mother, had wanted her son to have a friend after he left Augland Center, so she insisted Joao accompany Wolfe to all his classes. If there was anyone in Augland 54 to trust, it was Joao.

Wolfe took in a deep breath and spoke. "Then we have to move quickly because we don't have nearly the time I thought." He wondered if Warren had subpoenaed Ashton because of something Joao had said while under the influence of the Customer Service Initiative.

For the next hour, Joao and Wolfe discussed their new plan of attack, exhausting all possible scenarios until they came up with the most plausible option with the least amount of risk. They split up the to-do list: Joao would introduce Forest to Vic and create a plan to move Vic to safety and away from NeuroEnergy in case Warren came to find him before the trial concluded. They had a plan in place to protect the NeuroEnergy workers, assuming Warren was successful at the trial and would attack NeuroEnergy to get to the STEMP project. While Joao was busy with protecting Vic, Wolfe would be left with the most dangerous action item on their list: infiltrate Augland DC.

Joao left the apartment while Wolfe stepped outside his apartment doors and headed toward the outdoor NeuroEnergy market near the mess hall. They had plenty to do before they reconvened with the rest of the STEMP support crew for a status update. Wolfe sighed with frustration at Joao's revelation.

Wolfe's first thought was that Joao had betrayed him, but within seconds that thought had evaporated. Joao was one of the few he could trust and if he said that Warren did this—Wolfe had to believe him. They had been through too much together and when Wolfe needed

Joao he was always there, trusting Wolfe. The least he could do is return the favor.

It was midmorning, about nine o'clock on the second day of trial. Based on the time difference, it was roughly noon east coast Augland time. Though it was still early in the day, the sun was already showing high above him. No one was outdoors, other than a few stragglers who had walked to the mess hall for a late breakfast. Wolfe pulled out his interconnect and dialed his father, making sure to keep his distance from the others. Warren didn't answer, but sent him a message response. *Give me five.*

Wolfe waited, using the few minutes to grab himself an espresso with cream from the on-site coffee shop. Minutes passed. This was a crazy and impulsive idea, but if it worked, it could be just what was needed to buy them more time until their STEMP project was completed. His interconnect rang. *Warren.*

"Thanks for calling back," Wolfe said.

"Good timing, just ending our break between witnesses. How can I help you, Wolfgang? I figured given the abrupt ending of our last call that was the last I'd hear from you for a while." Wolfe had thought the same thing at the time, but since Joao's confession things had changed.

"I . . . reconsidered your offer; that is, if it still stands, of course." There was a pause while Warren seemed to be processing Wolfe's change of mind.

"The . . ." Warren paused, "the trial already started and I'm not sure what added good will come of your testimony, but . . . I don't think it would hurt. We'd have a very specific message crafted for you. And you'd have to commit completely, no double crossing." Wolfe thought about Warren implanting the CS chip in Joao's head. He undoubtedly thought he could control any situation.

"Of course, I'm sure you'll think of a way to ensure my compliance." Wolfe was certain his father had already thought of a way to do that.

"And you'll come back to Augland 54? Stop fighting me at every turn? I want us to go back to the way things were."

"I'm putting up my white flag, Warren . . ."

"Don't be disrespectful. I'm your father."

"Well, *Father*, I give up. You win. I just want to make sure Ashton comes home safe from the trial, and once I have that confirmation, I'll come back to Augland 54 and return to my old role next to you." Wolfe could sense his father's devilish grin from across the Augland countryside.

"Below me, you mean . . . I can't trust you yet, but I hope in time we will gain back what we once had. And, Wolfgang, I plan on testing that loyalty once you're here."

"I would do the same." Wolfe admitted.

"Be ready within the hour. I'll have a jet waiting for you outside the NeuroEnergy compound." Warren's voice was soft, but serious. "And Wolfgang?"

"Yeah?"

"You try anything—I don't think I have to tell you what will happen," Warren threatened without any hesitation in his voice.

"I know." Wolfe acknowledged Warren's very real threat against Ashton. Warren's highest priority was Wolfe returning to his side, regardless of the motivation that brought him back. While Warren was no "father" in the traditional sense of the word, he took pride in raising Wolfe to be strong, independent and powerful, but knew he had a weakness—empathy. Wolfe figured Warren knew the warning alone would keep Wolfe in line.

Within forty minutes, Wolfe had ordered two cups of espresso with steamed milk to go and had packed a bag with his essentials. He had even paid a quick visit to Joao's doctor to hear his opinion on the chip in Joao's head.

Wolfe plopped his packed bags down in front of Joao, who eyed him as they huddled in Vic's underground bunker. Rye, Hunter, and Vic gathered around Vic's computer system, mapping out different satellites. Forest had just arrived and was introduced to the group. "We leaving today?" Joao asked.

"I am. I'm going to go to Augland, DC. Warren and I made a deal to protect Ashton if I testify on his behalf. We already know the outcome of the trial, so we have to figure out how to get Ashton to safety and stop Warren from coming here for the scientist and STEMP project.

"How do you know he'll come here?" Rye asked.

"There is no way Warren will let something like the STEMP project exist without him controlling it. If Georgina is removed as CEO, I can only imagine he'll come straight here to find Vic. It's what I'd do if I were him." Wolfe confessed. "I suggest working with Rye and Hunter on our new plan—make sure Forest is working with them to help speed this up. And the sewer system, keep mapping it out just in case we need to make a quick getaway."

"Vic?" Wolfe turned his attention toward the scientist. "How long till we can give that thing a test drive?"

"I need at least a couple weeks."

"See what you can do in one week with Forest's help," Wolfe barked. It wasn't a respectful tone, even though Vic had been working day and night on the operation. But they were running out of time and Wolfe felt the urgency running through him like adrenaline.

Wolfe was terrified, but despite the circumstances he couldn't help but find the tension exciting like he once did when he was Security Director for Augland 54. He missed this, but not nearly as much as he missed Ashton.

CHAPTER 16

Ashton

DC, AUGLAND

Ashton's mouth remained open in shock. A familiar Suit stood in front of her, one she had heard Wolfe speak of only a handful of times as someone close to his father. "You met me, in Augland 54. At the gala while you pretended to be Charlotte." It clicked, finally, why she recognized the man in front of her. Warren had introduced her to him at the Predator Biome gala.

"The family friend . . ." Ashton was still against the wall, ensuring at least five feet of safety between them.

"Yes, the family friend." Reuben grinned and gave a slight chuckle. Warren, impersonating Wolfe, had said something about his loyalty, which caused her to question their history. At the time, champagne had clouded her memory, but she did remember the feeling that there was more to Warren, imitating Wolfe, and Reuben's story.

"Why are you here?" Ashton moved cautiously to the other end of the room, closer to the door.

Reuben took in a deep breath. "I'm about to tell you something that isn't going to make a lot of sense, but I'm hoping we can establish some trust before we move forward. Because if we move forward, you'll have to listen very carefully about what you'll be instructed to do next." Ashton frowned, still unsure of Reuben's motives for appearing in her quarters and scaring her half to death.

Did Warren send him? Reuben's eyes softened while he shifted his weight on the bed, becoming less threatening in stature and closer to eye level with Ashton. "I know what you're thinking: Warren must have sent me, but I have to say that my allegiance goes much higher than Warren."

"Higher than Warren? Like . . . the AEC president?" Ashton asked.

"No, it goes to an association called iHumanist." *He's a Suit! And he works for Warren, don't trust what he's saying!* Ashton's mind cautioned her.

"What do you mean?"

"I'm part of a society that is comprised of key members from AEC, Auglands and NeuroEnergies that believes technology has gone too far, and that, with the recent developments of VELIC and worker-targeted infertility, we need to change our community and develop a better governing structure. Our philosophy has loose ties with what you're doing with the UnSuited."

Ashton scoffed. It was insulting to make correlations between UnSuited and anything created by Suits. "Doubtful."

Reuben's eyebrows rose, but he didn't comment on her response. "In all honesty, the association didn't think much of you until the trial. You seemed to be more of an impulsive, wrong-place-wrong-time kind of girl." *That was sort of true, but still rude,* Ashton thought, shifting from one foot to the other.

"But that has changed," Reuben continued. "You know the level of courage it takes to get up in front of the CEOs of Auglands, Neuro-Energies, and AEC Senators and still hold yourself with such grace and dignity—even though the outcome wasn't what *you* expected," Reuben said with the hint of a smile. She looked away. That wasn't exactly how she felt in this moment—her courage seemed foolish and ill-advised for a worker in the House of CEOs, and unworthy of entertaining the support of someone she wasn't quite sure was trustworthy.

Reuben went on, "I think it's assumed that we all have the best interests of the workers at heart, but only the workers can confirm if that's their experience. We want you to join us, Ashton. Help us clean up the mess we've made with technology running amok, and work to create a more harmonious society." Ashton took a deep breath; this was a lot of new information to take in, not to mention an entirely different per-spective to the situation. *You've been burned by trusting too easily before.*

"I'll speak candidly with you, Ashton. You won't make it out of Augland DC, alive—and that threat isn't coming from me." Reuben stared directly at Ashton as he spoke, incredibly blunt and emotionless. His honesty was at least refreshing, Ashton admitted. "If you don't agree with my proposition, you die here in Augland DC. The UnSuited will be found and perish. All I'm asking is that you agree to work with me, and I will make sure you make it out of here alive and help you gain more favor with the UnSuited outside of Augland 54. I can help you achieve what you want."

Reuben was admitting what she had presumed about her chances of survival within the Augland DC walls. Frederick hadn't explicitly told her what would happen if Georgina lost—which it seemed she would—but Ashton guessed she wouldn't be allowed to go back home. She had so many questions about iHumanist, and how Reuben wanted to use her, but what came out wasn't something she expected.

"And what is it that I want?"
"You want Warren to be displaced. You want workers to have rights, and to stop Executives from dictating their existence in their homes, their lives, their . . . minds and bodies. You want the liberty we promised people to replace corporate tyranny that exists today. I can help you."

"Why are you in a Suit, if you don't believe in trusting technol-ogy?" Ashton questioned. Everything she knew that had ever come from Suits had been lies and manipulation, especially in Augland, DC. She was reminded of the Suits and NeuroEnergy CEOs at her dinner table. They were unable to even speak of worker treatment and liv-ing conditions, Georgina reprimanded her for even talking about their daily lives. How was Reuben different from them?

"Fair question. I do it for appearance. I still have my job as Chief of Operations for Augland 54, next to Warren and that gives me access to information and the ability to get my hands on things like blueprints and locations of discarded Artificial Existence Beings . . ." Ashton's eyes widened. His words didn't specifically say what he had done, but Ashton made the connection when she remembered that Wolfe's mother, Ana, had supplied Joao with Warren's discarded Wolfe Suit, helping free Wolfe from the NeuroEnergy prison so he could find and convince Ashton he'd told the truth about his father's impersonation.

"How did you—"

"I gave it to Ana to help Wolfe. I wish I could say it was for your love story, but I'm afraid it was not. We needed Wolfe to survive and the UnSuited to continue. This uprising is exactly what our cause needed to kickstart the change we've been planning for. It is what our cause needed to instigate change."

"I'm not sure I understand." Ashton crossed her arms. Reuben didn't move.

"You're a sweet kid, and it's unfortunate you got stuck in this mess. But seeing that the trial isn't going in Georgina's favor, we thought maybe you'd be open to another tactic."

Ashton didn't say anything. "We need you to send a message to the UnSuited, giving them orders for a coordinated attack from their respective territories or Auglands. Right now, you're not their 'official' leader, even though Frederick is trying to paint you as one. Some workers think you're a legend and nothing more—and we need to change that. Give them a face to follow."

"How?"

"The AEC; it's Warren's next plan of attack. He will use his control over the UnSuited to gain popularity among the CEOs, showing that he can stop the rebellion and restore order with the Customer Service Initiative. I can make sure he believes you can be controlled and used to become their *actual* leader, which will help him become the next president of the AEC. Instead of giving Warren power over the UnSuited, we will leverage his belief you can be controlled to undermine him and activate the rebellion."

Ashton had so many questions. The AEC already had a president. The UnSuited were not as successful and well-known as CEOs were giving them credit for. "And the workers. What will happen to them if we go with your, plan or . . . whatever you want? Why would you help the UnSuited?"

"iHumanist needs an army and the UnSuited need powerful people in Auglands, AECs, and NeuroEnergies. Look, you've already been marked as the instigator of rebellion, so we are using that platform to boost UnSuited territory and create a war against the AEC and Auglands. iHumanist wants to go back to the foundation of our nation—pre-technology, pre-corporate rule—and start fresh. We had a government once that helped create a framework for living peacefully with one another, but there was always freedom of choice and that goes beyond just freedom of the individual. It promoted balance and equality. But war is inevitable in order to return to a place of peace. We need numbers and that's where your UnSuited come in." Ashton shook her head. *He didn't answer my question.*

"I've sacrificed enough for corporations and so have the workers. I'm sick of constantly being in a state of fight or flight and getting stuck in-between one of your corporate feuds. That's how I ended up here," Ashton said stubbornly.

"You can wait to see the fall out after the trial or you can take a chance on a better avenue for reform and outcome for the people you care about."

"And if I don't?" Ashton retorted defiantly.

Reuben kept his eyes on Ashton. His once soft demeanor hardened as he lifted himself from her bed to a standing position. His six-foot Suit towering over her.

"You want Wolfe to go back to Augland enslaved by his father's will? Or Bez to be returned to the brothel, only for Joao to be forced to watch from afar, after being demoted? Or what about Versal and Hunter, separated and dispersed within Augland 54? Rye put to death for treason or Cahya labeled as a traitor? The Colony? Rico . . . and

NeuroEnergy employees forced into new lives as workers of Auglands? What about the Customer Service Initiative? Are you prepared for every worker to be under Warren's total and direct control?

"That's what you risk by saying no. That's the threat of an Augland takeover. Warren's end game—total control over Auglands and Neuro-Energies. You've demonstrated you are an empathetic person, driven by the needs of others and that's exactly why this corporation will punish you, and make an example of you. That is, if they don't decide to kill you first."

Ashton's throat tightened and she found herself at a loss for words. He knew so much about her, and she knew nothing of him. "And your *association*. How are they any different from Augland or the AEC?"

"We align in some beliefs, differ in others. Now, yours and my philosophies align. If we stop recklessly advancing technology forward, humanity will be saved. We need to rebuild as a human race and go back to basics. We want people to thrive, not just barely survive as the workers are doing now. With technology like VELICs already in existence, there's no end to the dangers of artificial intelligence that are waiting around the corner. Humanity is in real and near danger, and likely won't survive these advancements—and neither will the human forms living in pods."

There wasn't much to think about. Reuben outlined the impending threats one by one, taking care to note the dangers that awaited them in a future where technology was the highest law. Though Ashton agreed with him theoretically, she didn't know if she could trust him and his association after learning about both less than ten minutes ago. On the other hand, she was at a loss for her next move. They wouldn't possibly win at the conclusion of the trial, and they had no safety net.

"If I agree to your plan, how can I trust that you'll protect me?" Reuben walked toward Ashton, his strong build shrinking her stoic stance.

"You'll just have to trust me."

"I didn't say I agreed," Ashton called out as she watched Reuben walk toward the exit.

Reuben paused to look back at her with a piercing gaze. "Yes, you do agree," he said seriously. "You sold Georgina out to Warren because you thought it would save that little girl. You knew you might die. You knew it would hurt NeuroEnergy, and you did it anyway because you care about people. You will sacrifice whatever it takes for the people you care about, and if you don't? It was nice knowing you for our brief exchange today."

Reuben turned and opened the door, but not before he turned again to say one last thing. "And if you even try to breathe a word about what the iHumanist are or tell anyone about me your life, and the lives of those close to you, will end. I hope you're smart and choose wisely because though I'm an honorable man, I won't sacrifice the iHumanist cause for you." The door closed and Ashton was left with the threat Reuben had uttered ringing in her years.

What he proposed was a solution but, like trusting Georgina with Charlotte's Suit, she feared that the iHumanist cause would somehow hurt the workers and the UnSuited. Reuben was right about one thing: she may not have a choice. If she said no, then what would happen to everyone she cared about? NeuroEnergy or the Colony?

It was only minutes after Reuben disappeared that VELIC was turned back on.

"I can play some soft music . . . it has been proven to help relax individuals suffering from panic attacks or anxiety," the VELIC reported, continuing as if it hadn't been turned off for the last ten minutes.

Ashton was still speechless, ignoring the VELIC's unfaltering, customer service-like behavior. Soon, her break would be over and she would need to return to trial.

Ashton was unable to pay attention to the steady stream of witness after witness who provided testimony when the trial reconvened for the late-morning session. Even during the rest of their break there was little Ashton could think about after Reuben's iHumanist ultimatum.

You may have fallen into another trap, you know that. You know members of these corporations can't be trusted. Let alone a Suit you know is the right hand of Warren. Ashton's mind argued with herself as she contemplated Reuben's proposal.

What other choice do you have?

"We have two more witnesses, Mr. President, before we plan to rest our case." Ashton tuned her attention back into the exchange between Silver and Beaugard. The trial was almost over and soon she would need to decide: play nice with Reuben and iHumanist or hope that she could think of a better plan to save NeuroEnergy and the workers of Augland 54.

CHAPTER 17

Ashton

Warren's team had asked for a recess while their last two witnesses prepared, and Ashton took full advantage. She quickened her steps to take her outside the auditorium and away from the other CEOs, escorted by her two security guards. The air in the House of CEOs was suffocating her. Once outside and away from the capitol building, Ashton felt the wind against her, and the warm sun beating down on her. She closed her eyes and inhaled in the fresh*er* air.

The cherry blossoms near the capitol pond fell and were reflected in the calm surface. Ashton felt anything but calm. Following Reuben's conversation, all she could think about was what his proposition meant for her immediate future. Maybe he would free her, and if so, she would owe the iHumanist movement a debt—which meant her cooperation with the UnSuited rebellion. His timing was *interesting*. She had never heard of the iHumanist association before, and Reuben had waited until the hologram showing Ashton's confession was revealed at trial. It was then that he approached her—before her fate had been sealed and while Georgina's chances of winning the trial appeared to be growing slimmer.

Ashton tossed around the idea of what working with the iHumanists would mean for her and the rebellion of the UnSuited. If she did agree to ally with Reuben, did that mean the Colony and NeuroEnergy would be safe from Warren as well?

Ashton couldn't predict what would happen now. Warren's team had done a great job of highlighting Ashton's leadership of the UnSuited, and tying Georgina to Ashton wasn't difficult given the video footage. If she didn't agree to Reuben's terms, the House of CEOs and the AEC, would never let her leave.

To keep herself from completely spiraling into panic-ridden thoughts, Ashton turned to acknowledge her security Suits. "You two have names? Or am I just supposed to call you 'Thing 1' and 'Thing 2'?" She snorted at her own joke. The idea of the nicknames was thanks to a children's book left behind by the previous tenants at her Hood Canal home—written by someone called Dr. Seuss. The two security Suits didn't answer and instead stood as statues, watching her from the corner of their eyes.

"Could you give us some privacy?" A voice from behind Ashton spoke sweetly.

Georgina gracefully guided herself next to Ashton on the cement step and sat down. The two Suits appeared to compromise and turned away, not leaving their post, but at least turning their backs.

"Is it really safe to be seeking me out right now, and in front of those two? For someone who's been careful not to be seen talking with me, you seem to be around me quite a lot."

"I think we both know it's too late to worry about what everyone will think of us communicating." Georgina looked up, letting the Augland DC, sun beat down on her face before turning toward Ashton on the House of CEO steps, "I'm sorry you were put in the middle of this. That I put you in the middle of all this . . ." She placed her hand over Ashton's clasped hands. The admission was sincere and remorseful, and while Ashton could forgive, she would never forget.

"I'm sorry too. I tried, Georgina," Ashton confessed.

"This was a long shot anyway. I tried to stop this trial from even starting . . . I wish I hadn't listened to Frederick when he said we had a chance. Not that it would have done any good. The trial would have happened one way or another. Warren has a way of getting what he wants." This was a regret they both felt, which mingled with the palpable danger they sensed in the air surrounding them while in Augland DC.

"What will happen to us when they make their decision?" There was part of Ashton that wanted to confide in Georgina about the alternative potential that Reuben suggested, but one thing he had made clear was that Ashton's silence was required.

Georgina took a deep breath. "That's up to Beau and what Warren's side suggests as a punishment. Most likely he will strip me of my CEO title." Her voice wavered; she didn't like the suffocating stench of stagnant defeat that hovered around them. "If I'm found guilty, I'll admit to my role in everything and hopefully they will let you go home and let me take the punishment." Ashton presumed that was doubtful considering Auglands were known to cage people for less.

"What happens to NeuroEnergy?"

"I don't know. That depends on what the AEC dictates. I hope Beaugard will make a fair decision regarding the future of Pacific Northwest NeuroEnergy. I'm just not sure I'll like it."

The uncertainty over what would happen following the trial was worse than coming to terms with their inevitable defeat. Georgina and Ashton sat in silence, watching the continuous loop of blossom petals falling.

"You know what disappoints me the most?" Ashton didn't respond. Georgina stared ahead. "I think even if you were somehow able to force Warren to admit that he was creating his own energy initiative, I'm not sure the AEC would have punished him for breaking the treaty with NeuroEnergy. I think . . . that maybe this company is too far gone to uphold their founding philosophies of what's right and true."

Georgina sniffed, then pushed up from the step and swept her hands down across her pencil skirt to smooth the creases. "I think you might have been right, Ashton. When you first approached me, you asked for an army to back you if you were to go against Warren, and I didn't believe we were at a point where the imbalance and power had shifted to necessitate a war. I was wrong." Ashton could only stare back, speechless.

It was only minutes that they waited in silence before being called back to continue with the remainder of the offense's witnesses. Georgina would then have her opportunity to convince the CEOs of her innocence despite the mountain of evidence stacked against her. Ashton wasn't privy to the whispers of the CEOs, but she felt their alliance further solidifying behind Warren after the show his team put on.

———

The two witnesses for Warren were on the stand for less than an hour, both speaking highly of his long-standing leadership over Augland 54 and the resources he had provided for the Colony and NeuroEnergy over the years. If Ashton hadn't known better, she too would be convinced that he was a good man with an altruistic mindset—but she did know Warren and he was not honorable in any capacity.

"Thank you for your patience, Mr. President, as with every CEO in this room. We had a last-minute addition to our witness list and were waiting for his jet to land. He's arrived and is ready to testify."

Beaugard nodded. "Please call your witness. And I do hope this is the last surprise of this trial, Silver. We need to move this along to the defense as we are nearing our third day and have yet to hear from their side."

"Of course, Mr. President and rest assured, it is. We'd like to call forth Wolfgang Igor Warren as a rebuttal witness."

Ashton did a double take to make sure she heard Warren's representative correctly. She knew Wolfe's full name. It was taken from his mother's lineage. Anastasia's father had required Warren and Ana's first-born son to have the middle name Igor, which Warren had initially agreed to but later attempted to alter along with the terms that Wolfe's grandfather had included as a prerequisite of their marriage. Ultimately, Ana was successful, and Wolfe was named after her father. Wolfe had said that he and his father had many conversations about

Wolfe's first-born sharing Warren's name to continue his legacy—that was before he knew about worker infertility.

Ashton's eyes went wide in disbelief as she saw Wolfe in a pressed suit stride through the doors and toward the witness stand with his typical pulled-back hair and rough beard. He stood tall and quickly glanced at Ashton without expression.

He pulled the chair out and sat quietly.

"You realize a rebuttal witness can only be questioned around information already entered into trial. And the witness cannot provide new evidence." Beaugard insisted.

"Mr. President, we will only need him to testify regarding the issue of the blueprints, which were mentioned by Frederick during his opening statement. He referred to them as 'documents,' which we believe has stirred some questions among CEOs and for which we would like to clarify." Silver and Frederick were both standing on their respective sides while Wolfe sat at the podium where witnesses were questioned. Ashton leaned around Frederick's standing figure to look again at Wolfe, who appeared at ease.

"Mr. President, we never presented any evidence concerning the blueprints because they were never admitted into evidence, and I've had no time to create a narrative or questions for if they were admitted." Frederick was stammering. It was just as much a shock to him as it was to Ashton to see Wolfe presented as a witness.

"Yes, but Frederick opened the door in his opening statement by discussing the potential documents, which he claims are the reason Georgina kept the Augland 54 workers," Silver countered.

"Doesn't that meant the blueprints can now come into evidence?" Frederick questioned.

Beaugard silenced them. "Silver, you discuss blueprints, I'll be inclined to let them come into evidence and Frederick can use them in his defense."

"Yes, sir," Silver conceded.

"Proceed then."

"Wolfgang, please state your full name." Wolfe did as Silver instructed.

Ashton's mouth was hanging open in shock, and Frederick must have been just as stunned because he tensed as he looked from Georgina and then back to Ashton.

"Only a few questions for you, sir." Silver continued.

"Do you know Georgina Raylen?"

"Yes." Wolfe answered. Ashton studied him, hoping for some insight into his agenda for showing up so unexpectedly. He would not come here to support his father willingly, not after all the evidence Ashton and Wolfe had prepared at the Colony to present against him.

"How do you know Georgina Raylen?"

"She took me captive after I saved Ashton's life and returned with her to NeuroEnergy."

What is he doing?

"What did you give her for your freedom?" Silver asked.

"Objection, Mr. President, he's testifying!" Frederick yelled.

"He's right, Silver," Beaugard scolded.

"My apologies. How did you escape Pacific Northwest NeuroEnergy?" Silver asked.

"I had my associate provide her with, from what I was told afterwards, falsified blueprints of Augland 54 energy initiatives."

"So, you gave her the documents in exchange for your freedom?"

"Yes."

"That is all."

Alarmed by Wolfe's testimony, Ashton frantically bent forward to speak with Frederick.

"Ask him about Warren! Ask him about how he went to save us. The head of the Suit!" Ashton's whispers were fierce and forceful as she was out of her witness chair and whispering loudly to Frederick.

"I can't. He didn't ask about those specific events. I can only ask questions about his testimony regarding the energy blueprints or knowledge of related initiatives. That's the rule. Unless you know that he didn't know the documents were false?" His tone was belittling. "I could call him as our witness but I'm not sure we want to open the door to what he knew about Georgina after he left Augland 54."

He cleared his throat, "Mr. Beaugard, I'd ask for an exten—"

"If you are asking for a further delay, my patience has been tried here. We have one more day to get through your defense, so any time wasted is your time. Please, proceed with your questions."

Frederick cleared his throat.

"How do you know the documents were falsified?" Frederick questioned.

"I don't, not for certain." Wolfe answered.

Ashton was dumbfounded.

"Did your *associate* ever say how they received the blueprints?" Frederick pried.

"Mr. President, we can't know for certain if the person who provided those documents knew they were falsified. He could have said they were verified as accurate. Wolfgang didn't find those documents." Silver stood, countering before Wolfe had a chance to answer.

"Wolfgang, did you ever know of any energy initiatives created by your father?" Frederick conceded and redirected his question.

"Again, he wouldn't have knowledge of that information. Not as Director of Security, not even as Head of Security—" Silver clearly did not want Wolfe answering that question.

"But as an Executive, he would be privy," Frederick argued.

"Then ask him if it was ever discussed," Beaugard said with a hint of agitation.

"Mr. President, this is absurd. Here we have a witness who is unable to testify to the validity of these alleged blueprints. The entire basis for Wolfgang being called as a witness is to clarify any knowledge he had concerning energy initiatives his father may have been drafting. We need to know if Wolfgang received this knowledge firsthand. This is the only way to verify if the blueprints were real." Frederick's frustration was obvious.

"Not my job Frederick. Proceed."

Frederick smacked his lips in annoyance, "Wolfgang, were energy initiatives ever discussed?"

"No, no such energy initiatives were ever discussed."

Frederick paused. "Did you ever tell Georgina that you thought the blueprints were falsified?"

Wolfe hesitated. "No."

"Then tell me, did you imply that the information was accurate?" Frederick asked.

"I didn't confirm or deny." Wolfe responded.

"So, there was no reason for Georgina to believe that the information wasn't true? And it would benefit you for her to believe that it was?"

"Mr. President—" Warren's counsel started voicing disagreement again.

Frederick sighed in relief. "No further questions."

He gave Georgina a sly grin of satisfaction before returning to his seat. Ashton failed to not this hopeful exchange between the two, as she couldn't take her eyes off Wolfe. He refused to look at her, not even for a moment. She needed a glance so she could read him, understand what was going through his mind—why he now supported his father.

Silver declined to redirect any further questions toward Wolfe, and his side rested. Beaugard announced that they would close for a short break before the defense team could begin. The witnesses were dismissed, and the room began to awaken with chatter. Ashton's security guards came close and one of them pulled at her arm. Ashton's eyes surveyed the room for Wolfe one last time before she gave in and let them take her out. After he had left the witness stand, he disappeared from her view.

Ashton closed the apartment door with a sigh after her security Suits had escorted her back to her room. She was met with silence inside the four gray walls. She had been dismissed for the defense unless she was recalled, which Ashton doubted would happen considering how upset Frederick was with her over the hologram footage. She still had her hand on the door handle when she sunk her head against the cool wood door. She closed her eyes, exhaling in exhaustion from the day's events. *One more day.* This caused Ashton to feel both relief and dread. Ashton heard a shuffle in her bedroom and her eyes went wide. She nearly called out for Reuben before she inched closer to the open door to her bedroom.

When Ashton saw who had broken into her space her eyes went wide and she yelped, jumping back in surprise. Wolfe sat on her bed with his hands clasped between his legs. He stood as Ashton ran toward him, barreling directly into him, unable to pull back.

"What are you doing here!" She nearly yelled as she clung tight to him. He wrapped his arms around her tightly.

"Not here." Motioning to the VELIC walls, Wolfe silently acknowledged that it would be recording everything except when manually shut off, as Reuben had done for their conversation.

"You testified for your father." Ashton whispered and Wolfe sat back down on the bed, so he was closer to eye level with her. "Willingly?" She asked and Wolfe nodded. "Why?"

"It was a smart move. We aren't ready to go up against him yet . . . and coming here to side with him at least bought us time—and you, safety. Georgina isn't going to win this trial and Warren will likely have a proposition for you once he wins. I need you to accept his offer, willingly." Wolfe was right that Georgina was likely not going to win the trial, unless there was a miracle, but she hesitated when he spoke about a proposition. Ashton's brow furrowed wanting to ask why, but before she could Wolfe spoke. "We can talk more tonight. My father has invited us for dinner."

"You and me?" Wolfe reached for Ashton's hand, interlacing his fingers with hers.

"Yes. He wants to talk to both of us. I don't think we are going to love his proposal, but we will need to listen to him. I can't say more than that. Promise you won't fight it and please do whatever he says." Wolfe's eyes asked her to trust him and Ashton sighed in frustration. She knew Wolfe would not stop asking if she didn't agree—even though she had a hundred questions that couldn't be asked in front of VELIC.

The most pressing question she wanted to ask was . . . *What did you do?* She didn't think Warren would come to them with any proposition if he were already poised to win the trial. There was a long pause while Wolfe gently traced Ashton's curled fingers. Wolfe's tone softened as he asked, "how are you?" It was a simple question and a welcome one after the probing questions and accusations of the last two days.

"I'm okay. I'm mad you came here, but happy to see you. I feel like punching and kissing you at the same time." Ashton smiled and Wolfe gave a slight chuckle.

"I'm always thinking of ways to keep you on your toes . . ." Wolfe smirked.

"I did bring you something." Wolfe reached into his pocket and pulled out a lengthy string with a white marbled stone with wire wrapped around it. His fingers interwoven with Sheva's stone necklace. Ashton smiled in surprise and gratitude. "You went back home and got it for me?" Ashton's voice cracked with emotion.

"Yeah, figured you would want it. I was a little surprised I found it; you never take it off." Ashton inspected the small stone, rolling it between her palms. She went to loop the string around her neck, only for Wolfe to reach up and take over the job. She rarely ever took off the necklace but for their hikes and she wasn't even sure why she had left it behind this last time—most likely the fear of losing it. Ashton stared down at the moonstone where it was clasped in her fingers, it brought her comfort, providing something real and meaningful to ground her in the madness of the House of CEOs.

"I should go. Warren will wonder where I ran off to. Your guards will escort you to Warren's home later tonight. Everything is going to be fine." He gave her a kiss, "See you at eight." Then he wrapped Ashton in an embrace.

Ashton was left with silence and loneliness once Wolfe left, and she felt the shift from worrying about the trial outcome to what Warren would ambush her with at dinner tonight. They hadn't been able to talk about what they needed to, not with the VELIC being so near to them. If Warren were listening through the VELIC, which was a constant threat, Wolfe hadn't wanted to tip him off to any trick plays he had up his sleeve. He must have taken a great risk to come and see her.

CHAPTER 18

Hunter

"I don't understand. What are you saying?" Hunter's blank expression would have been considered condescending to anyone else, but to Vic and Forest, he only came across as bewildered. They'd repeatedly informed Hunter about why the satellites were going in and out of service, but the technology nouns were enough that Hunter became frustrated with his limited understanding of the STEMP project's inner workings.

Hunter stood in a mess of technology cords and high-resolution screens running with active code. The NeuroEnergy dungeon was more cluttered than it had been the last few days when they all stood celebrating their pet project that could be their salvation. That was partly due to Forest and his demands for additional technology to help support Vic in the STEMP project. Wolfe had left NeuroEnergy two days ago and relayed specific instructions that the project was to be done in a week. Hunter seriously doubted the feasibility of that task. "English, please!" Hunter shook his head in disbelief, raking his long locks back with his fingers.

Vic sighed in audible frustration. "We aren't there yet . . . the satellites are located and yes, we can connect to them and, yes, we could do what we've been saying, but the connection can only last for a minute, maybe five at most. Connectivity will begin again, but the moment the satellites move a short distance, which is what satellites do, we lose our ability to reach them. It's pointless when we only have so much time to connect. The satellites must be above us at the precise moment—and once they move significantly, I can't connect anymore and . . . poof! Our control is gone. I really don't know how to explain this any differently."

That explanation finally registered in Hunter's brain. It was already too late in the evening, and with each passing day they seemed further away from a STEMP project success.

As Hunter processed this, Vic continued, "I told Wolfe the same thing before he left. Yes, we have some satellites, but to keep acquiring more is going to take time. If we can get access to enough satellites, then moving from satellite to satellite will help maintain connectivity." Vic emphasized the last few words. "I told him like I'll tell you. A week is not enough time; I've been working on STEMP for the last month."

"Maybe there is a way to lengthen the connection time for one satellite. We could do five minutes, then wait and do it again or maybe an auto-connect function?"

Vic's head swayed in disappointment. "You don't get it." Vic's dejection worsened.

"Oh, I get it. Unlike you, I'm trying to think of solutions." Hunter spouted harsh words, recognizing that now wasn't the time to be sensitive to people's feelings.

Every move since Hunter and the others had found out about STEMP was calculated because they needed the possibility of STEMP in their arsenal to win the impending war—which hinged on Vic and Forest's ability to crack the VELIC firewall and gain access to more than a handful of satellites at one time.

"We can try, but Wolfe said a week and I can guarantee this won't be resolved by then. It could take months, years maybe." Vic's baggy eye lids were more swollen today than usual, which told Hunter he wasn't sleeping. *Join the club.*

Hunter stormed out of the underground bunker and headed toward his NeuroEnergy apartment. He wondered why Wolfe and Joao had put him in charge of the STEMP project when Rye was much more capable. But really there was no other option—not with NeuroEnergy needing to function properly and Rye not having the time to dedicate to both. Hunter was mentally exhausted when he opened his apartment door and saw Versal busy hosting an elderly couple.

Versal shot him a dirty look. A few moments passed with Hunter standing frozen in the doorway before the meaning of her disappointed glare registered. Hunter hadn't realized how late he was—the clock said 10:00 p.m. The air was tense with disappointment over Hunter's forgotten promise to be home for his dinner-hosting duty. He recognized a few of the starry-eyed guests.

Hunter had become a celebrity once out of Augland, and many of the workers now looked to him as their hero. He had released them from their cages and led them to the Augland 54 supply boat that freed them from the park. At first, he enjoyed the recognition, but soon the weight of his celebrity image made him uneasy. He had always possessed a natural charm and was drawn to the feeling of popularity. In his former life in Augland, he was considered popular and likeable, which is what had landed him in Land of Legends to begin with— Augland managers didn't appreciate his sense of humor.

Not that he minded that now, the transfer had introduced him to Versal and Ashton in Augland's torture park. It was the weight of being pulled in so many directions that was beginning to affect him. Hunter wasn't sure what had changed, but the weight of the imposter he portrayed rested heavily on his conscience, because he didn't feel like a hero. While many judged Ashton for disappearing to Hood Canal and NeuroEnergy, he understood her reasons and envied her. She wasn't one to embrace the notion of being a heroine, whereas Hunter, at first, thought he was up for the job. But he was mistaken. There was simply too much responsibility.

"I'm sorry, Versal," said Hunter. "I—I forgot we had dinner plans tonight. Rye has me working on a big project." *And Wolfe informed me that Warren knows about Vic and STEMP . . . and Warren told Joao he will invade NeuroEnergy if he wins at trial to secure the not-so-secret device for Augland's use.*

Hunter hadn't been open with Versal about the plans or the STEMP project. Not many people knew about it—or Warren's plan to overtake NeuroEnergy. Those that did know were the people in the immediate inner circle—Vic, Forest, Wolfe, Joao, and Rye. The only person besides Versal who had yet to find out was Bez, and from what Joao was saying, he wanted to be the one to let her know. He was undoubtedly waiting until he felt more comfortable that their plan had a viable Suit-disrupting mechanism, and that the invasion of NeuroEnergy was plausible. But Hunter presumed Joao wanted to keep the truth from Bez because he didn't want her to panic knowing that for Ashton, Versal, and Bez, returning to Augland reign was worse than any nightmare. At least Versal left things alone and didn't pester him.

"It's fine. We were just finishing up, but a couple of the guests wanted at least to say hello to you before heading home." Versal's usual easy smile was forced, and her hazel eyes roared with disappointment, but she maintained a sweet demeanor in front of the guests. She took on the responsibility of fame with grace, but that didn't mean she didn't expect something from him in return.

"Not sure if you remember," said the elderly woman in a wheelchair, "but we were located on the third and fourth floor of the cages. I hadn't seen my husband in four years, not until the rescue boat. It was because of you we were reunited." She wheeled over to Hunter to give him a hug, her weak arm muscles shaking as she wrapped them around him. He presumed the Customer Service chip procedure had left her partially paralyzed—it was one of the many side effects he had seen in those chosen for the experimental surgery.

"Can't thank you enough for your hospitality," said the gentleman, clasping Hunter's hand. The man was at least a foot taller than Hunter. His left eye was missing, but that wasn't uncommon either for many of the workers who were imprisoned in metal-barred boxes Hunter had led out of Augland.

Their kindness warmed Hunter's heart, deepening the guilt he felt from his absence. The formerly caged workers gave him more credit than he deserved. For the first few months after their escape, he hadn't minded the constant acknowledgement and claps on the back from the workers. Now, with Ashton away, Wolfe's sudden disappearance to infiltrate Augland DC, and Bez and Joao planning their travels to Augland 54, he felt more like a shallow-faced hero than the actual one people seemed to see and need. He welcomed the diversion from hero to his new role as STEMP Project Moderator, giving him some self-worth.

"Thank you so much for stopping by." With a sweet voice and inviting grin, Versal held the older woman's hand close to her. She had spoiled their guests with an absolute feast; she was a talented cook even with a less-than-ideal and limited food supply. Versal shut the door after they said their goodbyes and whipped around to give Hunter a scathing look.

"You promised," she reprimanded him. Her eyes narrowed.

"I know, I know I promised but the—"

"Yes, I know the *thing* you don't talk about with me. But you don't realize how much these people need you! You're the one who rescued them. The least you could do is show up when they come just for a moment of your time." Versal stacked the dirty dishes in the sink before turning to blow out the tapered candles she had lit. Hunter followed behind her.

"Versal, it's not over. I'm still trying to rescue them. Do you know what happens if Ashton isn't successful at trial or this new project doesn't go well? They will be taken right back to Augland 54. Back to the cages, back to where they are poked at, treated and tested on like animals, and left for dead." Hunter's eyes softened when he caught her around the waist as she stood next to the kitchen sink. Hunter rested his head on the back of her slender shoulder and Versal closed her eyes. She hated the gruesome truth. She was much better at pretending the world was not like it was and that they could resemble a normal, willing population if they just didn't think about the reality of their situation.

Versal turned and faced Hunter and with it a forgiving smile that instantly melted his heart. She folded into his embrace and sighed heavily.

"You'll save them again; I know you will." Versal's reassurance spoke to her true nurturing and supportive nature.

"I hope so . . ." Even though he knew he couldn't. Not unless the STEMP project succeeded.

"What about Ashton? Any news?" Versal changed the subject. He didn't have the heart to tell her the shaky reality they were facing. Wolfe hadn't abandoned them on a whim. Hunter knew why Wolfe had gone to Augland DC: to give them enough time to prepare *in case* Warren decided to overtake NeuroEnergy—which was likely. Joao's confession that he was under the CS chip, and Warren's knowledge of their secret STEMP project, thwarted any surprise attack they could have had over Warren. Not only that, but the trial was not going well, which made the reality of his invasion on NeuroEnergy territory a likely possibility. Everyone danced around with the idea that they were now scrambling to be in a better position. If word got out that Georgina was at risk of losing the company, there would be chaos amongst the NeuroEnergy employees and the ex-Augland workers who resided at NeuroEnergy, and possibly the Colony. That couldn't happen.

"No word just yet. I'm sure she's just fine. It's Ashton . . . warrior princess for the Vikings." Versal laughed, believing the lies as he smiled to hide the fear that triggered a tidal wave of doubt now coursing through him.

"She'll hold her own; she's strong and will come out of this. She always does." She pushed back slightly from his embrace.

Hunter wished he could see Ashton right now; her presence was always so comforting. He recognized their relationship was a bit unusual, but Ashton was like family to them. Though they had only spent a handful of time together—usually when Hunter and Versal sailed on their boat *Freya* to visit Hood Canal—they had easily transitioned from friends to something closer. She was family. During each visit, Hunter could see Ashton was thriving outside of Augland and relishing in her sovereignty, but there was always a hint of darkness in her eyes. Her deep hatred toward Augland 54 and Warren hung like a mist around her, often pre-occupying her thoughts.

————————

Later that night, Hunter lay awake next to Versal thinking of the elderly couple who had been crippled by the Customer Service Initiative, and Joao's predicament. The worst thing that could happen to them would be if STEMP were to short-circuit and fry their brains. Hunter didn't know his thoughts could wander in such a direction but now it was a deep-rooted concern.

As Versal slept, he crept out of their apartment and began the ten-minute trek toward Georgina's dungeon for a status update on the STEMP project. If Vic and Forest couldn't sleep because of their responsibilities, then neither would he. As predicted, they were head-down reading their monitors, barely noticing his arrival.

"I brought food. Versal made some soup last night; I thought you guys might be hungry." It was a peace offering to make up for the way he had snapped at them just hours earlier.

"You know I'll eat whatever that young lady makes. She's a gifted woman." Vic was stumbling across wires and cords to get to the food. He gratefully grabbed a bowl and placed it on the only open space he had on a side bench. Forest wasn't far behind him as he smelled the savory soup and rushed over along with Vic.

"Have we thought about how this will affect workers with the CS chips?" Hunter was reminded of the Customer Service Initiative after seeing the one-eyed man and wheelchair-bound woman in his living room. There could be hundreds impacted by CS chips within the Augland 54 walls, and he worried that messing with the satellites could somehow hurt the chipped workers as well.

"I think we should focus on the improbable success of our satellites first, before going down the path of 'what ifs'," Forest said as he slurped down a spoonful and groaned in satisfaction, scarfing down the remaining soup. He was an ex-Augland worker, at least from what Hunter had gathered from Joao. He was a smart man who had leveraged his intelligence to launch himself to better standing in Augland. It was this same skillset that had helped him devise a plan to evacuate Bez, Ashton, and the Augland Apparel workers out of Augland through the train system.

"Get good rest boys. Tomorrow—well today—is going to be another long one," Hunter said, turning around and heading back home while giving them space to eat in peace.

CHAPTER 19

Ashton

DC, AUGLAND

It was thirty minutes to eight and Ashton was pacing in her room, counting down the minutes before Warren's dinner. There was no sense dressing for the occasion. VELIC had asked her at least twice if she wanted help getting ready, which she declined. She anticipated Warren's reaction to her presence would be revulsion. *Asking an ex-worker to be your dinner guest.* This time Ashton wanted to be in control and that started with wearing the clothes she knew all too well: black pants and a T-shirt.

She walked back and forth, wondering if Reuben would think Wolfe's plan was a good idea. In all honesty, Reuben probably already knew more than she did about this dinner. The meeting with Reuben—and then Wolfe's involvement—was too much of a coincidence.

Ashton heard a knock and she opened the door. The faces of her two security Suits' greeted her in the door frame. She didn't offer any pleasantries, as they stood nonchalantly, ready to escort her to Warren's home.

"You ready?" It was the only comment directed at her and came from the tall, tan-skinned Suit—"Thing One," she had named him. Back in Augland 54, no security guards were awarded Suits, but here in Augland DC, every worker, whether guard or waiter, wore their own Suit. These two probably loathed babysitting a rogue ex-worker and no doubt thought it beneath them.

"Yes, I didn't realize you two were invited to dinner." Ashton attempted to engage them in some kind of discourse.

"Let's go." Thing Two grasped Ashton by her arm and yanked her forward toward the long hallway. "And we don't need your smart mouth."

"He speaks!" Ashton chirped. "Huge breakthrough, Thing Two. Maybe we can play drinking games when we get back—but I'll warn you both now, I'm very good at cards." Her comment was met with zero response and Ashton shrugged. She rolled her eyes before taking a step to the side, motioning with her hands for them to lead the way. That last comment had a little too much sass, but her control was slipping by the moment and there weren't many moments left, considering the verdict would be decided the next day. She would take this time to exert a dusting of power. It wasn't much but it was all she had left to show the authority of Augland, and it would begin with her insolent attitude tonight.

———

During the car ride to Warren's, Ashton re-played in her head every horrible thing Warren had done. Several times she tried to shake the thoughts, because she knew spiraling down a rabbit hole of anguish wouldn't help her control her anger when confronting Warren. But in the silent car ride, the way he made her feel and the anger that had once transformed her into a broken version of herself, continued to overtake her thoughts.

She hated that he got under her skin, and even more that he showed no remorse for what he had stolen from her. Ashton's thoughts rewound to the day Sheva was taken. Her crepe-like skin against her own, holding her arm for stability while the twist and turns of the Augland train rounded from park to park. She thought of the moonstone necklace Sheva had given her for her birthday. The pleasant memory was disrupted when she thought of Sheva's death and the interconnect demand to shoot at them that Warren had made to his goons.

Ashton's thoughts continued to spiral at a rapid pace as she thought of the Colony's children, Bez being tossed to the brothels, Niall's eye patch covering his eye socket where he had been mutilated, the woman who had found her in her pod, entangled with the Customer Service Initiative . . . and finally she saw Jagatha. This rampaging train of thought screeched to a halt as grief flooded through her once more over her young friend's pointless death. Warren's face wasn't in every memory, but he was the person who had committed these atrocities. He was the only common denominator.

She looked out, seeing her reflection from the car windows passing by car. She breathed, counting one, two, three in and one, two, three out, attempting to calm her nerves and anxious excitement. Wolfe knew she wanted revenge. He'd come to save her, which meant he had a plan to thwart whatever Warren was plotting. After processing everything that had happened while Warren was wearing his Wolfe Suit and rec-onciling the fact that Wolfe had never really been the one to hurt her, she'd reached a point where she could trust him implicitly once again.

They drove for what felt like hours, but according to Thing One, it was no more than fifty minutes. Ashton had seen at least two parks since leaving the House of CEOs and now, finally, they turned off the main highway into a snowy and mountainous park—Snowcadia.

The weightless snowflakes floated down on the automatic VELIC vehicle that had brought them to Warren's remote getaway. Ashton's foot crunched down on the compressed piles of snow as she carefully exited the vehicle and looked toward the lights of a log home mansion. Dark wood beams cascaded from a small bridge over a frozen creek that led to the grand stone entrance. Smoke billowed from the chimney of the three-story home. Ashton inhaled, and the fresh smell of snow and burnt ash filled her senses.

Both security Suits exited the car and flanked Ashton as they headed toward the entrance, which looked more like a fortress with its oversized logged entrance and umbrella of stones over a dark steel door. Before they could knock, the door swung open, and a familiar face greeted them with the most stoic of smiles. Ashton's heart skipped a beat. The effects of her calming technique earlier in the car dissipated as Niall greeted them. She was prepared for meeting with Warren, but not Niall who had been her first childhood friend. A boy with whom she'd transferred from Victorian to Maya Bay, whom she'd watched grow into a man and become her protector. The last time she had seen him was in Maya Bay when she was disguised as Charlotte and even then, she couldn't contain herself.

"Welcome, may I grab your coats? You must be freezing." His gaze met Ashton's but the man in front of her was vastly different from the "brother" she had known in Augland 54. She noticed the signs of the Customer Service Chip instantly, and realized Niall was no longer the man she'd known. He was as handsome as ever, but his dark skin had paled and there was a marked emptiness in his eyes. *Didn't he wear a patch over his eye last time I saw him?*

"Oh, Niall." The words escaped before she could refrain—she was lost again and her hard exterior melted. She couldn't hide from heartache. *At least the chip didn't shift the color of their eyes anymore.*

Niall's expression didn't change.

She moved closer to him and put her hands to his face, cupping his cheeks that were at least a foot above her. "Niall, I know you're in there." She now saw the slight difference in his left eye, the mechanics hard to pass as a real iris.

"Yes, ma'am. I'm right—"Niall said mechanically.

"No, the real you; I know you are in there." She studied his face carefully, but his expression never wavered, never revealed a hint of who he really was.

"Ashton, welcome!" Warren's voice rang throughout the hall, reaching the entrance to the cabin home. Ashton dragged her eyes away from Niall and took in the scene unfolding in front of her. The entryway led into the great room where a fire in the background gave off a luminous light as Warren appeared before them. She could see Wolfe's outline as he sat in a chair further back in the room.

"That will be all, gentlemen. You can wait for Ms. Ashton outside." Warren spoke directly to the two security Suits that trailed behind Ashton.

She dropped her hands from Niall's face but couldn't tear her gaze away from him. The shock turned to anger that now flowed through her veins as she felt a disgust creep up like bile.

"That will be all as well, Niall," Warren commanded, and Niall stood straighter and stepped away from her. Ashton took a moment to compose herself before slowly making her way toward them, not believing for a moment that this place was safe for her even with Wolfe only several feet away.

The reflection of the fire flickering in the background sparkled in her eyes in the darkness as she walked hesitantly toward them. Warren looked the same as he had at the trial, but this time his attire was much more casual than his typical creaseless suit: quarter-zipped charcoal sweater with neatly pressed jeans and comfy-looking black wool slippers.

"I hope you like steak. I had Niall go and get the real thing for you both since I'm dining among some mortal life forms tonight." Warren attempted to ease the tension that clung in the air, but it was a constant reminder that he was untouchable as a Suit.

She set her sights on Wolfe, who remained seated, resting his elbows on his knees as he looked at Ashton. He stared at her, silently communicating his discomfort about the reunion as danger hung stagnant in the air, confirming her intuition.

"Sounds lovely. I want to thank you for kidnapping me for dinner." Ashton said.

"Kidnapping! Ha!" Warren laughed out loud. "Well, Wolfgang, you didn't tell me how comical she is. Sarcastic humor is my favorite." He pivoted his attention to Ashton again. "I thought it would be nice for us all to get better acquainted. It's been long overdue. Trust me, this is less of a kidnapping, more of a family gathering."

Ashton cringed.

"Can I get you anything to drink before we eat? Wine will be served with dinner."

"No, thank you." The politeness was out before Ashton could filter it. Warren was the last person who deserved any courtesies.

"Very well. Just for me then." Warren disappeared into the kitchen and as soon as he was gone Wolfe was out of his chair and on his way to Ashton, who stood awkwardly near the front door where Niall had left her.

Out of Warren's view now, Wolfe wrapped his arms around her. She remained tense against him as she felt his rapid and erratic heartbeat, which only furthered her resolve that this was not a safe place. She felt his hand fidgeting at her hip.

"In your pocket—something for later and open it alone," Wolfe whispered before loosening his grip around Ashton and placing his hands on her face to give her a deep kiss. It wasn't a sensual kiss but pressured, almost pained, like he was afraid he'd forget the feeling. He withdrew from her and gently gripped Sheva's necklace in his hands, examining it before placing it back against her chest. *That was weird.*

"Wolfe, what's happening . . ."

He drew near her and whispered, "Be cordial and this will all be over soon. I love you."

Ashton's eyes swam in his crystal blues. She wanted to know what was in her pocket, but more so she wondered why this felt like a goodbye.

Warren appeared again, drink in hand. "You two make a precious couple. But alas, it's time for dinner. Please, sit." Warren gestured to the dining table set for three. "I was hoping to have a few minutes to chat before we ate, but *you* were a tad late this evening." Warren tsked while Ashton took hesitant steps forward in front of Wolfe. He trailed close behind, putting his hand near Ashton's lower back to give her a reassuring touch that he was with her. Ashton exhaled, diffusing her internal conflict—she was angry, scared, and fairly certain something was about to happen—and it wasn't going to be good.

———

Niall poured Ashton a generous serving of red wine before filling up Wolfe and Warren's glasses. Sitting down at the dinner table, it was the first time she had gotten a close-up look at Warren since their poker game, and he looked just as devilish as he had that night: perfect and flawless complexion with a goatee peppered with white to show maturity. His eyes were icy blue, like Wolfe's.

The rich wine provided a distraction for Warren until he pointedly looked at Ashton. "I forgot, Wolfgang mentioned you know Niall. I brought him here because I figured it would be nice for you to see a friendly face without that God-awful scar and tacky patch he wore. I'm happy we were able to fix him up." Ashton's eyes burrowed into Warren's side profile, her fingers tightening around the knife she hadn't yet used to cut her steak. "He's been such a great help since arriving here; I think I might just keep him when I go back to 54." He gave an approving smile toward Niall, who reciprocated. Warren's tone was deliberately friendly, but his raised eyebrow clued Ashton in that his choosing Niall was deliberate and intended to hurt her.

"It's sad you have to force people into serving you. Do you have to do the same with your friends?" Ashton attempted to embarrass him, but in truth it was to mask her own surprise at seeing Niall here. That was something she would not give Warren the satisfaction of.

"Ashton," Wolfe said, giving her a disapproving look. He didn't want her poking at Warren. Ashton shifted her eyes to Wolfe. *How can he defend him?* Wolfe spoke through his gaze, reminding her to remain civil—just like Frederick and Georgina wanted her to be.

"Yes, Wolfgang, why aren't you reining her in yet?" Glancing back at Ashton, he started in again. "It's as if those years at the Center did her little good. Neither did your Land of Legends experiment." Ashton could see the muscles in Wolfe's jaw tense as he refrained from speaking what he truly thought.

"Father, that's enough."

Ashton scoffed out loud, "Reining me in—"

"We're done." Warren's tone was casual, nearly dismissive and it carried across the vaulted ceiling of the living room. Ashton's anger was discernible. Dinner hadn't even been served and there was already an argument at the table.

Niall returned from the kitchen with dinner and set the serving platters in front of them. Warren continued to antagonize Ashton, and it might have worked if she hadn't anticipated as much—except for Niall; that was a surprise and she would need to do better at concealing any further reaction.

"Father, I think we should get straight to the point." Wolfe was uneasy and Ashton could see it in the way he gripped his fork and knife tightly. Ashton stared down at her plate of food, hunger slipping away from her as she waited for Warren's next move.

"How's Georgina doing, Ashton?" Warren ignored Wolfe and studied Ashton as he took a bite of his synthetic food.

Ashton glared at Warren's dismissal of Wolfe, thinking how to respond appropriately. "She's fine. I mean, as fine as one who is being framed can be." That made Warren laugh out loud before coughing and swallowing his bite of food.

"You know, you aren't as much of a damsel in distress as I initially thought. I read your file: docile, a little streak of insubordination, but for the most part never a smart mouth. And that display as Charlotte. I thought you were this shy, meek, little thing," Warren joked.

"I guess you bring out the worst in me. I don't take kindly to psychopaths." Warren tensed at the accusation, which made Ashton smile momentarily.

"So, you're not scared?" Warren rose to her barb with a retaliation of his own. "You should be. I'm going to win tomorrow at the trial. Preliminary numbers are greatly stacked in my favor and will give me the opportunity to take everything from both of you. I *could* take everyone from Northwest NeuroEnergy and make them work for Augland 54. I *could* take back all my caged workers. I *could* take the Colony. The UnSuited." Warren listed out his many threats, silencing Ashton. Wolfe's gaze was on his father, but he said nothing. "You know, I was really hoping for a cordial dinner. Like I've told Wolfgang, I've decided to make allies out of you both, not enemies. Wolfe has clearly returned to my side once again and I am willing to offer the same opportunity to you."

"Well? I'm listening," Ashton spat, trying to hide her fear after the threats he'd made.

"*When* I win, I'll let NeuroEnergy stay intact of course. Once I find that scientist working on the STEMP project, I'll leave the Colony alone with a treaty of fifty new recruits a year until the cure for infertility is complete. I hear that NeuroEnergy is close to a breakthrough."

"Scientist? STEMP?" Ashton blurted out before she could think. Wolfe's expression hardened but he didn't respond. Ashton looked alternately between Wolfe and Warren in confusion.

"What? You don't know about the STEMP project at NeuroEnergy? Looks like a lot has happened since you've been away at trial— that or Wolfe hasn't been forthcoming with you." Warren pointed out. "Better not to keep secrets from your significant other. Take it from me, they don't like it—your mother especially didn't."

Ashton sat in baffled silence.

"Allow me to bring you up to speed. NeuroEnergy has someone manipulating the satellites to turn off all transmissions from pods to our Artificial Existence Beings. I, of course, can't let that kind of power be in NeuroEnergy's hands. So, when tomorrow's proceedings end, Augland security will infiltrate NeuroEnergy and secure the scientist."

Warren pivoted toward Wolfe, eyeing Ashton's expression, which was drained of both color and emotion,

"So why are we here, if you just want to get to NeuroEnergy?"

"You're here because my representative wanted to show the hologram of you admitting Georgina's involvement, which will help me win at trial and remove Georgina as Pacific Northwest NeuroEnergy CEO. As for Wolfe, well, we've come to an arrangement. If he came to DC to speak on my behalf at the trial, I promised your safe return to Augland 54," Warren divulged.

"How altruistic of you."

"That's a big word for such an uneducated lady." Ashton bit her lip to stifle her reaction, but her eyes narrowed.

"All right, Father; that's enough," Wolfe said, slamming his fist down on the table. Ashton grinned, feeling vindicated by Wolfe's defense.

"You're right, Wolfgang. I think I've had enough fun with Ashton, so I'll get to it."

Ashton remained silent.

"Once I have NeuroEnergy and the scientist under my control, I plan to take over AEC and I'll need both of you to support my campaign for the presidency," Warren announced, finally revealing his endgame.

Ashton eyed him without reaction. The news of Warren becoming the next AEC president should have been a surprise, but Reuben had already warned her of Warren's intentions.

"I plan on running for AEC president after Wolfgang helps me tie up a few loose ends. You'll help me gain CEO support because they already believe you started the UnSuited riots and if they know you can be controlled, they will believe the UnSuited can be controlled as well." Warren spoke freely.

"That wasn't the deal we talked about," Wolfe chimed in, but something told her that Wolfe absolutely expected it. "She's not supposed to go with us on the campaign," Wolfe said.

"Plans have changed. I said I would deliver Ashton back to Augland 54 safely and I will; I just didn't agree on when."

Wolfe scoffed in response. "Ashton will become the unofficial
leader of the UnSuited. She won't truly be leading them, but image
is everything and so we will spread the news of her 'success' across
Augland CEOs." Ashton suspected that in Warren's mind, this was
a done deal and whatever reservations Ashton or Wolfe had would
be ignored.

"You said you're running for AEC president? What happens to
Beaugard?" Ashton whispered, still unsure exactly what was happening.

"Beaugard's death is imminent."

"So, you kill him so you can run for president," Ashton said out
loud, connecting the dots to Warren's plan. Not that she condoned the
idea. She didn't know Beaugard personally, but she was beginning to
feel exhausted by all the pointless deaths.

"I feel like I've been fairly clear, but I do forget that you're still
young and naive."

"Rude," Ashton said under her breath while she stuck a fork in
her steak.

"What I'll need from you, Ashton, is to help me convince the
CEOs you can control the UnSuited. And that I control you."

"How do you even know the other CEOs will care about the
UnSuited? It was barely anything in 54, and most either escaped Augland or died trying," Ashton pointed out.

"I know there are more UnSuited, because I've already aided in
spreading your rebellion's message. How do you think the word of
the UnSuited made it out of our Augland 54 walls?" Warren's cryptic
confession helped piece together the answer to a question Ashton had
wondered for some time: who had incited UnSuited rebellions outside
of Augland 54?

"Why would you spread word of the Augland 54 rebellion?" Ashton asked.

"Well, Ashton, if a rebellion happens in my backyard, it counters my ability to effectively rule my own kingdom, but if it happens across several, it gives me allies. Then when I fix the issue—hence the reason you are even in this room—I become their savior."

Ashton exhaled, shaking as she gripped the knife she held mid-cut in her steak. It *would* be just like Warren to use an event as serious as a rebellion for his own gratification.

"I can't believe you did that." Wolfe spoke out loud the words Ashton thought. "You didn't, for even one second, think that the rebellion was your fault? Instead, you use their cause to help your political campaign?" Wolfe chuckled sarcastically. "Did you ever think that maybe, just maybe, you should take ownership of how you toss away human life and learn to change your ways? Oh no, of course not. I mean, you were willing to take my life in exchange for power, so why wouldn't you believe you could take the workers' lives. I mean, look at Niall!" Ashton stared as Niall perked up from behind a pile of dishes he'd been washing to see if he was needed.

"Wolfgang, be quiet. I've chosen to allow your autonomy, but I can take that away too." Warren let out a breath. Ashton instantly straightened at Warren's implied message. He immediately continued his thought with, "Have you thought about what would happen if workers stopped working? If NeuroEnergy took over, or AEC intercepted? This has been the way the world works for longer than I've been in power. Even the Colony, in some ways, works the same. You don't follow rules, you're out, and as a leader of Augland and with the stakes this high . . . I do what I have to do to save Augland 54."

"What's he talking about—allowing you?" Ashton questioned Wolfe, who remained silent.

Warren rotated toward Ashton, ignoring that she had asked Wolfe a question. "Do you honestly, truly, believe that Georgina would treat your workers any differently? Has she given them employment?" he asked.

Ashton thought about it—not that she knew the answer, but she wouldn't provide him with any new information either.

"Has she built them homes outside the NeuroEnergy walls? Or better yet, take the Colony as an example, has NeuroEnergy made their lives any easier? They generate electricity, but do they offer protection against attacks? You're so focused on making me the villain of your story you have no idea what other monsters are awaiting for your fall." His words rang with some truth and Ashton hated herself for understanding and, in part, agreeing with his perspective. "Thought so . . . at least I own up to my behavior, for the most part. I don't pretend to be the workers' salvation, but the workers' rebellion will only hurt them—I'm just using this as a way to gain favor."

Wolfe scoffed at his father's admission. "You'll help me build up UnSuited, even if it's only a rumor of it, and once I'm president, I'll let them be. Then everybody lives. Isn't that nice?" Warren cut into his steak-like product again, popping another piece into his mouth while Ashton and Wolfe sat frozen, in shock.

"Have you ever cared about what happens to us? Without us, your precious kingdom, that you protect so aggressively, falls," Ashton said before thinking.

"But my dear, that's why we have VELICs . . ." The audacity of his statement and the realization of what it meant was like a slap to Ashton's face.

"Then you can get rid of us, let us die out, and let humanity fail." She used a word that Reuben used when he spoke about the iHumanist movement.

"If you become enough of a problem, maybe we will. You may not believe me, but I'm one of the few that still believes workers are useful. Many of my fellow CEOs would rather eliminate them and use VELIC instead—less of a hassle, especially with the rebellions. Ashton, if it's not me, there will be another man, or woman, maybe even Georgina, who takes the initiative to revolutionize Auglands.

You don't know her like I do. She may carry herself well but she's just as ruthless as me."

There was no choice in this. Warren wanted power and he was dead set on using the UnSuited to help him scare the other CEOs into siding with him.

"And if I don't agree to help you?" Ashton asked, because now she understood what Warren needed from her. He wanted her cooperation.

Even though Wolfe had told Ashton to agree to Warren's offer and that he had a bigger plan, agreeing to work together with Warren went against every fiber in her being.

"I'm sorry, I think there's been a misunderstanding. I'm not asking you to agree to my terms. I'm telling you what you *will* do. You don't have a choice."

Ashton's brow furrowed; she was unsure what he meant.

"Here, let me show you what I mean." Warren pulled out his inter-connect and pressed a button on his device before turning to Wolfe. "Wolfgang, kill her."

Wolfe's back straightened and his eyes went dark as he stood abruptly, moving toward Ashton with his steak knife still in his hand.

Ashton's eyes grew wide in fear and confusion. "Wolfe! What are you doing?"

Wolfe didn't answer.

"If it's a choice you want, *I'm* giving you a choice. Join me and bring the UnSuited to my side . . . or die." Warren said, delicately placing his utensils down on top of his finished plate of synthetic food.

Wolfe was suddenly right next to Ashton. She tried to jump out of her chair but he was too quick; Wolfe yanked her by the back of her black shirt, bringing the knife up to her throat as he held Ashton against him.

"Wolfgang stop." Warren ordered. Wolfe's rapid breathing brushed against Ashton's face, frantic and shallow. She could feel the tremble in his hand as he held her against him. But he did as he was told. The sharp knife remained against Ashton's throat as she tried to claw desperately with her hands to wrench herself from Wolfe's arms. Her fear evident in her eyes.

"Wolfe!" She screamed his name again, but still no response. Like a punch in the gut, the unfathomable became all too clear to her. His blue eyes had gone gray, and his gaze was cold and vacant.

"Fine! I'll do it," she relented.

"Wolfgang, drop her."

Wolfe obeyed the command and released his hold on Ashton. She fell to the hard wood floor. Her wrist had twisted back and she winced from the pain, but that was nothing compared to the realization of what Wolfe had almost done to her, and to what she'd just agreed to so she could prevent it.

"You're mad."

"Perhaps. You'd be surprised what I'm willing to do in order to preserve our way of life."

"So what now?" Ashton remained on the ground, too stunned by what Wolfe had just done to move away, even though the threat was gone.

Warren brought his napkin to his face and patted it to remove any remnants of his dinner. He scooted his chair back and came toward Ashton, placing his hand out to Ashton's. She ignored it and rose without Warren's unnecessary, and unwanted, help.

Warren shoved his hands into his jean pockets. "Something I'm sure you didn't expect when you came to my home tonight . . ."

Ashton began to back away, piecing together what he meant by that vague and daunting statement. He wasn't asking for her support, wasn't going to give her anything for her help with the UnSuited. What he meant was that he was going to force her to comply. Ashton shook her head while Warren moved a step toward her.

"Wolfgang, subdue Ms. Ashton."

Wolfe moved with such fluid motion she barely heard him approach, but that didn't mean Ashton wasn't prepared, this time to fight. Ashton dodged right, heading straight for the kitchen island and away from both Warren and Wolfe. The kitchen wouldn't be safe; there were no exits. Ashton ran past the island and bolted toward the living room. *Exit, find an exit!* Ashton searched the dark room for another door beside the front door, which happened to be behind Warren. She scanned the room quickly: two couches, fireplace, coffee table, and finally a door.

"Stop running; you won't escape." Warren said, too casually.

Ashton nearly ran into the couch situated in the spacious room as she bolted toward a solid oak door that looked as though it would open to the backyard of Warren's home. She looked behind her briefly to see Wolfe's nearly grey eyes staring back at her. He was now too close for comfort.

"Wolfe, stop, please." Ashton whispered as she took to reasoning rather than attempting to outrun him. Wolfe didn't say anything.

"Wolfe, please!" Ashton begged as she backed up, nearing with each step toward the back door. She was two steps away. If she acted quickly, she could open and close the door before Wolfe had a chance to grab her. Ashton's breath quickened in anticipation as she did just that, turning quickly and finding the cold steel of the doorknob and turned it . . . but nothing happened. Ashton tried again, but the knob did nothing, and the door remained closed. That's all it took before Wolfe was on her, wrapping his arm around her waist and dragging her from the door.

"No! Wolfe, no!" This time, Ashton shouted, but both Warren and Wolfe ignored her cries.

"Wolfe carried a still-fighting Ashton back to where Warren stood. "VELIC, please prepare the Customer Service Initiative surgery for employee number JR105."

And that was the last thing Ashton heard.

CHAPTER 20

Wolfe

Wolfe's head was pounding, making it hard to concentrate on the trial unfolding before him.

He sat behind Warren with the other witnesses as the procession of CEOs made their way into the auditorium. Ashton wasn't allowed back in for the defense because Frederick claimed he no longer needed her as a witness, which dismissed her from the proceedings. By the end of the final day of the trial, Frederick's defense rested and Beaugard gave a break so the CEOs could prepare to vote.

Wolfe had only seen Ashton once since dinner at his father's the previous night, when the Customer Service chip had been installed in her head. She rested now, but he knew her head must be in a similar state. His neck hurt to turn, and his eyes couldn't adjust to the light without extreme pressure pulsating behind them. That wasn't even the worst of it. While he hadn't been certain his father would submit him to the Customer Service Initiative, Wolfe had hoped his own father wouldn't make him a slave to his will—but he was wrong to be hopeful.

The moment Wolfe landed in DC, his father had ushered Wolfe to his home in Snowcadia where he profusely advocated that this was *their* opportunity to mend—to be a family again. It was also the time he made promises to bring Ashton back to Augland 54 safely and without harm. Soon after, his father drugged him with a sedative in his food and when he awoke—the Customer Service Chip had been implanted.

What was unfortunate was that the engineers at NeuroEnergy had only one prototype that could interfere with the customer service transmission and had no time to create another in the short amount of time before he had left for Augland DC. When Warren said that he wanted Ashton to join them for dinner as well, Wolfe quickly realized his father's intentions. He had no other choice but to disguise the prototype in Ashton's necklace so she wouldn't suffer under Warren's control. That was the hope, at least.

As Warren's plan was put into motion, Ashton would now be the face of the UnSuited and needed to act based on her will alone, which meant that Wolfe was left to suffer, chipped and under Warren's control. His father still loved him, in his own narcissistic sort of way, and wouldn't kill him. So, Wolfe had no choice but to prepare Ashton for the worst. He had done what he could, slipping her a letter explaining about the transmitter and what he needed her to do. He didn't have time to prepare himself for his new reality. Warren had used the CS to force Wolfe to nearly kill Ashton if she didn't cooperate. The fear in Ashton's eyes would haunt him for the rest of his life. Ashton was just another pawn in Warren's unrelenting game for power, easily expendable—so Wolfe needed to prepare her to play her part.

Warren had turned off Wolfe's chip earlier that morning before the proceedings began, which Wolfe appreciated because, when turned on, the effects of the Customer Service Initiative were torture. At any minute, his reality could be plunged into a dreamlike state where he had no control of his actions. His thoughts would be clouded and when Warren activated the chip and ordered a command, it would drain him of all energy until it was switched off. Warren had only allowed Wolfe's mind and body to rest overnight and into the early morning because he knew that, in a flip of a switch, Wolfe could be paralyzed and compelled to do his father's bidding.

Beaugard appeared after their break for the conclusion of the trial. He sat in his elevated chair overlooking the entire crowd. "Thank you all for your time these past three days," he droned. Wolfe cracked his neck back and forth and thought of what he wouldn't do for some extra sleep and to see Ashton again—to make sure she was okay when she finally awoke from surgery.

"We will wrap up the trial with each side offering final thoughts before we open it up for a majority vote. We've spent a lot of our time on this trial so please be brief in your closing remarks." Beaugard cleared his throat.

Frederick stood. "Before you conclude, Mr. President, may I ask that our defense be permitted to offer our closing arguments first?"

"I don't see why not . . . Silver, do you mind?"

"Not at all, Mr. President." Silver said.

"Very well . . . proceed with closing remarks. Frederick, you may begin," Beaugard said nonchalantly.

"Thank you, Mr. President. I'll be very brief, not to waste any more time here. Georgina is innocent. She's not the leader of the UnSuited rebellions; there isn't proof of any wrongdoing against Warren. She will admit to only this; she did employ counterintelligence to find out what was happening in Augland 54. At the time, there was sufficient evidence documenting that Warren wanted to overthrow NeuroEnergy. Yes, Georgina used a former worker to help obtain this information and decipher Warren's motives. *Yes,* she knew that the energy resources provided by Augland 54 had declined and prompted her suspicions, but in terms of a conspiracy that would violate the treaty, there is no proof of intent. She only wanted to gather intel and expose Warren's secret energy plans. That information was kept from you because this incident of treason reaches beyond this feud between Georgina and Warren. This stems from political power and how far Warren is willing to go in order to gain favor beyond his borders. This trial was rigged from the beginning and only allowed for the evidence and witnesses that supported—"

"Enough, Frederick; you're on thin ice," Beaugard warned.

"No, I won't be silent. You'd already determined the outcome before we even came to trial," Frederick argued. He stood tall as he accused the corporate government of the highest level of treachery.

"I won't have any more of that!" Beaugard spat.

"Don't you see what's happening here? Georgina is being framed for trying to illuminate the truth, Beaugard, and Warren has been masterminding this outcome for the entirety of this trial." Wolfe glared intently, ignoring the throbbing pain in his head as Frederick exposed their position.

"Silence! I will have order here! Frederick, you are way out of line." Beaugard's tanned Suit shook in frustration.

"That's fine. I've said what I wanted to say." Frederick's southern accent was thick as he enunciated every word. He stepped down from the platform and slammed his interpad onto the table as he sat down next to Georgina. She gave him a small, defeated smile. She didn't seem surprised by Frederick's outburst, as she reached up to his hand and tightened her grip. Wolfe's brow furrowed. He hated being on *this* side, but because he had seen the trial while Ashton was here, he knew he had no choice. Frederick only hoped his last attempt to reach the CEOs who may still have a conscience could sway their decision in Georgina's favor.

Beaugard's frustration came out in small huffs of breath. "Silver, anything on your side?"

"Only that what Georgina's counsel just admitted to what we already knew. She conspired against Warren and abducted his workers to aid in her attempt to overthrow him. I warned you all before we started with this trial that at the end I'd ask you who the real monster is. We all know what Georgina planned to do. We should not fall for her innocent act. We appreciate your time here. With this new admission, we ask that Georgina be immediately removed, and Warren placed as interim Pacific Northwest NeuroEnergy CEO in order to search for false documentation she has hidden at NeuroEnergy headquarters. That is all, Beaugard."

Frederick stood up to protest, but Beaugard's hand went up to silence him.

"We will vote now on both the status of the accused and, if found guilty, the corresponding consequence. Please cast your vote now using your interpad and VELIC will tally the final numbers." There was a long pause, with the only sound in the room being muffled tapping of fingers on interpads determining Georgina's fate.

"All votes are accounted for." VELIC confirmed.

"Please read the verdict," Beaugard instructed.

"With the charge of conspiring against Augland 54 in an attempt to violate the treaty, we find CEO Georgina Raylen guilty as charged, with votes tallied at 79 for to 21 against. As a result of the guilty charge, the punishment is removal of CEO Raylen from her current position as CEO of Northwest NeuroEnergy and designation of Owen Wolfgang Warren IX, CEO of Augland 54, interim CEO of Northwest NeuroEnergy, yes, 79 for and 21 against."

"Then as President, I, Beaugard Hollenberg, designate the punishment for treason. Georgina Raylen, you are stripped of your CEO title immediately and placed under AEC arrest until an appropriate detainment term is determined. We are adjourned. Safe travels, all." With a final wave of his hand, Beaugard dismissed the CEOs.

Warren immediately shot up, embracing his counsel and turning to Wolfe. He stuck his hand out and Wolfe hesitated for a moment. He narrowed his gaze at his father, the face of a man whose DNA he shared but nothing of his character. He had been so accustomed to the scowl Warren usually wore that the twisting on his face made him nearly unrecognizable to Wolfe—for the first time Wolfe could remember, seemingly a genuine smile. He brought his hand out to shake Warren's, not because he agreed with what Warren and his team had accomplished, but because this was not the battle to fight, especially since Warren had all the power.

Playing this role made him feel like a puppet, like he had at dinner last night with Ashton. He knew every time Warren spoke, he was inciting Ashton's emotions. Wolfe wanted to physically fight back for the way he spoke to her—ridiculing her lack of education, exposing how he had used Niall, and even worse, how he was planning to use her and the UnSuited. But he had to maintain control. Ashton had stood her ground against Warren, forcing Wolfe to stand by and watch Ashton fight on her own. What had kept him up the night before was the horrifying memory of how, when Warren activated his chip, he had been forced to nearly take the life of the woman he loved.

Wolfe knew he was playing a dangerous game, trusting his father. He knew Warren wouldn't kill him, but he knew Warren wasn't opposed to killing Ashton to keep him pliable—and that scared him more than anything.

As Warren was congratulated, disagreements rang throughout the auditorium. Wolfe turned to search through the rows of smiles for those who didn't agree, most likely the twenty-one voters who believed Warren had manipulated the trial to start the first phase of a major NeuroEnergy takeover. They weren't wrong. Likely, the other NeuroEnergy CEOs were either corrupt, paid off, or unwilling to see today's verdict as anything but the first domino to fall in a long line of crimes that would ultimately crush them all.

The grumblings grew and shouts began to come from every direction, quickly turning into a screaming match. Warren grabbed Wolfe so they could sneak out of the auditorium during the rising unrest. But Wolfe couldn't take his eyes off the stage—ground zero for the injustices that had been committed today. CEOs were out of their chairs and the room rumbled with loud voices—some for Georgina's execution, others maintaining Warren as the righteous one.

Wolfe scanned the crowd with a look of disgust. Everyone in this room should have known that Warren had only won because he had manipulated the facts both openly and by omission, all to tip the scales in his favor. Suits maneuvered left then right, and others started pushing because they all understood that the new reality was war between NeuroEnergies and Auglands.

Before being escorted out, Wolfe spun toward Georgina, who sat very still with her hands gently placed on the table in front of her. She appeared to barely noticed the chaos erupting around her. Her eyes held a dazed look and Wolfe presumed she was likely pondering what would happen now that she had been found guilty. Two security guards approached her as the door he exited closed, and Wolfe guessed she would be detained.

Warren and Wolfe left the auditorium as the shoutings continued. Little did the CEOs know that Warren cheating in order to win at court was exactly what he had wanted because Georgina would him of doing exactly that, and Beaugard would have no proof and would have to dismiss the allegations against him. So when Warren did eventually kill Beaugard, Warren could blame the man's death on a revenge-seeking Georgina and her supporters, further convincing the CEOs of Warren's innocence.

CHAPTER 21

Joao

Joao felt a small vibration in his skull, then heard a *click*. He could always tell the moment that Warren decided to turn on the customer service chip buried in his skull. After the click came a *beep*, indicating Warren was calling him.

Joao had heard plenty about the Customer Service Initiative, because he was one of the security men instructed to bring in caged workers for the early experiments. Since then, apparently Warren had made many advancements, including being able to erase one's memory. It was a horrible reminder of what Joao had unknowingly let happen.

Wolfe created their new plan once Ashton had left, and after Wolfe had discovered that Joao was chipped and had exposed their STEMP project to Warren. It was useless to continue with their original secret attack plan, considering what Warren knew now. Wolfe had made Joao promise to keep acting on Warren's bidding. Even if it meant leaving NeuroEnergy vulnerable. They knew they still had others like Rye and Hunter to help draft a counterattack.

"Rye! Warren's calling." Joao knocked and spoke loudly as he approached Rye's office door.

"Now?" Rye asked, standing suddenly. Joao hadn't yet proven to anyone that the Customer Service Chip was real and that the conversations between him and Warren were legitimate. While Warren's Customer Service Initiative put both Wolfe and Joao in a precarious position, as Warren had access to their secret planning, it also gave them an opportunity to change the narrative by feeding Warren false updates about STEMP.

Joao closed Rye's office door just as he answered his interconnect.

"Hello?" Joao answered the call, immediately placing it on the speaker so Rye could overhear the conversation.

"Hello, Joao." Warren said.

"Hello, sir."

"I need you to go to Augland 54 and help run things, as I'll be out of town for some time." Both Rye and Joao looked at each other in surprise.

"Run things?"

"Yes, in my place and as Head of Security. Reuben will be with me as we now campaign for my AEC presidency, and I don't want the others to make decisions without my consent."

Rye mouthed *to talk about NeuroEnergy.*

"Did you still want to send Augland Security to NeuroEnergy?" Joao asked.

"Most likely. Unless you think you can take the scientist to Augland 54 with you?" Rye mouthed no.

"I don't know where they are keeping him." Joao knew they couldn't expose the scientist to Warren.

"Hmm . . . I'd see if you can find that out before you leave. Has the scientist found a way to control more of the satellites?" It was another piece of information that Joao didn't intend to tell Warren, but now it was clear he had given away absolutely everything.

"They have only secured one more satellite." Joao admitted because, in fact, the scientist had a few more than that at his disposal.

"Unfortunate. Well, then yes, we will continue to send an Augland security team. I'll send word to Augland, and they will be there by tomorrow."

"Understood." Joao said.

"Back to running Augland 54. I'm not sure how long I will be gone, but I trust you'll call me and keep me abreast of anything going on. We will need to implement a lockdown and strict worker compliance policy. I'll call daily for a status report."

"Yes, sir."

"Good. I need full discretion here. I don't want anyone at NeuroEnergy or 54 to be alerted to my plans until my return. And you will tell no one of our conversations. We are going to need a fortress, Joao. I'm counting on you to make sure there are no mistakes. Eventually, NeuroEnergy will discover that I know about their destructive tool. When I send men to their compound, in retaliation they may try and attack Augland 54, or worse, hide *our* scientist. You need to make sure that doesn't happen. I need you to protect us."

The air between Rye and Joao thickened with dread and anticipation. "Of course, Warren. Anything you need . . ." The words felt bitter as they left Joao's mouth.

"Good. You will leave today for Augland 54." With that instruction, Joao's heart dropped. He hadn't heard what the results of the trial were, but he could imagine that if Warren were happy with the outcome, it also meant that Wolfe had been right and that Warren would invade NeuroEnergy in search of Vic.

"Yes, sir. I will leave within the hour."

"Good man. I will be in touch."

"Yes sir." Joao hung up and noticed, this time, that the buzzing in his head remained, which could only mean Warren had decided to keep it on. Both he and Rye remained silent. So it was happening. Warren had won the trial and now looked to overtake NeuroEnergy.

Bez plopped down on top of their bed, staring at Joao as he packed a duffle bag of clothes. Her smile was infectious, and her spirit something to be reckoned with. It was what entangled him the moment he met her.

He was working security; Wolfe would go and visit to check in on her at the brothels and sometimes brought him along. It was never for the purpose of visiting the brothel—Wolfe had known her before she had been sent there and regularly checked in on Bez to make sure she was okay. Bez was partially Augland-broken then, but her spirit was still thriving, and Joao couldn't take his eyes from her. Augland had done just about everything to her at this point, but the brothel was by far the worst of her punishment.

"Are you going to tell me what's going on or am I going to have to torture it out of you through my incessive questioning?" she demanded. Joao was hard to break, but Bez was his weakness.

"We are going back to Augland 54. It's part of the—"

"If you say 'plan,' so help me . . ." Bez countered before Joao could finish.

". . . plan." Joao already knew that statement would come with an interrogation.

Bez rose, narrowing her penetrating gaze at Joao, who dodged the stare. "Back to Augland? That's the *plan?* The one you refuse to give me any details on whatsoever because you and Wolfe seem hell bent on pretending Ashton and I can't take care of ourselves? That plan?" Bez's brown eyes were now intently fixed on Joao.

"Bez, that isn't fair. You both can take care of yourselves, but this is a bigger plan than just you two. This is about taking down Warren and, no offense, neither of you know him like we do. Especially, how Wolfe does," Joao confessed.

"How does going back to Augland help us in any way? We will be imprisoned the moment we step foot there," Bez countered.

"No, we won't. You'll stay with me, and you'll be safe," Joao said with too much confidence. In reality, he hadn't told Warren he was bringing Bez with him, but there was no way he was leaving her at NeuroEnergy—not when he knew of Warren's impending attack disguised as a "visit."

"Oh. I will, will I?" Bez's fierce side surfaced, and she rounded the bed, cornering Joao. "So, your brilliant plan is to go back to Augland 54, hoping that they don't imprison us immediately for you releasing countless workers and me inciting an Apparel rebellion because you say so? Actually, no, you're right. They've probably forgotten all about that." Bez's sarcastic tone drilled holes into Joao's affirmation. "And why wouldn't I be safe here?" Bez was smart and it was silly to think that he could get anything past her, but again, it was for her own safety. She couldn't find out Warren was sending him to Augland 54 because then she would refuse to go along with Joao's charade. If NeuroEnergy was bound to be under Warren's rule either way, it didn't matter where Bez was, and it would be safer for her to be with him.

"Could you just not fight me on this? Please?"

"Not a chance."

Joao sighed, frustrated. "B, please."

"How can I not fight you on something when I have no idea what's going on and why we are going back to Augland 54? Now who's not being fair?" Bez pointed out.

If Joao confessed that NeuroEnergy was going to be under attack, she'd want to stay. If she stayed, then he wouldn't be able to focus on delivering his performance to Warren of being under his Customer Service control. Besides, he needed her help while he ran Augland in Warren's absence. Joao had confided in Rye and Hunter that to ensure Vic was safe, he needed Rye and Hunter in on his game, even though it may appear to Warren that he had spilled his secret. That was leverage NeuroEnergy wasn't willing to hand over to Augland.

Rye would relocate all elderly and small children to the Colony; those willing to stand up to Augland would remain. Warren didn't mention anything about punishing the NeuroEnergy members; he was only searching for their weapon that could be used against him—and Joao knew better than to trust the over-simplified narrative Warren shared. In order to keep the people of NeuroEnergy safe, it was better to evacuate the weak.

He shifted so he faced Bez. Her eyes were still angry but infused with curiosity. She had never been a woman to sit on the sidelines.

"When we get to Augland 54, I'll tell you everything, okay? So please, just go and pack up your things—we need to leave soon." Joao's tone was serious. He was desperate, and hoped that with the promise to bring her into Wolfe's plan once they were back in Augland 54, Bez would accept taking this first step without knowing the rest. He would need Bez with him if their part of the plan was to succeed—but selfishly, he didn't want to leave NeuroEnergy either. This entire plan had each of them—Ashton, Wolfe, Hunter, Rye, and Bez—all working together but independently with each owning piece of the puzzle.

Joao held Bez's gaze for some time. She wanted to fight him. He could see it in the tense position of her shoulders. Her brow scrunched while she weighed her options and soon she rolled her eyes in defeat. "You'd better . . . if we get captured and have to somehow fight our way out of Augland again, I'll kill you myself." With that, she began maneuvering away from the bed, but Joao put his hand out and captured hers. He gently guided her close to him. "Deal."

"And if Augland security does decide to attack us, I can take care of myself," Bez emphasized.

Joao chuckled. "I have no doubt about that . . . I need to check in with Rye and Hunter for a few minutes before we head out. I'll be back soon." With that, Joao left before an unsure Bez changed her mind.

———

Rye and Hunter were down in the basement, packing up all the computers and tools needed for Vic to continue his work. Forest would accompany him so they could continue their work as a pair. He was brilliant with computers and had already helped Vic gain access to one more of the vital satellites. At this rate, with Vic's know-how and Forest's hacking skills, they could have the STEMP project completed within weeks.

"How'd Bez take the news?" Rye asked, knowing Joao was heading to Augland 54 soon and Bez would drag her heels about having to go.

"Ha! That girl will go back to Augland kicking and screaming," Hunter joked, but he wasn't half wrong. He bent down, spooling up several wires and wrapping them around his fingers and elbow.

"She'll be fine. Any word from Wolfe or Ashton?" Joao asked. It was unlikely they would have sent a message, as every communication out of Augland DC would be tracked by Warren or his team. Joao walked toward Hunter, looking around to make sure the others were occupied with packing their tools and supplies. He picked up another cord and started wrapping it in a way that mimicked Hunter's method.

"Change the location where you're hiding Vic and Forest. Don't tell anyone where you are going," Joao said quietly.

"And where do you expect me to take them?" Hunter's voice was a harsh whisper.

"Warren will tear apart any and all NeuroEnergy locations and won't stop until he finds them. The Colony is no better. I need you to think on your feet here. If any of us know the location, and we're forced to tell Augland security where you're hiding them, then we are done for. It's imperative that those two aren't found—not until the STEMP is finished," Joao countered.

"Geez, Joao. This was not how this was supposed to go."

"Plans change. We need to adapt."

CHAPTER 22

Rye

NEUROENERGY, PACIFIC NORTHWEST

Rye pulled his glasses off, rubbing his eyes as he leaned back in his chair. His private office, located on the third floor of NeuroEnergy's headquarters was now, nearly vacant. Twelve hours earlier, he had received word from Frederick that Georgina had lost at trial and Warren had been named interim CEO of Pacific Northwest NeuroEnergy. Before leaving for Augland 54, Joao had confided to Rye what Warren was planning to do—which did not sit well with him in the slightest.

Thanks to Joao's warning, Rye had a window of time before the attack would take place. Rye had hoped Wolfe's initial fear that his father would come for the scientist and attack NeuroEnergy for hiding him was paranoia—but that was wishful thinking. The general population of NeuroEnergy had all left for the Colony; only those who could defend themselves had chosen to stay in the compound. Rye was prepared for battle even though the entire point was to surrender with no casualties, as they would have a new CEO soon. *What a mess.*

Joao and Bez had left.

Hunter, Vic, and Forest had disappeared.

Ashton and Wolfe were in Augland DC.

Georgina, presumably, was still in Augland DC as well.

———

Hunter had made arrangements for Versal's care while he was away, but it was the weight of all the others at NeuroEnergy that haunted

Rye more than anything else. He cared more for the people in this compound than he did his own life. It had been a mistake to intertwine their affairs with Augland 54 workers. It had brought a potential war to their doorstep, but that was inevitable, and Warren's blueprints were the proof. There was bound to be a final showdown, and if it wasn't now, it would surely be soon.

The office had emptied out, and many of the employees were either readying for the attack or sheltering at home with the families who had stayed at NeuroEnergy. Technically, he should have gone home too, but he wanted to be here when the guards of Augland approached and searched the headquarters. All documents, plans, and procedures had been wiped from the mainframe, and only general information for NeuroEnergy remained in the operating system. Everything of value that had been stored on a NeuroEnergy computer was now in the hands of Forest and Vic, hopefully miles from the compound by now.

Rye thought about the last communication he'd had with Wolfe before Wolfe had taken off for Augland DC and what had brought Rye, and NeuroEnergy, to this moment of surrender:

"You're as mad as Warren if you think this is going to work," Rye had said.

"The new direction we decided on will work, Rye . . . give it a chance," retorted Wolfe, "Georgina was right. This trial, Warren's manipulation in Augland DC, and what he hopes to gain from invading our community—it's all a political game so we will need to win by outsmarting Warren."

"No, *you* decided this 'new direction' will work. And what game are you talking about? This isn't a 'game' if we're trying to stay alive—you're putting *my* people in harm's way! NeuroEnergy is no army of trained soldiers. We are engineers, scientists, data analysts; that's what we are!"

Rye was fuming. He wasn't usually an angry man, actually just the opposite. He was intelligent and preferred to spar with his mind, not weapons. He hated confrontation as much as he hated Augland 54, but this needed to be said. Wolfe and Joao had their pack of secrets, keeping everyone out of the circle in the name of 'protection.' But these secrets seemed to be doing more harm than good, and Rye was sick of it. He noticed the stares from his NeuroEnergy employees once the conversation turned heated, so he had pulled Wolfe into his office.

Rye shut the door before taking a seat in his office chair. Minutes of silence simmered between them. Finally, Wolfe sat down on the opposite side of Rye's desk in a chair and leaned in. Time had diffused the tension between them. "You know, I don't think I've ever really told you much about Warren. I'm his son, you already know that, but if you think I'm as mad as him you're mistaken. My father will do anything for power. He will kill, he will disarm, he will lie, cheat and steal. And he's had a lifetime of perfecting his technique."

"You think I don't know your father? I've researched and spied on him for ten years. I know everything about him, about you too. I know you started Land of Legends; I know you ran away and hid for days because you couldn't handle the violence and bloodshed. I know deep down you've tried to outdo your father and every time he comes back swinging and beats you at your own game."

Wolfe's head dropped into his hands, shaking as if to say "no" as the ugly sound of the harsh truth unfiltered Rye's lips. "Wolfe, there's more at stake here than you, Ashton . . . the Augland workers," Rye confessed.

"You don't think I know that? You think I'm taking this lightly? We have no other choice, Rye. Georgina will lose. She lost the moment she set foot in Augland DC. We didn't see it when she and Ashton left together, and Georgina didn't see it because she thought her relationships and political sway would be enough to convince the other CEOs to side with her. And when Warren wins . . ." Wolfe narrowed his eyes. ". . . he will come for NeuroEnergy. He will come for your scientist and every technology leverage you have in your headquarters." Rye refused to break eye contact with Wolfe.

"But you know how we can beat him?" Wolfe didn't wait for a response before continuing, "By weaponizing Warren's loneliness. He keeps me around because he wants someone to provoke and engage with—someone he can pass down his 'skillset' to. More importantly, he wants me to see what he's capable of. So, while yes, the plan changed and yes, NeuroEnergy will likely be his target, we know our opponent's weakness. You don't trust me, that's fine. I don't care. But my plan *will* work. I just need you to play your part. If you want to keep the people of NeuroEnergy safe, then you let him take over. It's Warren against all of us. So, while you may not like my decision making, this is what we are doing because apart we are nothing, but together we at least stand a chance."

Rye's fists tightened in frustration. Wolfe wouldn't divulge every facet of his plan, saying it was for his safety. Wolfe was right. Rye absolutely did not trust Wolfe or the direction of this new strategy.

Suddenly, sirens blared throughout the NeuroEnergy compound, snapping Rye back to the present. The fire alarm was followed by the showering of water from the sprinkler system, which would ruin everything meant to be destroyed. This was one of their strategies that would convince Warren that he was the cause of the damage. Rye let the forced rain beat down on him and knew: it was the start *of the end.*

Rye placed his glasses back on, reviewing the feed from the cameras surrounding the compound and its perimeter. It was his job to always anticipate turmoil to NeuroEnergy. He was used to being on constant alert after all he'd experienced in Augland 54, during all those years of surveillance. That was something he and Ashton had in common—always waiting for the worst to happen. They were more alike than anyone would have guessed. She not only saw, but lived through torture, hurt, and killing. He had watched the events unfold on the battlegrounds and brothels. He had seen the Victorian workers forced into fistfights for Suits to have a "game" to bet on and pass the time. He'd witnessed the torture of caged workers who were forced to be test subjects for the Customer Service Initiative, enduring inhumane installation procedures.

Through the camera feeds, he saw Augland guards break formation and surround the area. They were closing ranks around the NeuroEnergy members that had volunteered to stand in protection of their community. While Warren's 54 security guards had the appearance of being on the edge of violence, they refrained from engaging and instead headed straight for the headquarters in the heart of the compound. Rye switched views through his glasses to capture the front entrance of the building. NeuroEnergy guards had been called off for their own safety. The Augland soldiers filed in two by two, ready for a fight that they wouldn't get. The elevators were open, no longer requiring a password and keycard for access.

Floor by floor they searched. Rye watched the activity until the flickering of his glasses went black from the water pouring down from the safety valves, destroying them in the process. The water coating the third-floor concrete was at least an inch deep by the time the men reached him. Rye put up his hands in defense. He was behind his desk, the only man in the building—as intended.

"Hands where we can see them!" Instructions were shouted and Rye acquiesced. The soldiers' feet splashed in the water that had pooled on the ground beneath them. Rye was drenched. Strong arms yanked him out of his chair and threw him onto the ground. Rye groaned in pain as his face crashed against the hard surface.

"Hands behind your back!" Rye tried to breathe and bring his mouth just above the water line. The guards were rough, putting a knee behind his back and shoving him harder into the unforgiving, puddled ground beneath him. They forcefully took his hands and locked them together in handcuffs behind his back. The cold steel cuffs wrapped around his thin wrists and tightened so much against his skin so he couldn't move beneath the weight of the soldier pinning him to the ground.

Between the safety water pouring down and the sleet-soaked carpet, the room quickly turned colder than ice. The Augland soldiers forced Rye from his office and dragged him toward the stairwell that would lead them outside. Sparks erupted as the electrical equipment short-circuited around them, melting down and exposing hard drives and microchips.

With a sinking feeling, Rye realized everything around him was ruined—everything he and Georgina had built together. He was glad she wasn't here to witness its destruction.

THE CAMPAIGN

CHAPTER 23

Ashton

AUGLAND 44

"Ashton!" Warren yelled from the other room in a low, smug voice that she had grown to despise. Ashton could feel the Customer Service chip pulse when it turned on, which tipped her off on how to react, or not react to anything he said. There were moments it was hard to control, but her years of servitude to Suits made the blanket stare and masking of her thoughts that much easier. She was good at playing natural abider, but that façade was becoming harder to maintain as her anger grew with each passing day. Warren had once ridiculed her lack of education from Augland Center, but what he hadn't realized was the power it gave her when having to face customers or even people like Warren. She was able to hide her emotions well—for the most part.

"Yes." Ashton responded. They had been at Augland 44 for two days now and staying in an overwater bungalow. Ashton had her own room; so did Wolfe, Warren, and Reuben. The rooms were large enough for each of them to have their own space, but small enough that the quarters guaranteed every movement could be monitored. Ashton came out of her room to the living room where Warren sat next to Wolfe, whose blank stare and stiff posture had become the new normal. Warren sat at the living room table sipping coffee as the wind from the outside blew in from the fictitious ocean breeze.

It had been three weeks since the end of the trial. At first Ashton thought Warren hadn't yet tested the CS chip when she awoke in his home after surgery. However, after finding the note Wolfe had given her the night of Warren's dinner proved otherwise. Wolfe had assumed his father would attempt to violate her with the Customer Service Initiative after losing at trial, but Wolfe had given her something for protection—Sheva's necklace soldered with its own chip blocker that shielded her from any mind manipulation.

The morning after her forced surgery, Ashton woke up in a dark room, her head pounding. Trying to focus, she raised her hand up to the source of her pain. Her hand touched the tender spot on her head and an instant sinking feeling was present in the pit of her stomach.

VELIC, please prepare the Customer Service Initiative surgery for employee number JR105. Warren's words were the last thing she remembered before Wolfe had pricked her skin with a fast-acting sedative. She had no time to react—to fight.

There was an inch-wide patch of hair shaved on her scalp where the Customer Service chip had been implanted. Ashton remained on her bed in a maroon-painted room, brilliantly colored from walls to the ceiling. It was chilly and quiet . . . too quiet. Ashton inched her way off the mattress and toward the closed bedroom door. She turned the knob, and to her surprise, it was unlocked. She opened it slowly, looking out into the vast hallway of Warren's log home. Daylight poured into the windows surrounding the living room. Ashton crept around, but still nothing stirred. It was empty.

In a panic, Ashton contemplated leaving because she knew what the Customer Service chip meant—she was no longer in control. She rushed to the front door, ready to swing it open and run as far from Warren as she could get. But as soon as the idea of leaving surfaced in her mind, it abruptly left because Warren still had Wolfe.

Ashton's hand hovered over the knob to the front door. *Wolfe.* She backed away from the door, realizing she could not leave him here—not with him. On instinct, her hand fell to her pants pocket.

The memory of the night before was coming into full focus, and she remembered he had left her something. Ashton looked around, not trusting that this home did not have cameras; she rushed to the nearest bathroom. Slamming the door shut, she pulled a piece of paper from her back pocket.

Ash.

If I've given this letter to you, it means my father went through with implanting the Customer Service Initiative into me. I only assumed he already has, or will, do the same to you.

This must be very confusing for you. A lot has happened since you've been in Augland DC (by the way, I'm so proud of how you handled yourself on the stand! It takes a lot of strength to stand up like you did!)

To fill you in on what's happened. Warren knows about a defensive program that NeuroEnergy has begun to create and plans to commandeer it after he wins the trial. Vic, he's the scientist who created something called STEMP, I think you'd like him, and Forest (I believe you remember him from Apparel), have been working on it. The weapon can turn Suits off for a time, maybe even permanently. So, we need to buy them time so they can complete this task.

Joao's been chipped, which is how I knew what Warren was planning. Warren doesn't know we know, and we need to keep it that way. Warren thinks he's winning now, not knowing we know exactly what he will try to do. What we need now is time . . .

The necklace around your neck has a chip on it that stops the transmission of the CS even when turned on, which means you'll need to always wear it, no matter what.

We spoke once about doing this together—and I know that is still true. Warren will test you and I need you to convince him that you're under the control of the Customer Service

Initiative—like you're playing a part. When the time is right, we will find a way to defeat him.

You and me, Ash.

Ashton folded the letter and breathed a sigh of mixed emotions while leaning against the bathroom door. Wolfe had protected her, like he always did, but at a cost.

———————

Ashton stayed at Warren's in DC for a few days following her surgery, but she barely saw Wolfe. Warren, Wolfe, and Reuben had come home on her third night, but Wolfe left that evening for a few hours. During that time, Reuben had come to visit her, letting her know of Warren's victory at the trial. He also informed her that Beaugard had mysteriously died in his chambers. Apparently, his Suit had turned off—and when they opened his pod, they discovered his nutrition streams had been poisoned.

Warren was quick to insinuate Georgina, given the recent events of the trial and that spark lit the flame of conspiracy. Georgina had been kept in AEC chambers under twenty-four-hour surveillance until there was enough evidence to confirm she was the killer. Ashton was sure Warren had planted something to incriminate her. Since then, the CEOs had gone home, and Warren had started his campaign to become the new AEC President.

The chip's features were all or nothing—controlled, or it allowed its host to control everything. There were times when Warren turned off Wolfe's CS chip, but those moments became more infrequent as Wolfe's uncontrolled fits of anger became more frantic once his own conscience took control again. Wolfe hated not having control over his own thoughts and movements. Those outbursts were frightening at times, especially when Ashton could see his control slipping away for the few moments when he was truly himself—and it troubled her to see him in so much pain.

This first week with Warren was difficult. He kept Ashton and Wolfe separate for the most part. He discussed travel arrangements and kept Wolfe busy with errands while Ashton waited for the next meeting to which Warren would require her presence. Ashton knew it would be difficult to tame her emotions, but given what Wolfe had gone through to ensure her safety with the transmitter was something she could not let fail. It fueled her progression and eased her back into being the worker she once was—pliable, docile and non-combative.

There were times when she could release her tension. Warren would turn off the chip and she'd be quick-witted, which he found amusing. Each day she learned more about Warren's behavior, analyzing it to benefit their situation. Warren liked tempered banter but didn't like accusations. He preferred witty humor and spoke much of plans and manipulations he intended to impose on others. Ashton astutely listened, which Warren seemed to approve. He thought himself the smartest man in the room and if Ashton didn't belittle him, he gave Ashton some privileges—unlike Wolfe.

Reuben had decided that using Ashton's worker status during Warren's presidency campaign would benefit the iHumanist movement by uniting the UnSuited at each Augland they visited. Three weeks had passed since their first scheduled "rally" in Augland 2, for which Reuben prepared a speech for Ashton. How Reuben had managed to keep it from Warren, Ashton wasn't sure, but so far it had worked. However, what neither of them had expected was an apparent public-speaking fear that paralyzed Ashton on stage.

As she stood in front of twenty or so UnSuited, she blanked on the speech and stared off stage for what felt like an eternity. Reuben called it "first-time jitters." Ashton thought it was the most humiliating moment of her life. She was petrified to attempt it again—but

Reuben convinced her he'd help her through the fear, instilling the "importance of more UnSuited for their rebellion and a leader they can follow."

She doubted Reuben was convinced that she'd be the leader he needed. Nonetheless, he scheduled the meetings in each Augland and, over time, Reuben helped Ashton find her voice. Reuben hadn't said as much, but Ashton could feel improvement with each rally.

"You coming out?" Warren said, forcing Ashton back to reality, where she remained standing in the doorframe next to her bedroom.

"Yes, sir," Ashton said and moved slowly toward the dining table where Warren and Wolfe sat.

Warren crossed his legs while he viewed something on his interpad. "We have a meeting this morning with the Senators of Augland 44, after we meet with CEO Tasley. Not that Senators have any power these days other than resource allocation, but they are essential for a good political strategy. They're good for us to work with, and have influence with the other CEOs and Executives."

It had been the same in Augland 2, 60, 12, 10, and 33. Warren was making his rounds to visit different Auglands and campaign for his role as new AEC President. He used Ashton as leverage against the UnSuited, showcasing her failure as their leader and her inability to organize and overthrow Auglands. Warren assumed the CEOs would believe either that Georgina had in fact been manipulating her all along, or that Ashton's CS chip was successful in controlling her behavior. Either belief was fine with him.

"Reuben will be here soon and can go over details. Augland 44 has had the most rebel outbreaks so we will need you to convince the CEO that you have control over the UnSuited here."

"Okay, will Reuben provide a new script or are we using the same one as before?" Ashton asked. Reuben had suggested that memorizing the scripts ahead of time would help with her nerves.

"We should likely switch it up . . . breakfast? I asked Niall to make Eggs Benedict because I know it's your favorite." Warren was evil incarnate, but he did have a knack for getting others to warm up to him, despite any initial resistance. He was both nice, and cruel—nice, like when he gave Ashton her own room with a view of Augland 44 Historical and a renowned Florida Key beach or when pampering her with new clothes and Augland excursions.

But he also tortured her by surrounding her with the two men she loved dearly, now only shells of who they'd one been and unable to truly connect with her. He did this to keep Ashton in line. But what Warren wanted and what he got were two entirely different things. He thought surrounding her with chipped people and chipping her own mind as well would weaken her, but it only fueled the fire within her, each day burning hotter and brighter.

Unlike Wolfe or Niall, Warren only kept her chip on during the day, which meant he wanted her to be who she really was at night. She now would stop at nothing to tear Warren down from his pedestal once she aided him in climbing to the top. *I'm going to kill him. He's going to die by my hand, and I'll take everything from him like he has me.*

"Thank you." Ashton said coolly as she scooted into the chair next to Wolfe. She took a moment to study him. His eyes were shallow, both in shadowed discoloration and depth. The once whites of his eyes were lined with red from lack of sleep. His shoulders were tense. She knew he had trouble sleeping and the fact his father couldn't see or care about the abuse he was subjecting on his son made her tremble with anger.

Niall brought over her breakfast and placed it in front of her. He gave her a smile before he headed back to the kitchen. "Have you ever gone snorkeling?" Warren's interpad was down on the table and he glanced up toward Ashton.

"No, sir." Ashton picked up her fork and moved her potatoes around. She wasn't hungry but would need to muster up the desire to eat in order to keep Warren from becoming suspicious.

"You should try it out here on the island of Coastal View Park. It has crystal-clear waters . . ." Warren said before scooping up another mouthful of synthetic eggs and Hollandaise sauce.

"Yes, thank you for the recommendation." Ashton responded nearly robotically.

Warren glanced at his interpad. "Look at the time. Be out here in a half hour and wear something nice. We will have to leave soon." Warren pushed his plate back, signaling breakfast was over, then left without a second breath. When he was out of sight, Ashton spun toward Wolfe.

"Wolfe?"

His face was stone. Warren had told him not to look or speak to Ashton. She went to touch him, but he was out of his seat before she could, turning from her and heading back to his room. She could follow him, but it would do little good because he would keep moving out of her reach—because the CS chip commanded him to do so. Every day she tried. Someone else may have given up but each day she thought he might crack the CS code—if anyone could, it would be Wolfe.

Warren kept Wolfe's CS chip on now all day and night. Rueben mentioned that anyone with the CS chip application could control it, but, so far, Warren seemed to be the only one who had it. Ashton had nearly begged Reuben to install the application on his interconnect, but he told her the risk was too great. So, the only relief Wolfe received was when Ashton snuck into his room and wrapped herself around him, placing the moonstone necklace's chip so it touched both of their skins. She'd lie awake, sometimes she would let him sleep and only stroked his hair, allowing peace to reach his mind for a few hours. Other times, he would wake up and be completely numb, even speechless—telling Ashton how difficult the mind control was and what Warren was forcing him do. It broke Ashton's heart. Wolfe told her to stop coming into his room because it was too dangerous, but she couldn't stop. It was the only time in their long, drawn-out days that they could be *normal* together.

As if on cue, Reuben made his way into the dining room. Ashton looked at him and back at her plate of untouched food. "Where's Warren?" Ashton nodded toward his room. "Let's go outside for a minute."

Reuben led Ashton outside, and the bright lights shown down on the tropical paradise and the beach residence that Warren had rented during their few days here. Reuben turned to her after scanning the area for anyone or any*thing* listening. It was a remote sight with only a gentle wind and chirping birds.

"I'm working now on getting us another meeting with the UnSuited this week; my sources say they meet in Augland 44's Settler's Park. There's a group of around fourteen UnSuited from various parks that will be there. They all represent separate clans, so meeting with the UnSuited leaders from each group will be important."

"We can't keep telling them to look for the sign to revolt against the Auglands because I don't even know what the sign will be. It's been three weeks, Reuben. I need more than 'tell them to be ready'."

Ashton eyed Reuben. Her faith in him was tenuous because he had, at one point, threatened her friends and it was their protection she exchanged for her cooperation. Since then, they had grown a little closer and she felt comfortable now telling him what she was thinking. *But was there really any choice?*

The iHumanist movement was still somewhat a mystery to her, but they had come through with some good information. For one, they confirmed that Joao and Bez were safe in Augland 54. Warren had entrusted Joao to run Augland 54 under the control of a Customer Service chip, and he had been able to bypass the chip like she had. Ashton had kept silent about her necklace, but Reuben had been much more observant than Warren and sensed something was off. He tested his theory by downloading her chip's application onto his device and caught her in the lie. Since then, Ashton had been more than careful to notice the indication that the chip was on, but her brief lapse had forced her to tell Reuben everything.

"Any news on how to get Wolfe back?" She could tell Reuben was getting sick of this question, but until they had answers, she would keep asking him to keep this at the top of Reuben's mind. She needed Wolfe—the real Wolfe—back.

"We are working on it."

Ashton sighed, disappointed again. "Warren has me leaving soon for a meeting with the Senators and CEO Tasley."

Reuben nodded, "You're doing well." He stepped closer to her, putting his hands on her upper arms and turning her to look at him.

"You've grown to be so strong, you know that? Not a lot of people would be able to put themselves in front of these men and hold their own but you have. Especially how you've convinced Warren of his control over you for so long." Ashton's eyes searched his synthetic ones. She would never fully trust Reuben, but to have a "real" friend amongst those around her, who still had a grasp of their own consciousness, was necessary. In a way, he knew that.

"Reuben, just hold up your end of the bargain."

Reuben released her arms, squeezing gently first. "I'll see you at ten; meet you right outside the pub."

———

"Tasley!" Warren opened a dark stone door inlaid with concrete spikes. They entered a dark room with red carpets and copper framed artwork. Ashton's heels echoed in the darkness, lit only by the candles that covered most of the walls. Wolfe stayed a few steps behind her and despite this, his physical presence made the room feel smaller.

Augland 54's Land of Legend's Vikings camp mimicked Tasley's aesthetics with similar dark tones and tapestries which highlighted the medieval stone and carved bone art. Tasley was a thin man with long, black hair, broad shoulders and a pointed nose. Unlike Warren's suit and tie, Tasley wore an elegant robe littered with swirling patterns projecting the image of a king. All that was missing was a golden scepter, Ashton thought wryly.

"Ashton, come here. Meet CEO Tasley." Warren motioned for Ashton, who immediately straightened her posture and silently worked up the courage to play her part. She painted a grin on her face and walked toward CEO Tasley, the man who ran Augland 44.

"Sir, it's a pleasure to meet you."

Tasley eyed her, both suspicious and amused at the same time. "Warren, how on earth did you manage this change of heart? At the trial I was certain this girl planned to kill you. That was the rumor swirling around the Executives at dinner."

Warren let out a laugh. It was the same conversation repeated at nearly every Augland they visited.

"Once she realized Georgina had manipulated her, we found common ground. And given she leads the UnSuited, I wanted it known that we are able to . . . control those issues." Warren rummaged through his pocket for his interconnect and pressed down on an app feature that controlled CS chips. Instantly, Ashton's jaw tensed as the vibration in her head began. It was a soft hum in her mind reminding her to not give away her position.

"You're not worried she'll turn on you?"

Warren gave a chuckle in response as Tasley voiced his reservations.

"She can't," he said. And he motioned to his own head to indicate where the chip was located within both Ashton's and Wolfe's heads. They both evoked an unholy laugh and Ashton bit her cheek to temper her reaction.

"No kidding! And it works?"

"Like a charm."

Not exactly. Ashton put her head down to hide the gleam of triumph that had likely seeped into her smile. She looked toward Wolfe, but her eyes fell as he glared straight ahead with a blank stare.

Tasley motioned for Warren to take a seat. She could see Warren sink down into the plush leather couch as Tasley faced him in the adjacent armchair.

"What can I do for you?"

Warren took a deep breath. Ashton could essentially recite what he was going to say, just like he had done with all the other CEOs and Senators they'd met at the various Auglands.

"When the trial ended and Beaugard was taken from us, it got me thinking about how the future state of AEC should look. What

Auglands need and how we can better collaborate with NeuroEnergies." There was a long pause.

"I believe it's the Auglands that need to rise and help our economy to truly thrive and become the best it's ever been. I don't think Beaugard did a bad job at all." Warren had told Ashton that Tasley was a Beaugard supporter. "He will be missed greatly, and what we need to make sure of is that the next person in line for power is someone who understands the importance of what CEOs provide for our customers."

"Someone like you?"

"If the shoe fits. I've got years of experience under my father. As CEO, I did expose Georgina, which, Tasley, you can't deny has made you question your own relationship with your NeuroEnergy counterpart."

Tasley remained still, putting his hand up to his chin in thought.

"The UnSuited has become a problem for you, hasn't it? A rebellion in a few of your parks."

Tasley's eyes narrowed. Most CEOs wanted to keep the rebellions under wraps, but Warren always knew when and where they were sprouting up. "I can stop them." He nodded at Ashton.

"Ashton, come here." Ashton moved as if from his command to face him and Tasley.

"How strong is the UnSuited?"

"The UnSuited is very strong. We have ties across most of the western Auglands and growing numbers on the east coast."

"Do you control them?"

"Yes."

"And if I told you to tell them to expose themselves in Augland 44, would they?"

"Yes."

The answers rolled off her tongue quickly. They had played that same card at several different Auglands. Warren did his homework, understanding the inner workings of every CEO he encountered. With some CEOs, he weaponized Ashton as a dangerous threat, and for others, Warren let them know he was pulling her strings. He didn't care what they believed, as long as they believed him and voted Warren in as president. Some wanted to know more about the Customer Service Initiative and Warren took the opportunity to show off his control, asking her to do something or Wolfe to employ fear tactics. At first, it made her nervous what he might ask, like for Wolfe to kill her or a CEO, but after this much time she knew Warren wouldn't do anything that drastic.

Conversations continued until Tasley seemed satisfied.

"Can I count on your vote then? A favor with the future AEC president isn't a bad thing to hold in your pocket."

Tasley thought for a moment before putting his hand out. "I'll have to think about it, but I don't see why not." Warren placed his hand in Tasley's, shaking it as if they had come to some agreement.

"I understand. I plan to be here till tomorrow, so reach out if you have questions."

They walked out of the room and Ashton could feel the tingling of her chip stop and she knew Warren had turned it off—though she didn't see him reach for his interconnect. *Finally*, she thought to herself. "At this rate you'll owe every CEO a favor."

Warren smiled ironically, "Tasley will agree. He's too scared of the UnSuited."

"You don't think at some point they are going to figure out that I don't have these connections to the UnSuited?"

"By the time they figure that out it will be too late. I'll already be president."

They walked in silence for some time. "Ashton, may I ask you something?" Warren asked.

"Do I ever have a choice?"

Warren chuckled as they strolled together. "What does it feel like—the chip?"

Warren could have asked his son, who trailed slightly behind them as they entered the VELIC-driven vehicle back to their home, if only his son had the ability to respond of his own volition. Ashton wasn't certain, but she thought there was a part of Warren who didn't want to know what his son was going through because Warren, deep down, did care. Struck all over again by her anger over Wolfe's situation, she bit out, "I'd be happy to put one in you so you can feel the full force."

Warren smirked. "You're so violent sometimes. It's endearing because you remind me of a feisty kitten." Ashton rolled her eyes, finding his amusement of her threats even more infuriating.

Ashton sighed. "It feels like . . ." *Make this sound believable.* She looked at Wolfe in the front seat. His shoulders were perpetually tensed. She didn't know what it felt like but knew how it felt to see someone she loved withering away to nothing. She knew how much it destroyed her to see him in so much pain day after day. "Like you've run out of oxygen and all you can do is focus on the breath coming in and out, even though each breath is more painful than the last. It's never enough either, but somehow you still survive. The voice in your head panics, wanting control but every move is not yours; it's coming from another source. Like a puppet, almost. Or a dream . . . where you're watching everything unfold and you can't stop the nightmare." She paused. "Now can I ask you something?"

Warren just nodded.

"Does it hurt to see Wolfe like that?" *Like it does me.*

"I wish it was different. I wish I didn't have to control him."

"Can I ask why you turn mine off? And not his?"

"You can't hurt me."

"He can't hurt you either."

"He would find a way . . . someday. When I don't have so much at risk, I will."

"Is he still here . . . still your son if you're forcing him?" There was an awkward pause where she could feel Warren's reservation. She looked over at him and noted that he did take a moment and look at Wolfe in the front seat, likely seeing the same thing Ashton did. She hoped for one moment that it tugged on his fatherly heartstrings to see his son in so much pain. In a flash, it was gone and again he was busying his mind.

"I have calls to make. I'll have Niall make supper tonight, so be ready at 6:00 p.m. sharp." There was no use pushing the subject further.

CHAPTER 24

Hunter

NORTHWEST DISTRIBUTION CENTER

A muffled growl rumbled in Hunter's stomach as he mentally prepared himself for the food run he was about to make. Or at least he thought it was his stomach growling—it just as easily could have been from Vic or Forest. It was hard to tell anymore how many days they had existed without food.

Though Hunter had led them to the safety of the distribution center, their challenges were far from over. Food was plentiful, delivered daily by train and sorted, but out of reach—except for a few minutes every five days. Routine software updates paused the automated machines at that five-day mark for just a few precious minutes and it was up to Hunter to dash in and out of the facility with enough food for the three of them. Those food dashes had to last until the next software update. The only inch of the warehouse not covered with cameras was the supply closet, which they all three had been calling "home" for the past three weeks.

It had taken about a week and a half of them starving outside the warehouse in the cold for Hunter to figure out the camera system and routine software schedule. Having a scientist and a computer genius on the team didn't bode well for survival skills, especially out in the Northwest elements with zero electricity. Neither did the weight or amount of computer gear Vic claimed were essential to have brought with them.

However, in the weeks since they had broken into this middle-of-nowhere warehouse, they had been able to hole up in the distribution center. Forest and Vic hammered away at the STEMP project in hopes of completing their salvation. And Hunter oversaw the water supply and food rations.

Hunter didn't need to go far to find food, but it was sneaking around the machinery he needed to perfect. He thought at first workers could spot him and alarm Augland, but since they'd arrived, he hadn't seen anyone—only wires and metal. Once assured that no human was in the warehouse, he then began exploring. He had found the hidden nooks and crannies of the machine-only warehouse that housed the real food for distribution to Auglands, NeuroEnergies, and Colonies. Supplies would come from various Auglands to then be sorted by conveyer belt, compiled, and sent to other areas across the Augland nation. The location was especially useful when they needed wiring or technology, as they had plenty of resource material around them. In addition to providing life-sustaining nourishment, the warehouse also was a treasure trove of wiring, cables, and various discarded bits of technology—much to Vic and Forest's delight.

Hunter ducked down and peeked out the door of the supply room, as there were cameras hidden everywhere and he needed to remain unseen. Even with the software update shutting everything down, there was a chance the cameras would swivel to where he was and spot him. It was just easier to maneuver by sliding against the walls than out in the open warehouse space, which was twenty-two steps, taking him ten seconds if he raced full speed from their supply room. He had a minute forty-five seconds to make it to the palleted supply area and back to the storage room. Fifteen of that would be his chance to run away—timing calculated for him by the now annoyingly too smart Forest and his all-too-important numbers.

Please, let there be meat. Beef. Or even chicken . . . preferably beef." Hunter muttered to any higher power that may have been listening and drooled a little at the thought of something besides citrus and vegetables. This time he needed to grab any kind of protein. During the last three software updates, he had only found canned corn and fresh oranges—which were hard to live off of. Protein would be hard to come by because it most often was shipped out a day after it arrived, but they would make do with just about anything at this point. He wasn't sure how much more of a nutrition deficit their bodies could handle while they waited for STEMP to be completed or for Augland 54 to leave NeuroEnergy. He wondered how much longer they could last here. It had been nearly three weeks since they'd left, and no good word had come from Rye on when they could go home.

Joao had told Hunter to tell no one where they they'd gone and to install an app on his interconnect to scramble the coordinates of their location. Hunter kept that secret, but that didn't stop Rye and Hunter from communicating. The use of the interconnect kept them in constant danger, because if Rye were tortured and forced to reveal the interconnect, it could be used as leverage against them. But to date, Rye hadn't asked their location and trusted they would reach out if and when help was needed.

"I'm about to go; we've got a minute before the update. I'm hoping they had some sort of meat delivered, but if not, I'll try and grab enough of *anything* this time to last us for the next week." Hunter addressed Forest and Vic, who sat on either side of the tiny closet.

Forest's eye sockets were a hollow grey as he struggled to keep his eyes at least half open, staring blankly ahead. Vic didn't look much better. His permanently hunched-over posture shortened his already limited height and lack of food was quickly shrinking his deep belly. They were living in a cramped, closet and while they had learned to make it "homey," it was still too close a quarters for them. Hunter desperately missed Versal. He missed their home, which if Vic and Forest couldn't crack the code on the satellites successfully. And that assuming Hunter could keep them fed and alive in the meantime.

Hunter's conversations were mainly with himself because his two housemates weren't social, or comforting, companions. His worst fears projected out in front of him daily with visions, like Versal under arrest, Ashton in prison for treason, and Joao's and Bez's lives torn apart by

Joao's servitude to the Customer Service Initiative. In comparison, every scenario he imagined had his friends in a similarly distraught state as Hunter, Forest, and Vic. Shifting from his mind back to his dismal reality, he concentrated on the need for food to survive. They could starve and die in a distribution center miles away from the Colony. Never to be found again. And it would be his fault. With those thoughts weighing on his conscience, Hunter glanced once more at his watch before darting out of the closet to restock their food supply.

CHAPTER 25

Ashton

AUGLAND 44

Ashton sat quietly during the car ride home following their meeting with CEO Tasley. Warren didn't miss an opportunity to continue his campaigning and made call after call, speaking cordially with most of the recipients on the other line.

One call that was most interesting was the one he made to Joao—or at least Ashton presumed it was him because Warren asked about the Augland 54 boardroom discussions. Ashton couldn't decipher how Joao responded, but Warren seemed satisfied with his report. Ashton didn't dare ask anything about the call because she was sure Reuben wasn't supposed to have told her about Joao's current job working with Warren as his eyes and ears in Augland 54.

By the time they had returned to the water villa, Niall was making preparations for dinner, and Ashton only had time to wash up. Sometimes, Warren was away for an evening as he had frequent dinner arrangements with CEOs or Senators, so Reuben would be put in charge as her temporary captor. Warren exploited every opportunity to wine and dine and gain the favor of those with influential standing. What Warren hadn't anticipated was Reuben's double crossing as he continued to work with Ashton in secret to build up the UnSuited ranks. The only downside to Warren's absence was that he usually dragged Wolfe along on the outings.

But tonight, both Ashton and Wolfe were expected to dine with Warren. Following her new routine, Ashton sauntered out of her bedroom to the dining room table where Wolfe and Warren were waiting. Warren nearly always enjoyed a cocktail with Wolfe before sitting down to dinner. Ashton would occasionally listen in on their conversations, but typically their discussions were brief and hushed unless Warren decided to turn off Wolfe's chip—which he hadn't done in two weeks. As the days went on, she constantly worried Warren would ask Wolfe to confess something they both needed to stay hidden—like the fact her necklace had a transmitter to stop her chip from functioning properly. She also wanted Warren to turn off the CS chip and let Wolfe be himself again, who knew how long Wolfe could keep being himself, who he truly was as a person.

She wore her typical black attire, which she considered her new uniform, she thought wryly to herself as she donned her dark "worker" clothing. Warren had bought her nicer outfits to wear when they were visiting CEOs, but during their downtime, she preferred to be in something more familiar. Wolfe usually wore a business casual ensemble— per Warren's direction, no doubt. He sat straight, so straight it often looked painful, prompting Ashton to realize that no matter how many days passed, she still struggled seeing him in this state. His soul-less eyes were glossed over, and his back was constantly tense, like every interaction they had—stiff and forced.

Warren looked up at Ashton and smiled. She forced an empty smile in return before sitting at her assigned seat at the table where Niall had carefully arranged her place setting. Niall didn't fight the CS chip like Wolfe did, which is why Niall appeared more relaxed and at ease in his movements. But she knew the longer the chip remained on, the harder it was to fight against it. Seeing Niall completely adapted to his new persona reminded her they were running out of time. She imagined Wolfe's strained demeanor meant he was not giving in, but the days were long and soon weeks would become months. She wasn't sure how long he could hold on. Eventually, it would be easier for Wolfe to give into the chip and accept defeat, and she wasn't sure if the real Wolfe would or even *could* ever return.

"I'd like to ask you something, Ashton," began Warren, "and I'd prefer to just ask, rather than demand."

This is new. Niall approached the table and placed down serving platters of salmon and risotto, which smelled divine. "Again, you ask me like I have a choice," she said. The smart remark was out before she had time to catch herself. Warren merely chuckled, Ashton thought it weird that he enjoyed their light banter when he could just as easily make her regret her word choices. Though her tone was light, she meant for her words to be offensive.

"Did Wolfgang ever tell you why he left Augland?" Warren asked while keeping his eyes on an expressionless Wolfe.

"I'm not sure I understand what you're asking. Wolfe left because he had to."

Warren looked away, as if embarrassed by his next statement. "I know he was angry when I kept him in my home and ran Augland 54 in place of him. And I can understand why he was upset, but we are blood and I figured he would soon see why I had to do that. With the Customer Service Initiative barely past pilot, and plans for Augland 54 remodels for elite status, we weren't ready to have him take over."

"*We?*" Ashton asked.

"Yes . . . if he would have given me a chance to tell him before plotting to overtake me . . . and just cool down. I'm sure he would have understood why I had to do what I did." Warren paused for a moment. "At first, I was angry, and I knew he would be too once he was released, but we always move past our issues—he always comes to reason after some time." Warren's finger tapped nervously against his whiskey glass.

Ashton paused, analyzing Warren's reaction. "Wolfe was betrayed by you," she said in a measured tone.

"He betrayed me first." Warren shot back.

"He felt he had no choice but to take over the CEO title."

"That's not true, I've given Wolfgang more authority than any other Augland 54 member, even an Executive. He had privileges as my son, and he spat on that honor . . . I don't even know why I'm talking to the likes of you about this. You don't understand."

Ashton kept talking. "Warren, I'll tell you why he left. Wolfe left you because he actually cares about people. He doesn't believe in the same 'perfect' Augland as you do. He wants Augland to be different where people like me can live a life as equals."

"You really think that, don't you?" Warren shoveled a bit of synthetic salmon and rice into his mouth. "He never did anything for workers until he met you. If he had these dreams of helping workers, then why would he create a park to help rehabilitate them?"

"Stop it!" Ashton thought, knowing exactly what Warren was attempting to do. "You can't change my mind about Wolfe or his motives. I know him. I know more about him than you." Ashton's cheeks grew hot with her rising temper. She didn't want to be baited into a debate with him, but she couldn't help it. "He has always pushed hard for workers and reform, ever since you made him Director of Security. Even at Land of Legends he protected us while all you cared about was another five-star customer service record."

Warren laughed, truly laughed. "Is that what Wolfgang told you? That he created an entire park, that mind you, still, as you put it, murdered workers, under the pretense of giving workers a fighting chance? I gave him that project, a rehabilitation project, to showcase to the other Executives that he would be a good successor for CEO. He knew workers were going to die."

"I don't believe you."

"Doesn't matter to me if you believe me or not . . . it's the truth. I doubt Wolfgang has been honest with you, if as you say he's convinced you that he's been against me his entire life. That only started when he met you."

Ashton's palm hit the table, "I won't listen to your lies!" Her breath quickened and she locked eyes with Warren. "I doubt you have ever known your son. He has told me all about your relationship—or lack thereof. He's resented you his entire life. So you can try all you want to twist his story to make you feel like a better man, but I think there is a reason you're asking me and not him. Because you want to convince me he's like you, and I can't—won't believe it." Ashton's eyes narrowed. She wouldn't believe Warren. He wanted to drive a wedge between her and Wolfe—she wouldn't allow him to create that divide.

"I think you don't want to hear the truth. Even if you don't believe everything, there has to be some truth to what I've said. You know what? I think you've been out of your mind long enough." Warren's hand dug into his pocket for his interconnect and Ashton knew exactly what he intended. Her chipped hummed against her skull and it took every ounce of will to bite her tongue because if she responded, he'd see the chip had no effect on her.

"How's your salmon cooked, Ashton? Mine's a little dry . . ." Warren carried on like nothing had happened, but even as a bystander to what had just occurred, the cruelty she'd witnessed hardened her body and attitude. Dinner continued in silence, but beneath her well-crafted customer service façade, Ashton fumed with anger.

Dinner ended when Reuben walked through the front door.

"Warren." Reuben's grin was contagious. "I think we should have a small celebration tonight." Reuben's pearly white smile was broad. "Current rankings indicate you are favored as the new AEC president at 74 percent of all House of CEOs."

Warren sat back in his chair, eerily grinning at the news. "Wonderful . . . I couldn't agree more, Reuben. I say we celebrate . . . Ashton, you're dismissed." It was the display of dismissal that created a crystal clear picture for Ashton—Warren meant to create the divide between them. She had to bite back a response.

Ashton could barely sleep over the ruckus Warren and Reuben made just outside her bedroom door while Wolfe was silent. At one point, glass broke, and she heard thuds of something heavy hitting the floor, followed by the roar of laughter from the two seemingly intoxicated Suits. They celebrated like Warren had already won the presidential election.

CHAPTER 26

Wolfe

AUGLAND 44

Wolfe was dismissed after a few hours from his father's celebration while Reuben and Warren continued their night-long festivities out in the park. Sleep didn't come easy to Wolfe that night, but if he was honest, it hadn't come easy to him in some time. As long as Wolfe remained complacent and within the chip's protocol, the chip allowed his mind to wander. The days had turned into weeks, and now he had to admit he was losing himself. His body lay motionless with his eyes closed, but his mind refused to bend. He could hear his father and Reuben from outside his bungalow bedroom—celebrating, laughing, and drinking to their hearts' content. There wasn't much he could do. If he tried to escape, the CS would activate, and he would be forced to comply with the demands Warren set on the Customer Service application.

Wolfe could hear the crashing of the waves, which was the only thing that soothed his nerves nowadays. *How had things gotten this bad?* Wolfe knew his father would put him under the CS chip, and he'd figured it would be difficult to navigate, but he was losing his mind. And worse, he didn't know how to get himself and Ashton out of this mess. Ashton, at some point, would be found out, and what then? He was failing.

Worse, he had begged Ashton to trust him and look at them now. Each night, this was all Wolfe could think about. He was stuck in his own head, rattled by thoughts of failure and guilt. He thought of

Joao, who was spying in Augland 54, and Hunter, who was hiding the scientist. He also thought of Versal and Bez, women with whom he'd worked relentlessly to keep outside of Augland's walls again, and what would happen if he and Ashton failed.

Warren's roar of laughter trickled into Wolfe's isolated room and distracted Wolfe from his spiraling thoughts. *Looks like he had fun out on the town.* If Wolfe could sigh and roll his eyes he would have. *Just go to sleep.* Counting did the trick and after some time, Wolfe found his much-needed sleep.

"Hey." The heavy whisper abruptly woke Wolfe and he bolted upright, ready to strike the person in front of him.

"Relax!" hissed the intruder, gripping Wolfe's shoulders tightly. Wolfe's eyes adjusted and his breathing was labored as he looked around. He was still in Augland 44's water villa. It was pitch black outside, which added to the mystery of the person in front of him.

"Wolfe, it's Reuben. Stay calm and get up."

It dawned on Wolfe that he was thinking more clearly. His rigid posture had loosened, and he could freely turn his head from side to side. He ignored Reuben and tested the liberation he was sure was some hoax, a dream he was yet to wake from. His father hadn't turned off his CS chip in weeks—why now?

Wolfe's vision absorbed the darkness, allowing him to assess the figure crouched over him, an anxious.

"Get up now. We don't have time for pleasantries."

"The CS—"

"Is off . . . Warren's out cold and he'll be convinced he accidently turned off your chip; he had a little too much fun tonight." Reuben smiled.

"You're helping me." It wasn't a question, but more of a statement of confusion because Wolfe wasn't sure how, or why, Reuben would help him. His brow furrowed as he thought of the tricks that were part of his father's and even Reuben's, political games.

"Get up, Wolfe. Go get Ashton. Get out of here. Make a run for it and see if you can get her out before it's too late.

So many questions flipped furiously through Wolfe's mind.

Reuben waved an interconnect in midair. "It's Warren's. Now, I'm going to turn on the chip and give you instructions to never tell anyone that I had any involvement. And when Warren awakes, he'll find his interconnect and turn it on and hopefully you've gotten Ashton far enough away that she can make a run for it and find somewhere safe to hide."

Wolfe instinctively jumped out of bed, ready—he may not have answers, but if there was even a chance Ashton could break free, he was all in. Wolfe grabbed his pants and shirt. "Why are you doing this?" Reuben's face was now visible in the darkness as Wolfe's eyes adapted.

"Your mother, of course. And there's more, but not now. Just hurry—you don't have much time. My suggestion is you follow the path along the water to the edge of the park and use the ventilation ducts to find a way out."

Wolfe wasted no time after Reuben left his room. Reuben had done as he had said, and turned on his Customer Service chip and spoken the words that would absolve Reuben if—well, when—Wolfe was eventually questioned once his father realized they had run away.

The hallway was dark and he swore he heard his father's drunken snores from across the hallway. It felt foreign having control of his movements back. His mind cleared and he was finally released from fighting against his own limbs. Wolfe slowly moved down the hall to where he knew Ashton lay, slowly he opened the door and saw her sleeping peacefully. Her unruly, still-dyed red hair was draped across the pillow and for the briefest moment he flashed back to visions of Ashton while they lived in Hood Canal . . . and their days together . . .

He shook past the memory as it tugged at his heart more than he cared to admit. He missed her; he missed their old life, and if they ever got back to safety, he'd never leave her again. He would whisk her away to whatever town, home, and country she wanted to seclude herself in. He'd stay in a cocoon in their world for the rest of their lives.

"Ashton," Wolfe said as he inched closer to her. He put his hand on her cheek. "Ashton," he said a little louder this time. Ashton's brow furrowed before her eyes slowly opened and her head quickly sank back into her bed in surprise.

"What the—" Ashton said before Wolfe could shush her.

"We don't have time to talk. I need you to get up and follow me outside. Right now, Ash."

His words were meaningless, as Ashton was certain this was a trick and remained motionless. "Wolfe?" she said questioningly, as if her mind still couldn't imagine what her eyes were seeing.

"It's me, Ash. We have to go." Ashton shook her head, undoubtedly thinking she would get her questions answered later, like how he was functioning outside of the CS Initiative. Wolfe grabbed her by the arm, the risk of everything crashing down on them hit him hard. They didn't have time; they needed time, and it was his and Ashton's only chance to get away from Warren.

Ashton's room was on the ground floor, which made getting out much easier. They both hurried out to her front patio and Wolfe looked around, hoping for a boat or other means of travel—but of course there was nothing to aid in an escape. Wolfe bent down low on the edge of the wooden deck, putting his feet first into the frigid water. Slowly he inched down into the water, afraid someone would wake. Ashton was quick behind him, sitting down on the water's edge while Wolfe helped her submerge into the midnight blue water.

In silence, Wolfe began swimming away from Ashton's patio, keeping his movements quiet just in case there were security patrols who could alert his father of their escape—not that anyone would think that right away. For all anyone knew, both Ashton and Wolfe were willing participants acting under the CS chip control.

"Wolfe," Ashton said under labored breath.

"Not yet," Wolfe replied in a hushed whisper. They were still too close to other customers of 44.

They swam under the moon until the bungalow village was far enough away and the vacant beach was in sight. At times, Wolfe would look back and make sure Ashton was still with him. It had been at least an hour now, and swimming through the water was becoming difficult even for him.

"You. Got. This." Wolfe whispered through labored breath. Ashton didn't respond, undoubtedly needing the oxygen more than she needed to respond to him.

After two hours, both were reserving their strength for each stroke. Wolfe periodically glanced back to make sure Ashton was still with him.

Finally, the current propelled them both to the waves edge that were crashing onto a white-sand beach. Both Ashton and Wolfe collapsed, their muscles burning and lungs aching after the two-hour and half-minute swim.

Ashton choked, coughing up water as she struggled to breathe, both lay exhausted on the shore. Wolfe wasn't much better—gulping in deep breaths as his limbs shook from both the cold and exertion. The cool sand beneath him trapped a frozen feeling deep in his bones.

"Ash."

She looked up and stared at him intently for a moment. The intensity caught Wolfe off guard. She didn't say anything, only studied him.

"Ash," he said again, not sure what to say as he finally stood to face her. It had felt like they had been apart for so long, though they were physically close to each other during their captivity. But their mental separation had created an ocean of distance. He saw her every day but couldn't touch or talk to her.

"It's you," Ashton said softly, still with some level of disbelief.

Wolfe chuckled. "Of course it's me."

"Shut up." She said it before she closed the distance between them, needing only two strides before barreling into his chest. They were both soaked from the water, and she shivered, but there was something that told Wolfe she wasn't shivering from only the cold. For how hard their separation had been on Wolfe the past month, it had been just as hard on her.

"I can't believe it. I was so scared that—" Ashton's voice caught, and she needed a minute, which nearly tore Wolfe in two. "I thought that maybe you would end up like Niall." Her hands dug into Wolfe, gripping him fiercely like she feared letting go.

"Sh . . . it's . . ." Wolfe trailed off, unsure of how to describe their current plight. Were they all right? Was everything all right? So instead, he would acknowledge that he understood. "I know, Ash."

He stroked her damp hair. Such a simple motion brought so much comfort. Feeling the strands, he reminded himself how many times he'd wanted to do just this when he was under his father's control. They had to leave and hurry on their way, but this moment felt too important. Too vital to their existence because he wasn't sure how much longer they had together. Each stolen moment created a thousand memories in his mind that he vowed to revisit should anything happen.

"It's okay. It's going to be okay. I promise." She was going to begin to hate him someday for his promises that he never seemed to keep, Wolfe thought.

"Is this it? Are we getting out?" Her face tilted up and away from his and Wolfe looked down at Ashton.

Not we—only you. Again, he would be forced to twist the truth to protect her. "Yes."

Wolfe led them on the border of the beachline, hidden by the jungle that lined Augland 44's beach park. He didn't know this park well, and trusted Reuben's suggestion. Chances were that any beach park as large as this one either had a massive lake or was a natural coastline and on the outer rim of the Augland park.

"How did your chip get turned off?" Ashton's pace quickened to close the gap between them.

"Reuben. I guess that Warren drank too much, which gave him the opportunity to turn off the chip. He told me to leave."

"You trust him?"

"I trust that he doesn't want to make an enemy of my mother . . ."

Ashton took a deep breath, "And what do we do when we get out? And *how* are we getting out?" Unfortunately, Wolfe didn't have the luxury of time to think that far ahead. He only knew what Reuben had said: "Get her out and follow the beach path to the venting system."

"How much time do we have? If Reuben only turned the CS off, Warren is going to figure out sooner than later that we're gone and where we are through his interconnect."

"That's why we don't have a lot of time. We have to move fast and get outside the walls of Augland. And when we are out, catch the resource train until you—we—get somewhere safe."

There was a long pause. "Go home?" Ashton asked quietly.

That threw Wolfe because he wasn't sure she could go home. It depended so much on what his father would do when—not if—he captured her.

"We will find our home, even if it has to be a new home." Wolfe looked back briefly, and Ash's head was twisted up, facing the faded, black sky where the sun threatened to make its appearance, reminding him they were running out of time.

"Warren said NeuroEnergy was attacked. And he talked about a scientist. Is it true?"

Wolfe's face fell, "Yes, that's true. Warren has overtaken NeuroEnergy and is hunting down the scientist who created the STEMP project . . . once you left for the trial, Joao, Bez, and I went to NeuroEnergy and found out there is a program to destroy Suits that Rye has been creating.

"To be honest, it was the only reason I came to get you. I thought they could figure out the technology in time and we could fight against Warren." The next part was hard for Wolfe to admit. "But I made a mistake—trusting that it would take only days to finalize and going to my father too quickly. Putting you through this all and risking your life every day with that monster." Ashton's hand touched Wolfe's and he couldn't bear to be given any gesture of comfort and pulled away. They both had suffered because he'd thought he could win against the Customer Service Chip, but he had hurt them both, subjecting them to the horrors he knew his father was capable of.

"Wolfe, I don't think there was a better outcome. It was this or getting imprisoned like Georgina, maybe even killed."

Wolfe kept walking.

"Wolfe—"

"We need to move faster. The sun's already starting to rise, and we could be hours away from the ventilation system." Guilt hit him like a ton of bricks. Ashton would forgive him because that was her nature—but he wouldn't let himself off the hook that easily.

CHAPTER 27

Ashton

AUGLAND 44

Big, tough Wolfe—that was how he always was—or how he wanted the world to see him. After what he had endured in the last month, Ashton was hoping for deeper conversation, honesty, not him shutting down. They were about to get out—out from underneath his father and the man who had dismantled an entire society.

They wouldn't let Warren win again.

"We should have grabbed water," Wolfe said, two steps ahead of her.

Ashton circled toward the waterfront. They'd been walking for nearly two hours and who knew when Warren would be up. They did not have time for this, but maybe they needed this. Ashton needed this.

A break from their reality.

A break from constant fear.

Ashton looked down at the tank top and shorts she'd worn to bed that night, noting the sand that now clung to half of her feet and calves. She glanced back out at the water, glistening with blood reds and blinding oranges that reminded her of Hood Canal. Ashton had stopped for a quick rest, breathing in and remembering their home for just that minute. The morning swims she would take. Walking this beachline didn't have the same sea salt smell, but it eased the tension in the air that surrounded both Ashton and Wolfe. She closed her eyes again She wanted to feel again, especially the closeness she once had with Wolfe . . . just briefly, to keep her going.

Ashton opened her eyes, turning toward Wolfe, whose brow was furrowed in confusion at why she had stopped walking. And she smiled in return, knowing that she was about to take a detour from their death march and spark a moment of play, and Wolfe would chase her—like he always did. It was the game they played.

Wolfe paused, seemingly reading the situation perfectly. "No, Ash, we don't—" But Ashton didn't wait—she was off. The sand sunk underneath her feet and the cool breeze whirled around her.

"Ash!" She could hear Wolfe close behind her. Ashton wrapped her arms around herself and lifted her shirt over her head. It was freeing to lose. She took another step, but this time she shimmied her pajama shorts off, leaving only her underwear and ran until she reached the water's edge.

Wolfe laughed. "What are you doing?" he called out, and all Ashton could do was turn to look behind her and smile. There it was—the half grin she had waited to see—then the shake of his head before his shirt came off and he followed her into the waves.

Ashton had swum out just enough to cover herself and where the waves would lift her up briefly before setting her back down on the sandy beach floor. Wolfe waded in to her depth, and Ashton grinned, knowing exactly what he was thinking.

"Always chasing you." He said finally, coming close enough to where they were face to face in the water.

"At least I always let you catch me." Ashton said as she wrapped her arms around Wolfe's shoulders and his eyes met hers.

His laugh was hardy, "Let me, huh? I'm fairly certain I've always caught you, whether you liked it or not." He chuckled again and tightened his grip around her waist.

"This is . . . nice" Ashton said, as she gazed into his eyes. Wolfe didn't look away, knowing what she meant. He knew that they both had been lost for too long and finally, finally they were feeling at home again.

Wolfe kissed her for several long moments, staying there and not letting her move more than an inch away from him.

"We *will* get out of here, Wolfe, and you were right. We need to do it together, and this time, we have to work from the same playbook. We will go back to what life was and find another way to fight your father." Wolfe's smile quickly faded, as he slowly moved from her while she stood mesmerized at the sun rising above the water's edge. "We should go." Ashton's brow scrunched in confusion; sensing Wolfe was again holding back.

"At least I got you to forget for a second." Ashton smiled.

"You're a distraction; that has never changed," Wolfe said with a flirtatious smile before turning and splashing out of the water toward the jungle's edge.

As the hours passed, Ashton could sense tension building between them. Wolfe was never good at hiding his emotions from her.

"We're nearing the wall." Wolfe said as he brushed past another leafy plant on the beach edge.

"How can you tell?" Ashton looked ahead, but all she could see was the beach, which looked like it was going on forever.

Wolfe paused, pointing in the distance. "There's this kind of shiny look that all the computers have and if you aren't looking for it, it might look like infinite sand. It's the cameras and monitors projecting more beach."

Ashton smiled at his textbook explanation. "Did you miss being a know-it-all?"

Wolfe laughed. "If you mean smart, handsome, and cultured, then yes. I may have missed that."

Ashton nearly snorted. "*Cultured* . . . didn't realize you thought so highly of yourself."

Without notice, Wolfe spun around and picked up Ashton, swinging her over his shoulder.

"What are you doing?!" Ashton screamed in gleeful surprise as her gut hit Wolfe's shoulder blade.

"Not putting you down until you agree how cultured I am."

"No, your ego is already too big," Ashton teased as she looked for a way to change her awkward position.

"You can carry me, Wolfe. I've been tired of walking for some time," Ashton joked, but she hoped he would put her down.

"I'm actually keeping you here for your safety."

"And why is that?" Ashton toyed.

There was a long pause. "Because you're about to hate me."

Ashton realized the tone of their playful banter had changed and her body stiffened. Her smile drifted from her face while dread seeped into her pores.

"Why . . . why would I hate you?"

Wolfe paused, avoiding a large tree as they approached the camera-plastered wall that was nearly invisible. They had trudged for the last four hours and had finally reached their destination.

"We're here. The ventilation systems will be hidden but should be between trees, that's at least how it is in Predator's Biome."

"Why am I going to hate you, Wolfe?"

"When you crawl through the vent system, it should lead right out to outside. From what I remember, Augland 44 is southeast to other Auglands. So, head north to find the train station."

"Wolfe." Ashton said, swinging herself upright against his shoulder and sliding down until her feet reached the ground. Wolfe bent over and began pulling green shrubs and roots away from Augland's wall. Wolfe kept pulling until the concrete wall exposed a steel grated vent that hummed with forced air.

Wolfe focused only on the vent, refusing to meet her gaze. He turned to find a thick vine to help him tug against the vent's grated system. "Remember—you'll have to find the tracks and eventually the train." Wolfe wedged the vine between the wall and grate. He pulled hard to where there was enough space so his fingers could get a hold. "It should be stocked with food and supplies, so you won't starve. Stay on the train until you get far enough away, maybe even make it to the other coast. That's going to be west . . . you know how to track west from our hiking trails. Just keep going west, Ash." With that, the vent's cage gave way and a two-foot space opened—enough for Ashton to fit through.

"Wolfe," Ashton said with more conviction this time. She recognized he was speaking like he was leaving her and that was not going to happen.

"Don't go to NeuroEnergy, but you could find the Colony again. And ask Cahya if you can hide at her house for at least some time."

The shock hit her like a punch to the stomach. "You said we were going to do this together! You *just* said that!" She went in to punch Wolfe across the chest. He could block her, she knew that, but that didn't stop the fury from taking root and propelling her arm forward—and Wolfe didn't try to stop her. Tears came as the realization hit too hard. Wolfe was leaving her.

"You said it, not me."

"Semantics? Really Wolfe?" Ashton's hands planted on her hip. "In the letter you gave me you said we would do this together. And you do this now to me? Everything, and I mean, everything, we have been through the last month will be for nothing. Is that what you want?"

Wolfe sighed. "I know, I'm sorry. But this is for the best. I don't need you here with me and it would be best if you went home where it is safe."

Ashton scoffed, dramatically wrapping her arms around her waist.

Wolfe continued, "I thought NeuroEnergy's weapon would be ready in days, not months, and I didn't think it would get this bad . . . but every day that you're back there with him? Pretending to be under the CS chip? You know all he has to do is ask me and I'll be forced to tell him that you aren't controlled. What do you think happens then?"

"I've done fine since we started! He has no idea that I can't be controlled. I thought you'd be thrilled at how far we've come . . . given you've been convinced I'm too impulsive. I think I've done extremely well, given Warren still has no idea the chip doesn't work."

"Yeah! And what happens when he decides he wants you to kill someone, or torture them—can you do that without being forced and live with yourself?" Wolfe's eyes grew wide in frustration. "Tell me, because I know for a fact you couldn't. Not the woman who sacrifices everything for others. You'd break in a second! And that's not me being harsh, that's reality."

Ashton fumed, but he was right. Their time undetected while living with Warren had been pure luck and at this point, he hadn't figured it out.

Ashton backed away, finally turning from him.

"I'm right, Ash. Go home and I'll find a way to get a message to you when the tech is ready to launch against Augland."

"No, we won't, not when he's got control over you. He'll never let you leave. I know that! He's asked me how to fix things with you so he can keep you. He wants you with him. Wolfe . . . if you stay under that chip, you'll die. You'll fight for as long as you can, but eventually you'll have to give up. Your mind will turn like Niall's—dead inside. I can't let—"

"We have no other choice. And right now, we don't have time to argue. Any second, Warren will be awake and when he finds me missing, he will search for the chip control. So, I'm hoping that we have enough time to get out."

"So, you lied when you said all we had to do was get outside the walls."

"Yes. I lied," Wolfe confessed.

"So that's it. You're giving up? After everything that has happened . . . you're taking the coward's way out." The words spilled out of her, and immediately she regretted them—because Wolfe was no coward.

His face fell, and as she anticipated, the words stung with a hurt Ashton intended. But guilt radiated through her.

"Please, just—" Ashton heard the abrupt pause before Wolfe could finish his sentence. The buzzing of the service chip alerted them that Warren was turning it on. Panic dripped down her spine, freezing her in place as Wolfe's eyes glossed over. His expression melted into one of tension. Ashton wasn't ready to lose him.

A ding brought both of their attention to Wolfe's pocket as he pulled out his interconnect.

"Wolfgang! I can't believe you two were idiot enough to try and leave. You know I can track you both! Come back now and bring Ashton with you." Warren sounded hoarse, like he had just woken up.

"Yes, sir." Wolfe's eyes slowly drifted up toward Ashton as he hung up his interconnect.

She knew what that meant and began to back away.

"Wolfe don't. We don't have to listen to him. You can fight this!" Ashton pleaded, knowing her efforts were futile. The influence of the CS chip was too strong, which is why Wolfe had brought her here and away from his father. Wolfe's fist tightened as he took one step, then two steps closer to her.

Ashton cursed as she felt her adrenaline surge and she ran toward the now-open ventilation system. Ashton ducked inside, pushing herself into the small space. All she would need to do is get far enough in, where Wolfe wouldn't be able to fit. Her hands scraped against the metal as she propelled herself forward inching through the metal tunnel as she heard Wolfe clang against the edge of the wall.

Ashton pushed harder, but she could feel Wolfe's hand snake down through the opening and brush against her ankle. She searched the four walls of steel for anything to grab onto as she swung her foot to rattle Wolfe's tightening grip.

He yanked hard and Ashton felt like her hip bone nearly came out of its socket. Instant panic spiked inside of her as she scraped her fingers against the slick metal trying to stop him.

"Wolfe, no! Don't!" But it was no use, she was ripped from the ventilation system and slammed against the wall like a rag doll. Ashton screamed as finally felt the full force of Wolfe's strength used against her. Fear made her eyes panic as she looked at the man she loved dearly, not seeing him anymore. His crystal blue eyes had darkened, and she knew she'd lost him.

So, it left Ashton with no choice. She braced his shoulders and brought her knee up to Wolfe's groin—a defense move Wolfe had taught her during their time at Land of Legends. Instantly, Wolfe recoiled and dropped Ashton. He coughed and toppled off balance. Ashton took advantage of the moment and pushed him over and raced in the opposite direction of the ventilation system. She dodged bushes and trees while frantically looking for a new route to take to get away from him. Wolfe may have been stronger than she was, but she was faster and with the head start she could possibly get away— but not for long. She didn't dare look back and instead scanned ahead at her options.

Trees or water. In an instant she had to decide.

Trees.

Ashton quickly latched her gaze on one with low enough branches—probably not the most strategic move, but she was running out of options. Wolfe would catch up soon and her only hope was that he wouldn't see her climbing. Her breath was ragged from the intense beating of her heart and adrenaline running through her veins. She pulled herself up onto a branch, then the next, and next. She started gaining speed as she quickly glanced behind her. She didn't see Wolfe, but when she looked straight down, she saw his eyes targeting her. She could have screamed in frustration in that moment; Wolfe chasing her as an enemy was never a position she thought she would be in—again.

The air squeezed out of her lungs as she felt his presence gaining on her. She would run out of trees soon, *Maybe the water would have been better.* But the thought of either drowning or falling took hold and she felt the world was fighting against her. Sweat gathered, pooling down her face and back as her hands trembled from exhaustion. When Wolfe had pointed out she was thinner, that was true, but she was also weaker. The five-hour hike and initial two-hour swim had left her drained. But

Ashton wouldn't give in that quickly. She climbed higher. *Go faster! He's gaining on you,* her mind screamed.

Snap!

In an instant she slipped, trying to grasp onto anything near her but found nothing and fell, hitting the ground from at least ten feet up.

Ashton's stomach recoiled as the wind was knocked out of her and she could barely move from the force. Her vision went fuzzy. And then, her world went dark.

CHAPTER 28

Ashton

AUGLAND 44

Steam rose from Ashton's bath and swirled around her as she gazed ahead blankly, her mind occupied by last night's escape—or attempted escape. The taste of liberty and those precious moments with the real Wolfe replayed in her mind. Ashton had fallen from the tree, giving her a nasty concussion that was tended to once Wolfe managed to get her back to Warren's home. Warren's only comment when they returned was, "Serves her right."

Reuban was instructed to care for Ashton's medical needs, which he did but not without letting her know she needed to be ready for another UnSuited gathering later that evening. She berated him for the idea that she leave without Wolfe. His exact words in response were, "We might as well keep working—and that means another meeting tonight."

Ashton still had her reservations about Reuben, even though Wolfe had said he'd helped turn off Wolfe's CS chip and made it look like he did the same to hers. He'd also convinced Warren her fall had disrupted the chip, causing Wolfe to drag her back and had promised to have the doctor examine it—saving her from a rather unbelievable explanation. *That was a close one.*

Reuben hadn't divulged her secret blocking transmitter necklace to Warren and had also been someone she could talk to about Wolfe and the UnSuited. Although she appreciated his support, she would not be surprised if Reuben had some ulterior motive. She thought she should interrogate him more when they spoke of the iHumanist, but since she was often surrounded by Wolfe, Niall, or Warren when in Reuben's presence—there was little to no time for her questions. Plus, she had no friends and couldn't afford to push Reuben away with her suspicious behavior.

Instead of focusing on Reuben, Ashton needed to find a way to release Wolfe from Warren's hold again. After last night, it was unlikely that Warren would get drunk enough to forget about Wolfe's chip anytime soon. She mentally replayed how livid Warren was when they returned—verbally assaulting Wolfe for his attempt to leave. Warren left her alone, placing full blame on his son.

Ashton sighed. It was closing in on the ten p.m. deadline and Reuben would be waiting for her near the Augland 44 pub.

Rising and letting the warm water drip from her, Ashton wrapped the plush robe around herself and found clean clothes ready for her to change into.

Her friends drifted through her thoughts, one by one. They seemed to spend their days waiting for things to change. Ashton couldn't help but think the worst. *What if the waiting was never ending—and what if nothing about this life ever changed?* Ashton shivered in fear at the thought. Nothing about her day-to-day thoughts and movements were normal. And if they couldn't escape, then she had a riot to incite—beginning with an escort from Reuben and meeting with UnSuited members after the house quieted for the night.

A soft knock disrupted her thoughts.

"Ashton?" The voice wasn't more than a whisper. Her hope was Wolfe, possibly again woken from Warren's spell, or Niall, who she hoped would come out of his nightmarish CS haze, which hadn't happened yet. "It's Reuben."

Ashton sighed, still lost in her thoughts. She wished she could stop all this. She wanted to press pause on her life and curl into her bed. She wanted to turn off her emotions and pretend like it didn't bother her that Wolfe was back under Warren's control, or that Joao was in Augland pretending to be an extension of Warren for who knew how long.

In her solitude it was safe to face her fears, but out there with Warren, Reuben, Wolfe, and Niall, she had to be much stronger than she felt.

"Just two minutes." Her voice cracked, but she cleared her throat, hoping Reuben didn't notice. If she let Reuben see her like this, he'd lecture her on the "greater purpose" or how the 'iHumanist had a plan and she needed to be patient, and her personal favorite, "stay strong." Her forced alliance with Reuben perplexed her. One moment she felt she could trust him and the next she was sure his smooth talk was filled with venomous manipulation—like Warren.

Ashton needed to pull herself together. She finally blinked, letting the remnants of her sadness well up and disappear all in one drop and swipe. She dressed in black leggings and a sweatshirt and pulled the hood around her face. She opened the door to face a similarly disguised Reuben, also in black attire to shade his movements.

"I thought we were meeting near the pub," Ashton whispered.

"I know, but I wanted to check in on you first. Are you okay?" Reuben's face showed concern. Reuben, most of the time, stayed in the same residence as Warren, and the current bungalow was one of those instances. Warren rarely invited Reuben to attend campaign dinners unless Warren was away, which Ashton thought was odd. But that wasn't why Reuben had asked if she was okay. No doubt it was her attempt to flee, falling from a tree and her concussion. Even though he had not been at their table, she had no doubt he had heard the commotion the night of Wolfe and Ashton's breakout attempt.

"I'm fine, Reuben." Her body shifted past Reuben as he scrutinized her carefully. It was times like these that she was convinced Reuben cared more about her than he let on, but if true she refused to let that cloud her judgment. While he was thoughtful and caring, she knew he had his own agenda.

The old pub was smaller than the other UnSuited venues, but it was far enough away from any Suits that it would do. Some Auglands had worker-specific areas of recreation, and bars like this one were a popular choice.

It was packed inside, which was to be expected. Workers from all Augland 44 parks were gathered, waiting for Ashton. She still wasn't sure how Reuben was able to get messages out to them for these meetings, especially so last minute. But she was pleasantly surprised by the turnout. The large-scale support and attendance had given her the status she needed. She would never have guessed that after her dangerous Apparel escape, she would be here, leading a revolution.

Commanding attention and leading the UnSuited wasn't as easy as someone might have thought. No one knew what she looked like, only that she was someone who claimed to have started the rebellion in Augland 54. Every pair of eyes followed her as she walked into the noisy room. She stood at the edge of the room, trying to mask her anxiety and hoping no one could hear how loudly her heart was beating inside her chest as the room went silent. Reuben insisted that he stay back at the car—which was most likely a good thing. It would be hard to explain her relationship with an Executive Suit of Augland 54 while leading a rebellion against the C-Suite.

Ashton surveyed the room and held her chin high with the most confidence she could muster, looking for their spokesperson. She could always tell who they were by their suspicious glare.

There he was—a young man with a dimpled chin and crooked nose, like it had been broken two or three times. He analyzed her carefully before pushing through the crowd. He walked directly up to her until he was standing too close for comfort, and for a moment she wanted to step back from his imposing presence. But Reuben said any kind of deference would show weakness, so she bravely remained in place and tried to take up as much space as possible.

"So, you're the redhead then." *Woman in red,* Ashton corrected mentally. She had heard it all now. Fire Wielder, Red Ash, Axe Woman . . .

"Ashton is fine." She hated the nicknames people insisted on assigning to her.

"And why should I let you speak to *my* UnSuited?" He had sandy brown hair that swept across his eyes. Ashton thought he couldn't be much older than her—maybe a year or two.

"I'm only here to bring a message, hoping to unite all Augland UnSuited together," Ashton stated firmly.

"You're younger than I thought you'd be." It came out more like a criticism than a surprise.

"And?"

He gave a quiet laugh. "These people will listen to *me,* and only me, so let's get that straight first. You're here to convince me, and then I'll decide who we follow."

"And who are *you*?" Ashton asked, giving him as much attitude as he was dishing out to her.

"Aiden."

There was a long pause while he stared back at her, attempting to intimidate her with his raised eyebrows and silent glare. Ashton was not flustered in the least. Aiden had no idea what she had lived through, and what she had done to survive. Knowing how much hung in the balance, Ashton wouldn't let him feel he was in charge—him of all people—especially since she refused to cower before someone as powerful as Warren.

"Well, Aiden, if you feel you can take down Augland 44 without help, then, by all means, go for it . . . but I have a suspicion that you're starting to see your numbers dwindle the longer CEO Tasley paints you as a problem. I imagine he's ordered search parties to hunt your group. No doubt, he's already interrogating people to discover the name of the man that leads this UnSuited. My sources say that he's calling in favors with other CEOs to help with his . . . UnSuited problem." At this, the color drained from Aiden's face. But despite her statement, Aiden didn't let the scowl fade from his face.

After thinking over her words, Aiden scoffed before stepping to the side to allow Ashton room to access the stage. Now, this was the part she truly hated: standing up in front of a group of strangers. She had given herself a mental pep talk earlier, when walking from the car to the meeting spot. The steps creaked beneath her feet as she moved herself to center stage. The room was still silent, except for a few snickering whispers, as everyone waited in anticipation for what she would say. She stepped forward into the dust-filtered light that illuminated the raised platform.

"Hello . . ." Ashton began, her eyes grazing across the many different faces of Augland 44. No one smiled, no one moved, but at least the snickers had died down. But now the silence was deafening. Aiden crossed his arms as he leaned against the bar top from among the audience.

"My name is Ashton and I'm from Augland 54, where I *was* a worker. First, I think it's important to explain why UnSuited began in Augland 54. I know my story might sound different, compared to the life you are living here, but it really is the same experience we've all had. Not long ago, I was sent to a 'rehabilitation' park, Land of Legends, where the Suits would kill people—flat out kill. They created a 'game' for the Suits . . . we were on a battlefield and they'd . . . just . . . kill people. Us. For fun." *You need to work on your synonyms.*

"My friend was forced onto the battlefield and when a Suit attacked her, something moved in me. I can't explain it, but it was in that moment I felt deep in my being this wasn't how we were supposed to live. That our purpose was greater. We are more than just pawns to be played with for their entertainment." Her words generated some nods around the room.

"I did escape—barely, but I wanted to rescue others from the Augland world and show them there is life outside. A different life than we've all been living, where we have independence. There are colonies of people living and thriving outside these walls. I came back and experienced firsthand at the Executive level what they are willing to do to ensure our servitude: installing chips in our minds to make us comply." Ashton's mind flashed to a vision of Wolfe, as he finally took a deep breath and momentarily relaxed after Warren had turned off his CS chip. His mind was in a prison *of the worst kind*.

"I'm telling you, this not because I think my story is unique, but to show you that I know Auglands just don't want your body to experiment on and torture. They want your mind. They want to destroy your thoughts, your feelings, your autonomy. And if it hasn't happened here yet, it will soon."

Ashton's voice rose above its typical octave. "Gone are the days that you have any liberties at all because they will strip you of everything."

Shouts of outrage spewed from the audience as they became infuriated with the news. Ashton's breath quickened, because she too felt their anger. She felt their pain. "What gives them the right?" She paused. "What gives them the idea that we will go willingly?" Ashton felt like she was no longer trying to convince the crowd of her leadership ability, or their need to understand the depth of evil that Augland was planning for them. This moment, in front of 44, was for Ashton to release what she had held captive inside—after being stifled by Warren for so long.

"Augland has tried everything to break my spirit and body. When I was sent to Apparel, they thought they had broken me. They abducted and murdered my best friend. They killed a little girl in front of me to shatter my will to live. But guess what?!" The room's rumbling continued to escalate. "They couldn't! And we escaped and survived. We fought them and they fought back, but you know what? They want to destroy UnSuited because they fear what we are capable of." Ashton could swear she felt the floor vibrate as stomps reverberated within the wooden flooring.

She was invigorated. She channeled her own anger to show them that they too held the same power.

"You know what terrifies them? Our numbers! So, are you done with their control?!" Ashton shouted.

"Yes!" the crowd shouted back.

"Are you going to allow Augland to enslave you anymore?"

"No!"

"Do *you* deserve to live a great life?" Ashton yelled, mocking the Augland slogan.

"Yes!"

Ashton recalled the speech Reuben had made and rehearsed with her countless times. "Then I ask each of you: when the time comes . . . will you join with me, and the rest of the UnSuited, to take over their Augnation and set ourselves free? To build a society we deserve! Our rights honored; our autonomy guaranteed." The roof felt like it might fly off from the excitement and passion crackling through the air. Ashton would soar on this high for the rest of the evening, and it was exactly what she needed to erase the memory of that night's horrible dinner with Warren.

"Keep wreaking the havoc you cause! Make them pay in every way—even down to the smallest petty action because when we are finally united, we, the UnSuited across Auglands, will be unstoppable."

Red!

Red!

Red!

Red!

They all chanted "Red"—paying homage to her Land of Legends moniker. Ashton put her hand up to quiet them and shifted her attention to Aiden, motioning for him to join her on stage.

"Aiden will send out the message when the time comes and we'll have our plan of attack ready. I can't tell you when—maybe days, months, a year. But the time will come, and we *will* be free." It undid the crowd all over again, and Aiden raised his hands up to show his support. Winning over 44 tonight was an absolute victory—much like their previous meetings with the UnSuited groups hidden in pockets all over the Auglands. *Let's just hope this works.* Ashton's high suddenly peaked and took a sharp dive down. She hated thinking this could all be a ruse, but in response to this fear she reminded herself that, so far, Reuben had stayed true to his promises. She had every hope that they would soon be sovereign.

———————

With only an hour for their clandestine meeting, Ashton focused on socializing among the group, meeting as many members as she could.

"That was better than I expected," Aiden declared in a surprised tone as he approached her. His demeanor had changed since their initial interaction. Though it was possible he still didn't believe her story, he appeared to support their cause and that was good enough for her. Ashton smiled, still slightly buzzed from the adrenaline coursing through her nervous system, reliving the uproar of the UnSuited support.

"I'm glad you found me." She pulled an interconnect from her canvas backpack. "This is how we will communicate; other leaders are on channel 45912. It's without Augland interference. Do not use it until I contact you—it's strictly for sending the signal to get ready," Ashton warned. Reuben had cautioned her about limiting contact with the leaders, which for some UnSuited, raised suspicion when given their interconnect. But Aiden seemed content. She agreed with Reuben—if Warren ever found out about the channel, all their hard work, sacrifices, sleepless nights and time spent with the UnSuited would be for nothing.

"I need to go. I can't stay here long, but we will be in touch Aiden." Ashton smiled as she handed him the device. He held it carefully and looked at Ashton almost reverently—needing proof this was real. Ashton was real and the rebellion was real. Ashton couldn't help but feel the rollercoaster of emotions as the hype began to fade and she remembered what she'd felt only hours ago—hopelessness.

"This is really happening then." Aiden's smile grew.

Ashton smiled back but couldn't help the twinge of guilt and doubt—especially if Reuben was somehow manipulating her. Ashton had mostly agreed to help because she didn't believe the UnSuited had the numbers that would warrant a war, but now that they had gained traction, this was becoming much bigger than even Ashton could have hoped.

Aiden headed back to his group of UnSuited. Ashton noted the time and left.

Ashton walked along a dark, beaten dirt path toward the vehicle Reuben had commandeered for them and quickly climbed inside. Reuben looked up from his interconnect.

"So?" he asked as she melted into the leather seat of the VELIC automatic car from exhaustion.

"Done." Ashton sighed in relief.

"And you gave the leader the interconnect?"

"Of course I did." It was late and Ashton was tired but tried not to sound annoyed.

"Good job." He concentrated his attention on the road. "And how are you feeling?"

"Fine."

"Your speeches are truly inspirational. You're sounding more and more like a true leader, Ash. Night and day from when we first started."

Ashton didn't say anything. She knew Reuben liked to listen in, somehow, to the meetings.

"I was hoping you would escape, you know?" Reuben sighed, as if the confession caused him pain.

"I'm surprised you helped. Given that you've been so explicit that you need me to rally the UnSuited."

"Well, if I would have known you'd blossom into the speaker we saw tonight, I might have thought differently." Reuben chuckled at his comment. Ashton eyed him, not loving the comment.

Reuben cleared his throat. "We would have found another way." That realization stung, not that she needed to be the face of the rebellion. She'd much rather have her freedom. But, to have *purpose* revitalized her, like it had tonight.

"Is that why you helped Wolfe? So I could escape?"

"Yes and no. I knew he wanted that more than anything—for your safety primarily. Wolfe could use less distraction and you both have powerful people rooting for you who requested my aid in your escape." Reuben remained cryptic in his messaging.

"Yet you knew that he couldn't come with me. You knew he'd leave me." Ashton turned so she faced Reuben.

"You're hell bent on making me the enemy, Ashton," Reuben's accusation hung in the air. "I'm not your enemy and the sooner you begin—" He was about to say *trust*, but Ashton stopped him. She was done talking about Wolfe to Reuben.

"Listen, I'm the one putting my name on the line, promising these workers they have hope! That we are bringing them a reason to hope and offering the solution for how to break out of this horrible reality. You couldn't even help us break out of Warren's control! How are we going to instigate and succeed in a coup?" That may have been a tad harsh. Frustrated, Reuben drove, taking full control of the system that was fully capable of navigating toward home without a driver. When they rode with Warren, VELICs controlled the automatic car, but Reuben had said he didn't want the location recorded on the VELIC system in case Warren checked the history.

Ashton went on, "I want to believe that what you say is true, that you want to help me, help Wolfe, and the UnSuited. That the whole iHumanist movement does have the workers' best interest, but I need something besides your word."

Reuben stared intently at her. "You want blackmail?"

"If that's what you want to call it. I want information of high value to the iHumanist as collateral. The UnSuited workers are beginning to trust me and I'm gaining their support without knowing whether or not your story is true or made up to manipulate me. I've been tricked too many times, Reuben. I won't keep making promises to the UnSuited with only your word to guarantee any iHumanist support."

Ashton sensed Reuben's disappointment, but he quickly hid his emotions under a blank stare. Three weeks had passed with Ashton trusting *the process*—as Reuben phrased their symbiotic relationship. She feared now more than ever that her work with UnSuited would make them vulnerable and that Reuben could easily exploit all of them in the end. She refused to blindly trust *anyone* ever again, not when people like Warren, the Senators, and the AEC existed. She knew first-hand how dangerous it was to her very existence to trust without proof.

Reuben chuckled in amusement. "You've learned so much. I can't say I'm not a little proud." Reuben's smile was innocent. "Sure, Ashton. If you want reassurance, collateral, I'll give it to you." Ashton sighed with relief. Hearing that eased some of her stress and dampened her theory that Reuben might be playing a game with her.

The house was quiet when they returned. Reuben hurried to his bedroom and Ashton did as well, but only to give Reuben the appearance she was going to bed. When Ashton heard the click of Reuben's door shutting, she knew it was safe for her to slip into Wolfe's room. She stood silently in the hall, straining to hear if there were sounds of anyone else awake. The only sounds she heard were the waves lapping in the background.

She tip-toed to his door, opening it slowly to make sure he was in a deep sleep. If Wolfe woke up before she was able to touch him, he could panic and raise the alarm, exposing their late-night meetings. Warren would find this especially odd given that he had turned her chip on after dinner. Her behavior would alert him that her chip was suspiciously malfunctioning again after Reuben had convinced him the doctor had fixed it after her fall.

During the first week of the campaign, Ashton had left Wolfe alone, but she became increasingly lonely as the nights passed and had begun a routine of sneaking into his room she missed him. She would enter his room and draw him close before he woke up. Her necklace worked its magic as long as it touched them both.

Ashton held her breath and stepped into Wolfe's room. At that moment, he was still asleep as she crept to his bed and put her head close to his soft features. In sleep, he wasn't locked away from her. His eyes were shut, and his body relaxed. She eased herself next to him and made sure the necklace was on both their skins before stroking his hair. He slowly drifted out of his slumber and with a start, his eyes snapped open in alarm, his chest heaving with labored breaths.

"Shhh . . . it's okay, you're okay," Ashton whispered.

Wolfe's eyes darted around the dark room in confusion before he landed on Ashton and his posture softened in relief. His eyes began to water with the inevitable relief and sadness of these moments. "You okay? I saw the fall after Warren turned on the chip . . ." He wrapped his arms around Ashton, leaving no space between them as he took deep, steady breaths.

"I'm fine, Wolfe," she said, breathing in and allowing the silence to engulf them. Instantly, she could feel his guilt following their failed escape attempt and that was the last thing she wanted him to feel when he was with her.

"You remember that time in Hood Canal, you—" Ashton quietly chuckled at the memory, "were crabbing for the first time and the trap you set had flipped upside down in the water as you brought it up and our dinner escaped." Wolfe's breath lightened as her hand wrapped around his bare chest and lightly touched his head, which now lay across her shoulder.

"Yeah, I got so mad. Dove in after the crab. I think I still have the scar from his pinchers."

"You aren't a bad human crab trap." Ashton could feel his smile spread across his face as he rested against her.

"You're never going to let that one go, are you?"

"Never . . . wait until we get back and I tell Joao. I think I've kept your secret long enough," Ashton joked and Wolfe had to muffle his laughter. "Shh . . ." Ashton said while restraining her own giggles.

"You wouldn't dare." Ashton smiled. *Try me.* The darkness surrounded them as they held each other, and Ashton let the silence take him for the moment.

"You sure you're okay?" Ashton hadn't even noticed that Wolfe had tilted his head up toward her, knowing something was off balance.

"You promised we were going to do this together . . . you lied to me. And I need you to swear that you won't, ever, try that again. We get out of here together, Wolfe," Ashton scolded.

"Ash." His brows scrunched in sadness, and he traced a finger across her cheek.

"I'm worried you're losing yourself and every day, I'm afraid I'm going to wake up and see what I see in Niall. See that you've stopped fighting. And I'm afraid if you stop fighting . . . I will too. I just want so bad for us to go back to—" Ashton couldn't finish her sentence. "And that means not giving up. That means not abandoning each other."

"Stop that. I'm not done fighting, and neither are you." Ashton needed his confirmation because she could not do this without him.

"So, no more secret attempts to get rid of me?"

There was a long pause before he finally gave in. "I swear."

Satisfied with Wolfe's vow, she stilled her anxious thoughts. Ashton wouldn't need to bring this subject up again, and relief spread through her body. They fell into the silence and slept until the early morning. Wolfe hated it when she fell asleep in his bed—it was too risky. Warren could wake up and notice that his CS wasn't engaged, but tonight they both needed to be held and falling asleep in each other's arms was worth the risk.

The sun rose and peeked above the crashing waves. It was the same way they had woken up many times in Hood Canal with Ashton's red curls sprawled across the pillow, and her face laying on Wolfe's rising and falling chest. She glanced up at him, his face soft and at peace. For the first time in so long she finally saw in daylight the unbothered, unworried, and unchipped side of Wolfe. They were playing a danger-ous game—it was early and Warren would be up any minute. For just the briefest of moments she let him be. She soaked in this pure side of Wolfe—the man she loved dearly and would soon miss as their night together ended. She gently moved herself away from him and as soon as the rock around her neck travelled only inches from him his face tensed and she knew the Customer Service chip had taken its hold on him again. Her stomach twisted, but she whispered defiantly.

"I won't let him have you much longer."

CHAPTER 29

Rye

Rye was startled awake by an early morning dream, only to find the faint hum from his computer at his side. His office had been transformed into his living quarters at night as he was letting Versal stay at his house—not that he had time to go home. Augland security had commandeered many of the NeuroEnergy homes for their hopefully temporary stay in NeuroEnergy.

He could almost laugh when thinking back on his previous life. If he thought Georgina's nine a.m. to six p.m. hours were long, they were nothing compared to the brutal expectations of Augland 54 personnel.

––––––––

Augland security arrived swiftly at NeuroEnergy and were met with limited resistance as they overtook their entire operation. At first, they scoured the offices for memos, technology, classified information, and, of course, the scientist, which they didn't find. Rye had destroyed everything that remotely pertained to satellites, STEMP, and Vic's work—well, mostly everything.

Before Wolfe left, he called an emergency meeting with Joao, Hunter, and Rye. In the room they discussed how and what Warren knew about the STEMP project. Joao admitted he had been unknowingly chipped by Warren and supplied him with all their secrets that would have made Augland's demise quick and seamless. Wolfe was relentless about changing their tactic and allowing the overtake of Northwest NeuroEnergy to serve the bigger picture and aid in their countermove.

The *new normal* weighed heavily on him. At first Rye was locked in his office while they covertly tortured him for information. Warren's instructions included the Augland guards subjecting every NeuroEnergy employee to distress until they cracked and confessed to where the scientist was hiding.

Fortunately, Vic's hiding place was kept confidential and it was only Rye who knew of his location. He would not throw away what he and his team had worked toward just for Warren's cronies to swoop in and steal victory from their hands. Shortly after the takeover, NeuroEnergy employees couldn't step foot beyond their homes without being escorted by Augland 54 security guards. But after weeks with no activity or information gleaned, the rules had become more relaxed. Rye, and the other directors had more privileges. But Rye took no unnecessary chances. Augland security had gained access to the still-functioning security cameras around the compound that had not been damaged by the water. As one of the men who had installed them, he knew the distance and scope of each one that was still active.

Rye's watch dinged, which told him it was time for breakfast, that is if any supplies had arrived from Augland. He didn't care about breakfast as much as the company it provided—breakfast meant he would get to see Versal. He told himself it was because he had promised Hunter that he would take care of her that he sought her out, but it was for selfish reasons he did so. She was beautiful, funny, and sophisticated—and the list went on. Versal was a bright light in the darkened sky, and he couldn't help but be drawn to her. He couldn't understand why she was in love with Hunter. Hunter had charm, much more than Rye possessed, but he was arrogant, insufferably sarcastic, and selfish—his mouth alone had almost gotten him killed in Augland 54. Hunter had worked for Rye as an engineer before his mission to infiltrate Augland 54 for the energy secrets, and if he was honest with himself, Rye blamed NeuroEnergy's "situation" on Hunter.

His mind drifted back to Versal and how her smile was so becoming. She was always asking for updates or whether Rye had heard from Hunter. He was forced to lie and say he hadn't—no one could know Hunter and Rye were communicating.

Rye cursed himself for being distracted by Versal—like in this moment when he should be keeping NeuroEnergy safe. But even when he actively didn't want to think of her, his brain refused to cooperate, and he found himself lost in daydreams. Rye needed to focus, there were so many moving pieces he needed to manage, and *everything* needed to go as planned or his people would suffer even more. Every detail, every piece of information he researched was fed to Augland's pursuit of information about STEMP and the separate investigation into the workers' infertility. He focused on the infertility because it limited them from pressing for more STEMP information. Versal, while a beautiful distraction, was just that.

He straightened out the wrinkles that had formed on his once-pressed, button-up shirt and adjusted his sweater vest. Rye tried to focus but there were several tabs on his AI glasses that he had opened late the previous night to do more research before falling asleep. Taking off his glasses, Rye rose and headed for his office door.

"Morning, Jay." Rye opened the door and spoke to the guard stationed just outside. Rye began walking toward the elevator and Jay, his personal security guard, followed him. Jay didn't ask where he was headed because it was routine to go to the cafeteria promptly at eight-thirty a.m. every morning.

"You weren't out long. Feels like you're going for a record number of hours worked in a week."

"Well, my new *boss* is relentless. Told me I have till the end of the week to find him something about this fictitious scientist he's convinced we are somehow hiding when security has literally swept every inch of this place." Rye was referring to Warren. His threats, parroted by the guards, were crystal clear. At least Jay was one of the good ones; Rye preferred being followed by him to any of the others.

"He knows you're hiding *something*. You don't just work that close with Georgina and know nothing about her secret dealings."

That's where Jay and Warren were both wrong. It wasn't Georgina who had developed the secret program to shut down Suits. It was him. He knew he must divulge some information and planned to release crumbs of details that he wanted Warren to know. The information would be false, of course, and hopefully send Augland forces on a wild goose chase. Until he developed a strategy, he was under pressure. That was the reason he had been up all night. He didn't know what details to give up, and time was ticking. Rye chose not to respond, opting instead to walk in silence.

———

The cafeteria bustled with activity, as usual. The once-virtual library had been deconstructed to create an open space for a cafeteria of sorts. The first few days the Augland soldiers had refused to feed them until someone stepped forward with information about the scientist. But after the first week and with no news of the scientist, Augland forces had shifted focus to the fertility viability research, giving them a reason to feed the NeuroEnergy employees. Now their allotment was two meals a day which was barely enough to sustain them. One egg and a handful of beans.

Rye walked amongst the clanking of forks against plates. He was late and there most likely wouldn't be much food to choose from before all breakfast options were gone. He scanned the room until he found her, *Versal*. She looked beautiful. Her long, dark hair swayed in waves as she moved gracefully, greeting one employee after another down the rows of tables. Everyone at NeuroEnergy loved her; it was hard not to. She was kind, magnetic, and focused on serving those around her, finding ways to bring joy to others rather than dedicating her own resources for her benefit alone. Rye saw it, though. She was getting worn down, just like the rest of them. He rarely used this time to approach her directly. Actually talking to her was out of the question; he was far too intimidated. Besides, it wasn't smart. *She's a distraction. And if they know I care about her or consider Versal a friend, they'll use that against me—and her.*

Just at that moment, Versal eyed him and began to walk in his direction. Rye could feel his palms begin to sweat as she walked toward him. If he didn't redirect, she would run right into him. *So awkward,* he groaned inwardly. He slowed his steps, but it was too late. Her eyes glided up and met his gaze. Rye's cheeks grew warm from her stare.

"Rye!" Her grin grew wide, and her eyes crinkled at the edges in a genuine smile. Rye melted—but his face remained emotionless.

"Versal." He said so matter-of-factly, hiding his admiration for her.

"You'd better hurry, breakfast rations are a little low today. I can grab some if you'd like." She spoke so sweetly that he felt badly to even decline her offer.

"No, no, I'll be fine, but thank you." She lingered for a moment, not saying anything but he knew what her questions were—he could see them in her eyes. She wanted to know if there was word from Hunter. Realizing he was little more than a conduit to deliver news about Hunter, his eyes dropped to the floor—he didn't want Versal to read the disappointment on his face. She was just using him to gain information.

"Better go. I'll see you around, Versal."

"Yes . . . see you around." The disappointment clouding her expression was palpable. He needed to separate her from Hunter, even if that breached the agreement between the two.

Rye finished breakfast in a hurry, leaving him completely unsatisfied—as per usual. The egg and beans only gave his cavernous hunger a few minutes of satisfaction before the aching need for substance returned. *You were lucky you got anything,* he told himself.

"Rye, boss wants another update. Anything new from yesterday's findings?" Jay asked.

"No, I mean we thought of a new avenue of utilizing pods as a source to contain a fetus, but we would need an actual pod to test that theory. We believe that once the fetus has matured to a certain degree, it can sustain life in the uterus. If Warren is willing to supply testing pods . . . and maybe some additional technol—"

"That's not what he wanted to know." Jay interrupted him.

Rye figured that Jay wanted to know about the STEMP project but he would not be forthcoming with any of that information.

"I guess you're going to need to be more specific, Jay." Rye said sarcastically, now one full stride in front of Jay on their way back to the office. The thing was, their resources were focused on fertility research because without Vic, they were helpless to improve on the STEMP project. Vic was the only tech scientist in the region who knew about the pre-war government connections to satellites. Without Vic, they couldn't build intelligently on what already existed. Rye paused and slowed his gait even though he had reached the steps of headquarters. He could give them something benign to mull over, but he would need to ensure it wouldn't backfire, and that would take a quick call. Jay glanced over at him with a neutral expression,

"Guess he's getting tired of waiting. My boss says that he's flying in a VELIC system, one from DC to help start up and monitor interrogations again." Jay's tone was almost empathetic.

"That might get someone to crack, if what you want is truly out there." Rye knew of VELICs and the ones in the DC market recorded everything. They'd have less liberties soon by the sound of things, but then the thought hit him.

"Just the software?"

"Nah, they'll send androids to install. It's like twenty boxes that will be stationed around NeuroEnergy. Might take a few days for every building to have it." Jay pulled a foiled-up breakfast burrito from his pocket and opened it, taking a massive bite. It reminded Rye how well the security guards were fed and treated compared to his people.

"Hmm," was all Rye could say. During the late nights spent with Forest, Hunter, and Vic in his "supervisory" role, Rye hadn't absorbed all the technical details of the project—but he did recall Forest mentioning that they would have to crack through VELIC technology in order to capture control of more satellites. If VELICs were coming to NeuroEnergy and Forest needed to hack through their firewall, having one nearby might help them achieve STEMP success faster.

"What is it?" Jay looked at Rye, whose mouth gaped open as he was deep in thought over VELIC's impending arrival, and how this could be used to their advantage.

Rye quickly shut his mouth and turned to Jay. "You know Jay, not feeling great. I think the lack of sleep is catching up to me. Mind if I go back to my home office, maybe take a shower?" Rye asked. He wouldn't have gotten away with that request with any other security guard, but Jay was actually a decent person.

"Really, man?" Rye looked down at his watch, noting it was almost ten a.m., which meant that Jay's shift was about over. He was Jay's overnight watch and Augland security quarters were on the other end of the compound, across campus from where Rye stayed.

"Is Sal taking over for you? Just have him meet me at my place. You can head out. I'm just taking a quick shower to try and wake myself up so I can be more productive today. I'll be good after that and can hopefully hit my metrics." He had built trust with the guards and used this trust to his advantage, when necessary, which gave him some liberties.

"Uh . . . yeah, I mean, I'll just have him meet you there. I don't want to have to walk all the way back over here in ten minutes. Just don't do anything stupid."

"Scout's honor." Rye innocently smiled at him.

"All right man, see you tonight."

"I'll see you later. Get some rest, man."

Immediately Rye's thoughts returned to what Jay had revealed. VELICs were data and security systems with a feature that supported any ask of Suits. It was AI everywhere that recorded, tracked, and deciphered movements, speech patterns—everything. Rye knew the dangers of having a VELIC in his NeuroEnergy, but was conscious there might be an advantage if he was able to gain access to one onsite.

Rye practically ran to his dormitory, trying hard to avoid suspicion from his quick pace. All he needed was five minutes to get this communication out. He casually walked to his bathroom, locked the door and turned on the shower. He left the shower running and crouched on the tile floor near the toilet. Prying up a chunk of tile by a loose edge, he carefully lifted out the interconnect that would route directly to Hunter. Interconnects were confiscated the moment the Augland guards took over, but Rye had stealthily hidden this one—and so far, had not been caught.

"Hunter," Rye whispered, tapping on the connect button.

Silence.

"Hunter, it's Rye." Rye whispered louder this time. Again, he was met with silence. Rye looked at his watch, noting it was three minutes till ten when the new guard's watch would begin. There was no doubt that Jay had given Sal the message.

"Hunt—"

"Of course it's you . . . who else would it be." That was the sarcastic humor Rye despised.

"Any luck with the satellites?" Rye asked.

Hunter exhaled. "Still just the five we were able to get prior to escaping. Forest says he needs access to the direct system or something like that. He's working on it, and hopefully soon he'll be able to access more satellites . . ."

"If I have a VELIC here and work on accessing its mainframe, could Forest use that?" Hunter didn't answer, presumably relaying the question to Forest and Vic.

"Forest says if you have access to a VELIC, that it would be helpful. But Rye, only Augland DC has VELICs . . ."

"Okay . . . tell him they are sending a VELIC to NeuroEnergy and to message over instructions on what I need to do here so you can bypass their systems to access the satellite coordinates."

"Oh, seriously! Yeah man, I'll get them working overtime. I'm done with this place." Hunter perked up with the good news, and so did the adrenaline within Rye.

"Good, I'll be in touch."

"Wait! Rye, how's Versal? They aren't hurting her, right?"

Rye hated being the middleman in their relationship, especially given his newfound crush on Versal.

"She's fine . . . I mean, she's good. Saw her today," Rye answered, trying to keep his tone even.

"She say anything?" Hunter questioned and Rye could feel the longing in his now soft-spoken question.

"No, just . . . was there in the cafeteria, said hi, but she's fine . . . Hunter, I have to go. I'll be in contact soon." The knock sounded right at ten a.m. and Rye quickly turned off the interconnect and returned it back under the tile. Sal had a key—even to the bathroom—and could open the door at any moment. Rye hastily disrobed and stepped into the shower, right as the door opened slightly, as if on cue.

"Do you mind? Just finishing up," Rye said as he peeked behind the shower curtain, meeting Sal's suspicious gaze.

"I swear I heard voices."

"Nope. Just me . . . I talk to myself in the shower. Helps me think—." Rye's voice nearly cracked on the lie.

There was a pause, but soon Sal shut the door completely, and Rye sighed in relief. Now, he needed to figure out how to break into the VELIC system before it could be used to find Hunter and Vic—because while he'd never reveal the secret of Vic and Forest, VELIC could and would force him.

CHAPTER 30

Warren

AUGLAND 13

"We leave at eight tomorrow morning for Augland 27 . . . I'm looking forward to being back on the West Coast," Warren announced to Reuben before taking a long draw of his cigar as he sat on the bow of the eighty-foot yacht. It was a short stay in Augland 13, only about a day and a half before they would leave for Augland 27, which would take them to the desert-themed Augland.

The campaign was taking too long. They had been travelling across the nation for a month and there was new chatter of other CEOs running for AEC President. And as Georgina spent more time rotting in an AEC prison, her sympathizers would have time to rally and save her life or find evidence against her involvement. So, Warren had decided to expedite these trips and begin targeting the CEOs that would likely vote against him.

Reuben strolled up to Warren and took a seat next to him, handing him a glass of whiskey as the sun set. The deep orange bled across the water horizon. It almost looked like the line dividing the ocean and sky was on fire as it swayed in reaction to the waves. Augland 13 had only four parks to choose from: the Isles de Beautés, Secret Garden, Land of Gods and Goddesses, and Little Rome. Warren nearly always stayed in beach-themed parks—and 13 was notorious for Isles de Beautés and its near-perfect clear waters, white sandy beaches, and mountainside chateaus surrounded by luscious green trees.

Every twist and turn of the last few weeks weighed heavily as Warren drew in his breath and exhaled.

Killing Beaugard.

Groveling at the feet of other CEOs to gain support.

Ordering the murder of those who would not vote for him.

Balancing his home life with Wolfgang.

The sun threatened to disappear as the water cradled the boat.

"We should be all set for our meeting tomorrow with CEO Cea'vine. It took some convincing for her to agree on a meeting with me."

"You have one of those for me?" Reuben asked. Warren tossed over a cigar that Reuben caught easily.

"How's Ashton? She asked to leave for bed early this evening," Warren noted. Ashton hadn't been herself since he had turned on Wolfgang's chip four days earlier, during dinner. She had been more reserved and sulkier.

Reuben gave a slight smile. "Didn't know you cared."

Warren shrugged. "She's feisty, that's for sure. I guess I'm surprised that I've taken a liking to her—I wasn't expecting that to happen." He took a swig of his whiskey and let the smooth and sweet scent of vanilla and buttery notes of caramel run down his throat. It paired nicely with the smokey oak flavor of the cigar.

"I've noticed you keep her Customer Service chip off during the day."

"She knows it's there if she decides to act out. I'm pleased she's chosen to play nice." Warren took another long draw of his cigar.

"So why keep Wolfgang under? You can see he's suffering. He's not succumbing to its' commands as all the others have," Reuben questioned.

Warren paused. He knew exactly why he hadn't turned it off. Wolfgang pushed every boundary and bristled under every instruction. Of course, it wasn't his fault that Wolfgang couldn't see the bigger picture. He would someday, and by then, Warren would have his son back. Their relationship had always been rocky and untenable, but once Warren became AEC President, he could show his son the power he truly possessed as an heir. Warren's path to success was methodical and carefully designed. For Wolfgang to reach his potential as a leader, he would need to first be broken. Between trying to overthrow him as CEO and blowing up the Centauri star, there was significant damage to Warren's trust that would need to be repaired. He couldn't let those discretions go without consequences. He needed Wolfgang to surrender.

Reuben had seen the errors of siding with Wolfgang and had faced the consequences firsthand when he'd positioned Wolfgang as CEO the previous year. Reuben was the only other person who knew the truth—that Warren had created an AEB of Wolfgang, despite his public denial. Playing the long game, Reuben hadn't exposed Warren to the rest of the Executives—which had built a measure of trust between them. Warren had threatened Reuben against ever exposing him, and he had wisely kept that secret. While they had known each other for years, Warren refrained from bringing Reuben into all the inner workings of his grand plan.

"There is too much at risk right now. Once I'm President, he'll understand the reasons for my actions and what we are trying to create here. We need NeuroEnergy folded into Auglands and then he will see all the good that can come from our consolidation. The infertility solution is viable, and who knows, maybe expansions into other areas of technology could even be possible."

"What about the workers?" Reuben pressed, expelling a plume of smoke.

"What about them?"

"What's your plan?"

There was a pause while Warren thought how best to answer. "Customers have always said they prefer interacting with real humans over androids, which we can maintain with the Customer Service Initiative. VELICs will be key for Executives, but for customers, I don't see why we can't continue with our current operations. People like Ashton and her UnSuited will just need to adapt . . ." Warren tsked. "We are getting ahead of ourselves. We first need to worry about the vote for the Presidency, and it is rumored that Augland 13 has an alliance with Neuro-Energy. I need to convince them otherwise." Warren sighed, noting his cigar was nearly at the end. He was accustomed to Reuben's blind support and wasn't sure what angle he was working with his questions this evening. Warren would need to be vigilant while keeping an eye on Reuben.

It was a restless evening for Warren. His mind was occupied with numerous questions and nagging comments provided by Ashton and now Reuben. So, as soon as the sun rose the next morning, Warren summoned Wolfgang to his room. As commanded, Wolfgang's hair was combed and parted in a traditional style and his beard shaved as Warren had requested, with the CS chip forcing his compliance.

"How'd you sleep?"

"Fine, sir."

Warren lifted his interconnect and turned off Wolfgang's chip. His once tensed shoulders relaxed and he blinked while he eased into control over his movements.

"Stay calm. I wanted to talk to you."

Wolfgang remained still but his eyes glowered back at his father.

"I know how much discomfort you are in. I'd like to trust you without help from the chip, but your outbursts—when not under its influence—give me no choice. I can't trust you without it."

There was a pause while Wolfgang settled his fidgeting, composing himself after the long hours under the CS spell. Warren was making his best effort to connect with Wolfgang and dropped his guard for just a moment. But it was too soon. Wolfgang lunged at him with such ferocity and spontaneity that it surprised him. His fists came center with Warren's face, but the pain was barely noticeable. Warren recoiled, feeling his son's grasp on his shirt and the continuous pounding of knuckles against Warren's face. Wolfgang's blows slowed briefly, giving Warren an opportunity to push Wolfgang off him. He righted himself and came after his son, determined to correct this outburst. Wolfgang was prepared, arming himself with a nearby lamp and brandishing it toward Warren like an axe. Warren quickly shot his hand up to smack it away. He raised his fist and threw his best punch at Wolfgang, landing the blow above Wolfgang's right eye before he pivoted to the left and went for his gut. Wolfgang spit blood with more dripping from his face as his eye began to swell from the impact of Warren's fist.

I should stop, Warren thought. It wasn't a fair fight between them, but his rage took over. Wolfgang's anger only heightened. He composed himself and swung left, right, then left again. With the last blow, Warren put his hand up to his face and felt the bio-synthetic skin peeling from his cheek.

"Wolfgang, stop!" Any more damage and Warren would need to repair his AEB before continuing his campaign and that was time he did not have. "Or I'll put you back under." Wolfgang breathed heavily, blood spouting from his nose and lip, but he didn't seem to care. The adrenaline he felt only supported his urge to continue the fight, but reason appeared to set in, and he didn't want to lose moments of freedom, no matter how brief.

They stood in silence. Warren straightened his white linen button-up shirt and leaned his weight against the table.

"Feel better?" Warren asked.

"Got a good few blows in," Wolfgang said through ragged breaths.

"I don't feel pain, Wolfgang, you know that," Warren laughed.

"Doesn't mean it doesn't feel good."

"Anyways . . . as I was saying, I wanted to talk to you."

Wolfgang took a seat, spitting blood onto the ground and wiping away the remnants of their fight. "The Senators here at Augland 13 are NeuroEnergy advocates and have poisoned the CEO against supporting an Augland takeover."

"You want me to take care of the Senators . . ." It was a statement, not a question.

"Yes." Warren was direct, leaving no room for confusion with his order.

"And if I do this, you'll stop turning that thing on?" Wolfgang's anger was palpable.

"Yes, *if* you do this for me and *if* we have good behavior then I won't turn it back on. I want my son back. I've been open about that."

Wolfgang gave a small, ironic laugh as his fists tightened unconsciously. "So, the last month, living under control of the chip was to show me what *could* happen. Smart tactic, show me how much I don't want to live this way, and give me the chance to stop it from happening again . . . except now I become your *willing* assassin?" He referred to Warren forcing him to put the poison in Beaugard's feeding tube, strangle and stage suicide for Southwest NeuroEnergy CEO Roan, and drown CEO Chase and CEO Graingley in their own pods' plasma. Warren could have erased those memories, and maybe he would in the future, but he needed his son to know that one way or another, Warren's new reign and restructuring of society was going to happen and he'd prefer to have his son as a willing participant.

"You don't think the CEOs will connect you to the murders of their colleagues?"

Warren shrugged. "And if they do, why would I care?"

"They wouldn't vote you in as president."

"And end up like their 'colleagues'? Besides, I haven't committed any murders . . . I have an alibi for nearly all of them. For all they know, it could be anyone."

Silence fell between them. Wolfgang had a choice to make and Warren's eyes clouded dark with unspoken threats as he watched Wolfgang's wheels turn, weighing his options. He hated the possibility of losing his control more than anything, and when he told Wolfgang that he would need to prove his loyalty, *this* is what he meant. They both knew each other all too well, and it was understood that Warren would make good on his threat if needed and Wolfgang needed control of his own life and choices—even at a cost to his moral compass.

One thing Warren knew for certain; he would get his son back in his life and standing next to him—one way or another.

CHAPTER 31

AUGLAND 13

Ashton stood in front of a mere eight members of UnSuited. It was clear that Augland 13 had only just begun their rebellion efforts. It was a smaller group of UnSuited supporters and from what she'd gathered from Reuben, Augland 13 was considered a boutique park. The UnSuited rebellion had barely built momentum, or if it had, this was not the sort of turnout Reuben and Ashton were predicting.

Or maybe Reuben couldn't draw the gathering in such short notice, given he had to scramble to schedule their meeting after Warren decided they would be leaving tomorrow. He had mentioned Warren wanted to quicken his campaign and focus on certain influential Auglands before the vote for the next AEC president.

It wasn't the ideal accommodation, staying on the yacht, anchored just outside the Isles de Beautés coast of Augland 13. Ashton and Reuben had "borrowed" the yacht's smaller vessel to slip away for the UnSuited meeting. It was more difficult for them to maneuver without being seen or heard, leaving late at night on the smaller boat.

Ashton had been speaking to the handful of UnSuited for the last twenty minutes without much confidence, but her message was gaining their support.

"What we need," she said, "is to spread our message of rebellion and solicit more workers out there. It will be risky to grow and expand to the numbers we need without any recourse from Augland 13. Trust me, I know it's putting a lot of you in danger for our cause, but we aren't alone and if we want change, we need members. Aren't you sick of being controlled? Pushed beyond your limits? Underfed, silenced . . . eventually the Customer Service Initiative will come for you, and you'll have no freedoms left—not even in your mind." Ashton had been able to bend her message depending on the size of the audience. But eight members was not enough to take on Augland 13. It certainly wouldn't be enough to take on any of the individual Augland 13 parks.

"Word is you're with an Augland CEO," called out one of the UnSuited. There was no specific leader for Augland 13's UnSuited, but this particular worker was speaking up more often than the others. "How do we know this isn't a trap?" That question made Ashton pause. Not many workers knew she was here with Warren.

"I'm here with one . . . yes, but it's only to benefit our cause. I've gained the trust of several CEOs, and they believe I can control the UnSuited and dissuade you all from rioting, but that's not my intention. My intention is to unite us. And then . . . release us from their control. If we fight against them, we can win. We have the followers outside of these walls and by sheer force we can take them. We also have weapons and are gaining favor with Colonies and NeuroEnergies."

That last bit was a stretch; Ashton had no idea if other Colonies or NeuroEnergies outside Pacific Northwest would side with them, but Reuben had instructed her to do or say anything to help build the rebellion. He wasn't wrong. If UnSuited felt like they had even the slightest chance, it would be easier to grow their followers. She had seen that firsthand in 54's rebellion.

"Then we need proof." Their acting spokesperson was short in stature, disheveled like he had slept on the streets, but it was more likely he played a role as a farm keeper on a Suit estate. "We want weapons. If you're going to be our leader and you have such prestigious *friends*, then that's what we demand in order to trust you," the man shouted as the rest of the group murmured their agreement.

The conversation shifted and Ashton was distracted from her practiced enthusiasm for her memorized speech. "I, I can try, but . . ." Ashton didn't know what to say.

"You want us to follow you and stake our lives on this cause *and* recruit others to join, but you also say you're here telling CEOs you can control us. Maybe that is exactly what you want to do. And you'll tell the CEOs who we are so they can hunt us down. If you're telling the truth about leading us and double crossing Augland, then it should be easy for you to get your hands on a few weapons for us."

It was useless to speak after that. The man had convinced the few others present that there would be an exchange of goods for trust. Her remaining words were drowned out by their demands.

Ashton couldn't deny the parallel between their reservations to blindly follow her lead and her own skepticism when it came to trusting Reuben. Making demands of Augland 13 was the same thing Reuben had done to her, and she wasn't willing to mindlessly follow either. The group may be smaller in size, but they had passion and intelligence that surpassed some of their larger groups. UnSuited in other Auglands were angry and would follow nearly any cause to start a war against the Suits, but here they weren't just aggravated at Suits—they mistrusted any system that told them what to do with no recourse. It was impossible to make them trust her without giving them leverage or collateral— and that was something she wholeheartedly understood.

These thoughts had clouded Ashton's mind all the way back from the meeting location to the dock. Ashton sank down into the soft padding of the boat's back seat. Reuben glanced up while the lapping of the waves tilted them back and forth.

"It went that well, huh?" Reuben spoke sarcastically to Ashton as she crossed her arms. He swiftly began untying the ropes, mooring them to the dock.

"You didn't see?" Usually, Reuben had ways to infiltrate the meetings and hear her speak.

"Nah, not enough time to set up surveillance this time," Reuben confessed.

"Is it me or are these clans getting smaller and smaller in size?" Ashton complained.

"It won't be the same everywhere; some places will be harder to rally than others. The point is you are gaining favor with these workers and getting the message out about the rebellion—maybe they will begin their own recruiting, which is a good thing. Even if they don't start building up their ranks, just the rumor of masses can be quite powerful, even if it's not the entire truth."

"Gaining favor" was an overstatement for the group this evening. What Ashton was stuck on was the how, when, and where the UnSuited showdown would come to life—and what they risked by rebelling against power.

"How are you so certain that an UnSuited war will succeed? I'm telling these workers that if they become the UnSuited and fight against Suits, then we can defeat Augland. I don't want to lie to them, Reuben. I won't. Those deaths will be on my hands if we don't succeed."

"Patience, Ashton. It will work."

Ashton's hands flew up dramatically. "Walk me through what happens. Warren wins the whatever title of president and we go back to Augland 54 . . . then what?" Reuben dropped the second to last rope, keeping them still against the current and looked evenly at Ashton.

"Joao is moving weapons from the security vault to a location that the UnSuited can access."

"You're in contact with Joao? Recently? Is he okay? Bez?" Ashton questioned.

"Not with him directly, no, another iHumanist supporter that I trust . . ." Ashton sighed heavily in frustration. *All these secrets!* "When the time is right, you'll have your UnSuited. Hopefully NeuroEnergy will complete the STEMP project, and we can use that to our advantage. I've already begun campaigning with those who fear Warren's complete take over—"

"You mean the ones that Warren is forcing Wolfe to kill? Those supporters."

"I'll admit, that's a setback."

"Oh! A setback."

"Will you let me finish?" Reuben demanded. Ashton rolled her eyes. She didn't know why she was feeling so obstinate this evening and by the sound of it, Reuben wasn't having any of it.

"The UnSuited will be given every opportunity for success across Auglands, with full support and established safe havens for workers who can't fight. The iHumanist will use our power as protection, if we can rely on the UnSuited for brute force once the battle at Warren's home in Augland 54 is won. It will give your UnSuited the leverage they need to fight against their independent Auglands."

"And—"

"Everything else will come with time, Ashton. I've told you more than I should because I want to earn your trust, which seems to have diminished instead of improving in the last couple of weeks. I thought at least I'd get some points for helping you and Wolfe with an attempt to run away. It wasn't my fault you didn't get out." Reuben hadn't been wrong. The more days that passed, the more UnSuited groups she spoke to and the more solitude she lived in—she was trapped in her own untrusting and lonely prison. Guilt filled her thoughts, as she was the last person she should feel sorry for. There was Wolfe and Niall who had it much worse than her internal suffering—the UnSuited, for example, who put their lives on the line to meet in secret. Ashton barely noticed Reuben approaching until he sat down on the bench next to her.

"Ashton." He turned to her. "I know this hasn't been easy on you. I've pushed you . . . and I've kept things from you for the best interest of—"

"If you say greater plan, I swear . . ."

Reuben laughed, hardy and authentic. He put his arm across her shoulder and tightened his embrace, letting Ashton's head fall on his shoulder. "Touché . . . but I promise to protect you and Wolfe, especially when dealing with Warren. I know you don't believe me, but I don't want to see either of you hurt in any of this mess. And once we are back home, and Warren is distracted by his AEC presidency, we will strike and he won't even know what hit him."

"I still don't understand why you're helping us and what's in it for you. Like when you helped Wolfe and me run, you and I had already started rallying for the rebellion . . . my disappearance would have stopped that and you knew Wolfe wouldn't have been able to leave. So . . . how does all of this help you?"

Reuben tightened his grip on Ashton. "It's not me you're helping. It's the iHumanist movement. Like I said, that request came from someone within my organization. But in all honesty, I didn't want to see you suffer anymore and I knew Wolfe wouldn't fight against his father until he knew you were safe."

Ashton breathed in, pausing for a moment before exhaling. Reuben, holding her like this, felt . . . nurturing, like he truly meant what he said. Even so, she couldn't let herself relax fully against him.

Reuben patted her on the shoulder before leaving her to focus on getting them back to the yacht, but Ashton wasn't quite done yet. She still hadn't figured out what he got out of the UnSuited rebellion, but she'd need to be careful how she broached that subject. Reuben was "testy" when it came to questioning his motives. "You told me that Warren has tasked you with finding the UnSuited in each Augland we visit. What are you telling him to keep his attention away from the real UnSuited we are rallying with? Is he buying it?"

"Well, I need to give him something." Reuben finished untying the last rope and turned toward the speedboat's helm.

"What are you giving him?" Ashton followed him, not particularly loving his vague answer.

"Decoys. People that don't have anything to do with the rebellion," Reuben said too casually as he started the boat and began heading toward the ridiculously sized mega yacht Warren had rented for their stay. Ashton nearly lost her balance at the sudden speed, catching herself on the passenger seat as Reuben propelled them forward. She whispered obscenities toward him, knowing he'd done it on purpose.

"Innocent people?" The idea triggered an unforgiving ache in Ashton's stomach. "You told me that you needed the UnSuited. That's the only reason I've been giving speeches and gaining their trust! Was all that talk two seconds ago a bunch of bull?" she nearly screamed over the buzz of the boat's electric motor.

"Ashton, we can't save them all. It's impossible. I'm doing what is necessary to get the word about the rebellion out without exposing the UnSuited altogether! I'm being as careful and selective, as possible when it comes to whom Warren or other CEOs find out about. Without feeding them some information, I'd be useless to Warren. Let me remind you that the only reason you are here is to help Warren convince the CEOs you know the UnSuited leaders. He uses the information I give him, says it's from you and that's his narrative. He'd never be able to convince the rest of the CEOs you have any power with UnSuited—even though he thinks you don't. Win, win, I find out who the *real* UnSuited leaders are, so I can protect them." She winced as she felt his anger grate against the very fiber of her moral compass.

"How do you find the real UnSuited at each Augland?"

"A lot of research . . . time spent reaching out to people I trust who then reach out to their own sources. Then, they help me spread the word about a gathering with location, date, and time."

"So, they're right to feel like this is a trap . . . because you're using the information you find out and I'm helping you confirm it." Ashton *needed* to understand her part in this plan. She'd never forgive herself if innocent people died because she was too naive to ask questions.

"Maybe some do. Others are desperate to know they aren't the only ones who want change and they're willing to sacrifice anything for it.

Many CEOs, Executives, and even NeuroEnergy members know there are internal communication streams; it's just they don't care to follow them because they haven't seen them as a threat before now. Other CEOs do sense a threat and use their own resources to find UnSuited and kill them. They're hoping these executions will discourage their workers from conspiring and joining the UnSuited, which makes it harder to find and gather them in one central location. I think we've been lucky so far."

Killing meant less recruited, which meant less UnSuited, Ashton mused. "Do you think Augland 60 has more supporters?" Ashton thought of their next campaign destination.

"Probably, maybe not, though. It's hard to tell since I haven't started to gather that intel. Their CEO is less inclined to follow Warren's ways but soon she won't have an option."

Reuben didn't elaborate and Ashton didn't question him further. He had gone to great lengths, both in time and effort to gather the UnSuited, and at his own risk. She struggled internally, wanting and needing to believe him and feeling like she was close. There was just one more thing she needed.

"What about that collateral . . ."

Reuben's eyes stayed focused on the waves and dark night sky ahead of them. He sighed heavily, as if reluctant to speak, "I've got the locations of our pods. The direct coordinates that at any point you could visit. Me, Warren . . ."

"The others in iHumanist?" Ashton inquired.

"Not their names. Just locations of the pods. Some aren't in pods, so I'll need to protect their identities for now."

"And what if these locations are secure? Somewhere I can't break into?"

"They *are* secure, but you'll have their physical location. Without the coordinates, it's nearly impossible to find the pods. I hope you can appreciate the potential devastation that comes with this disclosure."

His eyes had taken a break from staring at the sea and now focused squarely on Ashton's lack of appreciation of his gift of information.

It wasn't exactly what she wanted, but she grudgingly accepted it all the same. The coordinates would help, she had to admit.

"How do I know it's the real coordinates?"

Reuben sighed, stopping the boat in the middle of the dark sea and speaking with a measured tone, mixed with intensity and forced patience. "Again with this? Trust, Ashton. We need to trust each other. Want me to take you there myself when we get back to Aug-land 54? Because I will . . . at some point we need some faith between us. You could at any moment, tell Warren that I've been hiding the truth of the UnSuited leaders and rebellion, whom I'm associated with, and he'd kill us both." Reuben's tone shifted. Ashton couldn't tell if it was frustration or exhaustion from her incessive questioning of his allegiance.

"And *you* could betray *me* once you have all the UnSuited you need. I could be just another pawn to you. I won't apologize for my questions and suggesting that there may be some ulterior motive here. And to be honest? That's what I've experienced with literally everyone who said I could trust them. Georgina, Warren . . . you're asking me to *trust* that you're somehow different. That's a lot, Reuben. And I have people's lives at stake. I don't take that responsibility lightly."

Reuben nodded. "I understand, you have just as much to lose as I do and I'm trying to be sensitive to that. So, what else do you want?"

"I want Wolfe back!" The words blurted out before she could think. There was a long pause.

"Then you'll be happy to know he *is* back. Warren's made a deal with him. He's off the chip, not out of the woods yet, but at least for now he's himself."

Ashton couldn't believe what she was hearing and nearly asked Reuben to repeat himself. She wanted more than anything for it to be true. Wolfe was free? Ashton was left speechless, hardly able to contain the relief she felt. *Wolfe was free,* she repeated in her mind. Reuben started the boat's motor again.

"He doesn't have the chip anymore? He's . . . protected?" Ashton lightly touched Sheva's necklace, laced with the transmitter blocker that still hung around her neck. She hadn't been forthcoming in the beginning with Reuben on how she bypassed the chip, but he had figured it out. It was a rocky start for their relationship, but Reuben proved he seemed to be adept at keeping secrets from Warren—proving Ashton could trust his intentions.

"No, no, we'll have to wait till we're back at Augland 54 for that when I can work with NeuroEnergy for a spare blocker. Ashton, you need to remember that I may have connections, but there is only so much risk iHumanist is willing to take. For now, it's me and you, and that's it. If Warren even had the faintest thought I was looking into a chip blocker, there would be no ability to protect what we are doing." Reuben paused, but Ashton was still stunned by the news about Wolfe, unable to speak.

"Please, Ashton." Reuben nearly whispered, as if afraid Warren was listening in. "iHumanist, while having considerable resources, has only fifteen members. We're out of our depth here and are trying to stop an unstoppable movement between the AEC and Auglands . . . even NeuroEnergies. You have your reasons not to believe me. I get it. But we are both going to fail if we don't work together on this. I can't succeed without you and your influence with the UnSuited. You can't succeed without me and my ability to reach influential people within the AEC."

Ashton looked at him intently. She focused on his eyes and dove deep, trying to decipher if he was truly trustworthy or not. Trying hard to not let his aiding in the attempted escape attempt to persuade her. All the time they had spent around each other, he was honest with her—he had stayed true to his word and had not given away information about the transmitter hanging around her neck, but he was giving UnSuited names to Warren. He still worked for her enemy. His eyes were unwavering, searching hers as well. She softened. He had a point. If they stopped now, Warren would win regardless.

She needed Reuben's help, so Ashton reluctantly admitted, "Thirteen wants some sort of weaponry; something to prove we are strong enough for them to get more people. And, fun fact, they know I'm here with Warren." It was her peace offering—he was right that she needed to get over her reluctant and trust him. Reuben thought for a moment.

"I'll see what I can do."

"But none of their names get released to Warren. We can't afford to lose anyone in 13; there's barely enough members of the UnSuited as is. Growing our numbers here will help us gain additional leverage."

Reuben genuinely smiled. "Fine, as far as Warren knows, no one here is part of the rebellion." Ashton sighed in relief. Before tonight, Reuben and Ashton had spoken occasionally, but not with as much depth as during tonight's trip from the docks of Isles de Beautés to Warren's yacht. Reuben had gained her partnership for the moment, and if they were going to continue to build that trust, she would need more conversations like this.

"How'd you become an Executive anyway?" Ashton questioned, attempting to show Reuben she was finished with challenging him for the time being. Wolfe said that Reuben had been like a family member to him growing up and had tried to help him become CEO. But beyond that tidbit, Ashton was in the dark.

"I wasn't born into privilege, if that's what you're thinking. I was adopted at a young age as a worker. A Suit family liked me enough at eight to keep me around and, just like that, I was one of them."

"How did being part of this family lead to you becoming an Executive? Did they have special connections?"

"I worked hard. My adoptive father was a Senator and worked at the Southwest division supporting Augland 4 and NeuroEnergy. They controlled resource allocations and distribution between Auglands, then also to NeuroEnergies. Unfortunately, he was corrupt like so many of the CEOs that exist today. NeuroEnergy CEOs and Senators are always incentivized by Augland CEOs with more: luxury homes and promises of the very best in vehicles, technology, AEBs—all kinds of perks—if they side with what the CEO wants. I left when I was twenty to work for Warren, we had vacationed together because our fathers were close. When Warren took over as CEO for Augland 54, he thought I was suited for Operations."

"What changed?"

"I was approached to join the movement by someone I have known for a very long time and trust. I won't lie to you, it's not because of my morality. Even though I saw workers die in Land of Legends, along with the other cruel and unusual punishments, that's not what made me turn away. And although I do remember the days of living as a worker, essentially a servant and working long hours and never having a real childhood. You and I both share that experience, those feelings of bitterness."

"How selfless of you to admit your shameful worker roots."

"Look, I'm not perfect and I don't have this humanitarian viewpoint for a better world so we can all sit next to each other and hold hands in peace and love. To be honest, I could have lived with that chip on my shoulder and gone about being a person of 'influence' as an Executive without much thought of it. It was the infertility that raised my concerns about our society and the abuse that flowed from the top down. When Warren didn't see the problem with the eradication of human existence, it changed my perspective. I couldn't work beside someone who viewed workers as less than human—as disposable.

"There is a part of me that does not like the mistreatment of workers because I was one. I was just lucky and was able to experience both sides. Running a company is not easy, and I do respect Warren for working hard and seeing a bigger picture. But he's not working toward utopia. His vision has flaws and we are starting to finally see those issues for what they are."

"Utopia?" said Ashton. "What do you mean by that?"

"Utopia means . . . perfection. Like a world that lives in harmony."

"No, not a utopia, but can we get close? I think so, we once were—a very long time ago. We had a system in place that benefited everyone, instead of sorting and ranking each community. I think we can get there again, maybe better."

They neared the yacht where the boat's VELIC took over and roped it to the side of the massive vessel. Reuben placed his hand on Ashton's arm.

"Ashton, I told you more than I should have. I need you to promise me: don't say anything to Wolfe. Not while he's under Warren's CS. We can't compromise what we are doing with the UnSuited or iHumanist. If it somehow slips, all this would be for nothing." Reuben's hand slid from her elbow, letting her go. She understood why Reuben asked her to keep that a secret. Wolfe had echoed that message as well—which was the only reason she nodded in response.

"I'll still want those coordinates, though."

Reuben grinned. "Fair enough. Good night, Ashton."

Ashton moved quickly and quietly across the hallway deep within the yacht. She crept toward her room but stopped short to tiptoe into Wolfe's room at the last moment. She wanted to see for herself if the chip was off. The door opened slightly, and she saw Wolfe out on his balcony.

"Wolfe?" His broad figure was hunched over the rail as he stared out at the expanse of ocean. His face was shadowed by the night sky as he turned in surprise at the sound of her voice. She took two steps forward and Wolfe hurried toward her.

"Ashton, oh my God, where've you been?" She stopped short, finally noticing his face was now swollen with one eye shut and dried blood on his shirt.

"What happened!" She evaluated his face, putting her hand up to his cheek where he winced from the pain of even the lightest touch. The black and blue formed deep rings under his eyes.

"Nothing, I'm fine."

"You don't look fine." She said softly, "You'll need ice."

"I'm fine, really." He guided her hand down from his face. Looking at her with his one good eye, he laced his fingers between hers.

"Warren and I had some words."

"Looks like more than just words." Ashton continued to study his face for the truth of what had happened that day. "And you said I needed self-control." Wolfe chortled in response at the lighthearted jab. Ashton sank into him. "I'm so happy you're back, Wolfe." Finally, feeling the warmth of Wolfe's true, unaltered embrace was everything in that moment. She could step away from his side and not worry he would slip back under the CS spell.

Wolfe and Ashton spent the next few hours out on the balcony of his bedroom suite.

"After Warren and I fought, we talked . . . more about what he needed me to do. He wants me to play a more active role in his campaign, but without the chip which means that if I play the game *he* wants to play, then I can be . . . free."

"Wolfe . . . he'll make you kill people." Ashton's words felt sour as they left her mouth.

"Yes . . . and I knew that the moment we decided war would come eventually. I just thought it would be me fighting for our cause and not my father's."

"This . . . this is heavy."

"You're thinking it's the wrong decision? Agreeing to Warren's terms . . ." Wolfe winced as Ashton lightly placed the ice bag she'd snuck back in over his eye. They both sat out on the balcony with

Wolfe's chair facing hers. Wolfe finished explaining the terms of Warren's arrangement if he was to exist outside of the chip's commands.

"Do you think you could do it? Kill someone? I mean, like actually do it without the CS chip?" It was a hard question.

"I don't know . . . I mean, it's weird knowing I've already done it. I've interrogated people before but never killed anyone while being consciously aware of what I was doing." Ashton could sense the turmoil this caused Wolfe, and it hurt her that Warren's decisions spilled over into their time together. His presence was constant, and they both needed to feel something again—anything but Warren's manipulation or the risk of being caught while gathering the UnSuited. It was important, but right now what was more important was their time together, for their own sanity.

Silence turned to sleep and they ended the night in each other's arms, and it felt like home.

CHAPTER 32

Bez

AUGLAND 54

One month. It had been one miserable month since Joao had brought Bez to Augland 54. It was chaos. The first couple of weeks being back in the world where she had suffered so much and wanted so deeply to escape. Since arriving, she snuck around from place to place while Joao played the stand in Head of Security and sent word back to Warren about what was happening in the C-Suite. He barely slept at night when he came home from a long day.

Joao mentioned several times how the weight of keeping up the façade with Warren was becoming harder and harder to manage. Bez complained about being cooped up in the house all day because Joao said it wasn't safe to leave and possibly be recognized. It wasn't until she threatened to leave and return to NeuroEnergy that he agreed to take some risks and they both agreed she could venture out—his only ask was that she stay out of sight, which was nearly impossible given they were living in the city known for never sleeping. Venus was notorious for its wild nightlife.

Now Bez left late at night and stayed out until the early hours in the morning, scheduling appearances at worker-only locations like Victorian barns and Predator Biome watering holes. She attempted to make the UnSuited meeting locations easy to access, but far enough away from cameras and customers. She worked tirelessly with her connections to bring forth the UnSuited once again, but the lack of attendees and those willing to risk Augland 54's wrath left the meetings with disappointing numbers. Bez soon realized most UnSuited had all gone into hiding after the escape from Maya Bay.

While the restrictions on when she could come and go were less than ideal, bringing fuel back to the fire of the UnSuited gave her purpose, and she and Joao found their rhythm. But that did not mean that danger didn't weigh heavy on both of them. She could not forget when Joao confessed what Warren had done to him.

Joao had packed their things and convinced Bez to leave with him as they departed from the haven of NeuroEnergy. Bez's anger brewed slowly on their two-hour journey after Joao had suddenly asked her to leave, with only the promise to answer all questions she had once they left the compound. Bez was livid that Joao had kept the truth from her, but in reality, she was more terrified than angry—going back to Augland 54 meant reliving a nightmare that she had begun to heal from. When Joao and Bez first left NeuroEnergy, they'd travelled by hover bike until they made it to the former Colony refuge on Bainbridge Island, where they camped for the night. She trusted Joao—and there weren't many people in this life she could say that about. But she did not like being kept in the dark and that was exactly what Joao had done. She was angry with herself for agreeing to his terms.

Joao had made a fire and the bubbling canned chili simmered over it as the warm embers heated the former Colony member's home where they were staying the night. Bez hadn't uttered a word to him since leaving NeuroEnergy, because she was patiently waiting for Joao to confess all that he had promised to disclose. Her eyes threw daggers at the side of Joao's head, but he was overly concentrating on the food— which further agitated Bez.

Joao handed her a bowl filled with the hearty bean mixture, but Bez refused to take it out of pure stubbornness. If he wasn't going to begin the conversation, then she would.

"You've got to be starving." Joao said.

"I'm not eating anything till you tell me what's going on. And for real this time. I'm not some robot who's going to follow your direction without questioning your actions and motives. I've had enough of blindly following orders in Augland to last me a lifetime and I refuse to let my own partner handle me this way, Jo." Bez was more than comfortable standing her ground against this man who was twice her size. He was reserved at times, but he liked to do things on his own and Bez wasn't going to stand for it.

"Bez . . ." he began, giving up on her taking the chili. She could tell instantly he wanted to avoid the conversation, which meant he already knew she wouldn't like what he had to say. She wouldn't let him pretend the promises he'd made in their NeuroEnergy apartment weren't important. She deserved to know the truth. Before leaving with Georgina, Ashton had confided in her that Wolfe had kept her in the dark about his plans for revenge and the trial, which happened to be at the core of the only dispute between them. She had presumed their relationship was different—Joao wouldn't hide things from her. A twinge of hurt infiltrated the anger that bubbled up hotter within her than the chili she so desperately wanted to eat.

Bez put her hands on her hips for emphasis. "Don't 'Bez' me! You dragged me all the way out here with nothing more than a 'Please trust me, Bez'. 'I'll tell you everything, Bez.'" She mocked his low voice. "Well . . . now's your chance. I'm listening." Joao was lost in thought, allowing space for more words to spill from her mouth. "And don't say you want to wait until we arrive in Augland. I'm not playing that game either because if I want, I can march my butt right back to NeuroEnergy," Bez threatened. His silence only fueled the fire within her. *His confession can't be this bad, right? Did he just not trust me?*

"I don't know where—"

"To *begin?*" Bez stood abruptly, cutting him off and catching Joao off guard. He was still sitting down in his chair, holding the two bowls of chili. "You don't know where to begin in telling me the truth? When did we start lying and keeping things from each other?"

Bez couldn't contain it any longer. Her anger turned quickly to hurt. Her partner didn't think her capable of handling the truth—or at least, that was what her mind was telling her. Now, it felt like all her insecurities rose to the top of the list of things she needed Joao to feel. He had shut her out, had kept things from her, and now she couldn't stop an emotional wound from opening.

"You haven't been yourself for weeks! When did that become us, Jo? When did we become one of those couples who couldn't be themselves with each other? Maybe start there, huh? Start with the truth, because it is really starting to feel like I'm some damsel you're trying to protect and I'm not fragile, Jo. I'm not. While you may have helped me escape Augland, I was the one who saved myself plenty of times before you got there. So, I don't need protection; I need honesty. I want to know what the hell is going on!" *That* was honesty even Bez hadn't admitted to herself before it poured out of her before she could filter it. That had always been her problem—filtering how she felt and the words she said shooting out of her mouth like daggers. It had gotten her in more trouble in Augland 54 than she would ever like to admit.

"I'm chipped!" Joao rose, his green and blue eyes pained at the admittance. Bez took a step back, not from fear but because what he said was impossible. He couldn't have been chipped. What he said meant something else—she was sure of it. It had to be.

"What do you mean by chipped?" Because Bez couldn't come to terms with that truth—that fate alone meant that Augland 54 could never let Joao go and she wasn't ready to acknowledge that. They had escaped and lived a wonderful life. For six months, they had lived at the Colony. Granted, it was hard for Bez to agree to their relationship at first—Joao had admitted he cared for her long before she even knew of him. Joao occasionally tagged along with Wolfe when Wolfe came to make sure she was well taken care of in the brothels. After Joao came for her in Augland 54 and after she and Ashton were separated and she ran for the docks of Maya Bay, she was surprised and hesitant to allow his help. But Joao was patient and kind and loved her fiercely. So, she gave him a chance when they were outside 54's walls.

She had known of love once before Joao—and now could not trust loving others. There was a time and a place when that love she thought was real, turned out to be a ruse. That Suit had said wonderful, beautiful things to her. He had taken her to beautiful and romantic places in Predator's Biome and Maya Bay resorts. He had told her that she was the only one for him and that he would remove her worker status—that he would give her the life workers only dream of.

Bez had to stop herself from thinking of the Suit she had once, foolishly, fallen for—the man who had condemned her to the brothels for her remaining days—because Joao was nothing like that Suit. Bez knew deep down that she could love like that again, but trust . . . trust would be harder to earn. Because Joao was not *him who she would not name*—but the secrets? The chip? Going back to Augland? It scared her more than anything because Augland 54 only broke things that were once whole—and had given her only heartache.

Joao's answer drew Bez back to reality. "You know what I mean. The Customer Service Initiative, courtesy of Warren, was installed back when I filled in for Wolfe at some point. I don't know. Everything is a blur. The headaches were apparently a sign and when I went to go see the physician at NeuroEnergy, he confirmed it." Joao sat back down heavily on a chair.

The fire crackled between them and Bez was left—for once—speechless. Bez recalled the frequent headaches. They'd kept him up some nights and worried her when they couldn't find a cause. She searched her memory and could pick out moments when she'd noticed Joao's exhaustion, confusion, and general brain fog. *Maybe he really has been chipped,* she thought as she recalled his behavior.

Joao continued, "The doctor took x-rays and that's how he discovered it. Once I saw the scans, I knew instantly it was a CS chip.

I felt for the incision, and the scar was there. The Customer Service Initiative was so prevalent in the cages, and I watched so many undergo the procedure. I explained what it was, and the doc thought he could help me stop the transmission." Joao brought out a necklace that Bez had barely noticed. It hung around his neck and displayed a tiny rock that when turned over, blinked with a green light. "While this thing is around my neck, I'm safe from the chip turning on and taking away my ability to be myself. But Warren still thinks my chip is active."

"Does . . . does Wolfe know?" Bez stumbled back to the chair behind her and sat, trying desperately to comprehend what this all meant.

"Yes, I told him right after I left the doctor's office. Wolfe went to Augland DC knowing that Warren already knew about STEMP—"

"STEMP?" Bez questioned before the realization took hold and she answered her own question. "The project we celebrated that night we came to NeuroEnergy." It made sense to Bez now.

Joao didn't say she was wrong, which confirmed her thought. "And Warren would do anything to take it from NeuroEnergy." The room fell silent. Joao at some point had placed the chili down on the coffee table and leaned back in the chair, staring up at the ceiling. "I should have seen this coming because I was there in the room when he was experimenting on the captive workers. If Warren can imprison his own son, he sure wouldn't have any issue putting a chip in me. There was no way Warren would trust me to run Augland's security simply because Wolfe and I grew up together. We were close—I know him better than anyone. I'm *loyal* to him. And him, me." Joao's voice cracked with emotion in a way Bez had never heard before. She could feel the guilt radiating from him. "Point is, I should have seen this coming. I should have known and because I failed, Warren has used me to find out exactly what kind of sabotage NeuroEnergy has been planning and our specific plans to attack him. We are right back where we started when we first left Augland."

"You can't blame yourself. Not for this." The delayed confession now made so much sense to Bez. Joao hadn't confided in her because he was scared and embarrassed.

"I don't understand, that doesn't answer the question of why we are going back to 54." Bez spoke softly now, her anger gone and in its place, sadness or fear, like her mind wouldn't grasp the reality that Joao had explained to her.

"Warren still thinks he controls me through the CS chip. Wolfe and I decided it was best to let him continue to think that so we could try and get a step ahead of him. So, Warren called me and instructed me to run things as Head of Security at Augland 54 while he is out campaigning for his new role as AEC President. I'm supposed to be his 'eyes and ears' and report back any scheming from the Executives in his absence."

Joao brought his eyes up to Bez, meeting hers. "I couldn't leave you at NeuroEnergy because Warren . . . well, turns out it was me that sent security to invade and take over, with the intent of capturing Vic, the scientist who designed the STEMP project. With Warren winning at trial and removing Georgina as head of NeuroEnergy, our entire community was vulnerable. Warren is obsessed with finding Vic and forcing him to use his satellite expertise on the STEMP project—but using it for himself and his nefarious ideas."

Who's Vic? How much more has Joao kept from me? Bez had more questions than answers now.

"But, Rye and Versal. Hunter, and what about Forest . . ." Bez rattled off the names of their friends and allies.

"Hunter is with Forest and Vic, hidden away while they try and finish the STEMP structure. Rye and Versal stayed."

"Do they know that Augland will attack?" Bez asked.

"Rye does . . . Versal, she'll be looked after." Joao's eyes had finally found Bez as she absorbed everything Joao had disclosed. It was his turn to reach for her hand, but Bez pulled away.

She rose from her chair with mixed emotions churning within her. She was furious Joao had made so many decisions for her, and without her. There were still members of the UnSuited living and working in NeuroEnergy, and Bez had unknowingly abandoned them. As if he could read her mind, Joao assured her, "NeuroEnergy people who can't fight or want to leave are heading for the Colony today."

"You should have told me. Not now, but when it was happening. Instead, you went to Wolfe? And it's not just your life these decisions impact, Jo, it's mine too." Bez said, trying to keep her voice steady.

"It's complicated, B. I know I should have come to you and told you everything, but I wanted to protect you. In case," Joao paused, "in case there was nothing that could be done about the chip. I don't know what we would have done if there wasn't a blocker able to stop the transmission. All I wanted to do was to protect you from *me*."

"Stop protecting me by lying to me! That's not how this relationship works!" Bez stormed out of the living room and up the dimly lit stairs to the bedroom. She did so in fear that she might say something she would later regret or that she would be subjected to more lame excuses from Joao for keeping a monumental secret like the CS from her. Ashton was right to be mad at Wolfe for keeping their plan from them, and now she was overcome by that same anger at Joao—even if it was meant to keep them safe, they had no right.

When Bez awoke the next day, she noticed Joao hadn't come to bed. Instead he'd stayed downstairs and slept on the couch, giving Bez her space. When she came downstairs in the morning, he looked like he hadn't slept at all. Bez rounded the corner to face him. The night had brought her some peace because she wasn't going back to Augland for Joao, she would use their time to bring purpose back to her life—reviving the UnSuited.

"I'll go with you to 54, but no more secrets. No more lies. And you keep me in the loop from now on."

Joao nodded. "Fair enough." He stuffed his hands deep into his pockets.

"And you're going to help me find a way to bring 54's UnSuited back together." Joao stiffened, realizing the danger of her involvement. He'd meant to hide her away from danger, not encourage her to be the center of it. "That's the deal."

Joao paused for a moment as he considered her offer, but soon he just smiled. "Fair enough, again." Bez smiled back at him, satisfied she had made her point.

"All right, so let's go through it then. I want to know everything." And by the time they were finished, Joao had told her *everything*.

———

Victorian Park brought Bez a sense of both familiarity and déjà vu. For a world she once despised, she now felt gratitude. Knowing she would have died if Ashton hadn't disrupted her world helped ease, just a bit, the ache of being back here. She would have wilted away in hopelessness within the four walls of the brothel without Ashton.

Joao had never asked what happened in the brothel and Bez never revealed the truth because she did not want to revisit those memories. But here she was. Bez stood on the rickety steps, waiting to go through the swinging entrance doors to the brothel where she'd spent nearly two years. Her nausea and pitted feeling of her memories hadn't dulled, even after the last few weeks. It was just past two a.m. when she visited this particular spot, a time when the Suits would be gone or sleeping. As the doors creaked open, and she walked in slowly while a server stood where she once wiped down the bar from the rush of the prior evening.

"Closed for the night, hun; come back later today," Chloe said before looking up from her task of placing bottles back on the top shelf of the bar.

"That's a shame, I was really looking forward to a dance from a pretty thing like you," Bez joked as she pranced into the open bar like she owned the place.

Chloe exhaled sharply. "Gosh . . . you scared me for a moment."

Bez went to sit on a bar stool and swung her new long, blonde locks out of her face, part of her disguise to help her blend in. She wore a wig and Victorian attire to help blend, including a long, pleated beige skirt and flowing white blouse—typical for a Victorian worker. Joao had looped the cameras both within and outside from around one a.m. to six a.m. to give Bez the freedom to be in the room without the prying eyes of Augland security.

"We . . . good?" Chloe questioned, slowly moving her dark eyes around the room.

"Yup, we have a couple hours." Chloe's shoulders relaxed in relief without the fear of cameras recording them. "How are we doing on our stock?" Bez slouched against the tabletop.

"Five more came yesterday, three the day before. I'm running out of under floorboard space; so I think it might make sense to find another location." Chloe threw down her towel and leaned forward on the other side of the bar.

"I have some stored in my house and could probably take a few more. It should total about nine guns, with more coming. But if we secure any more, Joao said those outside his trusted security circle might start to notice they're missing," Bez confessed. "Joao is moving as many as he can. He thinks he can move a larger number and call it a 'routine inspection.'"

"Do you think it's smart to keep them in your house? Wouldn't it be safer to find another place?" Chloe questioned. After bringing her into the throws of the UnSuited, Chloe had been both ruthless and cautious about preparations, more so than Bez.

"Yes, he's working on it . . . any UnSuited newcomers I should know about?" Bez changed the subject. It was easier back when she was in Apparel and in front of workers to recruit her peers to join the rebellion. With Joao's restrictions and limits on whom she interacted with, Bez was left with only the people she knew and trusted. Chloe had worked with her once upon a time. She had been sent to Bez' brothel for a brief time after she was caught aiding Ashton in makeup and disguises to escape.

"A few. We've got many here in Victorian, but we need to start meeting somewhere else; there are way too many high-up Suits here to keep building our numbers—safely. Besides, we need to expand outside Victorian . . . too many young kids with big mouths here." Chloe was right. When it was just a few of them, they could maintain a level of secrecy, but to have the numbers of UnSuited now it made sense to move their operation. Soon, they would need to find a new safe space to meet.

"I'll figure it out." Bez said. Chloe came around the counter and plopped down on the barstool next to her.

"You really think our armory is going to make a difference against Suits?" Chloe's dark brown eyes glistened with curiosity. Bez couldn't tell her everything that Joao had confided in her in case Chloe was revealed as an UnSuited recruiter.

"Better than nothing, wouldn't you say?" Bez answered a bit too casually, because she too had been curious what weapons could do against Suits. Joao had been sure that they would only benefit the UnSuited, but Suits were costumes, and they needed to remember that.

"I guess . . ."

"Don't worry, Joao and I have things handled."

"I'm just ready to leave . . . I'm ready for this all to be over so I never have to step foot in this place again. I don't care how it happens; I just want it to end." Bez's face dropped, she knew that feeling all too well. The yearning to not let this be 'my story' or 'the end.' But Chloe was strong.

Bez reached for Chloe's hand. "Soon," she promised, even though she had no idea of when. Joao hadn't heard from Wolfe and Ashton, even Hunter, who had hidden the scientist while he completed the secret STEMP program. Rye was the only one from the group who had reached out and there wasn't much to say other than they were all under lockdown. Chloe grasped her hand more tightly in return, as if she meant to hold Bez to that promise.

For the next hour, Chloe and Bez talked more about their armory and potential hiding areas in Augland 54. Before long, Bez excused herself and headed home, promising she would be back with more news soon.

Bez made it back to their home without incident, arriving earlier than she'd expected. Typically, she stayed out until at least six a.m. and Joao was already asleep, but tonight she was home by three a.m. and Joao still hadn't come home from work.

Their place was a two-floor condo in the smaller park of Venus—the city that never closes. There were more people out during the evening, which made it safe for Bez to roam around the parks without looking out of place. This world with bright lights and talking Suits swirled around her, mixing her realities. When she first arrived, she wouldn't be caught dead walking around Augland freely. She had no desire to come back ever, but after talking with Joao she was able to see the bigger picture and she'd come around. She hadn't heard from Ashton but Joao had mentioned some connection with Wolfe when he had first arrived in Augland DC—since then, crickets.

Bez heard the lock on the door turn and Joao walked in, his footsteps heavy against the hardwood floors. Bez looked up from the kitchen where she had warmed up dinner. Joao's sunken eyes and strained shoulders only physically told her the kind of day he must have had.

"You're home late."

"And you're home early," Joao smiled. "How'd it go with Chloe?" Joao pulled his tie away from his neck and slid off his suit jacket. He placed his hand around Bez, grasping her tightly, not for her sake, but for his own.

She wouldn't ask about his day because she already knew. He didn't like to talk about what a day in the life of the Head of Security entailed, so she'd stopped asking. Instead, she discussed hers, which she realized was an easy distraction. "Good, they received a couple more shipments of photon guns. She thought we might need to move them to a bigger storage location. Have you thought any more about a new spot to house the weapons?"

"I haven't had time to find anything yet, but Chloe may be right to suggest moving our stash . . . I hear Warren may be heading back soon. He's ending his campaign earlier than expected. My guess is he's feeling confident in his supporters." Joao separated himself from her and leaned up against the kitchen bar.

"What does that mean for us?" Bez turned from where she was in the kitchen and faced him.

"Means we continue preparing." Joao looked more exhausted than usual. The sleepless nights were clearly weighing on him, and carrying out Warren's biddings kept him busy as did Augland 54 Executives with early-morning calls and late-night dinners. He was also sneaking out photon handguns and rifles and the risk of exposure or capture grew by the day.

While Bez didn't want to further put stress on Joao, there were things on her mind. "Jo, what if we don't have the numbers for the uprising? I haven't been able to recruit like I thought I would, and Chloe said now it's mainly just workers in Victorian—which is a joke. It's full of recent grads of Augland Center and they are the opposite of 'inspired for a rebellion'." Bez rolled her eyes in frustration.

"We've got the majority in the security team on my end, and you've got enough ties with the UnSuited that once they hear rumblings of a rebellion, they'll show up without hesitation." Joao came over to her, wrapping her in his embrace. Bez melted against him.

There was a knock at the door and they both froze instantly. Joao quickly released Bez, only to take her hand and guide her behind the pantry door in the kitchen and out of sight. Bez mouthed something to him, but Joao just shushed as he looked across their kitchen island and toward the knock. For the four weeks they had been back in 54, no visitors had ever stopped by, and given Joao's reaction, he wasn't expecting anyone either.

Joao walked over and opened their front door. "Wintefred, it's late." Joao sounded calm and collected. The Executive for Customer Success walked into Joao's condo without invitation. Wearing a stylish pencil skirt and matching blazer she strutted beyond Joao and into the kitchen, where Bez could barely make her out through the slit in the door.

"Well, you left dinner without saying goodbye to the Executives and I've been meaning to steal you away for some time. I hope you don't mind the surprise visit tonight." Though her voice sounded sweet and innocent, Bez knew she was anything but that.

"Of course not, I'm happy to have you." The strain in his voice was minimal, but Bez could tell it was there.

"Aren't you going to offer me a drink?" Wintefred asked pointedly.

Joao paused, "what would you like?" Joao went for the cabinets, reaching for two glasses before turning back to Wintefred.

"Cosmo. Please." She smiled. Wintefred side-stepped around the kitchen, not so subtly looking around before making her way to the living room table and taking a seat. Joao began concocting what passed for vodka in 54, with some makeshift sweetened cranberry juice for her Cosmo, and selected a bottle of stout ale for himself.

"Smells wonderful in here. Didn't grab enough *mortal* food tonight?" Joao passed her the drink, ignoring her comment of the food Bez had made for herself.

"It's missing a few ingredients, but hopefully to your liking. I'm sorry, I don't typically make . . . these here." Wintefred took a sip and nodded. "It's perfect and I'm quite impressed. You're a bit of a young bachelor; I'm sure Cosmos aren't exactly your drink of choice." *Is she flirting with him?* Bez nearly gawked. Joao laughed like he could read Bez's mind.

"I hear we should be expecting Warren back soon. Is that true?" Wintefred eyed Joao carefully.

"Yes, yes, from what he's told me he should be coming home within the next week or so." Joao stood at the island, casually putting his hand down to lean his weight against the table.

"Good. He's been missed here. I mean, between the trial and his campaign, his mind has been elsewhere and I think he'll be keen to hear about how our customers have been affected," Wintefred said.

"That would be your area of expertise, Wintefred." Joao volleyed.

"You are absolutely correct, and according to your security records, there have been no security breaches or instances of UnSuited rebellions since your return. Warren did confide in me that you previously helped workers escape from Augland 54, in addition to absconding with his son, but he mentioned that you've been 'rehabilitated'."

So Wintefred knew Joao was chipped!

"That is true. I have." Joao forced his hands into his pockets to hide his nervous fidgeting.

"It's just *interesting* that you show up, and we see nothing more from the rebellion, yet our customers have complained of insubordination among young workers. Senators have claimed some of their staff have been out late at night. There have also been workers reporting later than normal for job shifts."

"I'd hardly call that cause for a security concern. And there haven't been any outbreaks that I'm aware of—nothing reported. I respond to alerts and what has been reported directly to me, Wintefred. I don't see how this is an issue; usually it's a good sign when there aren't riots in the streets. But if you believe differently and have access to evidence, I should be made aware of them. You have my word, I'll look into that."

"Hmm, well, thank you. I don't presume to know anything about how your security team goes about sniffing for rebels." Wintefred got up from her seat, untangling her long, fake legs and walked toward Joao, getting closer as Bez backed away from the door and tried to get a better angle from her hiding spot. Their home was open and modern, very on brand with Venus futuristic floorplans, but the slit in the pantry made every angle hard to see.

Wintefred took a long look at Joao before redirecting her attention toward the living room. She headed briskly toward the couch, her long fingers reaching for something hanging from the armrest. She grasped Bez's Victorian wig with her fingertips and held it up in triumph. Bez held in a gasp—she had taken the wig off after returning home from her visit with Chloe and flung it on the couch without a second thought. Wintefred shot Joao a smile before putting down the blonde hair piece. Bez shut her eyes tightly in horror, knowing exactly what an Executive like Wintefred would infer from this find. Wintefred confidently strode around the room, her heels clicking on the hardwood floors.

"You wouldn't be the first or last Executive who appreciates worker *company*, but it is frowned upon by those in the C-Suite. Good thing we're friends, though, right? I mean, you wouldn't want that kind of reputation. A *new* Head of Security professional, a former UnSuited worker sympathizer, fraternizing with unknown workers. Some might draw conclusions that would be—well, let's hope word doesn't get out." The threat lingered between them uncomfortably before Wintefred spun around and stalked toward the door.

"It will be good to have Warren home, I hear he has gained strong favor as our future AEC President. I'm hoping for your support when I run for his vacant seat as CEO." Wintefred smirked, leaving Joao frozen in place where he stood in the kitchen. "See you tomorrow at the board meeting." She disappeared from the front steps of the condo, allowing Bez to come out from hiding and storm out of the pantry.

"Jo, this isn't good. She knows!" Bez rounded on Joao with eyes widened in terror.

"She didn't say she knew 'who' the person was, just that she assumed I had company," Joao said, but she could see he had come to the same conclusion about Wintefred's suspicions.

"She knows something and that's enough. You, under a CS chip, wouldn't be keeping company with a worker. Ah, why'd I leave my wig out! I was too careless." Joao grabbed Bez, focusing her before she spiraled out of control.

"We're going to be fine. Let me handle Wintefred. She's nothing, a pawn in Warren's game."

CHAPTER 33

Versal

NEUROENERGY, PACIFIC NORTHWEST

Things had gotten much worse for the residents of NeuroEnergy. Augland security had reduced the food supply and medical accessibility and tossed the remaining NeuroEnergy people out from all common areas. They were forced to live in to tents that littered the courtyard. Augland was clearly searching for something and as the days went by, the less NeuroEnergy looked like a town and more like a prison.

Rye hadn't given Versal much information, despite her near daily asking of the question they all wanted to know—why.

Why was Augland here?

And why were they punishing them and starving innocent people?

Why didn't Rye give Augland what they needed so the security men would leave?

Versal had no idea what had happened to Hunter and hadn't heard anything about Ashton, Wolfe, and the fallout from the trial. Or anything about Joao and Bez, who'd mysteriously disappeared without so much as a goodbye. All she knew was that Augland security had arrived with minimal warning, apparently looking for something and without much luck.

Since then, security had treated the NeuroEnergy members like social scum, evicting the residents from their homes to make room for the Augland security guards. Most of the community were now unhoused, forced to find or create alternate living arrangements.

It weighed on her more each day, seeing the crowds of NeuroEnergy people pitching tarps as tents to live in near the apartment buildings they used to call home. She'd been kicked out of her own apartment two weeks ago, and Rye had kindly let her stay with him. But she was mostly alone. The nights Rye did leave his office and return home, he'd sleep on the couch so she could retire for the night in his bedroom. He rarely ever spoke to her—other than a hello and good night when they crossed paths coming and going from the apartment. Maybe that was why she focused so much on the NeuroEnergy humanitarian crisis—it masked her own feelings of loneliness.

She could tell summer was coming to an end because the nights were cooler nights and the leaves began to transition in color. Only a month had passed since the takeover, but in that time, their home now felt like a detention center as they were forced to stay within its walls. Rye had helped her with organizing what supplies she could get her hands on so she could give them out to the community—items like toiletries, fresh water, and medical supplies, which were scarce since the Augland takeover.

Versal wrapped herself in a dark maroon crocheted sweater and stepped out of Rye's bedroom, looking into the living room where he sat slowly sipping his coffee on the couch. His brown locks were disheveled, and the AR glasses perched on his nose indicated he was concentrating on something intently through the lenses.

"Morning." Versal gracefully moved toward the kitchen to pour herself a mug from the coffee pot steaming with freshly brewed coffee. It wasn't very strong, as they were having to ration the coffee, tasting more like caffeinated bean broth. Still, it was better than no coffee at all. She glanced back at Rye. "Sleep well?"

Rye took a moment before pulling his glasses off and looking at Versal. "Sorry, did you say something?"

Rye confused her. She saw how much he cared for the individuals of NeuroEnergy, but he remained outside of their purview. He never spoke with anyone here, but Versal saw all he did with his planning and creation with technology—not that she understood any of it, but she had no doubt how much he cared for them. "Never mind, sorry to bother you."

"You're not bothering me. Sorry, sometimes I get too focused and I didn't hear you come in." The silence between them was strained, and Versal didn't understand why. She realized Rye kept secrets from her for one reason or another, so she did not press the issue. Although, she sensed that Rye could use an ally, especially in this strange, new world.

"What are you working on?" she questioned, hoping for some crumb of information hinting to a change in their situation.

Rye sighed. "Warren has provided VELICs to support some of our engineers and scientists here." Versal could sense he wanted to say more by the way his mouth opened to say something else but quickly shut as he second guessed how much to say.

"What's a VELIC?" Versal asked, coming to sit beside him on the couch.

Rye leaned back, diverting his eyes from hers and scooting further from her to leave a comfortable space. "Virtual assistance, essentially." He fiddled with his glasses. "Executives use them in vehicles, rooms, and their headquarters. It's like . . . artificial intelligence that becomes more intelligent the more information it's provided."

"Hmm, and why is it coming here?" Versal pressed.

Rye took a moment, "I shouldn't . . ." Versal didn't need him to finish the sentence before she stood.

"I didn't mean to pry." But that was a lie. She wanted to know why Augland was still here and what they wanted. Because if it was up to her, she'd give it to Augland 54 just to stop the starvation.

"No, you weren't . . . I'm sorry. Uh . . . how are people doing?" Rye clumsily changed subjects. "I've heard you've spent a lot of time with them," Versal wasn't sure who would be talking to Rye about her whereabouts, but she didn't press him on that. Rye worked long hours in the headquarters, but it would be nearly impossible for him not to see what had happened to his community.

"I think you already know the answer to that," Versal said gently as she set her coffee down on the kitchen bar table. She didn't look at him as she began to put her shoes on to leave. She hadn't seen his expression, but the silence told her he did know exactly how *his* people were doing.

"But in case you need a reminder—they're starving and soon going to die if things don't change here. And if you don't see what is right in front of you, then that's your own ignorance." Versal's voice was soft, but her words visibly pained Rye.

But Rye needed to hear it. Versal had done what she could to help prepare them for the cold weather that was soon to come. She had spent hours knitting sweaters and scarves. Thanks to her time in Colony market, she'd learned how to create clothes that sold well for their climate. She had also stolen food from the security team and scavenged in dumpsters for broken furniture to burn to keep the camps warm at night. The autumn chill and damp cloudy weather brought sickness, and she had already seen a few people fall ill in recent days.

Silence was stagnant around them until Rye spoke. "I know it looks like I don't see it, but I do . . . and I also see how they respond to you, Versal. I don't think I've said this before. But I want to thank you for taking such good care of them. I don't want to even think about what state they would be in without you." Versal stuffed a blanket she had crocheted overnight into her bag. "It's nothing really." Versal paused, debating if she should say what she wanted to next.

She ultimately did, only to fill the awkward silence. "I know you care about the people here, so if there is a way to end this, whatever this is, sooner than later . . . I hope you do. I know if anyone is capable, it's you." Versal decided not to wait for him to say anything because she assumed he would not.

"Wait," Rye said before she had the chance to walk any closer to the door. "What . . . how . . . are they?" Rye fumbled. Versal knew what he asked, knowing he didn't quite know how to articulate his concern. He had no reason to offer her a place to stay but he had done so without questions and given her his own home to help.

"They're hungry. Many of those who stayed behind didn't guess that their food rations would be restricted . . . or that they would be exiled from their homes to live on the cold streets. And the weather is turning now that summer has gone. There has also been a virus going around the camp." Versal's voice was calm, but there was the undertone of frustration mixed with sadness she knew she couldn't hide.

"What? What can I do? I want to help." Rye's admission surprised her. But when she thought about it, she wasn't sure Rye could do anything more. Where he belonged was behind the scenes, working his technology magic to protect his people.

"You're doing enough, Rye. I mean, unless there is a way you can conjure up vegetables and meat . . ." Rye looked away. "They know you're working hard at finding whatever the guards want so they can leave." Rye's head dropped, visibly pained by Versal's words. She sensed there was something deeper going on than a search for a *thing.* "I, I hope you know you can trust me. If you ever want to talk to someone." Versal hoped Rye knew that. It wasn't just her connection to Hunter that allowed her to find comfort in Rye. While many others saw someone reserved or at times aloof, and separated from everyone else, she saw him as who he truly was. He was caring and smart—but mostly he was selfless when it came to *his* people.

"I can see you care for them just as much as I do." Rye's leg pattered on the ground with a nervous tick. "And I hate seeing them treated even remotely close to how I've seen Augland treat its workers . . ." Versal knew exactly what he meant. Rye's work for the last decade with Georgina had been to spy on Augland 54.

"I know what you mean. It's hard to . . . see." Versal's empathetic heart ached for Rye because she could see he wanted so badly to fight through technology advances for his people but didn't know how to even speak with them, only how to look at them through the lenses of the cameras he was so accustomed to.

"VELICs are not here to help. They are here to find out what I've been keeping from them." Versal fought to remain expressionless even though she was sure her heart skipped a beat.

"We have something Augland wants. Something that Hunter is helping to protect. But VELIC . . . VELIC could ruin all of what our people have endured." *Our* people. He thought she was one of them and not just Hunter's partner that she was sure Rye had been asked to look after.

"You don't have to tell me anything you don't want to." Versal wished she hadn't said that, but she wanted Rye to feel comfortable confiding in her because she wanted to know what was so important that he let NeuroEnergy suffer for it. "But, if VELIC is what you're worried about, then why let it come? You're in control of NeuroEnergy until Georgina returns."

Rye chuckled to himself. "I'm not in control, Versal . . . and because VELIC access could be both our salvation and our downfall." Versal placed her bag on the ground and headed back to sit next to Rye on the couch.

"If it's worth it to be our salvation, I think it would be worth it to also be our downfall," Versal said. Rye looked at her, confused. "All I'm saying is that no matter what, this is the worst it can be. I won't lie to you. You had half of NeuroEnergy leave to go to the Colony and those who remained wish they would have left with them. It doesn't get much worse than this."

"Don't remind me . . . I feel like I've failed them."

"You haven't. I think everyone here knows you take care of them. I've been around them, Rye. You're respected. And appreciated." Rye gave her a wide-eyed look, like that was the first time anyone had said that to him. But was the truth. There were people here that thought Rye was the smartest man alive, saying, "if anyone can do it, it's Rye." But that wasn't what Rye needed, he needed to talk through what to do next. "I don't know what you're hiding from Augland, and you don't need to tell me. But I believe you know what is best for NeuroEnergy."

"How do you know? You don't know me enough to make that assumption." The words were harsh, and she wasn't sure Rye meant it that way.

"Well, in Augland, everything was horrible, especially in Land of Legends. You had no idea if you were going to live to see the next day. So, when we had the opportunity to escape, we took it. Not because we thought we'd get away, but because it was better to risk a chance at escaping than continuing to live a life not worth living—completely hopeless. Workers were being sliced open and mutilated. All I could think was it couldn't be any worse than this . . . if I was next . . . all I'm saying is that if you want to hide something from Augland to protect NeuroEnergy, it can't get much worse for your people now. I'd say, you do whatever to keep it from Warren—don't let him take what he won't protect."

Rye remained silent. At some point during her rant his eyes met hers, like he was trying to read further into her past than she was willing to let him see. "Anyway, if I can help . . . just let me know what you need me to do." Versal rose again, breaking the connection.

"How are you this selfless . . . you take care of them and you even . . . you even make blankets and sweaters for people you don't know very well, and you don't question me more about what we are doing to protect them? Question why I've allowed Warren to do this to NeuroEnergy?"

"I trust you. I know for a fact you care more about the NeuroEnergy community than you do for yourself, everything you do is for them." She smiled. "And I enjoy taking care of people."

Rye stood, taking a step closer so he was only a foot from Versal. "Thank you, for everything," Rye said. Their eyes locked far too long in silence before Versal smiled in return. Sadness came across her features because while Rye was strong—she knew whatever he kept from Augland 54 would lead to *loss* before there was victory.

CHAPTER 34

Hunter

NORTHWEST DISTRIBUTION CENTER

It is dark outside, the night sky littered with stars. Hunter stands on the steps of NeuroEnergy headquarters. This is it; you did it. Rye summons him to the headquarters of one of the distribution centers. It is colder here, but the fresh scent of dark dust pulls him into his surroundings. He is going on a mission, something Rye hasn't been too forthcoming about, but he is game. The work he does for NeuroEnergy is mundane and he has no passion for it anymore. Engineering is fine. He is good at it. He knows wires; he knows how energy works, how it flows, and that the NeuroEnergy technology funnels energy from one source to another. That, he can do. Finally he can work on something with more meaning. Something great.

The night sky is melting away now and he begins to step forward into Georgina's office. Rye joins him and Rye seems as nervous as Hunter as they stand in front of the CEO of Pacific Northwest NeuroEnergy. Georgina has asked for a recruit; one destined for a top-secret mission. Not even Rye knows exactly what the mission is or what it could mean, but Hunter doesn't care. The air of anticipation is building as they stand in front of such a powerful woman.

"Hunter, is it? It's great to meet you. I appreciate that you and Rye traveled all this way." She pulls out a chair and gestures for Hunter to sit. Rye stands just behind him.

"It's my pleasure. I'm happy to help." Hunter cannot hide his smile. Georgina responds with a grin, her hair perfectly pulled back, and wearing a bright orange dress that hugs her tiny frame perfectly.

"What I'm asking of you is dangerous and highly top secret, so I'll need your allegiance before I tell you more about the mission. Rye speaks highly of you—your skillset and your discretion."

"Yes, ma'am. I'm game for whatever it is you need me to do. If it helps NeuroEnergy, I'll do it. You have my word."

"Even if you don't survive? You must know that there are risks and at no time can you expose us." It isn't a question. Hunter pauses. He can't go back now; his curiosity won't allow it. He will survive. He is a survivor and he has gotten to where he is today because he has been willing to take risks.

"If you come back, you'll be part of our regime here at Northwest. I'll make you part of our ecosystem here." That has Hunter sold; it can't be so bad.

"Yes, I understand and I'll do it."

"Great." There is a long pause before Georgina continues.

"I need you to go into Augland 54. We'll send you in as a fusion electrical engineer, but what I'll need is for you to find information on their energy initiatives."

The world around him begins to fade as Georgina and Rye slowly dissolve into the black abyss.

He is somehow transported and moments later finds himself in Augland. Hunter looks at his hands which are stained red. He can feel the pulse of electricity as it scorches his skin. He glances around him; he is in the underground tunnels to set cables for the new Suit Spa. They provide no physical protection from the dangers of fusion energy, no help. He begins to drag the open-ended wires to where they can be connected above ground. He pulls and pushes while the space between him and the ground above become smaller. The dirt around him threatens to collapse on top of him. He grasps the wires tightly as he pulls them.

"Hunter!" comes a voice.

Hunter looks around, but nothing. He's suffocating under the earth moving around him.

"Hunter!" the voice yells again . . . then everything goes black.

"Hunter . . . Hunter!" A forced whisper and a hand on his shoulder Shakes Hunter awake. Forest's shadow-sunken eyes were huge and he had a concerned look on his face. Hunter focused his vision, his breathing quick from the dream—memory, really—he was forced to awaken from.

"What?" Hunter looked around, aware now of his surroundings and wondering what had happened.

"Shhh!" Forest reprimanded him. For a moment he'd forgotten where they were. The distribution center—they had to be careful.

"Better be good for you to wake me, Forest." The lack of food had caused his muscles to atrophy and made him more tired every day they didn't get any substance.

"I did it." His eyes were a mix of shock and excitement.

"Did what?"

"Got into a VELIC. I'm in, man. I'm literally inside the VELIC system."

"What does that mean?" Hunter was wide awake now.

"Means I can corrupt it. By Rye gaining access to VELIC, he got the satellite locators from the VELIC system. Unknowingly giving access, VELIC opened the door to its network—well, it left open a crack and I'm going to kick it wide open. It's going to work. We have what we need. We can do it."

"You brilliant man!" Hunter was up out of his makeshift closet bed in seconds, pulling a reluctant Forest into a handshake turned half-hug. "And what about the satellite locations?"

"Easy. Once VELIC finds and relays the coordinates, we will be able to use them."

"But then, wouldn't Augland have them too? Rye said they have other NeuroEnergy scientists looking into it—it's not just us and that's why VELICs are helping."

"Yes, so we will have to move fast. Get access and then change codes so they can't infiltrate again."

"So basically, block them from accessing the satellites once we have them?" Forest nodded in relief. "Well, let's get it! And get the hell out of this place. I'm starving!"

Finally, they were making progress and soon, hopefully very soon, they could head home. Back to NeuroEnergy.

CHAPTER 35

Ashton

AUGLAND 27

Wolfe had been gone since they arrived at Highland Park, a city within Augland 27. He had been ordered to run "errands" for Warren, who had decided to make a pitstop following their departure from Augland 60, which also happened to be on their way back to Augland 54. Neither Wolfe nor Ashton had slept last night because they had stayed up late, talking. It was good to have him both physically and mentally back where she didn't need to think about him under the spell, but to have him gone the entire day was just as bad.

Warren didn't have Ashton come with him while he visited Augland 27 officials. Apparently, these officials were already cooperative with Warren, and he most likely had their support—which begged of the question what they were doing there.

Reuben lay in an exaggerated casual pose on the couch while they waited for the evening activities. To kill time, Ashton had gone out shopping with Reuben, then rested on the balcony of the skyrise apartment for a while. She had raided the kitchen to make herself a snack and paced around the living room to release her nervous energy.

"Okay, I give up. What's wrong with you?" Reuben didn't even attempt to hide his irritation. Ashton stopped her pacing, glancing furtively around the room. She never knew when it was safe to speak. Warren's own paranoia and VELICs that may or may not be hidden anywhere in Auglands were always a concern. Reuben's hand waved away her fears. "We're fine. VELICs aren't installed yet and there are no cameras."

Ashton relaxed. "What's taking them so long?" she asked.

Reuben shrugged without breaking eye contact with his technology.

"You think they'll be home before we leave for the meetup tonight?" Ashton asked out loud.

"Why are you so bothered by how long it's taking; you haven't been before when they've been out running errands." Reuben glanced up at Ashton, who resumed her pacing across the room, clearly becoming annoyed.

"Something feels off. I don't know, maybe it's because it's Wolfe's first time out with Warren without his chip turned on." Ashton couldn't pinpoint specifically what bothered her about Warren and Wolfe being gone. It wasn't like they hadn't done "errands" before, but this time was different. Wolfe was himself and given how worried he was about what his father would make him do, she was concerned he'd come back under the CS spell.

"So?" Reuben asked.

"So, I don't want him going back under. And whatever Warren has him doing probably isn't good."

"Probably not."

"Hence, why I'm anxious." Ashton glared at Reuben, perplexed at how he wasn't understanding her perspective.

"Well, if it happens, it happens. You can't change anything. Besides, it's been a week and Warren hasn't turned it back on." Reuben shrugged.

Ashton sighed, taking a seat on the couch and resting back against the cushion, "Tell me something to take my mind off of it. Something about the UnSuited."

Reuben set down his interconnect. "Fine . . . let's talk UnSuited then. I've put together some data about members and who we have across the Augnations."

"Okay, is it good?"

"So, we've visited DC, 2, 4, 10, 17, 29, 33, 19, 13, 60, and soon 27. Out of all those visits, we have solidified numbers of at least 843

UnSuited. The numbers have grown over 30 percent since your visits and continue to rise. If our projections are accurate, we will continue to see that growth for the next few months." Reuben smiled.

Ashton wasn't good at math, but the numbers he had rattled off seemed better than she could have hoped. "How . . . how do you even know about the growth after we leave?"

"Ashton, I'm in Operations; it's my job to know how to project growth. Anyway, this is even better than we could have anticipated. Once we are back in Augland 54, we can begin working on distribution channels for communications, supplies and coordinating safe havens for workers. I believe Augland 60 would be perfect; their CEO is pro-human and may be our next member in iHumanist. You even said that it would be better to have more UnSuited numbers there. And I agree."

"You . . . you're planning a safe haven for workers?" Ashton couldn't hide the surprise on her face.

"Of course, not every worker will be able to rise against the Suits. We need some place for workers to go." Ashton was on her feet and walking toward Rueben before she could think. He had been so casual about safe haven, but it meant more to her than anything. She quickly put her arms around Reuben, who was taken back by her sudden show of affection.

"It's really happening, isn't it."

"Yes, I told you we could build an army if we were patient enough." His hand came and wrapped around her—his stiff demeanor softening.

"Thank you, Reuben."

"Saying thank you now? Who are you and what have you done with Ashton?" Reuben teased.

Ashton snorted as she hugged him tighter, but it was short lived when the front door burst open, and Warren and Wolfe both strode into the living room right as Reuben and Ashton broke apart.

"Well! Sorry we are home late. I hope you didn't have too much fun without us." Warren's sarcasm had Ashton nearly rolling her eyes. The buzzing in her head stopped her. "Ashton, did you have a good day?"

"Yes, Warren. Great day. Thank you for asking."

"Oh, forgot." He laughed. "Sometimes it's just habit to keep it on." He brought out his interconnect and Ashton instantly noticed it. The buzzing ceased once Warren pressed a button on his interconnect. Ashton loathed that tiny technical device. Warren felt invincible with it, and he *was* to everyone in the room because the moment they felt any power—he would take it away with the push of a button.

"Wolfgang and I had a great day. CEO Rogan was such fun. I forgot how much I missed being around that guy. I'm glad we decided to stop by on our way home." Warren made himself comfortable on the couch across from Reuben and Ashton.

"Wolfgang, tell Reuben and Ashton about your day."

"It was fine." Wolfe stiffened, and not from the CS chip for once.

"Oh, come on, give them details," Warren said maliciously, as Wolfe's jaw clenched tightly.

Ashton shifted her feet, wanting nothing more than to come toward him. His face showed more than just hatred. It showed defeat, the shift of a man losing part of himself—and it broke Ashton's empathetic heart.

Warren wouldn't let it go. He harassed his son, wanting him to bear witness in front of Ashton and Reuben. It was power, his power, his ruthless soul rearing its monstrous head.

"I found the UnSuited leader Augland 27. He was hiding away—"

"Tell them *how* you found him. This is great, you two. This is what makes Wolfgang a brilliant security professional." Warren beamed with pride as he motioned in Wolfe's direction with a flourish.

"CEO Rogan knew he was hiding in Rain Forest Park, so I had their security make rounds between the community of homes and ordered them to drop a few smoke bombs in the caves. The smoke bombs brought him out and we spotted him on the cameras. We were able to apprehend him and bring him to Rogan's office." Wolfe stopped talking; not wanting to continue.

"Oh, Wolfgang, you're butchering the story. So, Wolfgang brings him in front of Rogan and puts him on his knees where the boy is begging Rogan to spare him." Warren leans forward, enthralled and enthusiastic about retelling of the story. "Wolfgang then gives his photon gun to Rogan, who then puts him up against the wall and I kid you not, gives the boy his own photon gun. They did a western standoff! Ha! Can you believe it?

"They took five paces and everything, before turning and shooting. Oh my, it was hysterical! Reuben, we should think about creating a game like that in Victorian. I bet Senator Chandler would get a kick out of that." Warren's sole laugh was too loud in the room as Ashton remained stunned and Wolfe ashamed.

"He's dead?" Ashton asked.

Warren laughed sarcastically. "My dear, of course he's dead."

Ashton turned away from them, feeling her stomach revolt while hiding her emotions. She breathed in deeply, feeling the burden of the UnSuited again. She looked up to see Wolfe staring at her, emotionless. She shifted to Reuben, finding it difficult to keep the heartbreak from her face.

"May I be excused, Warren?" Ashton's voice shook and she hoped Warren would be too distracted to notice she was moments away from cracking and breaking down. Warren paused before nodding and turning her chip on like he did most evenings.

"You're excused to your room for the evening." Warren turned to Reuben, "Tough crowd, guess you had to be there."

Wolfe was trailing behind Ashton as soon as Warren dismissed her. Ashton's ears rang from the customer service chip and shock. She knew death was imminent for many in their rebel group, but after hearing of all their success with the UnSuited, to learn a leader had been murdered did not sit well with Ashton. "I had no choice," Wolfe whispered to her just loud enough for her to hear.

"I know." Ashton moved her hand behind her to graze his fingers. She let them go just before they parted to their own rooms. She was about to shut her door when Wolfe stopped the door from closing and quickly moved inside her room before shutting the door and making sure that no footsteps followed them.

"Wolfe, no . . . you should leave," Ashton whispered, trying hard to keep her emotions hidden. He drew Ashton into his body, harder than before.

"Shh, it's okay. You're okay." Ashton started to cry despite Wolfe's soothing words.

"I can't believe you're the one comforting me, when I wasn't the one who had to watch it."

"It's sad to admit but I've witnessed enough that now it's getting easier to shut out. I just know how important the UnSuited are to you—to us—and the news of one of their deaths, even if you didn't know him, is hard."

"What was his name?" Ashton asked tearfully as Wolfe released her and began walking toward her bed. He sat down and faced her.

"Crawford. That was his name." For some reason, knowing his name made it that much more real, important. Warren was unwilling to see them as people, just numbers and objects. Crawford was invaluable as a person, even if Ashton didn't know him personally. She assumed he was passionate about the UnSuited, and for that, he deserved respect.

"I thought you should know that Warren contacted Joao and let him know we should be heading back to Augland 54 soon. Warren is deciding today." Wolfe changed the subject. Reuben had told her about heading back to 54, but Wolfe couldn't know that the two of them had communicated, so instead she nodded in response. "I'm ready for this nightmare to be over." She was also ready to get Wolfe his transmission blocker so she could tell him everything about her secret work with the UnSuited and Reuben. He would be so proud. They truly were getting close to their revenge.

"Me too." Wolfe smiled, keeping his eyes on Ashton. "How was your day?" Ashton noticed, again, the quick change in topic.

"Fine, I went walking around the city for a bit with Reuben. It was nice to get out. He bought a couple new sweaters for me."

Wolfe chuckled and lifted one eyebrow. "Some retail therapy?"

"Need to fit in with your dysfunctional, yet well-dressed family." Ashton joked. "Look at us, having a conversation like a normal couple. I'm shopping to pass the time while you're out working too late. Should I dare bring up how I feel like we don't spend enough time together?" Ashton said mischievously. Wolfe chuckled, but the reality was that their life was anything but normal.

"We aren't a normal couple?" Wolfe pretended to be shocked, making the truth of the last comment slide, giving her a half smile that had her grinning.

"Hardly. I'm certain you tried to kill me the first time we met. I don't know many couples who can say that's how their relationship began."

"I seem to remember being a perfect gentleman when we first met."

"More like tormented me," Ashton teased.

Wolfe scoffed at her. "You're exaggerating."

"You were ruthless to me while training in Land of Legends." A smile slowly crept across his face as he likely remembered those first few weeks of training.

"It wasn't that bad." He gave a sly half grin. "I went easy on you." Wolfe leaned back against Ashton's bed post, now fully vested in the light banter and lighthearted atmosphere and away from Warren.

"Lies. I think you liked the fact I cursed you every day after practice," Ashton volleyed. "I really didn't like you back then."

"Now who's lying?" Wolfe flirted back. His eyes were now warming and the day with Warren seemed to be melting away from his mind. This was the Wolfe she missed.

"No, if I remember correctly, it was Versal who was swooning over you, not me."

"Was Jorgeon more your cup of tea then?"

"Eww, come on." Ashton playfully swung at him.

Wolfe propelled himself off the bed and came to her, wrapping his arms around her and before she knew it had fallen back on the bed. Ashton let out a yelp louder than was safe. But once she was sure no one had heard, she let out a laugh. They finally had their moments where they could pretend the world around them didn't exist, where they could be themselves for just a split second in time before reality settled back into their wake.

"I'm sure you're going to tell me you can't tell me, but you and? When I walked in it looked like he was comforting you. Am I missing something?" Ashton tensed beneath Wolfe and she could sense that he felt reservations. She was keeping something from Wolfe—she could sense it wasn't jealousy on his part, more like dangerous information—and he wasn't far from the truth.

"You should probably go back to your room." Ashton couldn't answer because the truth would lead to even more questions that she couldn't answer. Wolfe was still at risk of spilling their secrets without a transmitter blocker—that and she had promised Reuben. But the way his eyes shifted away from her, she knew that her relationship with Reuben bothered him.

"Be careful, Ash." With that, Wolfe kissed her on the forehead and moved quietly from her side and out her bedroom door.

Ashton waited. Time passed slowly and it seemed that Warren wanted to stay up and celebrate, making it impossible for her to leave for their UnSuited meeting at the caves. This was Warren's sick and twisted world, and they were the unfortunate witnesses. Wolfe and Warren played poker, while Ashton helped make drinks and Niall prepared dinner. Warren reveled in living in his delusional world of a happy family with his son Wolfe and "Uncle" Reuben.

Finally, Warren went to bed and Reuben came quietly knocking on Ashton's door. She dressed in black, keeping the lights off in case Warren or Wolfe thought she was still awake. She opened her door slowly and Reuben gave her a nod before sneaking down the long hallway of the apartment and toward the only exit. They passed the kitchen and opened the door to their escape.

"We're late," Ashton finally said as they both rushed toward the skyrise elevators.

"Warren wanted to stay up later than I expected, not much I could do there."

"What are we going to do? Their leader is dead now," Ashton whispered.

"Even more of a reason to get in front of them, Ashton. They will look to you to be that person now." A heavy burden of responsibility sunk in, seemingly more than any of their other risky gatherings with the UnSuited. It was remarkable what they all did putting their lives on the line for freedom. The anxious adrenaline hit Ashton like a ton of bricks.

Reuben drove faster than usual, making up precious time as they moved closer to the Rain Forest Park from the City Highland Park where they were staying.

Reuben parked about a mile away from the park. "I'll be out here, making sure no Augland security are patrolling. Here," Reuben said as he passed her an interconnect, while keeping one for himself. "This one is for you; if you need anything you call me."

Ashton took it. It was the second gesture that day that proved to Ashton she meant more to Reuben than he led on. That he cared more about workers than simple concern over the infertility issues but wouldn't admit it.

"Thank you." Reuben shrugged before motioning her to get going, which is exactly what Ashton did.

The road to the cave was dark, and the cave itself was colorless. She had taken along a flashlight to help navigate in the void. It was quiet, even more than the underground tunnels of Augland 54, and she heard nothing but the slight echoing of dripping water.

"Who are you?" A booming voice rang out and she looked around, trying to find its source.

"My name is Ashton."

"Why are you here?" It spoke commandingly again, and Ashton still couldn't identify the speaker.

"I'm here to meet with . . . supporters of the UnSuited."

"I'm not sure what you're talking about."

"Yes, you are." Reuben had mentioned the name they called her . . . *woman in red.* "It's the woman in red. I'm from Augland 54."

There was a long pause. "How do we know what you say is true?"

"Do I look like a Suit to you?" Ashton scoffed in the darkness, twirling around.

"You could be a spy."

"I'm not a spy."

"How do we know?"

"I'm unarmed. If I was with Augland they would already know you were here. They would have come after killing Crawford. They aren't exactly playing the long game right now." There was a long pause as Ashton spun in the darkness with only her flashlight to give her light. "You could kill me now. I risked that coming here."

The darkness remained silent and for a moment she thought the voice had left her. Minutes passed and Ashton started to fear that maybe she had come into a situation where she was not welcomed and given them the idea that she could be easily taken out. She started to back away as fear seeped into her being.

Then a light came on from the very back of the cave. The entrance narrowed intimidatingly from where she stood, but she went toward it anyways.

There were around fifty people crammed into the tiny space. They looked confused and terrified, their leader gone, and the loss hit them harder than she could have imagined.

"You know about Crawford? You said he's . . ." It was the regret she didn't see coming when she tried to convince them of her innocence. She had exposed something they hadn't yet heard.

"I'm . . . I'm so sorry. He died, yes." Ashton wouldn't tell them how, but maybe knowing would bring them closure. Cries were heard across the cave, and it felt like nails on a chalk board. They were suffering. Crawford was someone important to them all. Ashton tried to both comfort and instruct them "This cave isn't safe for you all anymore and you'll need to find somewhere else to go, to hide."

"He said you were coming to tell us about the rebellion, about the other workers in Auglands." Someone in the darkness asked.

"Yes! So many others at different locations across all Auglands." Ashton thought about Reuben's data from earlier. "You aren't alone." A young boy in a suit and tie came up to her, smudges of dirt on his clothes, most likely from his travel into the cave. He studied Ashton. "I want to go back home."

It broke Ashton's heart, and she knelt down to his level, exuding compassion. "Where's home?"

A man came up from behind him, putting his hand on the boy's shoulder. "He was taken from our Colony not more than four months ago."

She nodded in understanding before glancing back at the young boy. He couldn't have been any older than Jagatha. "You need a leader. I need someone to help guide you when the rebellion against Augland begins. We're close. I can't promise we will win, but we can't let Augland continue like this. We are done being sacrificed. And when we strike—it will hit their core." This wasn't like the meetings of the other Auglands; these people showed more reservations and was quiet, but the passion was exposed as they grieved their leader, and she wouldn't push for anger. Right now, they needed to know there was hope.

For the next two hours Ashton talked with the workers of Augland 27. She found most were taken from the outside the Colony at some point in their life. She also learned their CEO had reduced worker living costs by eliminating any bedrooms or beds dedicated to workers. He also had a twisted view on corporate punishment which mimicked Warren's evil Customer Service torture. By the time she left, her head was completely occupied by revenge against the tyrannical leaders of Auglands.

"We stayed out too late." Reuben said under his breath. Ashton ignored him as they made it to the steps of Warren's skyrise building, quickly making their way through the lobby and toward the elevators.

"I can't take it anymore, Reuben. We need to move soon. I can't keep making these promises and living with the repercussions. Their leader died . . ." She was almost shouting at this point. There was only so much she was willing to put up with and this was it. They needed to revolt and make changes so that these people could live a life outside of Augland.

"Calm down, Ash. We are getting close. We just need a few more Auglands."

"When! When will we have enough?"

"Be patient! Do you want to do this and lose or do you want to do it right!" Reuben was fed up.

"Right, but—"

"You expose us now and that's it. And those eight hundred and forty-three UnSuited members? All for nothing. The UnSuited will lose, and we can kiss all this hard work goodbye." Reuben sighed. "Get some rest, Ashton, we will talk more tomorrow."

They took the elevator up to their floor in silence and quietly walked down the hall towards their apartment. It was close to three a.m. and Ashton was exhausted. Reuben reached for the door, quieting Ashton before slowly opening it. The place was dark as they inched their way in.

Without warning, the lights turned on and exposed a shocked Reuben and Ashton as they acclimated to the harsh light. Warren stood waiting with Wolfe.

"Welcome home, you two."

CHAPTER 36

Ashton

AUGLAND 54

Ashton barely slept that night and was already awake and pacing her room when Wolfe came for her. Without any hint to what was going on, Wolfe instructed her to pack her belongings because they were heading back to Augland 54. She began to ask what was going on, but before she could finish her thought, Warren approached. She didn't see Wolfe again until they boarded the plane.

Now, Ashton stared out the window of Warren's private jet. Since campaigning with Warren, she had become all too familiar with the luxury travel Warren required. Typically, Ashton would be lost in the clouds as they travelled high above the world, but this time it was different. Her fingers twisted in her lap. She had knots in her stomach.

Wolfe sat across from Warren. At least Wolfe was still himself, shockingly kept out of the Customer Service commands by Warren. But he too kept his distance. He stared blankly out the window while his father swiped up and down, reading intently on his interconnect. His brows scrunched in a low "v" as he concentrated.

Ashton flicked her attention to Reuben, who sat just beyond the seat facing her. He too was on his interconnect. She wanted to steal a moment from him to find out what was going on. She was conflicted. Part of her was frightened for the future, but the other part hoped Warren was scared to death with the thought of how much damage Ashton had done with the UnSuited during the campaign.

Warren leaned in, whispering something to Wolfe before his eyes landed on Ashton. She watched Wolfe rise and walk toward her. Ashton looked up, searching his eyes for any indication of what was about to happen. His eyes showed concern as he looked at her. He crouched so he was now at eye level with her and in front of Ashton's seat.

"What's going on?" Ashton whispered. It was the first time he had communicated with her since reluctantly telling Ashton to pack her bags earlier that morning. He shook his head, indicating he had no idea. Ashton sighed.

"Warren wants to speak with you." Ashton looked from Wolfe to where Warren sat behind him, legs crossed and with a whiskey in hand. Ashton's heart raced, not just because she was afraid of what Warren thought of Reuben and her late night out, but she couldn't help but notice that Warren hadn't turned her chip on since turning it off when they'd returned the night before—which told her what was about to happen wouldn't be good.

———————

Wolfe motioned for her to move. Ashton unbuckled and slowly moved from her chair. Wolfe put his hand on Ashton's back, letting her know through his touch that he was not leaving her. Ashton looked at Reuben, who glanced up at her briefly before readjusting the screen on his interconnect.

Ashton slid into the chair facing Warren who kept his poker face on while continuing to gaze out the window, ignoring her. So much had happened in the last three weeks. Before she travelled to Augland DC, she was sure she couldn't be in the same room with this man without literally throttling him to death. The anger was still there as was the need for retribution, but she had more control over herself now. Up until this point, she'd thought they were on their way to winning this game against Warren, but getting caught last night could ruin everything. Wolfe took a seat facing Reuben, only an aisle away from them. Ashton's fingers twisted anxiously in her hands.

"I'm going to give you *one* chance to come clean with me. And before you decide to lie, remember I'll find out the truth one way or another." Warren still thought that his Customer Service Initiative worked on Ashton, what a relief. "What were you doing with Reuben last night?"

Ashton paused; what Warren didn't know was that Reuben and Ashton had discussed this exact situation. If ever they were caught, their stories would be the same. It came in handy, Reuben knowing Warren so well. He would ultimately go to both and see if their stories aligned.

"Reuben asked that I help him find the UnSuited. He thought it would be a good idea to have a worker around to help network with the community and find their group."

"And so last night you went where?"

"You mentioned that Wolfe had found someone important at the caves, so we went there."

"Did you find anyone?"

"No, unfortunately they had disbanded after losing their leader."

Warren's eyes narrowed accusingly before taking a sip of his whiskey and placing it down on the table next to his chair.

"And if I turn on that customer service chip, you'll say the same thing." Ashton's eyes shot back to Warren.

"Yes, sir."

Warren nodded. "Very well." Warren swiped on his interconnect and soon Wolfe's back straightened. She waited for the humming to start in her head, but nothing.

"Wolfgang, please hold down Ms. Ashton." Wolfe immediately got up and put two hands on Ashton's shoulders, pressing down firmly. Ashton instantly leaned away from him, but he was too strong.

"What are you doing?" Ashton tensed under Wolfe's grip.

"You know the one thing lacking with the Customer Service Initiative is that, for the operator to truly use the device to their advantage, one must be very specific with what information he wants, and what to ask. I must admit you were an amazing actress, Ashton. I thought you couldn't hide the hatred you felt for me, but I was wrong."

"Warren, I don't know—"

"I think you know exactly what I'm talking about . . . and now I know something about you, Ashton. You still think you can beat me. Like I said during our poker game in DC, I don't play games I know I can't win." He shook his head regretfully before Ashton could even question what he meant. "Wolfgang, please remove Ms. Ashton's necklace." Ashton's eyes went wide, and her hand immediately went up to the necklace that held the power to block the CS chip transmission. She hadn't fought back until now, but removing that necklace meant the end of their world, and Wolfe's plan would be ruined. "Wolfe, no, no don't do this!" But she spoke to a man who had no control.

"No!" Ashton shouted and she saw Reuben get up from his chair, but he quickly caught himself and sat back down. Wolfe's movements were fluid as he ripped Sheva's moonstone from her neck and tossed it away before Ashton could even reach for it.

"You're wondering now—how did I know?" Ashton didn't answer him, her entire body still in shock, awaiting his next move. One swipe of that interconnect and she'd be done and under the CS spell—and for real this time. All their hard work, down the drain, and he would have access to everything in her brain—and all the UnSuited they had spent the last four weeks working to bring into the rebellion. "Actually, it's embarrassing it took me this long to figure it out."

"Warren, please." She wasn't sure what she thought would happen. That their time together would pull at his nonexistent heart strings? That he suddenly, after all he had done to his son, to her friends, to Georgina, could have a conscience? She hoped. She knew he had grown fond of her. They had great banter and maybe in another world could have been close, but there was something so evil within him that Ashton could never forgive.

"I couldn't sleep. The anticipation of the AEC Presidency kept me up. So, to keep my mind elsewhere, I thought of the last few weeks, more so about yours and Wolfe's attempted flight. Something I hadn't realized that I missed initially. When I found out you and Wolfe were gone, I was too busy trying to figure out how I had accidentally turned it off and that I needed to turn his CS back on."

Warren motioned to his son. "But I didn't remember having to turn yours back on, Ashton. So, I went through the historical data of your chip's activity, and I was correct. Your chip was on the entire evening, even before your fall. He couldn't have forced you while swimming and your data shows that there was little distress about disobeying orders to stay in the home." Warren bent forward, eyeing Ashton and attempting to dissect her facial expressions for any crack to her hard exterior. She wouldn't give in to him.

"My initial thought was that I needed to run this by Reuben, I figured he would still be moseying around the home. And when I couldn't find him, I tracked him." Warren raised up his interconnect, showing how he had tracked Reuben. "I knew he was most likely doing some intel work on the UnSuited, but weirdly enough I saw you too. Your barcode is still in my system. That got me thinking. I never gave you permission to leave after hours. I had told you were excused *to your room.*"

Ashton tensed, looking down only briefly at the white tattoo left from when she was branded by Augland when she worked in Apparel. Ashton froze, suddenly feeling the jet's walls closing in on her. She knew exactly where this was going. "So, I woke Wolfgang up, turned on his chip and asked the question I thought impossible. 'Did the CS chip work on Ashton?' He said no, then I asked him, 'How?' and he told me about that block transmitter that he'd brought with him from NeuroEnergy."

"Warren there is an—" Reuben started to interrupt Warren but was silenced as Warren put up his hand. Warren kept his eyes squarely on Ashton.

"I know now that Wolfgang doesn't have one, that you have the only blocker. Now, being a logical man, I needed to know how . . .

and that's when Wolfgang told me about Joao and how he found out about his chip and . . . how to block its transmission. So, here we are." Warren clapped his hands with a flourish and Ashton stilled. He knew everything now.

"Warren, we are now preparing for our decent to Augland 54," the VELIC in Warren's plane announced over the intercom.

"When we get there, I'll personally make sure you're taken care of, Ashton. Once I assess the damage you've done these past few weeks." Warren's words bit through the shock and silent fog that had put a spell on both Reuben and Ashton.

"You know, I gave you a chance because I wanted Wolfgang to trust me again and maybe, just maybe, if you and I could work together this could have been a beautiful partnership. I could have had my son back and you could have been by his side. I was willing to overlook the fact of him settling for a low-life worker. Now Wolfgang will have to live with the fact that you're too far below our status to ever be our equal and will never be one of us." Warren tsked, "Only an ex-worker would be so ambitious, and greedy, to believe you can tear down a society that has worked for years. You don't even know what it means to work hard! You judge every non-worker and decide they don't deserve everything they've worked hard for, every rung in the ladder they've climbed. You want all of us to suffer because of your jealousy." The words cut, but not from his assertion that she'd never be like him; no, she would never be like Warren. What disturbed her most was that he still thought his son would be by his side, supporting every one of his sick, twisted, manipulative plays for power.

Anger radiated through her and Wolfe had to hold her back, pushing her down harder into the chair.

"I finally understand." Ashton spat. She had a chance to hurt him—if only with words. "You're so alienated and alone in this world that you have to force people to even be in the same room as you. You didn't keep me around for Wolfe; you kept me around because you can't bear the thought of being by yourself. No one would ever choose to be here with you, and you and I would have never been partners. Never been friends. And Wolfe? He'll always hate you!"

"I don't need friends. I need allies." With that, Warren pulled up Ashton's profile on his interpad and clicked. The buzzing sound hummed a split second before every muscle in Ashton's body pulled tight. She couldn't move or blink—could only think while her body was no longer hers to control. There was so much to consider at that moment. All Reuben and Ashton's hard work the past month, Wolfe staying out of the chip's control, figuring out a plan to get out of the situation she was currently in with Warren, but all Ashton could process was the pain. It hurt to sit, it hurt to turn her head. It hurt to uncurl her fingers from her palms.

Time inched by for what felt like an eternity in the final few moments before the plane touched down and they boarded a helicopter for the final leg of their journey to the Executive headquarters. Ashton couldn't fight against the chip. Besides, she was already fatigued from resisting in the short time since she'd been stripped of her chip blocker.

"I presume that Joao is under arrest?" Warren asked a security guard who approached them as they walked out of the elevators into the vast marbled floor of the Executive entrance.

"Yes, sir."

"Very well, please take Reuben with you as well." Warren walked along the opening entrance on his way to his estate in the old Seattle Space Needle turned Executive office.

"Warren, please. I can explain." Reuben had remained silent until Warren had directed security to apprehend him.

"And if you're innocent you'll be released, but right now Reuben, something's not right and you've betrayed me before. I haven't forgotten about your advocacy to replace me as CEO. We got past it; you paid the price for your part, but I won't be made a fool again." Warren scolded Reuben, and before he could respond, Wintefred came from one of the conference rooms.

"Warren, welcome back!" Warren's scowl quickly turned to a smile.

"Wintefred, thank you and it is great to see you again." Warren had given Wintefred a nod. "I'm sorry, I wish we could catch up, but there is much to do and—"

"Oh, I'm sure you're very busy. There is a call for you that just came in. They said they tried your personal interconnect but could not reach you; I presumed because you had some sort of disruption from VELIC while flying. Anyway, they are on hold in the conference room." Warren paused.

"Who is it?"

"Someone from DC. He said it was urgent. I thought maybe it had something to do with the election?" Wintefred beamed with excitement.

Warren stiffened, clearly thinking the same thing that Wintefred had just announced.

"Ashton, Wolfgang, please go back to my estate. I'll be along shortly."

With that, both Ashton and Wolfe obeyed Warren's orders to leave. Ashton felt relief to be out of his presence. She knew that what Warren presumed was most likely correct. The last month had led up to this moment for Warren, and from the reactions of many of the CEOs Ashton had corresponded with, it was doubtful Warren had lost. After all, Warren had once said to her, he rarely played games he wasn't confident he would win.

THE WAR

CHAPTER 37

Warren

AUGLAND 54

Someone from DC meant one thing—the votes had been counted. Warren hurried into the conference room where the call was waiting. He closed the door behind him, feeling nerves of uncertainty crystalize in his mind. He was a confident man. He didn't understand why he was so nervous, but that didn't mean his self-assurance was unlimited. Warren expected to hear soon about the vote. Yesterday, he had received a message on his interconnect requesting his vote, and Warren presumed the same message had been sent to the entire House of CEOs.

It had crossed his mind that Reuben had lied about his pre-poll standings—much like Wolfgang and Ashton had. To say he was disappointed in his son was an understatement. He had believed, at least for some time, that there was hope for him and Wolfgang to find common ground, especially if he could build a somewhat amical relationship with Ashton. Warren thought she could be easily managed, giving her some freedoms so that she believed she and Wolfe could be together. Warren learned a hard lesson after these last four weeks, thinking he was securing compliance from both Ashton and Wolfe, only to discover they were anything but.

"This is CEO Warren," Warren greeted the person on hold.

"Sir, this is Senior Senator Vallem, Executive Chair Member for the President's office at AEC. As you're aware we've conducted a vote on who our next AEC President given the late Beaugard's departure. I'm proud to say that you, Owen Warren, have been voted, by a majority, to assume the role of president."

After several minutes discussing the details of Warren's presidential responsibilities and upcoming plans to travel back to DC for the election ceremony, Warren grinned and leaned back in his chair. "Well, thank you, Senator Vallem, I appreciate your message and gladly accept the position. I shall prepare a speech to be broadcast to the members of the AEC by tomorrow morning." Warren hung up and placed both hands down on the marbled table in the Executive conference room. He took a deep breath in before staggering his exhalation. He had done it. He had done what others in his position were too scared to do, too weak to accomplish. Now, he would create exactly what his father had been too soft to implement. Warren saw Augland as incomplete and in need of renovation. Workers will be chipped and soon, used as a weapon to keep other workers in line—then, he would rule Augnation.

Warren strolled down the long halls of the Executive Suite. He had much to do and prepare for his speech tomorrow. He had messaged Wintefred and tasked her with helping to align some very important details before his commencement speech, but there was something he needed to take care of first—deciding on the punishments for Ashton and Wolfe.

Recalling the night prior, Warren hadn't been entirely truthful when he told Ashton and Reuben that he'd woken up and discovered them missing. Wintefred had called Warren, asking if he had received any updates about the presidency and casually let him know about her suspicions regarding Joao hosting a worker in his home. Fraternizing with any worker would not be allowed given the customer service protocol. Receiving this information made him think there was something suspicious going on. That, in turn, had made him think back to Wolfgang and Ashton's attempt at escape.

After Warren discovered that both Ashton and Reuben were missing from their rooms. Much like a light switch flipped off to on, the seeds of a conspiracy and the knife of betrayal blossomed. He felt foolish to not have seen this coming. He thought the CS couldn't be overridden, but here he was, learning firsthand of potential failures of the device. Catching Ashton in her web of lies was key to solidifying his theory—there was more than just her ability to block the transmission of the chip.

Warren had approached Wolfgang and once the chip was turned on, he shared all secrets now that he knew what to ask for. He interrogated Wolfgang about what had brought him to Augland DC, why he decided to be by his side, and finally, how he planned on saving Ashton and bringing her back to the Colony.

There were still some missing pieces. Warren wasn't sure exactly what Ashton and Reuben were up to, but he was on a mission to find out. He would have questioned Ashton the moment they were off the jet but decided to wait for the new software update on her chip, which had several fun new features he had yet to try out. It would also give him some peace of mind knowing that there was no way she could deceive him now. Concerning Reuben, all Warren knew was that he wasn't working with Wolfgang. It was either that Reuben was working with Ashton or he too was convinced of her influence. Either way, there was damage control that once again he was burdened to complete—but first things first: accepting the role of president.

"Close the door," Warren ordered as he made it back to his Executive estate and where Ashton and Wolfgang awaited his arrival. As they were commanded, Wolfe and Ashton stood stoically in front of him. He studied them. Rigid, tense, and . . . blank.

With Ashton truly under the control of the CS spell, he could *now* see the difference. Her eyes were glossed over, and her posture was armor-like from fighting back against the chip's control. She was a fighter; he'd give her that, and so was Wolfgang—but that was to be expected. Wolfe was his son, after all.

Wolfgang and Ashton hung just inside the doorway like statues out of place and for a split second the smidge of regret seeped in, but he quickly dismissed it. They both deserved the consequences he was about to impose because of their actions. Warren abruptly sat in his chair, putting his hands to his face. "Pour us all a drink, Ashton," Warren ordered. "Wolfgang, take a seat."

Ashton did as she was instructed while Wolfgang sat facing Warren. The only sound in the room was the clinking of glassware as Ashton passed around cocktails. He had missed the darkness of his sky-high lair and plush leather furniture of his suite at the Space Needle and now converted Executive headquarters and condominium. It had been too long since he'd finally felt like he was where he belonged.

Warren's daily life consisted of interacting with those under CS control, making genuine human engagement feel unfamiliar and foreign. He much preferred this version of people—predictable, malleable, and obedient. Warren relaxed back onto his leather couch, letting out a sigh as he looked around the room.

"Smile, Ashton. We're celebrating." Her face painfully contorted to a smile. "I did it," Warren said, mostly to himself. He rose, lifting his glass upward. "To power, to change, and to the presidency." Warren could feel his adrenaline rush with his announcement. All his work, all his years of servitude and scheming, and now he had finally won. "Cheers," Ashton said without provocation—a natural reaction prompted by the use of the word "celebrating" and a common response to cheers.

"Do you realize what I've just done?" Warren began, talking to no one in particular. Wolfgang and Ashton sat down on facing chairs.

"No, sir. What do you mean?" Ashton asked.

"I just made history." Warren pulled another swig of whiskey that barely tickled the back of his throat. It had a smooth vanilla and oaky taste, which washed over him with a sense of calm. "I just etched the Warren name in history."

"It's very exciting, sir." Wolfgang said.

"Yes . . . yes, it is." He wished they would truly see this moment as a monumental accomplishment and could genuinely celebrate his achievement with the enthusiasm it deserved. His lifelong, hard work had all been for this moment.

His journey had not been without setbacks; however, the trial had brought to light many who opposed him. But he could let those memories fade, knowing he'd triumphed in the end. He looked at Wolfgang, who sat next to him with his hands laid neatly on top of his thighs. Ashton sat upright, refined, with one leg crossed over, awaiting the next that came to Warren's mind. The silence was eerie.

He couldn't understand their resistance. They were powerless against the CS chip. Wolfgang always had his little fits of opposition, but he always did as he was told in the end. That was, until he met her. Now that Warren had borne witness, or better, been humiliated by falling for her lies, he now recognized that Ashton was a danger to them.

Warren narrowed his focus. Here, he could ask Ashton anything, but he wasn't ready to cloud his recent victory with the details of their betrayal just yet. But then again, he wasn't ready to hear their cries, being outside the initiative, either. He wasn't sure he wanted to know the specifics. Either way, she'd eventually pay for her sins against him. Warren glanced at his interconnect—*Software update, 70% complete.*

"I'm going to shower—big day tomorrow."

"Please let me know if you need anything," Ashton said without pause.

"Just . . . don't leave the house. You know what, don't even move. I'll summon you when I'm ready."

Wolfgang and Ashton remained still and as he left them, he turned, looking back at the lovers sitting only a few feet from each other and unable to move because of his command. They looked only ahead as they sat close enough to touch. It reminded him of dolls sitting still after a child was done playing with them. He should feel terrible. Perhaps he truly was an "awful" father, given that he was more terrified of losing his presidency than the happiness of his only heir.

Warren quickly shook the thought away. It was Ana's fault. Wolfgang spent too much time with his sympathetic mother and look how he turned out. Wolfgang would learn though, and soon understand the depth of his work. The sacrifices, lies, and manipulation had been for the betterment of the world. History showed that no one else was going to make the hard decisions and he was stronger than the other Executives because of it.

That evening, Warren remained in his quarters, thinking about all that had transpired. Tomorrow would be the day that the new future would begin . . . *his* legacy.

Wintefred had planned Warren's presidential acceptance in its entirety: the broadcast, his speech on the Interscreen that would project a realistic show with holograms and AI-infused room enhancements. All so those across Augnation would feel like they were sitting in the very room where Warren was about to speak. This was impressive, given that Wintefred had been given less than 24 hours to put it all together. She had accurately decided on a perched view in Predator's Biome—fitting, because Warren himself had transformed to just that: a predator lying in wait to rule his kingdom. The cliffside gave a sweeping view of the monstrous hills and mountains topped with lush, vibrant evergreens.

"Did you get what I asked for?" Warren approached Wintefred as she directed the workers rushing to set up the podium and camera. Ashton and Wolfgang trailed close behind him. He had collected them from his office just moments before, relishing the fact that they would be onstage with him but unable to sabotage this moment because of the chip's influence.

"Yes, Warren. She just arrived. We will bring her out after your speech concludes, just as you asked." Wintefred beamed; she had done well, and she knew it. Warren knew why she executed flawlessly on all his demands—she believed she could be next in line. He couldn't deny she'd be a good choice. She was fiercely loyal from all the other Executives here, she could be controlled.

"Perfect, let's begin." Warren approached the podium and turned toward the camera. He motioned for Ashton and Wolfgang to stand close behind him, to prove once more to the CEOs that his son and the unofficial leader of the UnSuited were supporting him and well under his control.

"Show time, ready, 1, 2, 3, and . . . go" Wintefred stood just outside the frame of the camera.

"Hello CEOs, and thank you for your audience today. I'm humbled . . . grateful . . . and inspired to be chosen as the face of the new era of the AEC. But first, a moment of silence for a great man, a man whose shoes I'm . . ." Warren faked emotion, appearing to nearly tear up, ". . . not certain I can fill: Beaugard Hollenberg. A man who brought us peace, prosperity, and the pursuit of corporate unity. I'm blessed to have called him a friend and leader." Warren paused.

"I must admit, the reason I pursued the presidency and campaigned at length was sparked from the injustices that occurred at the trial. The secrecy and separation of NeuroEnergy and Augland need to end. We can't prosper if we align ourselves with division, but rather we need to look at what makes us a great union.

I tell you, everyone: workers, customers, CEOs, Executives, and Senators, that as I run AEC, I'll be more than just a figurehead; I'll be dedicated to our own pursuit of perfection because we deserve to live a great life." Warren smiled. He had pondered if he was even going to say the next part, but it felt right. He needed to show the Augnation world what would happen if anyone disagreed with the new regime and fresh leadership. They would never obey if not motivated by fear; and Neuro-Energy, the Colony, and other Auglands could choose to break rank and thwart his efforts at consolidating their groups unless he showed them the power he wielded.

"What I'm about to say, and do next may seem . . . sudden, but it's necessary as we move forward into our next chapter. If we are to be a better union, we cannot hold onto the ways of our past and must move onward . . . if the trial proved anything, it is that we cannot, and will not, stand for those who seek for our demise. We must stand up against them and overcome any and all resistance." Warren took his eyes off the holograms of various CEO members and looked toward the security guard standing by, nodding for him to bring forward the *surprise* he had for the entire Augnation.

The guard rolled in a chair, stopping in front of Warren and facing it toward the podium. It was a simple dark brown wooden chair, but only Warren knew the secrets draped around its carved arms. But what was more interesting was its occupant.

Warren could see certain CEOs shifting in discomfort. *Good.* He wanted them to know they should fear him. He looked at the prisoner and knew soon there would be peace within him and finally, the wrongs of the trial—righted. It would hurt many, but this would surely cement in their minds the consequences should they defy him. Sometimes, drastic measures needed to be taken so people would learn their place. When individuals went against the greater good, what other choice was he left with? If he let her live, what would happen to the world he had sacrificed so much to control? Chaos and anarchy, constant threat of rebellions would be the result. Warren was done living in that society.

He masked her only for her own horrific surprise as she would now see the man she had tried to ruin—would be the one to ruin her. Warren's eyes stayed steadfast on the blindfold over her eyes. He took a deep breath in and watched as the security guard removed the cloth from her face. Her eyes fluttered as the lights from above shone brightly for the camera behind her. Her eyes widened as she searched the room around her until in confusion, she met Warren's. He waited for her eyes to find his own so he could see the understanding dawn on her face and know these were her last moments and his face would be the last she saw.

He had to admit, he had waited a long time to enact his revenge. Although now he had a bitter taste in his mouth, he once was in awe of her and aspired to be like her when she had worked alongside Beaugard.

Now, she was a different person entirely: her hair disheveled, her perfect dress tattered and smeared with dark mud from whatever holding cell she'd been dragged from. She no longer was the powerful leader he'd once admired. She was nothing more than a traitor, and he loved every minute of her downfall.

It was bittersweet, the ending that would be Georgina—more sweet than bitter. Warren regretted her demise in a sense; she refused to see what their partnership could have accomplished for Augnation.

Neither of them spoke of the night they fell out of partnership, but it was imprinted on his mind like it was yesterday.

It was thirty-two years ago, and seven years before he had met Anastasia. Georgina was a young Executive, working within AEC while Warren was learning from his father about what it took to run an Augland park. Warren accompanied his mentor to the House of CEOs for their quarterly meeting. He knew it would be the perfect night to ask her the question in front of their respected leaders, in front of the influential board where Georgina and he would eventually lead together—a perfect union of two powerful individuals. His father approved and was even proud that two prestigious Executives would join forces to create a bond between Augland and NeuroEnergy. Georgina had ties with Beaugard, and their philanthropy was world renowned—as a young Executive, he was impressed by her ability to garner generous donations. Warren was in line to be the youngest CEO in Augland history—they would have been the ultimate power couple.

He knew they could have changed the future between Augland and NeuroEnergy. They could have created a perfect world that now he was forced to implement by himself—a merger ultimately meant to be. Warren kept his eyes on Georgina as his mind flashed back through these memories. That night, when he planned his proposal at the quarterly meeting, he had no idea she would publicly humiliate him. It took years for the ridicule and shame to leave his reputation, and he had to work twice as hard to gain back respect. That was all because Georgina had refused to see the bigger picture—a life with him, which meant ruling both of their worlds together.

Now, she faltered only for a moment but masked her emotions strongly in front of him. Warren ignored her pleas; they were on a public platform. Georgina's whisper brought Warren back to this reality: "Warren, you don't have to do this." Even near her death, she wore the face of a true heroine. Besides, Georgina had wasted her opportunities to reconcile. There was no turning back now.

"Georgina Raylen, you stood trial and you were found guilty of the following by the CEOs of Augland and NeuroEnergy, as decreed by the late Beaugard Hollenberg: conspiracy against Augland NeuroEnergy Treaty, conspiracy against a fellow CEO, spying, and sabotage."

Warren's eyes shifted and now focused on the camera attempting to reach the other CEOs. "And finally, you gruesomely took the life of that same man—the man who only did great for this world by uniting NeuroEnergies and Augland alike. The same man who helped create the resource plan to expand and update current parks for customer experience. He, alone, had the allyship and respect of everyone on this stream. He brought NeuroEnergy and Augland together in corporate unity. He was an advocate for the highest level of customer success and served tirelessly for the last thirty years.

"Beaugard's legacy will be that of a true hero in our history, and I will do my best to follow in his footsteps." Warren took the moment to look directly at Georgina, continuing, ". . . and to be just like him." Georgina's brow furrowed and she stared deeply into Warren's gaze because both Georgina and Warren knew he was nothing like the pliable and equality-driven politician that Beaugard had been. Warren was going to own and rule everything and achieve his authority through any means necessary.

"Warren, you've gone too far. Stop this; stop before we go down this path."

"Anything *else* to say before you pay for your crimes?"

Georgina's pleas meant nothing. The moment she realized it, her eyes swelled with tears that she refused to let fall. Her brow knitted as she contemplated—this was her end. "Death will be the end of me, but I die knowing that what I did in this world was good. Unlike what I can say for the rest of you—and especially you, Warren."

It disgusted him, her altruistic sniveling. He ripped his eyes away from her and toward the security man and nodded.

"Georgina Raylen, I condemn you to death by fusion energy. Fitting for your reign over NeuroEnergy and the electrical terror across our Augnation."

CHAPTER 38

Ashton

AUGLAND 54

Ashton's gaze froze in shock. Despite the chip's control of her thoughts and behavior, a tear rolled down her cheek. *Oh Georgina.* When the chair was first rolled out, it looked harmless, but she knew Warren was anything but. He was all about theater and drama. Ashton first heard heels tapping on the floor behind them while approaching the front of the stage, and Georgina's dress came into view followed by a muddy and ripped jacket, she knew who had been chosen for today's sacrifice on the altar of Warren's powerful stage.

It was barbaric. *Electrocution.* The sparks shown bright in Ashton's eyes while Georgina's face peeled back as her muscles contracted from the pulsing of the electricity. Ashton could feel the reflux of bile creep up her throat. The awful stench of burnt flesh permeated the air while Georgina's once dainty and delicate hands gripped the side of the chair with such force that her fingers turned white, and her nails cut through the leather exterior. It was worse than she could ever have imagined.

She had seen people die before. Sheva was the worst; Ashton had witnessed her death up close as she bled to death. This, though, this was different—to see someone writhe and feel the radiating heat of their scorched skin sear across their body. Even the Customer Service Initiative couldn't minimize her feelings of disgust that she experienced. She wanted to save Georgina, but the CS control was far too overwhelming. She was powerless. Had it only been a minute or two—or longer? When would it end? Warren stood still, only feet from Ashton, but she could see he had his eyes trained on Georgina. The difference between Ashton and Warren were the feelings this horrific scene provoked within them. She, an unwilling participant in Georgina's downfall, and he, celebrating his victory and a fitting end to one who would have overthrown him.

Warren spoke into the microphone, but his words were muffled as Ashton's ears rang and her body stiffened with shock. Georgina's body went limp, even though the electricity still pulsed in her body, jerking her limbs and muscles. Warren continued speaking to the camera in front of him, but all Ashton could hear was a distant voice followed by silence as Georgina's body mercifully became lifeless. Ashton remained motionless, her reaction muted. From what Ashton could tell, Georgina was gone.

Suddenly, it was over, and it felt more like she was back where it all started—the distant days in Augland 54, Ashton as a worker and Wolfe under his father's thumb. This time, though, Georgina was gone. Warren turned as the lights shut off in front of the camera and he cranked his neck side to side, relieved when he heard the joints softly crack. "Wolfgang, I need you to leave immediately and interrogate Joao. I want to know exactly what has been going on this last month while I've been away. Use any measures necessary, I want him dead after he confesses to his crimes." Wolfe's posture straightened, his face stripped of emotion. Without saying a word, Wolfe walked away, following his father's directive. "You, Ashton, are coming with me," Warren commanded.

No, no, no! Not Joao! Ashton shouted internally, but instead she followed Warren. His steps were broad, and she found it hard to keep up with the CS's demands of her body. Her footsteps followed with little resistance, which mentally made walking down the pathway easier. All Ashton could think about was Georgina—she deserved better. Ashton now understood why Wolfe always held a pained expression. He fought it—the chip's influence, but ultimately always obeyed its command.

Ashton and Warren made it back to Warren's penthouse where Niall was preparing breakfast. The concrete ground was colder than Ashton remembered, or maybe it was Warren whose heart was so cold and hardened that it exemplified the coolness around them. His living quarters were minimalistic, but elegant. Leather couches and dark, painted walls and the glass doors that led out to the balcony—the scene of a past crime that haunted Ashton's nightmares. The memories came flooding back as she stood in his living room for the second time. She hated this room, because within its four walls, all she could hear were echoes of Jagatha's screams.

"Grab me a whiskey." Ashton's face turned toward Warren. *It's only ten a.m. in the morning.*

"Of course, Warren." In her mind, her voice was distant and seemingly belonged to someone else. Her words were an automatic response, not allowing a second for any filter to be applied. She wanted badly to curse at him. *Get it yourself; go jump off the balcony where you killed Jagatha . . .*

Her hands trembled as she tested her mental strength against the Customer Service Initiative. The bottle teetered only slightly, but the more she resisted, the more the constraints of her mind forced her to comply. Ashton could feel the sweat glistening on her forehead. She picked up the glass, turned toward Warren who sat lazily on his couch, and placed the drink in front of him. In a split second she won the war with her pointer finger and tipped the glass over. "I'm sorry, sir, let me get you another one." Again, spoken without thought or desire to fix her mistake, but to exercise that control over her finger felt like a win.

"The more you fight it, the harder it will work at controlling you. It was designed to be easier with one who is compliant and increase in intensity when sensing resistance . . . and the longer it's on? The more it seeps into your mind and controls even your internal thoughts; just look at Niall. He wasn't always so amicable." Warren spoke softly, but his words were dripping with evil threats.

Ashton tried to speak, tell him off. Scream. Yell. The words remained stuck in her throat and refused to come out, instead forcing her to hold her breath until she gave up.

"I'd save it for the interrogation. That's just me though. You saw how much Wolfgang struggled to compose himself, remember? Eventually it wins, and you will only have tired yourself out for nothing." Ashton handed him the fresh drink, trying again to tip her finger against its rim, but it was pointless. Her finger refused to cooperate with this small movement for a second time, her body unable to follow her commands. "Thank you, now take a seat."

Ashton didn't want to fight. She was already exhausted from trying to tip the glass over with her finger, so she sat down on the plush couch, her body visibly shaking. "See? Much better, isn't it?" He took a deep swig of his whiskey. Ashton's stomach twisted as she sensed Warren was beginning her interrogation.

"Now, we'll start off easy. Were you ever under the CS during the campaign?" Ashton's body writhed as she tried to lie, convince him she had been under the CS the entire time. "Breathe and be honest." She hadn't noticed that she had been holding her breath. *Say yes, say yes! SAY YES.* She struggled to draw in a breath as she tried to fight back with a lie.

"No," Ashton took in several breaths. Warren was right, it was next to impossible to fight because the CS always won.

"Was your plan to build up the UnSuited?"

"Yes."

"How?"

Ashton's body tensed harder, but the attempts to conceal the answers were quickly forced from her. "Reuben arranged meetings . . . with them . . . in each Augland, and . . . I'd convince them to follow me as . . . their leader. The long game . . . was, joining . . . forces and . . .rising up . . . against . . . Auglands."

"How? What was the plan of attack?" Warren remained quiet, barely flinching as her confession made her brow sweat.

"To gather . . . numbers . . ." *No! STOP!* She shouted internally, but again, it was no use. The harder she tried to conceal, the quicker the CS caused her to divulge and confess. The interconnect confession was on her tongue, ready to divulge.

"When, when was this rebellion going to happen."

"I don't know when. Reuben was going to tell me."

"So Reuben helped you. Did he know that the CS didn't work on you?"

"Yes."

Warren sat back, frustrated with this latest betrayal. "Your plan is ruined now? Was there an alternate plan for overthrowing me?"

"I don't know the other plan." Warren pulled his interconnect from his pocket and turned off the initiative. Instantly, Ashton slumped over, and her muscles spasmed from the sudden release from the constant state of fighting. She breathed a sigh of relief. Warren hadn't picked up on Ashton's use of "other plan" and assumed she hadn't heard of one.

"I'm so disappointed in you." Ashton ignored him. The first moment she was back in control of herself, her emotions came flooding in and washed over her. Georgina's lifeless body, her admission to their plan, everything. Her eyes swelled with tears.

"What is wrong with you . . ." Ashton said. He sighed before bringing the glass of mahogany liquor back up to his lips. Ashton was instantly out of her chair and in Warren's face. "No, seriously, it's pretty pathetic what lengths you have gone to, and you know that even your own Executives, Reuben and Wolfe, have all conspired against you! You have no one. No friends, no allies. Wolfe doesn't even consider you his father! You're completely alone."

Warren's smile faded. "Some say it's lonely at the top."

"I guess others will just mock the fact your own family can't even—"

"Think before you finish that sentence. I won't kill my own son, but you, I can get rid of easily. You're neither a customer, nor an Executive. You will always be a worker. You were born into a life of poverty and will die having nothing to your name. You'll die and your likeness will be draped across posters celebrating your death and all your UnSuited will die in vain following your own quest for equality. You're nothing, Ashton. And Wolfgang? He'll move on eventually—we all do."

"Is that what you tell yourself? The reason why Wolfe's mother left you? Ana, right?" Ashton had already lit the match and was now playing with fire. Ashton could have, in that moment, killed him with her bare hands but had to settle for words to strangle him. He could very easily kill her and use her name to dismantle everything the last month had built. But that still didn't stop her.

Warren lost it. He raised and threw his glass, shattering across the floor. "You don't know anything! Anything!"

"I know enough! Enough to know—" Warren didn't let her finish. His finger was on his interconnect and within seconds Ashton froze.

"You are a foolish, dumb, stupid girl. You are still defiant even now! You know what I'm capable of? What I have the power to do? Do you just not care about the consequences . . . Ashton, you *just* don't care about your life at all? I could tell you to jump off the balcony and have a precious ending like your little friend . . ." Ashton's eyes were glued to Warren's soulless ones. It was then that Ashton saw the vicious wheels turning in Warren's head. "No . . . no, you don't care about sacrificing your own life. You know what you care about? Workers . . . workers like . . . *Niall.*"

Ashton was paralyzed, but the words coming to mind were like daggers meant for Warren. "Niall, come here." That's all Warren had to say for Ashton to know what Warren had planned—the evil he meant to disperse to her world and how he would ruin them all with one chip of the mind.

CHAPTER 39

Wolfe

AUGLAND 54

To say Wolfe was tired was an understatement. Not only mentally, but physically as well. The toll from his father's demands and conquests were nearly unbearable—and he had trained harder than most and for most of his life. He'd had a taste of freedom and yet here he was, back where he started under the Customer Service Initiative doing his father's bidding.

The ironic part is that it wasn't much different than the life he led before he had escaped with Ashton. His father had always told him what to do and he had obeyed until he decided he was sick of following Warren's self-aggrandizing master plan. But Joao was his best friend. And to kill him would be a new form of agonizing torture. He fought hard, but even his attempts to throw himself off his hoverbike were met with Wolfe's thoughts continued to race but eventually went numb the closer he came to the interrogation rooms he knew so well. He'd been there once with Ashton before aiding in her escape outside of Augland and again with Hunter when he had helped in the escape of the caged workers.

As Wolfe approached the interrogation room located on the same level as the cages, a security guard stood intimidatingly out front. Wolfe ignored the typical stench of urine and iron from the bloodstained walls of the cages and focused his tired eyes on the man. His black attire was typical of Augland security guards. He had a red beard, longer than the standard shave meant for all security. Instantly, Wolfe's mind went to the standards he'd enforced when he was Head of Security, noting this lack of clean grooming would never have been allowed, but that was the least of his worries now. He was about to see his friend. And be forced to torture him to death.

"Sir," the red-bearded man said, correcting his lazy posture when he saw Wolfe approach.

"Open the door," Wolfe commanded. Wolfe could feel the sweat dripping down his back. His breath quickened.

The guard did as he was told, putting his key card in and opening the door. He internally hoped the guard would refuse, but then again Wolfe would be forced to find a way into the room. It would be delaying the inevitable at this point.

Wolfe walked in. The room was dark, yet the lights from outside illuminated the four corners of the cell and in front of him, uncuffed and leaning against a table, was Joao. He raised his head and looked at Wolfe. The room was silent, musky, and the shadow of Wolfe's frame seemingly took most of the light from the room.

"Wolfe," Joao said with a grin—like he was happy to see him. The ache in Wolfe's heart nearly broke him. If Joao had any idea why he was here he'd be less enthusiastic. Wolfe grew tense, trying to force his body to stop where it was and not move any closer. He couldn't trust his own body; he had no control of what it might do. The refusal made his throat close and his muscles shake. He couldn't kill Joao, even if it killed him. He refused to take a step further because he knew deep down what that would mean—Joao wouldn't confess, and so Wolfe would be forced to break him.

"Ronan come on, put the guy out of his misery." Joao's grin grew ear to ear as he remained eerily calm while he called out to the guard assigned to him. Wolfe sensed a presence behind him and instinctively grabbed the man's arm, catapulting him over his shoulder.

"Chill, Wolfe!" Ronan said through coughs, trying to regain breath as the wind was knocked out of him. Wolfe couldn't stop. He fought back, putting his hand down on Ronan's chest, pinning him firmly to the floor. Joao sprung up from behind Wolfe, who responded quickly, backing his elbow up so met Joao's nose. Joao recoiled as blood ran down his nose and chin. The maneuver afforded Ronan the seconds needed to break out of Wolfe's hold, but not for long. Wolfe jetted after the scrambling Ronan, but before he could apprehend him, Joao lunged and gripped Wolfe's arms behind his back. Wolfe snapped his head back in a reverse headbutt, making contact with Joao's cheek. It was survival—or CS survival—instincts that kicked in. Joao held on tighter and turned his face away from Wolfe's thrashing head.

"Do it already!" Joao screamed and Ronan reacted quickly, leaping up off the concrete and reaching for Wolfe, placing something against Wolfe's cheek. Wolfe winced, waiting for the blow he was sure would follow, but instead he experienced a full body instant relief, like plunging into warm water after freezing—needles prickling his tired muscles. Wolfe panted, realizing what was happening in a split second. Joao still held Wolfe's arms behind him, and Ronan breathed heavily with frantic eyes as he scanned Wolfe's fists for any sign of his next hit. Wolfe didn't move, praying that this was not some fleeting moment of CS disruption, but the tightening feeling of both body and mind control didn't return.

"Put the watch on him, make sure it's touching his skin." Ronan did as he was told, slowly moving the cold round steel from Wolfe's cheek down to his wrist. Wolfe was speechless and his mind volleyed between reality and what could only be a dream.

"It's a watch; it's got the transmitter deterrent in it and will disrupt the chip—it has stronger wavelengths on this one so the distance can be a few feet away, but the closer the better." Wolfe exhaled heavily, feeling relief in his breath. "It's okay, man, you're back." Joao patted him on the back while wiping away the blood from Wolfe's two blows.

Thus far, nothing had gone according to plan:

Ashton and the trial

Complete the STEMP project

Aid Ashton in her escape

Wolfe began to believe that luck would never be on their side—until this exact moment. He could have cried and even might have felt the faint tug of emotions because it wasn't just his freedom that had returned. Joao noticed Wolfe's relief and released his arms, switching his full attention back to the bloody ooze that continued to stream down his face.

"I think you broke my nose," Joao said, laughing. Wolfe had no response, only shaking his head as he regained his composure.

It took a few moments for Wolfe's body to return to normal. He had exerted too much energy trying to stop his body from taking him to the cages for the interrogation—now his muscles shook from overuse. He had expended a lot of energy, but he couldn't care less about feeling depleted. He hadn't been forced to kill Joao, and the relief nearly made him lightheaded.

Ronan brought them water. Wolfe finally gathered himself, sitting down across the table from Joao. The bleeding had stopped and now silence filled the air between them.

"I'm surprised you haven't ripped that thing out of your head by now." Joao only half-joked. If he only knew how much Wolfe had thought about doing just that.

"Trust me, if I knew how to without causing severe brain damage, I would have," Wolfe laughed before the room went quiet again. He looked around, noticing the two cameras in the room.

"Disabled." Joao answered Wolfe's question before it could leave his mouth.

Wolfe nodded. "Please tell me it's not just you and Ronan . . ."

"No, Wolfe, it's not just me and Ronan." Joao gave a gloating smirk, and Wolfe sighed in relief.

"Good. So . . . what's the plan?"

CHAPTER 40

Ashton

AUGLAND 54

*Warren is evil scum. The worst person alive and I should have killed him—
even if it was only his Suit. I should have killed him over and over again,
so he was in an endless loop of death and life.*

With everything Ashton had in her body, she twisted and turned,
trying to walk away from Warren. He called for Niall . . . *Niall!* She had
no idea where Niall appeared from, but suddenly there he was, standing
only feet away from them in Warren's living room. He wore his typical
plastered grin on his face, practically part of his uniform by this point.
"Yes, Warren. How can I help you this evening?" Niall said.

"Ashton . . ." *Don't say it, Warren. Don't say it, don't say it!* Ashton
screamed internally. She fought against her controlled muscles to move
from where she stood. "Go get a knife from the kitchen." *No, no, no,
no, no, no, no, STOP!* But she couldn't stop. Her left foot lifted, propelling her forward—then her right. She fought every single step until she
found herself holding her breath. *Breathe! I could pass out!*

But as soon as the thought came, it was like the muscles in her
throat cleared and she was forced to breathe, sucking in air. She brought
her hand to the marbled kitchen counter, hoping to grasp it, but only
a finger held on before she rounded its heavy corners and found what
she was ordered to find. The sharpened weapon. Her muscles felt as if
they might tear from her as she fought against grasping and holding
the knife. Ashton was so focused on trying to drop the knife that she
hadn't noticed her feet moving purposefully toward an unaware Niall.

Five feet. Four feet, three, two . . . before she knew it, she stood directly in front of Niall. His eyes a hazel brown and his smile warm and inviting like he always had been towards her. Tears began to form and without much resistance slid down Ashton's face. *No, Niall. I don't want to do this!* Flashes of past memories, back at The Hook restaurant where he would flirt with Suits, where he would lean against the counter and talk gossip around Maya Bay. On bad days, he would console her and make jokes about their boss Marius or Sandra who was the Suit that had a crush on him. He'd walk her home late at night to keep her company, so she didn't have to walk alone. The same Niall who had brought a semblance of happiness to her existence for the first sixteen years of her life. He was a bright light in all those years, he made Augland 54 . . . bearable.

Ashton remained facing Niall, awaiting further instructions. Warren hadn't told her what to do yet which was cruel and unusual. To draw out this sick and twisted punishment—but in the same breath as the seconds passed, she hoped he would change his mind. Warren stalked across the living room until he was only inches away from her. "I could say it and you'd do it. You'd kill him." His voice was more than a whispered threat, it was Warren's power play.

There was a long pause, as if Warren was deciding whether she would commit the act. He walked away from Ashton, disappearing from her peripheral vision. Ashton tried to move her head to see where he went. "If it makes you feel any better, the Niall you remember, even if I turned off his chip, is gone . . . the CS chip in his brain has already taken deep root and is now too ingrained, dictating his thoughts and feelings. It takes months for that kind of control to happen, but it always does. He wouldn't know how to function without the chip now. I could turn the chip off right now and he'd crumble to the floor with the mind of a newborn baby."

Sweat dripped from Ashton's brow as she worked tirelessly against the chip, giving up on loosening her grip on the knife. Her hands trembled with resistance and anger as Warren continued with his admission.

Oh Niall, poor Niall. "It's probably time to put him out of his misery, I'd bet you agree," Warren said. *How could he think that?!*

Ashton didn't answer. Warren spoke just one word: "Ashton." So it began, the words she dreaded hearing as the moments between their dialogue commenced. Her hand trembled again, gripping the knife she involuntarily brandished between herself and Niall. She couldn't bear to look, but her eyes wouldn't close so she placed her gaze gently in the dark brown eyes of the man she had known since childhood. Deep inside, she begged for forgiveness before the deed was even done, before she crossed a line from which she would never return. Before Warren broke her spirit into yet another piece. Her soul would shatter after this.

Fight against this! You can do it! Don't let Warren win, don't let him win!

I'm so sorry, Niall!

You can beat this, Ashton. You are stronger than this chip. He's not gone like Warren said. He's fine! He's Niall!

Forgive me!

You can . . . please keep trying.

Please, please forgive me, Niall!

She tried harder to fight against her own controlled mind—harder than she had any physical energy for. Her muscles spasmed and she could feel the joint from her shoulder dislocate as she pressed urgently against the command, but it was no use. Time seemed to stand still as Warren drew out the command she was sure would voice next. Her mind frantically sought any type of rescue that might save her— however unlikely. Wolfe could walk in and stop her, maybe another Executive would burst through the door and disrupt the words he would undoubtedly speak. Niall placed a hand against Ashton's cheek as if he understood how hard this was for her.

"Put him out of his misery." Ashton couldn't believe it. Her hand with the knife rose above her, and Niall's gaze stayed steady, as if through their stares, they could silently communicate. He still only smiled, even though death was right there. She could feel the pulse of command begin to draw the weapon down and this time, when she held her breath, her body didn't command her not to. Her hand came down despite her resistance, sinking into Niall's flesh, right next to heart.

Ashton's eyes followed the knife until she forced them back toward Niall's eyes, which had gone wide in pain. Ashton's hand tightened around the knife and time slowed. She pulled the knife out of Niall's body, and he sank down to his knees, his eyes never leaving Ashton's as she felt her heart shatter into a million pieces. She couldn't look away. She searched his eyes, hoping for hushed forgiveness and silently begging him to stand. Instead, his eyes shifted left and right before rolling into the back of his head and he finally collapsed against the cold concrete. *Dead.*

Warren had made her a murderer, and she knew that she'd never be whole again. Never truly be who she once was. Ashton could feel an involuntary nausea but it was extinguished by the CS chip.

"Ashton, come back." Warren commanded. Ashton blinked and her arm was midair again with the sharp blade only inches away from its target. Niall stood in front of her. Ashton was confused; he had just collapsed in front of her. The air felt too constricting, and she couldn't bring in oxygen into her lungs fast enough. "I think Niall needs that knife for food preparations. Please, hand it to him." *What just happened? How is Niall alive?*

Shock radiated through her senses like lightning, making her heart skip a beat in anticipation and her limbs tingle with numbness. Her mouth stayed closed, preventing her from making a sound, but the chip couldn't control her starved lungs from sucking in air. Niall's eyes found hers . . . unfazed. Her hand dropped the knife into Niall's palm.

"Niall, leave. We skipped lunch so I believe we would like an early dinner tonight." Niall's focus turned to Warren.

"Of course. I will begin preparing dinner now." Niall strode out of the room, leaving Ashton with Warren. She was incredibly relieved, but confused, internally urging him to move faster the moment Warren requested dinner, but needing to confirm her mind wasn't playing a trick on her—that he was truly alive.

"I bet you're confused. See, I waited to ask you questions because there a new feature to the Customer Service Initiative. It's a sort of like hallucination, a mind manipulation feature we can promote in the minds of workers. I haven't yet seen it in action but can sense it had quite an effect on you. You saw the death of your friend by your hand. And let that be a lesson to you. I can do much worse than making you kill your friend—I can make you relive that over and over again in your mind. I can make you go mad." She thought Warren couldn't be any worse of a human being, but this new CS feature of mind manipulation was terrifying.

"You may go, Ashton. I'd suggest staying in your room until dinner."

Ashton placed her hands in her bathroom sink and let the warm water wash over them, as if trying to rinse a darkness from her unsteady hands. Then, she let go, releasing all attempts to control her body. She didn't fight. She didn't try to elicit movement contrary to the chip, and whatever had connected Ashton's mind to her body evaporated and was now hidden deep within herself. Everything was on autopilot: the way her hands moved, her walk, and even breathing. The chip decided what to do and for the first time since losing her necklace, everything was easier this way.

Wolfe hadn't returned by the time Niall called them to the dining room. Warren and Ashton sat together for dinner while Niall served them in his usual formal manner. "Where is that boy? I've called him twice now." Warren referenced Wolfe, his irritation bordering suspicion regarding his absence.

"Would you like me to go find him, sir?" Ashton said.

"No, no, he'll come back when he's finished with his task, I'm sure. It's probably just taking longer than expected. Joao won't break easily," he said, without another word. Ashton forced her food down, thinking of what kind of potential evil action Wolfe had been instructed to complete.

"I know you're very angry with me, Ashton."

"But sir, I'm not angry—" Warren sighed and before she could finish he pulled out his interconnect and swiped through several screens until the CS released her. Ashton's body went and then, she emitted a prolonged, hideous sound. Every murderous emotion and thought trapped inside her, every heartbreaking moment she had been forced to bury. Everything rushed out, cleansing her mind of Warren's poison until she was empty. Ashton stood panting for breath after her lengthy scream drained of all strength. Warren eyed her, ignoring her banshee cry and continued through his first course of dinner. He calmly spooned several bites of soup into his mouth, waiting for Ashton's outburst to conclude. She breathed heavily while Warren ignored her and continued with the meal Niall had prepared.

"You. You almost had me kill him. I saw myself kill him," Ashton said shaking, her voice low and husky.

"And make no mistake, if you try undermining me again, I won't hesitate to have you do just that."

"You're . . . beyond cruel . . . you're the devil," Ashton nearly whispered.

"The next time you dare go up against me, I hope you think of the consequences of your actions. And don't underestimate the power of the mind—I can torture you in more ways than just killing people you love. You know, I thought, for a moment, Jagatha's death had taught you that. I thought you understood that I won't hesitate to take everyone you love away from you—and that was why you were so . . . amicable, with me, but I was wrong. Another lesson, I suppose." Ashton felt a certain coldness and couldn't stop the shaking from both fear and anger that pulsed within her. Without notice, he replaced her freedom with the chip's control once again, clearly bored of being an audience to her anguish and grief.

Ashton remained seated for dinner with Warren through the remaining two courses. On the outside, she was talkative and pliable to suggestion and every topic of conversation, but on the inside she replayed his words and her actions, Warren dismissed her, too wrapped up in his interconnect to continue with small talk. Ashton had no desire to be anywhere near him and welcomed the departure.

That night, Ashton lay in her bed against her will with her eyes closed but unable to sleep. She couldn't move as the chip forced her to mimic the posture of sleep, but her mind refused to comply. *Where was this sort of resistance hours ago?* while she recounted Warren's message, "putting Niall out of his misery".

"Ashton," a soft voice said, and Ashton was sure she dreamt it. Maybe her subconscious was fighting and she was finding ways to communicate beyond the chip's control. "Ashton," the voice sang again. Ashton's eyes opened and she blinked against the darkness. She sat up, seeing a dark figure inside her room and she flung herself off the bed and scrambled back. "Don't scream," the figure whispered, heading toward her slowly until Ashton's gaze adjusted, and could see an older woman with greying long hair. *Was this another mind trick of Warren's?*

Ashton shook her head in disbelief. The buzzing wasn't present in her head, only a deep ache within her soul. Ashton intentionally raised her hand and let it fall, testing the theory of her own voluntary movements. "Relax, you're okay, I'm here to help. I turned off the chip. I have Warren's interconnect." The voice had an accent, one Ashton hadn't heard before. She heard thick "r's", and as she glanced up, she met eyes she knew well even in the darkness. Bright blue, nearly translucent. Any other eyes would have deterred her trust, but these were too warm and familiar for her to ignore. She knew Warren's eyes mimicked Wolfe's, and these were nearly identical. The woman's hand came down on Ashton's as she meant to convey that she was here to help and Ashton immediately melted, letting the emotions take hold. She lost control and began to cry, unable to stop the tears. The mystery woman embraced her, sitting down on Ashton's bed and soothing her as Ashton tried and failed to pull herself together.

"Niall . . . Warren . . . I almost . . ."

"Shh," the woman said as she stroked Ashton's hair "Shh . . . it's okay, my darling." Her accent soothed Ashton and her gentle hands eased her pent-up tension. "We don't have much time. I need you to come with me now, we cannot stay here in case Warren awakes. Here, put this on." Ashton felt the woman release her hand and, in its place, was Sheva's necklace. She rose from her embrace, confusion marring her features.

"Where did you—and who are you?" Ashton whispered. But even as she spoke, she knew the answer.

"My name is Ana, I'm Wolfe's mother . . . Wolfe's with Joao in Land of Legends and once you are there, you'll be safe too, my darling." She stroked Ashton's hair as they sat next to each other. Her actions resembled those as if she was reassuring a young child—like Ashton had once soothed Jagatha. Ashton knew this could only mean one thing.

Wolfe hadn't come home.

Wolfe was safe.

Would she soon be safe too?

Ashton leaped from her bed. "How!? she exclaimed. "How did Wolfe get out? Is Joao still alive?!" Ashton fumbled for words.

"Everyone is safe, but there is no time—you must leave now," Ana responded, gently placing her hands on Ashton's shoulders to quiet her. "The only way out of here is down the elevator. Right now the hallways will likely be empty, but they won't be for long. You need to catch the train to Land of Legends, and quickly, before security starts to realize the influx of workers travelling there."

"Workers are going there?"

She nodded, "To seek refuge."

"Reuben . . . he's . . . okay?" Ashton asked. She hadn't seen him since they were separated once they had arrived in Augland 54. Warren had had him arrested moments after they landed.

"Yes, he's safe. We have more allies in Augland 54 than Warren realizes." Ashton instantly knew whom Ana was referencing, and what group she represented.

Anastasia—Ana—Wolfe's mother, a member of the iHumanist movement. *Maybe we have more allies in Augland 54 than Warren could ever dream of . . .*

Good.

CHAPTER 41

Hunter

NW DISTRIBUTION CENTER

Hunter opened the door to the distribution center. Long arms of technology sorted and clanked away. They were only moments away from the software update that would shut the machinery down for three brief minutes. Typically, it was just him scavenging for dropped food or breaking into pallets before they were sent out to the Auglands. Meanwhile, Forest and Vic worked tirelessly on cracking into VELIC and securing more satellites within their makeshift tech center.

Now, they were finally leaving this place and heading back to NeuroEnergy. After Hunter had updated Rye with the news of Forest's successful infiltration into VELIC, the next move was to head back closer to NeuroEnergy where Rye was working to take back Neuro-Energy from Augland security.

Hunter opened their closet door and peeked out into the main room of the distribution center. It would be hard to make it all the way down the rows and rows of machinery, with all their equipment strapped to their backs. If they didn't make it before time expired, they would need to find a hiding spot for another twenty-four hours until their next three-minute window—and Hunter hated that idea.

Hunter glanced over his shoulder. Forest and Vic were lined up behind him like two shadows. Hunter motioned for Vic to come forward. He was the weaker of the three, being at least four times their age and with a bad hip. Hunter would need to act as his crutch if they had any chance. He had stressed the importance of reaching the other end of the enormous warehouse before the three minutes were up. They had no idea what would happen if they were exposed, but Hunter didn't want to find out.

"Ready?" Hunter mouthed, taking Vic by the hand. Hunter tightened up the straps of his makeshift backpack—it weighed at least twenty pounds easy and was mounted on his back. He took a deep breath. This was it—the machines were about to shut down for the update.

The hum of working machines and the rhythmic clank of automation died instantly, and Hunter pushed open the closet door. His heart raced as he began the countdown.

180, 179, 178, 177 . . .

There weren't any cameras during the shutdown, or at least that is what Hunter believed. The entire Augland Distribution Center system shut down for three minutes to reboot and install security updates. Hunter pulled Vic along as they started down the first row of machines. The pattern of machines from row to row was so uniform that it took a minute for Hunter to realize they were making progress. It wasn't until he saw them pass the canned food station and then lumber area that he knew they were getting somewhere.

Hunter's stride was longer than Vic's, which made him lag behind him. He couldn't slow to Vic's pace for fear of not making it through the room. He should have tested their route and practiced to see if they could all three make it out in time, but getting the news yesterday didn't allow for even one practice trip.

142, 141, 140, 139 . . .

Hunter finally felt the effect of eating less the past few weeks as his body started to falter with fatigue. His breath came harder and failed to give him any energy. Forest and Vic were silent too behind him, he heard only their pounding feet against the concrete. They at least were making progress past the robotic arms sorting fabrics and onto nails and metal rods, but they were still too far from the exit to see it in front of them. When they'd first arrived, it had taken them two days to maneuver from the outer doors to the far wall of the distribution center where they had discovered the doors that led to the hallway and their closet space.

72, 71, 70, 69, 68 . . .

"Faster!" Hunter urged through jagged breath.

34, 33, 32, 31, 30 . . .

Hunter's eyes fixated on the row ahead of him until he finally saw the wall that meant the end of the endless warehouse. If he wasn't so exhausted, he would have sighed in relief, but they weren't there yet. But they could make it.

15, 14, 13, 12, 11 . . .

Hunter could see the door now, but as he glanced behind him, he saw Vic had fallen further behind him now and Forest had begun to pass him. His pack was just as heavy and bounced painfully against his back as his long strides sped him faster toward the exit. Vic's grunts became more prominent as he lost steam to continue. "Come on . . . Vic . . . you . . . can do . . . this." Hunter gasped in as the words were forced out between breaths. Forest increased his lead on them, refusing to give in to his exhaustion. They were so close. The steel door was close enough now that if they didn't slow down soon, they'd collide into the warehouse wall.

Forest got there first, pulling open the door that would automatically lock from the outside once it was closed. He left it open, now frantically looking at Hunter and Vic. The seconds ticked away as Hunter counted down in his head. They weren't going to make it. Hunter's hands were slick now from sweat dripping down his back and arms. Sprinting for three minutes was harder than he thought. He pushed harder, but his hand lost its grip on Vic. He turned to see a struggling Vic stumble as he lost his support. Hunter was nearly through the door as Vic lay helplessly on the smooth concrete floor.

"Come on, Vic!" He screamed.

5, 4 . . .

Vic scrambled up and began rushing toward the open door. Hunter stood in the frame and put his hand out. His eyes were wide as he silently begged the universe for only a few more seconds.

3, 2, 1.

Vic was a step away from Hunter's fingertips when a force behind Hunter pulled and yanked him outside into the darkness. Instantly, a steel gate slammed down, closing the two off from Vic, who remained in the main room. Hunter stumbled back as Vic panicked, banging on the doors as the machinery behind them hummed back to life.

"No!" Hunter screamed. He shook the steel bars hard, pleading for them to open again. Within a minute, Vic's movement set off the alarm. Both Hunter and Forest combined their strength to push up on the bars, but they didn't budge.

The bars started to slip between Hunter's fingers. He was exhausted from the running and the sweat made it impossible to keep his grip. His biceps shook. The alarm grew louder and louder.

"Help me!" Vic yelled as he put his hands through the bars and gripped Hunter's drenched shirt in utter fear. "We're trying, Vic!" Forest yelled through gritted teeth.

"Unauthorized Personnel. Unauthorized Personnel." The robotic voice spoke over the ringing alarm. Hunter didn't know what to expect next—they'd never set off the alarm before and he didn't know the security protocol.

"Stop moving! You need to hide, Vic. You need to hide! Forest, do something. Override their system. Something!" Hunter stopped and tried to focus on a panicked Vic.

"It's not on the same system as VELIC; there's no way to get into this system. At least not easily, I'd have to—"

Vic interrupted Forest, "No, no, you just need to open it! Open it, Hunter! Please!" Hunter couldn't take the pleading any longer.

"Unauthorized Personnel. Unauthorized Personnel."

The steel bars began to glow red and heat up and Forest yelped in pain as he tried to ignore the white hot pain while pushing up against the bars. Hunter pulled away as the steel bar escalated from hot to searing and burned the top layer of his skin. Vic had to step away too as the heat radiated from the gated door. The alarm continued and pulsed louder and louder.

"What do we do?" Forest was panting, looking at Hunter while Vic pulled at his hair, unable to think clearly through the noise and logically look for a corner to hide.

"Unauthorized Personnel. Unauthorized Personal." The alarm suddenly stopped. Hunter noticed it first, stepping closer to the blazing bars to get Vic's attention. At every station, steel arms worked away in an endless loop of motion, generating resources for Augland. When the update finished, an autobot broke from its sorting duties and wheeled around quickly, marking Vic as its target. Vic was still focused on opening the door and unaware of the steel monster approaching him. "Vic, you need to get out of here!" Hunter yelled as the ten-foot-tall appliance targeted his scientist.

Vic wasn't listening. He was paralyzed with fear, not able to process what was happening. "Vic!" Forest yelled, but it was too late. As Vic glanced over his shoulder, the mechanical beast yanked Vic's leg, forcing him to the ground and pulling him up beyond Hunter's line of sight from the outdoors. All Hunter could hear were Vic's bloodcurdling screams.

Suddenly, Vic's body came flying down before hitting the ground at such a force Hunter could hear Vic's bones crush. The eerie silence washed over him while Hunter stood by helplessly. Forest was ghost white as his mouth gaped open. Hunter forced himself to look at Vic's lifeless face and fixed eyes as blood pooled around him, from his head to his feet. Instantly, Hunter felt bile rush up his throat and he expelled it outward. He had only consumed half a bottle of water, so there wasn't much to throw up. His hands involuntarily covered his face; he couldn't look at Vic again. It was too gruesome.

"We . . . we should go. They probably know we're here by now." The words sounded distant as if he weren't the one speaking. Hunter faced away and toward the dense forest nestled around the distribution warehouse while Forest stood frozen in place, unable to look away from Vic. Forest breathed in heavily as shock overtook his mind and body.

"I'm, I'm not sure we can do this without Vic. He knew how to get into and control the satellites."

"You know exactly what he did. You were there with him. Every day you were there with him," Hunter said.

"Yes, but he knew everything. I've got his notes and data, but to actually make it work we need Vic."

"We don't have a choice, so you're going to need to figure it out, Forest. Got it? You. Need to figure it out." Hunter thought if he just said it out loud, Forest would understand the gravity of the situation they found themselves in. If Forest didn't get it together, these past weeks spent hiding and working grueling days while essentially starving, would be for nothing. And if that was true, UnSuited, the Colony, and NeuroEnergy had no chance.

CHAPTER 42

Wolfe

LAND OF LEGENDS, AUGLAND 54

Warren seemed to have little issue refilling the cages with workers after Hunter, Joao, and Wolfe had aided in the mass worker escape, Wolfe noted as he and Joao walked along the long aisle between cages. The occupants remained quiet as the group moved swiftly toward the exit. "We moved the stockpile of weapons last week from Victorian brothels to Land of Legends and are transporting the majority of UnSuited to the Viking and Saxon camps as we speak."

"How many people do we have so far?" Wolfe questioned as Joao led them along.

"Last count Bez did, we had over five hundred and thirty-two. More coming every time the train stops." Wolfe's brow raised in surprise. That was a significant number of workers, which was both terrifying and revitalizing.

"That's going to get Warren's attention sooner rather than later."

"Eventually, yes. Warren is going to figure out that we've taken over Legends and will bring the fight to us. But let's hope that with the presidency and meeting with his new AEC Executive team, we've got some time on our hands to prepare." Joao then explained their mission, step by step, to catch Wolfe up.

It's happening. Wolfe nearly pinched himself to make sure it was all real. One side effect of the Customer Service chip was that after time, it was hard to trust his own thoughts. Just moments earlier, Wolfe had been filled with fear and dread, knowing he would be interrogating and likely killing his long-time friend. That dark fear would haunt his dreams for the rest of his life. But he would believe this, everything he had dreamed of while under his father's thumb for the last month—nothing compared to its reality.

Joao had been one step ahead of them all and rallied a large group of security faithful to Wolfe and the UnSuited—under even his father's nose. Security guards now played double agents, like Ronan, convincing Augland that they were guards sworn to 54 while fueling the rebellion. Wolfe wouldn't deny that when Warren discovered Ashton's pretense of being under the chip's spell, that he was sure their plan had been foiled, even Joao's.

"Warren knows about the transmitter that stops the chip's function and likely won't be willing to overlook the fact I failed to kill you. Plus, I've already been gone too long." Wolfe thought about his interconnect, which he had ditched once Joao informed him of Land of Legend's rebellion location. His father was calling him nonstop at that point and no doubt tracking his location and wondering why he had been gone for the last five hours.

"We have no other choice at this point but to hide or fight. From what I know, Rye has been keeping Augland men occupied in Neuro-Energy after their takeover; Hunter and the boys have been hiding and finishing the STEMP project. The last I heard, Rye was working with Forest to infiltrate the VELIC system that Warren had delivered to NeuroEnergy." Joao's gait began to slow, and Wolfe glanced at him with a puzzled expression. "Nothing new with STEMP since I've been gone?"

"Rye's gone dark, but I'm sure it's just not safe to communicate yet. And I chose not to have any communication with Hunter, Forest, or Vic, in case something went wrong here, and Warren could use me to find him and the scientist."

"How long has it been?" Wolfe took two large steps forward to face Joao with his concern. Joao abruptly stopped in front of two double doors.

"Since we connected with Rye? A week or so," Joao said casually as he put credentials in the keypad to give them access beyond the doors.

A week? Wolfe thought to himself. "You think he's still alive?"

Joao shrugged, "I feel like if he had died, I would have heard. I'm still in contact with the security guard running point on NeuroEnergy's takeover." Joao was right.

"Who do we trust on Augland security side?" Wolfe was too far removed for comfort.

Joao shook his head, "I don't know names, but there are two that I feel confident in. It hasn't been safe enough for a NeuroEnergy debrief. I know my contact will reach out when it's safe and give us an update on Rye." Wolfe followed Joao into Augland's supply room, where Joao began placing photon guns and interconnects into his bag. "We need hoverbikes from the security locker and then we'll make our way to Land of Legends."

"I'll need a new interconnect too." Wolfe thought of Ashton and how he was going to get her away from Warren. *One thing at a time. Every step now has to be meticulously planned and executed.*

Wolfe and Joao stepped through the Land of Legends train doors and toward the vast greenery of rolling hills and deepening blue skies as night descended. The wind blew around him as the scent of campfire and fresh damp earth filled the air. It felt like an eternity since he'd been back in Land of Legends, and even longer since he and Ashton had been thrown into each other's world. Joao strode ahead purposefully while Wolfe trailed close behind him, as they walked along the path toward the Viking and Saxon battlefield.

"What about Warren's access?" Wolfe tossed the question in front of Joao as they reached a sloping hill where the Viking camp would soon come into view.

"We were able to disable most everything. It's technologically bare and anything that could be controlled by Warren has been disabled—even the gondola station. We thought Land of Legends would be best because there are no Suits living here, so we are able to overtake it more easily than any other park. We've also been able to recreate transmitters at a rapid pace, passing them out to new UnSuited like candy." Wolfe went down the internal checklist of all technology Warren could use against them: cameras, audio recorders, and CS chips.

Wolfe knew everything there was to know about Land of Legends, which made it a perfect place to house the rebels. At times he forgot that he was the one who had created this place—built it from the ground to reality. Quiet and peaceful. But Land of Legends was really a beautiful disguise because, at its roots, it held death and destruction. Each evening the sun went down on the hundreds of workers who were forced to sacrifice their lives and every morning their deaths were wiped away as if their executions had never happened. Even after every customer-driven battle, by morning the grass was green again, the birds chirping, and any evidence of the murderous worker experience forgotten. And he had helped create it—the monstrous bloodbath of a park. That guilt would never leave him.

This place was a curse and blessing, and it was ironic to have it be the place workers rebelled and exacted revenge. It was time Legends became just that—a land for transformation from workers to warriors.

Land of Legends' Viking camp hadn't changed much, other than the numerous makeshift tents that were the homes of workers now staying on the property—besides that, it was the same. Fur-covered tents littered the dusty ground. The massive tent where Ashton had once been the Viking princess who catered to the customers called Earls for entertainment. Wolfe began the walk down to the plateau between the tents and castle.

"And the people here, all workers part of the rebellion?" Wolfe surveyed the many individuals walking through the Viking community, and he presumed more were creating homes within the castle walls. Hundreds of people gathered, and Wolfe wondered how much, exactly, he and Ashton had missed while away touring Augnation with Warren.

"Any combat training?" Wolfe was nearly matching Joao's pace now.

Joao shook his head. "We didn't get that far. Right now, it's just trying to barricade the entrances here, in case security or Suits attack. We do have a group of people heading to the outer Legend's wall to see if we can dig an underground tunnel to outside the walls in case things get ugly and we are forced to flee." Wolfe winced. Fighting a war with a group of workers who had been groomed as actors most of their lives, trained by Augland Center, was less than ideal—it was madness.

"At some point we have to prepare to fight with or without STEMP," Wolfe said, mostly to himself. The people here were not an army, they weren't even security professionals. Most of the men who trained under him had years of experience in security before even holding a gun. Wolfe toyed with the idea of the right and ethical implications of putting unprepared workers through a battle they would likely not survive.

As if reading Wolfe's mind, Joao responded before Wolfe could verbalize his concerns. "Workers know what they are risking by coming here. We didn't force anyone to join the rebellion and if they aren't capable of fighting, then we find a way to help them escape." Wolfe nodded, but it didn't ease the tension building within him—they were preparing for war. *And how would war be any different than what Augland had staged in Land of Legends? Back then, the Suits slaughtered the workers by the hundreds . . . would a battle now be any different?*

Wolfe drew back the fur curtains that exposed a massive fire encircled by tables filled with workers eating an early dinner. But instead of joining them, Wolfe retreated to the shadows of the vast room, and was absorbing his new surrounding: smiling workers, noisy chatter, and *something else—revival?* It could be hope. They weren't cowards huddled in fear at what was to come—instead the groups laughed or demonstrated their own fighting and wrestling techniques as they ate and prepared for the days ahead, which left Wolfe speechless.

Joao had disappeared to gather key rebellion leaders who were reported to be near the Saxon castle. They all waited for their new interconnects that couldn't be traced by Warren and the Augland guards. Joao and, from what he relayed, Bez had been gathering UnSuited secretly since learning Warren was returning to 54. Wolfe still hadn't figured out how Joao knew his father would know about the CS chip transmission blocker, but he was thankful regardless. And with that thought, Wolfe briefly touched the new accessory on his wrist, the watch that prevented his own chip from controlling his mind.

Wolfe sighed as he soaked in the view from where he was standing now and all that had been accomplished in his absence. Handing over the reins to Joao was difficult, but Joao deserved this win. He had come through when Wolfe hadn't—his rash decision to go to DC and the aftermath following the trial would weigh heavily on him. But he reminded himself, that choice had been made to save Ashton. When it came to difficult decisions, he would choose Ashton every time, even if that meant giving up control.

"Relaxed is a much better look on you," said a deep voice and Wolfe didn't need to look over his shoulder to know who it was, but it was still a surprise to see him in this context.

"And how did you get away from my father unscathed, Reuben?" Wolfe's arms remained crossed as he continued to watch the workers eating and milling about.

"I have more friends than you might think."

"Or you're playing both sides like you tend to do."

Reuben chuckled. "You and Ashton are hard sales when it comes to trust. I truly hope it's not that way in your personal relationship."

The mention of her name caused Wolfe to shift his weight uneasily. Although Reuben remarked that Wolfe *looked* relaxed, he was anything but. He felt powerless at this moment and Ashton was hours away from him in another park with the most dangerous man he knew. If his freedom came at the cost of hers, he'd burn this whole place down. "She hasn't escaped from *him* yet," Wolfe responded with a clenched jaw.

"What's the plan to get her out?" Reuben inquired, shoving his hands into the pockets of his casual clothing. He must have figured out his typical Executive attire would do little in a rebellion campsite—his Suit alone would bring discomfort to workers.

"Still working that one out." Wolfe cleared his throat, confessing he hadn't designed Ashton's escape route yet. He couldn't casually stroll back into his father's home—not now. Warren was more than a little suspicious of his absence and likely had already sent a team to track him down, and ensure Joao was still in custody. Ashton's chip would also present a problem when planning how to extract her from Warren's presence. He'd have to render her unconscious to physically stop the chip from controlling her.

"Let me help you." Reuben lowered his voice to a whisper. "Another peace offering I'm extending."

"*Another* peace offering, Reuben?" Wolfe shook his head in disbelief. "Yes, you helped Ashton and me escape without asking anything in return. Nothing—you risked so much to give us a chance. You knew at some point my father would find out how you engineered the escape, which is a little suspicious. Let me remind you, I have a childhood of memories that remind me you can be just as manipulative, self-serving, and vindictive as my father. You've picked him over me my entire life. It wasn't that long ago that he imprisoned me after you supported me as CEO, then you turned your back on me. This whole thing could have been avoided if you would have been on my side and convinced the other Executives that Warren shouldn't be in power."

"You can't blame me for that. I did what I could to help you, Wolfe. He was still too powerful to go after and neither of us were prepared to go to battle against him. We both found that out the hard way when he outsmarted us by creating that Suit of you. I chose to step away at that point and regroup to find a new way to play this game of power against Warren."

"What's changed?" Wolfe growled, clearly agitated with all the secrecy. Reuben was clearly hiding something. Reuben's dark eyes met Wolfe's blue ones. "What's your end game, Reuben?" Wolfe asked, knowing it was a coin toss whether he would get the truth.

"My plans will be made clear with time, Wolfe. And while you may not entirely trust my motives, I've never been a liar." Reuben bit back in a similar condescending tone.

"We don't want any part of your plans. Leave Ashton out of it," Wolfe threatened.

"You need me whether or not you believe it. You will soon see. As for Ashton, I owe it to her. She's been an invaluable asset to me, but she knows too much, and our entire strategy is vulnerable every minute she remains imprisoned. Let me do this, Wolfe." There it was. Reuben wanted to help because he couldn't have Ashton exposing any of his secrets to Warren.

Wolfe's eyes narrowed, a pinch of jealousy creeping into his mind as Reuben casually dropped Ashton's name in the same sentence as "relationship"—which Ashton had failed to mention during their late nights together or during their escape attempt.

"I asked her not to mention anything to you. And if the surprised look on your face says anything, I gather that she was true to her word." Wolfe sighed deeply, releasing the need to control the conversation along with the plot to rescue Ashton. But that didn't mean it didn't hurt knowing that secrets had been kept from him. *You kept secrets too; don't be a hypocrite,* Wolfe's internal voice reasoned with him.

Wolfe chose to ignore Reuben's insinuation. "How would you get her out?" When Ashton was back with him, safe, he would dig deeper into her "relationship" with Reuben. He had known Reuben his entire life and while Wolfe was thankful for his help in Augland 27, that didn't make up for the years when Reuben chose to stand by while his father became the monster he is today.

"Relax, Wolfe. I've already made arrangements. She's on her way and will be here before the sun rises."

Almost as if on cue, Wolfe saw Bez, Joao, and Ronan hurry through the front drapes of the massive tent. Wolfe turned to Reuben, but as mysteriously as he had appeared, Reuben was gone.

"Wolfy!" A vibrant Bez rushed over, punching Wolfe on his arm. "You're not dead!" Wolfe laughed.

"Hi, Bez. Good to see you alive and . . . still got that mean right hook on you."

"It takes much more than Augland to take me out," Bez boasted.

"That I couldn't agree more on." Wolfe and Bez had a colorful history. After saving her from death after a Suit's wife accused her of fraternizing, he had checked on her often during her year at the brothel, making sure she was fed and taken care of. They had more of a sibling relationship and bantered endlessly—which they both loved.

"C'mon . . . you can say it. You're so impressed with what we did, Wolfy . . . that you couldn't have done this without us and we probably did it better than you ever could and you're forever in awe of how awesome and smart and charismatic we are." Her grin stretched ear to ear.

"And here I thought that your sarcastic and ever-growing ego would somehow be humbled by freedom."

"This *is* me humbled." Bez pretended to be shocked by the accusation.

"All right, enough you two," Joao laughed, "let's eat. I'm starving and there is a lot to discuss."

Joao was right. There was much to discuss. To start, how were they going to feed and supply their side of the war once Warren realized they had commandeered Land of Legends. Not only that, but how to restore communications with Rye to help aid in disabling the Suits once Augland attacked. But they were interrupted by a sudden commotion coming from farther out in the battlefield.

The entire field of workers suddenly rushed through the Viking camp, shouts filling the air. Wolfe spun around in confusion, trying to assess the source of the fear and chaos. One of the leaders crashed into Wolfe, yelling in pure panic that Augland security had attacked the train, trapping workers inside the train tunnel system. They were easy prey for security to capture and kill. The workers stood looking to Wolfe and Joao for guidance, for an order.

"Wolfe?" Joao's eyes shifted to Wolfe.

But Wolfe's mind was elsewhere—focused on Ashton's imprisonment. After the briefest hesitation, Wolfe darted through the tent, intending to sprint toward the danger. He heard a desperate voice call his name from the crowd, "Wolfe!"

But it was too late.

CHAPTER 43

Ashton

Sneaking out of the Executive Suites was surprisingly easy. That was all thanks to Ana, who guided Ashton from Warren's front door and toward the elevators, where she was ushered out into the dark night of Hollywood Boulevard. Ashton had thought Ana would accompany her to Land of Legends, but she'd declined, insisting she was needed elsewhere. There was still so much secrecy, especially as it related to Reuben and now Ana, but Ashton now had her suspicions that they both were part of iHumanist.

Having Sheva's necklace draped around her neck once again gave her a peace of mind she hadn't had in days. There was so much she didn't understand still, like how Ana had made sure Warren wouldn't know she'd escaped or how cameras wouldn't catch Ana aiding Ashton, or how she'd even found her in the first place.

But she hadn't questioned Ana as they tip-toed along the dark hallway of the Executive Suites. They barely spoke until Ana left her inside the elevator's steel enclosure.

"When the doors open, run, darling. Get out of here and don't let anyone see you. I can't help if Warren's security finds you."

"I can't leave Niall here," Ashton said with near desperation in her voice. Niall had suffered too much for her to abandon him.

Ana paused. "I'll find a way to turn off his Customer Service chip and get him to Land of Legends . . . but Ashton, you need to leave now." Ashton nodded as her eyes met Ana's cool blue ones, her soft smile giving more comfort to Ashton than a cozy blanket. She brought Ashton's hands into her own to focus her attention on the here and now. She saw many similarities between Ana and Wolfe. Wolfe might have Warren's smile, but his eyes were all Ana's. The shock of it all was still hard for Ashton to absorb.

"Thank you," Ashton whispered as Ana's hand slowly drifted from her own, right before the elevator doors closed and she descended to the streets of Hollywood Boulevard.

———

As she ran from the spherical Augland 54 headquarters, Ashton remembered the instructions she had been given: "Wolfe and Joao are in Land of Legends. The train station at 3rd and Stewart Street should be safe and will get you there the fastest." One moment she was despondent, knowing the Customer Service Chip was in control, and Warren was pulling strings and deciding her fate and the fate of those around her, like Niall. But out of nowhere, Ana had appeared, with hopeful news of Wolfe and Joao's safety and a plan to get her out. And most of all, she was safe from the ravages of the chip.

Ashton sped away from Ana and let her legs move at a speed driven by what she could only assume was adrenaline.

———

Ashton's lungs burned as she rounded the corner and passed the 3rd Avenue sign. It had been at least a year since she had taken the train at Hollywood Boulevard. She hurried, block by block, constantly scanning for danger. It was dark outside, past midnight if she were to guess, and there were only a few workers out and about, while some Suits walked along the dark alleyways and sidewalks between the one-way streets. The buildings were tall, crowding the skyline, and with each block, Ashton went deeper to the heart of the city. *Stewart, Stewart, Stewart,* Ashton repeated in her mind, hoping the next street would be the one she needed. *I didn't pass it, did I? No, I would have seen it. But maybe I did? I don't remember it being this far away.* The streets were familiar yet disorienting in her panicked state.

Ashton stopped, catching her breath for only a moment, not knowing how much time she had before security swept across the park or Warren woke to find her missing—again. But no one followed her; no one even seemed to notice that she was running for her life and away from the most dangerous man in Augnation. Ashton began jogging and by the time she made it three more blocks, her mouth was bone dry and her ragged lungs screamed in agony. But there it was— Stewart Street, and the downward staircase that would take her to the boarding platform.

Ashton glanced furtively around her, looking for any security coming after her, but still no one seemed to show her the slightest interest. Ana had done more than just save her; she had made it even remotely possible to escape and be reunited with Wolfe and the UnSuited. The crisp night air of Hollywood Boulevard and the twinkling lights of streetlamps were her last visions before she descended underground. One critical leg of her journey checked off and all that remained was a short train ride that would lead her back to Wolfe.

Ashton waited only five minutes before the underground train arrived. She now stood at the back of the train station, looking out the semi-soot-covered windows where a shadow of her own reflection stared back at her. Her freckles appeared more prominent against her pale skin and the bags under her eyes were shadowy. She couldn't tear her eyes away from her image, the screeching turns on the train reminding her of the days she'd spent travelling to Maya Bay. Most mornings she would look out, waiting for the underground tunnels to turn and slow. She never thought she would miss the days when the monotony of train rides and waitressing were all that happened in her day.

The flashback brought memories of Niall before his chip implantation, which nearly brought her in tears. She hoped whatever Wolfe and

Joao had planned that they could finally overthrow the newly appointed AEC president before he could do any more damage. She hoped it was soon, that the iHumanist movement was truly an UnSuited ally, and that maybe Niall could be saved. Ashton refused to believe that Niall was past the point of no return, like Warren had suggested. She hoped he could still be saved and return to who he truly was. The waves of guilt would drown her if they couldn't bring him back, if he had been sacrificed because the UnSuited failed to act in time.

ERRK . . . the train jolted to a stop as the brakes screeched along its tracks. Ashton's hand instinctively braced for the impact of the stop. Her eyes darted from side to side, looking for any sign of the Land of Legends train stop. But the black tunnel made it impossible to tell where they were. Ashton glanced around her. The nearby workers looked just as disoriented as Ashton. *Maybe a maintenance issue?* Seconds later, the train's interior went black and instantly shouts were heard in the surrounding cars. Ashton sprang to her feet, not letting the overwhelming sense of dread overtake the fight or flight reaction she felt and hurled her forward. The likelihood of this being a broken-down train was slim; in her seventeen years as a worker, taking the train nearly every day, she never once experienced it breaking down or in need of servicing.

Ashton couldn't help but stare into the darkness surrounding her as the screams of petrified workers echoed down the long tunnel.

Run.

Whether it was her internal voice or an audible command from a nearby worker, Ashton didn't hesitate as pellets of photon fire rang in warning of Augland's arrival, forcing some to freeze in fear and others to panic.

Ashton launched herself forward, putting her hands out in front of her to feel her way to the next car. She couldn't remember which car on the train she had boarded, whether it was closer to the front or back, but others around her were moving, so she found herself caught in the wave of shuffling movement and screams. Ashton bumped into another worker, nearly falling over before she reached the other end of the car, feeling her way along the train car's steel interior. Flashlight beams swirled behind her and Ashton looked over her shoulder to confirm the source. There was little doubt that the people wielding the lights couldn't be anyone other than Augland 54 security.

She picked up speed, keeping one hand in front of her to help guide her. She moved quickly and then she felt it, a subtle breeze. Ashton stopped, because a breeze meant an opening, and an opening was something she needed for escape. The outside tunnel was as dark as the train car's interior, but out there, she could at least try and make a run for it to Land of Legends—she'd be fairly close. Land of Legends was adjacent to Hollywood Boulevard, so on foot it would take only hours instead of days. Ashton stopped moving forward and instead crossed the tight aisle between seats and toward the windows where she had first felt the light wind. Ashton dragged her hands across the steel walls, trying her hardest to block out the screaming around her, along with the flashing lights that grew closer with each moment she searched for a way out. She could hide under a seat, but chances were the Augland security would easily find her.

Patience wasn't Ashton's virtue, but she would use that to her advantage. The packed workers couldn't budge past the one door to the next car but panicking like wild animals would get them all caught. Ashton backed away from the crush of passengers. Her eyes had finally adjusted to the darkness. Chairs, poles for standing patrons, windows, ceiling vents—*windows*. It would be a tight fit but there was still room between the car and tunnel walls for them to run toward the train stop.

Ashton quickly shed her jacket and wrapped it around her hand, knowing this next part was going to hurt and hurt badly. She recoiled her arm and with all her force punched the window, barely creating a crack in the glass. The pain in her hand was excruciating and Ashton stumbled back. Her panic was impacting the logical part of her brain, and she was making stupid mistakes. Instead of punching the window again, Ashton decided to kick the glass, which now, looking back, was a better choice. A worker near her saw exactly what she was doing and chose to help, which drew the attention of another, then another. Soon, there were ten workers taking turns striking the glass before the crackling of the glass finally gave way.

Air rushed into the train car as their way out opened. A male blond worker helped her clear the remaining glass shards from the window and began shouting to the others to abandon the car doors and head out through one of the open windows.

Ashton saw the flashlights getting closer and the screams behind them reached a deafening roar. The workers needed to get off the train *right now*. "Go!" Ashton began to yank huddled workers scrunched together near the train car doors and toward the open windows that would lead them out and give them a fighting chance against Augland security.

"Quickly!" The same man who helped Ashton break the windows began fighting through the crowd of workers next to her for Augland people to disperse and save themselves. "Go out the windows one by one!" Ashton yelled. But her commands were drowned out by the condensed train space and the alarm of the security. "Go!"

A loud whistle grabbed the attention of the surrounding workers. The blond man beside her commanded them, "Security is coming! You have to make a run for it in the tunnels. Not all at once, single . . . file!" His urgency compelled the people paralyzed by fear to listen. *Thank goodness for tall Blondie over here.*

Finally, the train's car began to empty, but that didn't mean they were out of danger. Minutes passed and instead of only the lights from the guards. Ashton began to make out features of individuals and outraged voices demanding they stop and surrender.

"You should go." The man whom Ashton had nicknamed "Blondie" instructed her as the number of workers needing assistance had lessoned. At this point he had jumped out of the window to help people make the five-foot drop from the window to the train tracks.

"We're close! Just a few more people," Ashton responded. They had time, or at least she hoped.

"Just get out here! You've done enough! You wait any longer and the Augland patrols are going to grab us both!" He had a point. The more seconds that ticked by, they were less likely to escape—and Ashton hadn't come this far not to evade Augland's clutches. She exhaled, knowing he was right.

Ashton stood on the train's bench, giving her leverage to fling her leg outside the open window. Her hand was useless, crippled by the pain from her punch to the window. Blondie seemed to understand and raised his arms, catching Ashton as she nearly tumbled out.

Ashton landed safely. "Thanks," she said, turning to Blondie with an appreciative smile.

His smile in return was wide. "No problem,"

"Hey! You two!" The intense light of a flashlight's beam blinded them.

"Run!" Ashton cried, nearly tripping over her benefactor.

The width between the steel car and the tunnel was only enough for a single file line. From where Ashton had exited the train car, she needed to run past at least five more cars before the tunnel opened.

"They're gaining on us." The man behind her panted between breaths.

"We're almost out."

One more. One more car until they reached the darkness of the tunnel and the much-needed space they needed to truly run from security.

Her legs felt like rubber as she expended her remaining energy. She could sense her new friend behind her, giving it his all. Finally, Ashton reached the front of the train and stepped onto the empty tracks and through the dark tunnel. A cluster of workers were still running toward Land of Legends. If they could keep the distance between them and the guards, there was a chance most of them would escape. They had to make it out, they just had to—and they had a decent head start. That was, until a familiar revving sound had Ashton whipping her head back to scan the tunnel behind them. *Hoverbikes . . .*

If that was the case, their chances had instantly dwindled. Panic rushed over her and the man who helped her slowed his steps too. "What's wrong?"

"We have to hide," Ashton instructed.

"Hide? Where? There's nowhere to hide in the tunnel," Blondie said.

"Then we have to run faster! They have hoverbikes. It will take them just a few seconds to catch up to us." Ashton couldn't help the fear that trembled her already shaky voice.

But they didn't get the chance to run, because as soon as the words left her mouth, she could feel the vibration as the hoverbikes drew closer to a group of stragglers, racing to cut them off before they could make it to Land of Legends. Ashton was glued to where she stood, realizing Augland had just tightened their noose around them.

Ashton's mind froze with dread. They were trapped.

CHAPTER 44

Wolfe

LAND OF LEGENDS, AUGLAND 54

Hunted down. Like *dogs*.

That was the image that flashed through Wolfe's mind when he learned security was tracking down workers on the train. He thought about what he would command his former security team to do in this situation. The train station was safe—that was, until Warren found out they were creating a fortress in Land of Legends. He thought for sure they had more time—*what in the world gave you that idea?* Wolfe's consciousness turned against him. He knew he should have gone to Ashton sooner. He ran faster and harder, creating less distance between the Viking camp and the entrance to the auditorium where he could make his way down to the train station.

Because there were only three options:

Ashton was safe with Reuben . . . unlikely, but he could hope.

Ashton was on the train, now surrounded by guards.

Ashton was still with Warren and his father would inflict retribution because of Wolfe's betrayal.

And he wasn't sure which possibility of the last two were worse.

As he ran against the crowd, he felt like a salmon swimming upstream. He dodged left, then right, as the dense crowd amassed and the auditorium doors grew closer. His eyes were constantly scanning the crowd, searching for her red hair.

"Ashton!" he screamed. "Ashton!" But he could hear nothing over the hustle of people forcing their way into Land of Legends, seeking asylum.

Wolfe stopped, unsure whether to comb through the crowd or continue his pursuit.

"Wolfe!" Joao screamed, racing over to him and passing him a rifle-type photon gun. "Go," he paused, catching his breath alongside Wolfe. "Go into the tunnels and I'll look here for her." Wolfe didn't need to respond; he shot Joao a grateful look and sped off, leaving Joao to continue his search in the crush of the crowd.

Wolfe didn't hesitate. At one point, he must have shoved someone out of the way, because they yelled at him in passing. He could sense that Ashton was close, which made him worry even more. It was an unknown mental connection they had. Something in his soul—he could just feel her presence. He begged whatever higher power would listen that she would be alive because one thing he was sure of: he couldn't, wouldn't, live in this ruined world without her.

Before sunrise.

That's what Reuben had said, and they were nearing that now. He would never forgive Reuben if any harm came to Ashton, even though Wolfe knew he'd only blame himself if she was hurt.

The auditorium was dark. The once-plush movie theatre turned Legends training center still resembled what it once was. Not skipping a beat, he moved closer and closer to the train station entrance, where he noticed workers pulling themselves up from the tracks and onto the platform.

The train. It had stopped before it reached the Land of Legends destination just as the workers near the Viking camp had reported.

Bang!

Bang!

Bang!

Wolfe could have sworn he felt life leave his body at that moment. The blast of energy from the photon guns echoing within the underground station was suddenly muffled by distinct, blood-curdling screams.

CHAPTER 45

Ashton

LAND OF LEGENDS, AUGLAND 54

"Stop! You're under arrest for evading! If you move, we will be forced to shoot!" It was clear Augland security had known everyone on the train planned to join the UnSuited.

Security closed ranks and rounded up the stragglers left on the train while the soldiers on hoverbikes created a flying barrier, trapping the remaining workers in the tunnel. *Corralled like livestock,* Ashton thought bitterly. Ana had mentioned those on the train were seeking asylum, but didn't mention that security would catch onto the escape so quickly. Now, nearly twenty dangerously armed men encircled the remaining workers—Ashton could only frantically guess at how many had made it to safety as there were still about seventy workers trapped underground.

Controlled chaos—their sophisticated strategy to keep the workers off-balance. The darkness combined with the use of photon gunfire and loud threats led to panic and confusion. The workers, unable to think logically, were easy prey.

"Get down and freeze!" *Bang, Bang! Bang!* Security warned with photon shots and shouted words. Ashton and Blondie had no choice but to listen. "On the ground, all of you!" The harsh voice was authoritative, demanding them to listen. From behind, a guard pushed them into a single file line, which Ashton it was true for all the remaining escapees.

Ashton complied immediately. She dropped to her knees. The dust below her rustled up as she raised her hands above her head. Blondie stood beside her, paralyzed.

"Get them lined up! Kneeling! Hands on top of your head!" A security guard barked from the darkness. Ashton felt the guards' presence growing as they quickly surrounded the line of workers. Several paced back and forth behind the rebels. One brutally jabbed Ashton with the butt of his photon gun, pushing her head down to the ground while another forced Blondie down, kneeling on Blondie's neck, spewing violent threats if he moved an inch. "Get down and stay down, you worker filth, or I'll make an example out of you."

Not good . . . Ashton and Blondie were near the end of the long row of workers closest to the train cars. Ashton kept her head down, keeping her eyes focused along the row of workers and the guards who patrolled their movements.

"We need to run. They're going to kill us if we stay," Blondie said under his breath. His jagged breath kicking up dirt as he whispered to her.

"They'll kill us if we run." Ashton reached for his hand, grasping his clammy palm and gently squeezing it to get his attention so he could see the calmness on her face—or at least she hoped it was convincing enough. Several security men trotted up from the rear, ensuring all workers were now captured and surrounded.

"Breathe." Ashton attempted again to soothe Blondie as he lay next to her.

"Sir, we caught most of the rebels near the train station opening and some right outside the train cars." Ashton listened as the guard detailed where all the captured workers were. "Looks like most were up toward the train station opening to Land of Legends. She could only hope that some UnSuited were be there to help them. "We were right; they were heading toward Land of Legends. One of my guards has even reported the park has been taken over by UnSuited." A guard relayed through his interconnect.

The guard scrutinized the long row of workers, marching between each one and shining his light on each face. Soft whimpers could be heard as the anticipation mounted the longer the guards kept workers in a holding pattern.

They are identifying us . . . the guard's feet spat dust up toward Ashton and her new friend as the guard blinded them with his light. He moved past Blondie quickly and stepped so his feet were inches from Ashton's face. She squinted against the light while raising her eyes to the guard. She couldn't make out any discernable features, only the shadowy silhouette of his frame.

He knelt in front of her, grabbing a lock of her unruly red hair and intertwining it between his fingers, examining it. With his close proximity she was able to see him now. Dark hair, short, like Wolfe's, but with calculating green eyes. He exuded danger and Ashton's instincts were to run far from this man. "Give me your wrist," the guard demanded. Ashton couldn't. She knew now that she was being hunted and there was no chance she would give up and be taken back to Warren. Not when she was this close to Wolfe. She would never go back to the Customer Service torture, no matter the price she would have to pay.

"Your wrist," the guard demanded again, hostility in his tone.

"And if I don't?" she asked.

"Give it to him." Blondie whispered under his breath, only loud enough for her to hear.

Her lack of obedience drained the guard's patience as he grabbed for Ashton's wrist, exposing the white shaded barcode with her employee ID of RT2—Rogue Tier 2.

Ashton yelped as his hand gripped her arm fiercely, twisting it to give him a better view. His interconnect scanned her barcode and instantly her identity was exposed. Her photo lit up the screen as the guard examined the image closely.

He roughly released her arm and Ashton nearly stumbled backwards. "Sir, we found JR105. Yes, sir . . . yes . . . yes, sir." That was all any of them could hear as the man continued to relay updates through the interconnect.

"There are about eighty or so," the guard continued.

"Understood." The guard cleared his throat after his conversation ended. The flashlight still focused on Ashton, blinding while highlighting her for the surrounding officers to focus on.

"Take her with us. Kill the rest," the green-eyed man in charge ordered to a nearby guard.

"Sir?" One guard questioned as the morbid command echoed against the underground train station walls.

"You heard me, kill them," the leader repeated. Silence was the only indication Ashton needed to confirm that his orders would be followed before he left and moved toward the other end of the tunnel.

'Kill them . . . that is what he said? You can't let them do that, they're innocent! Do something! A guard behind Ashton gripped her shoulder. "No!" She whipped around, hitting him in the ribs as she targeted her assailant. It all happened in a matter of seconds as Ashton instinctively went for the photon gun that the guard gripped across his chest.

"Get back!" the guard yelled, but it was too late. Ashton wasn't thinking as she wrapped her arms around the gun and wrestled against him. She wouldn't go back to Warren willingly and she wouldn't allow these men to kill the workers without a fight. Her actions weren't her own. Her strength came from somewhere she hadn't tapped into for a long time. She channeled the training she'd received from Wolfe and the years she had longed for true freedom. At this moment, being captured by Warren was worse than death, so if he planned on taking her or killing any of these workers, he'd have to break her first.

"Let go!" The Augland guard leaned back for leverage, but as soon as he did, he tripped on the track behind him, sending both Ashton and the guard forward. *Bang!*

The sound of the gun rang in Ashton's ears, temporarily shutting down her brain as the noise made thinking impossible. She began to check herself to see where she had been hit. Nothing felt different. She rose slightly from the security guard and noticed the shot hadn't hit her—it had hit him, directly in the chest where blood pooled beneath them and his face twisted in wordless agony. He looked young, only a year or so younger than her. His eyes went wide in realization of what had just happened.

"I'm . . . you're going to be okay." Ashton jammed her hand against his chest, pressing down and hoping she could staunch the rapid flow of blood. The darkness sheltered them from the other security men and workers. It all happened so fast. His face softened as life left him and Ashton was stunned at what had transpired. She hadn't pulled the trigger—but his blood was on her hands.

"Tye, you okay?" a guard from behind Blondie questioned. "Tye!" he yelled again. The man couldn't tell yet what had happened in the darkness. Ashton slowly rose, keeping her eyes on the young man she now knew as Tye. *Think about where you are; don't think about him . . . the underground train station. Blondie. Workers. Warren's directive to kill. What will happen if Warren gets his hands on you or any UnSuited.* Ashton's hands still gripped the weapon that was left in Tye's lifeless arms. The guard behind Blondie began racing toward them and Ashton made her move, tearing the photon gun from the guard and brandishing it at whoever was approaching them.

"Drop it." She brought the rifle-shaped weapon up and tipped the end of the barrel toward the nearest guard. The darkness benefited her now as it cloaked her motives to gain another weapon. He stopped, shocked and unwilling to move forward in fear of what would happen. "I said, drop it." Ashton repeated, her voice unable to hide the raspy shake of adrenaline. The man showed wisdom as he placed it down between the tracks and Ashton.

What now, what now . . . "don't say a word," Ashton threatened, hoping that the men closer to the opening of Land of Legends hadn't heard the commotion. "Blondie, come grab the gun."

"Me?" Blondie asked from behind the guard. Ashton realized she spoke his nickname out loud. She'd need to figure out his name for the future—hopefully there would be a future.

"Yes, you." Blondie raced to where the guard stood, reaching to the ground and grabbing his weapon as several workers were stunned and frozen in their kneeling position. It would be a matter of seconds before more guards arrived and they didn't have time to wait.

"One word and he shoots—" Ashton said. But before the guard could even respond, Blondie swung the butt of the gun against his head, causing the guard to fall hard against the ground. "That works too," Ashton said lightly as Blondie stepped back toward Ashton.

"What's the plan?" Blondie rotated the rifle-like photon gun upright.

What was the plan? Try and keep the upper hand. Right now, the other guards don't know you're armed . . . use it to your advantage. Bluff like you have control! "Take out the guards. Then run like hell."

"What are you—" Another guard's flashlight turned on them, creating a spotlight on Ashton and Blondie. He instantly fired his photon gun at the guard, but missed his target by several feet. The guard advanced with no hesitation, seemingly amused and even more daring now, convinced they couldn't aim their weapons.

"Workers. They have guns! South end of the tunnel!" The guard shouted across his interconnect as he ran toward them.

Blondie shot again and again, firing at him before silence finally took over and Ashton presumed that one of the seven shots had finally hit the mark. Ashton turned to see workers begin scrambling as the shots and disruption had officers chasing after workers now armed with weapons and those defenseless, fleeing in fear.

"Run! Get to Land of Legends!" Ashton shouted. "Blondie! Give that guard's gun to another worker." Blondie seemed to be reading her mind as he had already grabbed the gun and made his way back toward Ashton.

Blondie handed off the gun to a nearby worker. It was time . . . they all knew it. There was a palpable shift in the air, a sliver of hope spurring the workers into action. Collectively, they could feel the intensity building, sparking energy and rekindling their belief in the UnSuited.

Bang! Bang! Bang! Sparks flew and surrounded them. Ashton's back hit the tunnel wall, and she slid down, protecting herself as best she could from the photon fire. There wasn't anywhere to hide or recover—not that they had any time. It had been constant gunfire and fleeing hoverbikes for the last ten minutes. Many defenseless workers and unlucky guards lay sprawled out on the tunnel floor. Ashton lifted her gun, looking ahead as the sparks from the photon guns illuminated the once-dark tunnel system. Ashton rose and pushed off the side of the tunnel, now aiming at anything that threatened them from moving forward toward Land of Legends. There was no way to know if their side was winning. She had lost Blondie and several others with guns in the chaos and the closer she got to the north end of the tunnel system the more workers and guards there were.

A hoverbike roared to life as more photon guns sparks rang out at them. Ashton ducked again, feeling pellets of hot electricity sting either side of her. She needed to react, or the next hit would kill her. She pointed her gun and fired—miss. *Calm down, breathe. One, two, three . . . aim.* He shot, and so did Ashton, and this time, her shot hit the Augland guard. Ashton cried out as his shot hit her left arm. The pain was excruciating and she bit down hard as her body slumped against the tunnel's wall.

"You okay?" a voice from beside her asked, and Ashton saw the brown eyes of Blondie staring back at her in concern. Ashton nodded, propelling herself off from the tunnel wall, following the others as they moved forward.

"Retreat!" A voice rang out through the passageway, "Security needs to retreat!" Ashton's heart leaped out of her chest. The hoverbikes began to rev and race past them as Blondie and the others shot at the guards—taking only a couple of them out before a few were able to escape.

"Ha! Get out of here!" Blondie called out gleefully and the workers around them screamed in excitement.

Blondie turned to Ashton, giving her an unexpected hug while breathing out in disbelief, "Who are you?" Ashton winced as he squeezed her injured arm.

"Ashton. Friends call me Ash. You?"

"Shay, but I guess people who save my life call me Blondie."

Ashton smiled.

CHAPTER 46

Wolfe

LAND OF LEGENDS, AUGLAND 54

There were no screams, no sounds, after the photon guns and hover-bikes had retreated, only the rattling thunder of Wolfe's unrelenting stride within the long tunnel system. It was pitch black and the only way Wolfe was able to tell where the twist and turns of the tunnel system led were the steel tracks that he ran between. Every step without the faint sounds of . . . *anything*, caused more anxious.

"Ashton!" he yelled, but was met with only silence. At any moment, Augland guards could pounce on him, but he didn't care if he caught. All that mattered to him was making sure Ashton was alive. He'd never forgive himself if she died on her way to Land of Legends. *You don't even know if she was on the train.* He forced himself to think of scenarios where she was safe, and not dead.

"Ashton!" He tried again, but still—silence. Desperation now coated his words because, as the minutes passed by, so did the realization of what he might find—that Ashton had been in the tunnel.

Wolfe stumbled as something, or someone had blocked his path. Wolfe stopped suddenly. His chest tightened and he dropped his photon gun to one hand. It was a woman, most likely from Venus given the colorful nature of her elaborate tutu and black and green hair. *It isn't Ashton.* But the thought was only slightly comforting, because once this woman's lifeless body came into view, so did another . . . and another. And another. Men and women lay a few feet apart: lined side by side. Each body sent shivers down Wolfe's spine. It wasn't the first time he had seen a dead body, but that didn't make it any easier.

Wolfe slowly moved down the line . . . examining each dead worker both with hope and heartbreak as the massacre was seemingly endless. The overpowering smell of burning flesh had Wolfe tightening his grip on the rifle Joao had given him. His footsteps were light as he carefully navigated the blood-soaked path.

Suddenly, echoing in the distance, Wolfe could make out the hum of people approaching. Wolfe backed up alongside the tunnel wall, unsure whom of he would find when they reached him. He lifted his weapon, pointing it down the long underground passageway.

The muffled sounds became clearer as whoever was headed toward Land of Legends was undoubtedly going to pass Wolfe. Eventually they would see him and Wolfe needed to have the upper hand until he figured out if they were friends or the enemy.

One unsuspecting individual walked right past Wolfe, and he didn't miss the opportunity. He stepped forward, jabbing his gun right between the man's shoulder blades. "Don't turn around or I'll shoot," he spoke forcefully. Wolfe studied the group of five or so men and women who were dressed like workers from various Augland 54 parks, but they all had guns—Augland grade security photon guns. The thought crossed his mind that security guards disguised as workers would be a smart tactic to overtake the train. Hearing Wolfe's command, the others whipped around and raised their guns, pointing them at Wolfe and his hostage.

"Drop it, or I'll shoot!" Wolfe commanded. A man with sandy blond hair stepped forward, drawing his weapon on Wolfe.

"Better yet, how about you drop it!" *Noted, you're the one in charge,* Wolfe thought.

"Do what he says, man! Please! I don't want to die," the hostage beside Wolfe begged.

"Shut up! If I shoot him, you're a dead man anyway," the blond man said. "There are way more of us and only one of you." The man was fishing for additional details, hoping Wolfe would contradict him and tip off if he had more people hiding in the tunnel. He had no idea if Wolfe was alone or not.

"Maybe there's not. Maybe I have more men waiting at the end of this tunnel," Wolfe warned.

"You're lying. We killed most of your people, and the rest fled like cowards." *So, they were the ones to do this to defenseless workers—head shots with photon rifles. Who was really the coward?*

"You have no idea who I am or what or who I have with me. You're not getting out of here alive, even if I don't live to take another step. I'm not letting go of this man until I find what I'm looking for," Wolfe demanded. It was more likely he would stay alive with a hostage, especially given there were at least six of them.

"That's if you think I care about the person you've taken hostage. Maybe I'll shoot him first and then shoot you, save us all the trouble." The blond-haired man raised his weapon. Wolfe noted his horrible stance and lack of expertise holding such a large weapon, which made him pause. But then his hostage disrupted his thought with a cry for mercy.

Wolfe could tell by the look in the one in charge's eyes he wasn't bluffing and that only meant one thing: there was about to be a bloodbath. Wolfe scanned the tunnel as far as he could see. Strategizing that if he could toss his victim aside as a distraction then start eliminating blond hair first, then the two next to him. Reload, and go for the other two, all while encircling the group. There was no telling how prepared these guards were. *Okay, element of surprise, Wolfe. And—*

"Wolfe?" A soft and familiar voice spoke from behind him and Wolfe's bravado evaporated. He whipped around, seeing the disheveled red hair and bright blue eyes of Ashton. She cradled her left arm with a blood-soaked shirt—but she was alive.

"Ash!" Wolfe dropped his weapon, releasing his victim and took two steps toward her—forgetting about the remaining threat in front of him. Ashton collapsed into Wolfe and buried her head in his chest.

Wolfe inhaled. He placed his hand behind her head, cradling her tightly against his chest. There had been a small seed of doubt he'd ever feel her alive again and that scared him more than anything.

"I wasn't sure I'd find you alive . . ." Wolfe gently broke their embrace so he could assess Ashton for injuries. "You're hurt."

"Get away from her!" the man in charge yelled, misunderstanding the scene unfolding in front of him.

"Blondie, don't!" Ashton hadn't noticed the man's threat either until he spoke. *Blondie? Ashton knew these people?*

"What's going on?" a woman yelled, her gun raised.

Ashton released Wolfe. "Put it down! All of you. He's not a guard. He's with me."

Blondie took a moment, clearly agitated before he lowered his weapon. "Why didn't he say he wasn't a guard!"

Who is this guy? "What do you mean? I come over here and see dead bodies on the ground and you're the one with weapons—I'm also outnumbered! What am I supposed to think? You're trigger happy and should have asked questions before assuming." Blondie took a step forward, clearly irritated. *Blondie over there is going to be trouble,* Wolfe thought.

Blondie scoffed. "Enough, you two." Ashton stepped between the two of them, giving them both a look that said they were acting more like two derailed bulls than two civilized workers. Wolfe blamed the last twenty-four hours for his lack of control.

Blondie kept his distance, staying ahead with the others while Wolfe hung back with Ashton. Her face had grown two shades paler since leaving the tunnels and making their way to the castle grounds, but she insisted she was fine. Wolfe needed to find Joao, but first he wanted to ensure Ashton's safety and that meant getting her to a room where she could rest.

His hands shot out, supporting her elbow and relieving some of the weight she was placing on the stair railing as they climbed to the castle dormitories. "I'm fine, Wolfe. Really, I'll just need to patch it up and disinfect it and I'll be good as new," Ashton said as he brought her into a room Bez had prepared for them earlier. It would be their rebel home from this point on.

The spiral staircase on the northeast side of the castle would lead them up to where Joao, Bez, Ronan, and a few of the other security men had taken refuge. Bez had been kind enough to prepare their home before Wolfe had even entered Land of Legends. Wolfe glanced over his shoulder at Ashton, whose eyes now flickered open and close. "You're going to make it up there, okay?"

Ashton lazily smiled. "You offering to carry me the rest of the way? Like my knight in shining armor?"

"Ash, I'm serious."

"So am I," Ashton countered. "I'm just tired . . . that's all," she said.

Wolfe's relief that she was alive finally settled and the looming fear of an unstoppable war gripped Wolfe's every thought. During their brief travel to the castle, Wolfe learned how Ashton was able to escape and exactly what Reuben's involvement had been. Wolfe's mother had been the one to free Ashton, and for that he would be eternally grateful. If they survived this war, he'd find a way to repay her. She'd put her life on the line to help Ashton.

"I can't believe you made it out of that train station."

Ashton smirked. "Me too. I don't know what came over me. I just . . . attacked."

"Walk me through—" Wolfe began.

"Wolfe, I know we have a lot to talk about. Between what happened after your father found out about the chip to the battle in the tunnels, so much has happened—but I'm so tired." Wolfe was about to protest, because he needed to hear absolutely everything that had happened from the moment she left Warren's lair until now, either to know to what extent she had faced death and survived or to better understand the threat they were all about to face.

"Of course. I'll just wrap your arm and get you to bed." She was right. Everything could wait until tomorrow but he was feeling impatient. Ashton needed rest and recovery.

She was asleep as soon as her head hit the pillow. She hadn't fallen into this deep a sleep since living in their home in Hood Canal. That felt like ages ago—a different lifetime. He wished he could take her there now.

Wolfe counted the number of rises and falls of Ashton's chest, as sleep evaded him. His mind racing between Reuben's conspiracy, what his father was plotting in revenge for the failed train takeover, and the next Suit attack. Wolfe slowly rose from the bed, gathered his things, and glanced again at Ashton, who was still deep in sleep. Her brow scrunched as if she was concentrating intensely. Wolfe gently kissed her, making sure not to wake her before he slipped away.

Unlike earlier that evening, the Land of Legends' battlefield between the Viking and Saxon camps was devoid of any workers— most likely they were all asleep. Wolfe looked down at his watch, and transmitter, noting the time of four a.m. He continued on his mission.

Shortly after, Wolfe reached the train station entrance to Land of Legends where workers were gathering furniture from the auditorium and building a blockade to keep Augland security out. There were likely more UnSuited outside Land of Legends, which made the makeshift barrier not ideal, but Joao and Wolfe would find another way for workers to escape and enter their compound. The wall was nearly complete—stacked at least ten feet high with plush armoires, curtains, tables, and bunkbeds that he remembered all too well from his early training days. A worker caught Wolfe's eye as he struggled to lift a velvety chair higher than the five feet he had already climbed. Wolfe jogged toward him, lifting the chair leg and climbing the wall alongside him.

"Thanks," the man said as they both lodged the chair toward the top of the pile and climbed down, prepared to take the next one provided by the waiting workers. That's where Wolfe stayed and worked until the synthetic Land of Legend's sun showed bright above them and the wall had nearly doubled in size.

CHAPTER 47

Ashton

LAND OF LEGENDS, AUGLAND 54

"They will die—all of them," Warren says through gritted teeth. Ashton slowly walks around a marbled table within a room that feels vaguely familiar. Its overly exuberant and exotic bouquet of flowers from Predator's Biome, thick fur carpet, with white walls, and white cloth chairs that hint to its pristine and sophisticated elegance—meant only for Executives.

Where do I remember this room from?

Ashton glances out the window before she stalks from one end of the room to the other. Hollywood Boulevard spans across the view.

Augland 54 in the Executive Building. Yes, I was here when Wolfe had a meeting with the Board of Executives and Warren forced me to admit to infiltrating the Executive Suite while disguised in the Suit Charlotte.

Warren sits in his typical relaxed posture with his fingertips gently tapping each other as he speaks to another familiar face. Wintefred. . . .

She is Head of Customer Success. *Neither of them notices Ashton as she trails around the smooth corners of the golden streaked table and slips closer to where they are speaking. She is invisible in this room, like living in a memory. "Let them come together. The more workers, we know who intend on betraying us in Land of Legends—the easier we can target the UnSuited and wipe them out all at once. A revolution, while not ideal, will force them out of their hiding," says Warren.*

"Still, the optics on this aren't good," Wintefred responds. *"The AEC President allowing a full-blown attack in his home Augland, and they take over an entire park?"*

Warren smirks. "In the long run, it will be foolish for the UnSuited to stay rooted in 54. They don't have the loyalty within their ranks they believe they do, and soon others will turn when they see that the fight of a revolution is futile." Ashton's eyes dart toward Warren, teleporting herself only a few feet away from him. This is a strange dream.

"We will strike and take out their forces before word can even escape our walls. Let our customers know that there are necessary upgrades and new features being installed in Land of Legends, and we apologize for the inconvenience."

As soon as the words leave Warren's mouth, the snowy white walls begin bleeding . . . and red goop seeps from the corners of each wall, dripping down to the plush carpet. Ashton rotates in a full circle, and as each moment passes, more blood emerges from every direction.

A Suit opens the door, announcing, "You have a visitor, President Warren." Warren waves his hand to allow entrance to his Executive conference room, without noticing the bleeding walls.

Ashton continues to pace around the table as she strains to see the visitor entering the room. She continues wondering why and how the murderous red substance continues to ooze and stain the walls. As soon as the figure steps into the lighted room, Ashton's heart stops. Bez?

"Welcome, Bezanine." Bez looks so different in this dream world: her dark hair combed and pulled straight back into an elegant ponytail. Her lips have a slight glimmer to go with the dark maroon tint of lipstick. Instead of her typical worker outfit, she wears a vibrant coral dress that hugs her curves. She looks—stunning . . . professional. One of "them."

"Warren. May I?" Bez motions toward a seat next to him. Warren obliges. Ashton follows Bez, but the moment she steps forward her feet are drenched in a thick, red puddle. The walls are now a bloody mural, and the floors are soaked as the thick rivulets of gushing red liquid begin pouring, obliterating all available white space in the room. What is happening?

"Wintefred, I believe I haven't revealed our entire strategy or the assets we are using here in Augland 54. Bezanine has been a spy for me for the last decade. She's been a valuable agent throughout this pursuit, keeping me updated on Joao's whereabouts and UnSuited dealings." Bez's grin is demure and refined—not the woman Ashton knows at all. Her demeanor is devoid of any hint of every single sarcastic, smirky, and wild characteristic the real Bez possesses. She looks nearly robotic. This is a dream . . . this is . . . Ashton looks around her . . . a nightmare.

"And that's not Bez," Ashton speaks the last words out loud.

"You're right. It's a dream. Only a nightmare, Ash." Bez says. Now the three sets of eyes are entirely focused on her. Bez steps forward, closing the gap between them. The once expansive white room closes in on Ashton. The table and exotic flowers disappear, leaving only the two Executives and Bez, who quickly surround her.

"By tomorrow you and your friends will be dead." And out of thin air, Bez raises a blade toward Ashton, stabbing her in the stomach. A blink later, Bez is replaced by a mirror image of Ashton. "A fitting end to the woman in red."

Ashton stumbles back, stung by both the betrayal of her best friend and the slice to her belly. Blood rushes from the open skin as she tries to hold the wound closed with the knife still inside her body. Ashton's blood is now spilling onto the floor, which is already drenched in blood and sucking Ashton to the carpet. She inhales, but nothing happens as her body forces her to cough, the taste of metal coating her mouth. Bez's hazel eyes burn as she looks at Ashton, her gaze smug as she sees her betrayal has surprised Ashton more than the blade protruding from her body.

Ashton collapses on the ground, her head heavy and breath shallow as her face collides with the wet ground. Suddenly, Niall is beside her, his breath quickening like hers. When she looks down at his body, she sees that he too is suffering from a blade to the stomach. "Niall!" Ashton forces out, but he says nothing. What is he doing here? He only looks straight ahead at her, confused and in pain.

"Niall, stay . . . with . . . me."
Then, everything goes black.

Ashton woke up, panting, and still tasting the faint tang of iron. Sweat dampened her skin as the sun shone through the glass windows of the castle's rock walls, warming Ashton and Wolfe's room. Safe . . . she was safe . . . in Land of Legends. She raised her hands to her face, pressing hard against her tired body.

Shaking off the bizarre dream—scratch that, nightmare—Ashton slid off the side of the bed. She blamed her conscience. Whether or not the guilt of people losing lives was her fault, many people had unnecessarily died the previous night.

The last twenty-four hours had been stressful to say the least. She had witnessed many emotions from crushed hopes and the control of the CS chip, to experiencing a simulation of Niall's death, to the accidental death of that security officer—his lifeless eyes would forever haunt her. Ashton struggled, knowing death was part of their revolution and duty, but hating the repercussions of life lost. She'd add it to the ever-growing list of things she hated Warren for because he had given them no choice but to give up their lives in hopes of someday living free. Many people had died by Warren's command—and many more would die in this war.

Ashton needed to ground herself, so she focused on the specifics of their room. It was stripped of any useful essentials and instead was filled with gaudy decor that was likely for Suits' amusement. There was a bed and one mirror. The bathroom was more of a prop than a functioning toilet and shower and the lights were candles surrounding an electric fireplace. In the corner, a mannequin warrior with steel armor stalked the shadows, which she found creepy. While the furniture made it a livable space, it was cold and unlived, which made it feel uncomfortably stale.

When she worked in Land of Legends, Ashton was only allowed in the Viking camp, so she never was able to explore the interior of the castle. Versal, who played the Saxon princess and spent her time at Land of Legends in the castle, had described it once to her as cold and overdone—garish gold ornaments and lacking the necessary warm tones to be inviting. Wolfe, since he had created the park, had told her he'd suggested bareness of trinkets and unnecessary decor, but Jorgeon had taken over the aesthetics, which Wolfe later described as "off-putting," to be nice. With all that, Ashton suddenly realized the empty space on the other side of their bed. *Where was Wolfe?* Ashton grabbed her sweater and quickly moved toward the door.

Ashton examined the common area on the first floor of the Saxon castle; it still must be early as there was little movement and sound around the castle even as the sun shone bright through the stained glass. The mansion's expansive living space echoed with whispers of small groups coming together around the castle, pacing back and forth from one section of the first floor to another. "Ashton?" A voice had her spinning around. "Man, it's good to see you."

Joao's tall frame and warm smile came several feet closer, and he embraced her. It had been so long since it had been just the two of them, and, as if no time had passed, his presence was comforting to Ashton. Joao was genuine, loyal, and protective. He had helped her when she had been framed as Charlotte, when his sympathy could have gotten him killed. But he had risked it because he was loyal to Wolfe. Seeing him now after so much time away knowing he had put his life on the line to help the UnSuited, she regretted not staying closer to him after they had left Augland the first time.

"I know Wolfe was worried yesterday, I'm glad to see you made it out mostly unscathed." Joao's eyes glanced down at Ashton's bandaged arm as she pulled the sweater over her head. "Does it hurt much?" Ashton had nearly forgotten altogether that she had been shot the previous night.

"Not bad—" she began, but as soon as the words were out a worker approached, clearly wanting Joao's undivided attention. "Uh. Wolfe? Do you know where he is?"

Joao nodded toward the worker before answering her. "He's been working the perimeter since early this morning. I think they've moved from the train station to the outer wall. We're looking to blow a hole in the wall to allow people in and out of Augland, so he's scoping out the best location for that." Ashton's brow furrowed. Wolfe left her without saying anything, and from the sounds of it, before the sun even rose. "He should be back any minute now." There was a pause. "I think we were all hoping to get together for breakfast and discuss next steps . . . that should happen within the hour." Joao's hand went up toward Ashton's crossed arms as he silently examined her. His voice lowered so the worker beside him couldn't hear.

"You okay? I know how hard it is to deal with that thing in your head and from what Wolfe told me, you both have been through the ringer with Warren." The concern on his face was genuine. And he, of all people, knew exactly what it felt like to be Warren's puppet. But she was fine—she had to be because she wouldn't give Warren the satisfaction of knowing that Niall's death in her virtual reality nightmare had any impact on her psyche. *Niall is fine! He doesn't have that power over you anymore. You have the chip blocker.* Ashton's hand went to the stone around her neck before she nodded, forcing a smile.

He returned it, but Ashton sensed he didn't entirely believe her. "Do me a favor and find Bez. She should be running around here somewhere. I know she's been dying to see you since Wolfe let us know you made it here safely." Ashton tensed as the image of Bez plunging the knife in her stomach and the blood pooling around her hands, flashed in her mind.

"You sure you're good?"

"Yes. Totally fine," she said, smiling again, and this time selling it. "I'll try and find Bez and leave you to it." She motioned for the very impatient worker behind him to approach.

Ashton didn't remember the last time she was truly alone, and it was bittersweet to be back on the battleground where her war against Augland began. As she stood there, grass swayed left then right as the wind shifted and Ashton looked out above the valley toward the Viking camp where workers were gathered on the grounds. Some were wielding swords, while others digging trenches or moving heavy objects toward the backside of the campground. A smile tugged at Ashton's lips—it was completely involuntary as the swell of pride blossomed within her. Seeing the workers completely devoted to the UnSuited cause reminded Ashton why she would protect them at all costs.

She walked for the next hour the different Viking camps and stations dedicated to supporting the UnSuited rebellion. She even walked along the train station border where furniture was lined up at any opening to prevent the rest of Augland from infiltrating Land of Legends. All this work in such a short amount of time was truly remarkable.

"That red hair is getting a little cliché don't you think?" Ashton jumped as a voice behind startled her. Bez' smirky grin widened.

"You're funny," Ashton said, stopping and putting her hands on her hips, exuding the same amount of sass that Bez ran with constantly. To see Bez in her typical crazy on-top-of-head bun and sun-kissed cheeks was refreshing and reminded her that last night's visions were all just a nightmare.

She skipped toward Ashton, wrapping her arms around her with such force it nearly brought them both to the ground.

"Seriously though, don't scare me like that again . . . I thought you were dead. I mean, Wolfe bolted out of here faster than I've seen anyone run before. He left without saying a word, and we know Wolfe always has something to say," Bez said, still squeezing Ashton tightly. "There's just so many times you can escape death, I swear." Her hands reached for Ashton's arms as Ashton pulled away, wincing from the pain from her photon wound.

"Nearly escaped. Got nicked again." Bez loosened her grip while Ashton slid aside her collared sweater, exposing her shoulder and the white cloth Wolfe had wrapped her in the night before. Bez tsked, examining Ashton's wounded arm more closely.

"So . . . how'd you survive a month with *him*?" Bez' asked with a noticeable change in her tone.

Ashton shrugged, "I don't know. I pretended like I was under the CS and he never questioned it." Bez nodded in understanding, waiting for Ashton to continue, but there wasn't much more to say. Besides, Ashton still wasn't sure if she should talk about the UnSuited outside of 54, or Reuben, especially if she hadn't yet talked to Wolfe about him. So, Ashton shifted the conversation. "I mean, this!" Ashton looked around at the UnSuited, still practicing and preparing for battle. "You and Joao did this?"

Bez didn't mind the topic change as her eyes lit up and a beaming smile spread across her face. She was immensely proud. "Cool, huh?" Ashton nodded and for the next hour Bez listed key moments of the 54 UnSuited revival. She spoke of Chloe in the brothel, their run-in with Wintefred, and even their sleepless nights using the underground tunnel system to smuggle weapons into the camps. Down to the few nights before Warren and them came home, Joao had shut down Land of Legends with a potential security issue, giving them days to prepare for Warren's return instead of hours.

"Yikes. We've got to go . . . Joao wanted to meet at ten." Bez pulled at Ashton's good arm, circling back toward the castle from where they had walked and talked.

Bez guided Ashton into the secluded dining hall where it appeared Joao had created a war room. Breakfast had been prepared and laid out while they all came together. On the table were a couple of pieces of fruit and sandwiches. While it wasn't much, the scent of sweet fruit and bread made Ashton realize how hungry she was. It had been at least twenty-four hours since she'd last eaten and with the blood loss from her photon wound, she felt more lethargic than ever. Joao was already seated, and so was another man with reddish blonde hair that Ashton didn't recognize. Bez bounced over to Joao and he looked up at her and smiled, asking her something while Ashton surveyed the room. Everything was darker within the castle walls. The light glow of candles burning everywhere gave the impression they were nearing mid-day.

"I was looking for you this morning." Ashton turned quickly to face the familiar voice. But the sudden movement made Ashton light-headed, and she swayed. Wolfe was in front of her within second*s. I guess the long walk with Bez took it out of me.* His hair was dusty and his shirt reeked of sweat. "Whoa, careful," he said, steadying Ashton.

"I'm fine," Ashton said, convinced she only needed to eat.

"You should have stayed in bed. You lost a lot of blood yesterday." Wolfe's concern was obvious as he looked her over from head to toe and then abruptly wrapped himself around her, cocooning her in his embrace.

"She was out with her people, Wolfy—get over it." Bez sat down and patted the spot next to her, signaling for Joao to sit down. Ashton and Wolfe followed as well.

"I'm starving, we ready to get this meeting up and running?" Joao said before diving into his own breakfast that at some point he had already plated.

"You're starving? Which one of us has been working since dawn?" Wolfe volleyed.

"So, you snuck out of our room before dawn?" Ashton added, digging at Wolfe's early disappearance.

"Tsk, tsk . . . someone's in trouble," Bez poked.

"It's exactly why I didn't tell you. That, and you would have wanted to come." His half grin had Ashton rolling her eyes, but he wasn't wrong. She would have wanted to help, but she was here now and ready to learn how they would start, and win, a war against Augland—which all had been conceived while she and Wolfe had been gone.

"Okay, let's get serious . . . sorry, Joao. I don't think I want to get in more trouble with Ash than I am and that will likely happen if I try to defend myself." Wolfe's admission stopped any retort Ashton had.

"Bez and I are happy to prolong conversations for a lovers' quarrel. It's entertaining when it's not your own." Bez' fist hit Joao's chest before he could protect against it. "Ouch."

"Wolfe's right; we should get down to it . . ." Joao said as he rubbed the spot Bez had punched him. "What we have is Warren knows about Land of Legends being the central hub of the UnSuited rebellion. What he doesn't know is what we plan to do now."

"And we have a plan?" Ashton asked sincerely.

"That's why we are here. Land of Legends gives us access to the Augland fortress. We use their guns, supply chains, and hopefully Warren's desire to keep his home Augland intact, and won't bomb the park. Given how much time Venus was down after Wolfe blew Centauri, I doubt he's feeling he can afford another Augland project that extensive. Besides, we start with Legends and work our way to Maya Bay . . . taking over the port and any supplies Warren needs," Joao surmised.

"And we are sure that we can overpower Warren's guards? What if they attack with Suits?" Bez asked.

"STEMP will eventually aid in that. Joao and I were able to briefly connect with Rye right before we met up here. Hunter made it back with Forest, but the scientist was killed as they were leaving. The good news is that, before they left, Forest infiltrated VELIC and we are able to identify the satellites that can turn off a Suit invasion," Wolfe reported. Relief swept over the dining table.

"That leaves us with our next course of action. While we wait for Forest to target Land of Legends with STEMP, or what we have of the STEMP, we prepare the workers for physical battle. We will be up against a powerful Augland army of security men and women. They have training, guns, and the manpower; so we need to be prepared for that."

"What do you mean *what we have of* STEMP?"

"Well . . . it's not fully activated yet. We need additional satellites, but the good news is we have enough to sustain about an hour or two of attacks before Rye and his team need to regain access. It's as good as it will get for right now and will buy us enough time to stop Suit invasions."

"What about food?" Bez asked.

"We were thinking of taking out a supply boat coming into Maya Bay. It should have supplies to support our efforts for a long time. That or we need to work on one of the distribution centers . . . but those can be dangerous. The centers are equipped with death traps to keep out the Colonies," Joao said.

"And we what? Plan to take over Augland 54? Go up against the entire AEC?" Ashton asked.

"That's precisely what we do. Once we take over 54, we go after another Augland and another until we make it to DC." As Joao was speaking, Ashton caught herself before the doubt was written across her face. Their plan was bold. Ashton would give it that, but wasn't that what they wanted? She didn't want to question them, but Joao and Wolfe spoke like generals, not men leading a group of insurgents. The UnSuited weren't an army . . . yet. But what they were right about is they didn't have the time to reevaluate or adjust a plan of attack—they were going to war. If they didn't act now, there would not only be no changes in Augland 54—there wouldn't be change in *any* Augland in the nation.

"One last issue we need to discuss now that Ashton's back . . . so far, she's been the face of the UnSuited. I was thinking it would boost morale to keep her in the forefront of the battle prep. She's given workers something to believe in, and they need to have that beacon of hope now more than ever . . ." Joao said, Wolfe's head whipped around, eyeing Joao with silent disagreement.

"So, front lines?" Ashton asked.

"Maybe not front lines—we can't risk your life like that," Wolfe said too quickly. Ashton eyed him.

"You want me to be the face? And then hide behind them as they fight this war I've encouraged?" Ashton demanded. "That's it. Keep dying my hair red so that I can be the UnSuited symbol?" Bez chuckled as if she were silently telling Wolfe and Joao, "I told you so."

"It's more than that, Ash. Joao and I aren't the ones they follow and whether you, or I, like it, that's the way it is. We need you to be with your workers—the ones that followed you and Bez out of Apparel and across Predator's Biome—and that means keeping you safe."

"Bez was there too, but you're not telling her to *pretend* to be a part of the rebellion."

"Well . . . in fairness, I just helped. I'm not part of any of the *legends* of a woman in red decapitating a Suit or a superhuman magician who miraculously escaped Augland . . . twice."

Ashton glared at Bez. "You're not helping," she muttered under her breath.

Before another word could be spoken, an out-of-breath worker barged into the rock-built room. "I've got—" he swallowed, "I've got news from the interconnect. President Warren has issued a strike on Land of Legends. He's sending troops in tomorrow morning."

CHAPTER 48

Ashton

LAND OF LEGENDS, AUGLAND 54

Four hours after they learned of Warren's plan, Wolfe had nearly every able-bodied worker practicing different defensive and offensive fighting techniques. It was quite impressive how quickly they were able to assemble. Augland Center, the only formal training workers received, wasn't known for combat training. It was more for etiquette and which fork went where on a Victorian dinner table.

Ashton walked past several groups of UnSuited practicing how to hold their guns and aim toward targets on trees while others were practicing hand-to-hand combat. Once she had made her rounds, she found Wolfe near the entrance of the Viking main camp, where he was hunched over a table deep in concentration.

"How are we looking out there?" he said without glancing up. Sprawled out in front of him were hologram blueprints of Augland 54. She still needed to talk to him about being the "face of the UnSuited" and not their leader heading into battle. Ashton understood his fear. He had spent the better part of their relationship protecting her and that habit was nearly impossible for a protective man like Wolfe to break.

She never thought of herself as a leader of the rebellion, even when the UnSuited escaped from Apparel. But since then, things had changed—especially considering what she had accomplished with Reuben and the UnSuited outside of 54.

"Well, like they've been training for hours and not years, but they're aiming a gun and that will be more useful than the axes and swords we had." Ashton stood beside him. He was rigid, nearly frozen with tension.

"The worker overhearing Warren's plan could be a trap," Wolfe said. "Warren would know that we are tracking interconnects as I'm sure he is tracking them as well."

"Or it's not. I doubt Warren cares whether we know he's coming to attack. He knows they're workers, not weapons—like Suits," Ashton said, looking down at the hologram in front of Wolfe. His scribbles and circles detailed the map of Land of Legends.

"He also has our, well, Augland security." Wolfe shook his head, remembering that it was no longer *his* security. "We need STEMP to work."

Ash nodded. She agreed it was their best hope for survival at this point.

"Joao and Bez are going to work on getting Rye and Hunter on a call, see if they can get STEMP aligned before tomorrow—even just a few satellites will do enough damage to the Suits they decide to send." Wolfe reiterated the plan they'd discussed before leaving the castle. "If Warren plans to invade through the train station, we can keep them at bay by attacking all sides of the station's opening. We already have barricades constructed, which will help, unless he blows those up . . ." Wolfe sighed. "Or, he may come in from the engineer doors between parks."

Wolfe pointed to the three areas on the map where hidden doors in the park's walls gave access to Maya Bay, Hollywood Boulevard, and Venus. "That would likely be if he wanted a sneak attack overnight. There is no way to get a lot of people through the doors all at once." Wolfe shook his head. "That's all I can see him doing. Unless he plans damage to his parks by launching an explosion, but I doubt he'd do that."

"So, we know he'll likely come from the train station, so we start there. You can always have our people stationed at the doors." Ashton added in an attempt to help.

"Yes, but spreading us too thin would risk people at the train station and too many would leave us vulnerable at other access points . . .

best case, we have one wave and two backups and hope that he plans only the train station approach. We could have two to three people keeping post at the three entry points to alert us." Silence filled the air between them while Wolfe struggled to find the right answer.

"What can I do?" Ashton asked.

His eyes diverted from the plans to her. "Be with them." He nodded his head at the UnSuited workers preparing for battle. "I'm sure most have no idea what to expect, and they're looking to you . . ."

"No, they're not." Ashton turned to watch those preparing in the nearest Viking camp.

"They may not know you but they know *of* you, and I think you could help prepare them for what's to come." One after the other glanced over her way. She'd been so wrapped up in the whirlwind of the attack she hadn't noticed the people staring. The fact that they were looking still . . . it tugged at something in Ashton's core.

Ashton ignored the feeling. "I should go practice with a photon gun—my aim was horrible in the tunnels and if I'm going to be on the front lines, I don't want to embarrass myself." Ashton attempted to joke, but the realization of war and what that meant was difficult to make light of.

"You hunted with similar guns all the time back home," Wolfe said.

"Yeah, well, maybe I'm a bit rusty. It's different hunting animals versus—" She stopped, unable to conjure the words.

"Versus killing people?" It was a reminder that murder was something Wolfe had grown accustomed to after what his father had made him do, and Ashton had yet to digest the impact those actions had on both their lives. Just the false memory of Niall dying by her hands or the blank stare of the security guard she had accidently killed in the tunnel rattled her significantly.

Ashton turned to walk away. "Ash?" Wolfe stopped her. "There's no way you'd stay back, is there? If I asked you to?"

"Would you?"

"Would I ask, or would I stay back if roles were reversed?" The vulnerability in his voice made him nearly unrecognizable to Ashton. Wolfe fiddled with the hologram stylus he had used to draw on the blueprints in front of him. She could see he wanted to ask her to stay back, but assumed Wolfe knew how unfair it would be to directly ask her. Augland took just as much from her as any other worker, and she would not sit back while others defended what she had asked—freedom.

"It was selfish of me to even suggest." She remained quiet at his confession and Wolfe nodded in response, recognizing what she had not said aloud. She wasn't just the face of the rebellion, she was more and that meant not hiding.

———————

Ashton raised her rifle, bracing the butt of the gun against her shoulder and closed her right eye to concentrate on the thin Douglas Fir many yards in front of her. She breathed in and out, steadying her hand as the pops of guns around her sparked while workers trained. She squeezed the trigger—direct hit. A grin tugged at the right side of her face. *Maybe it's just a bad aim when it's at someone and not something.* Wolfe was right, she was a fairly good shot when hunting. Ashton aimed again, hoping it wasn't just good luck. *Aim. Shoot. Hit!*

"Not bad . . . Ash, or should I say Woman in Red." Blondie stood behind her, his own weapon draped casually across his shoulder. People needed to stop sneaking up behind her, especially when she held a weapon.

"I nearly shot you." She turned back to the task at hand. One more successful shot and she would be convinced her aim was as good as ever.

"I was looking for you after we made it into Legends. I wanted to thank you for saving my life . . . and then earlier today I saw you with that Augland guard-looking guy, someone said you were the one that started the rebellion and led the first escape out of Augland." Ashton could feel the crimson creeping up her face and coloring her cheeks, so she deflected his statement with a shot. *Third hit!* Ashton smiled, feeling accomplished.

"So, it's true?"

Ashton turned toward him. His sandy blond hair wild and his brown eyes not hiding his attempt to figure her out.

"It's really not that big a deal."

Blondie scoffed, "You kidding me? You're the reason most of these people are even here. And now that I've seen you in action, I mean, you saved us in the tunnels . . . you're legit."

"It's . . . really, I—" Ashton fumbled over her words. For so long she had felt misplaced as the UnSuited leader, like it was a false title bestowed upon her only because she had accidentally beheaded a Suit. Or because Bez had used the tale of the Woman in Red to bring Apparel workers together, who then died trying to escape. Even as Reuben had positioned her in front of the secret crowds during Warren's campaign; gathering underground UnSuited leaders to join a cause that would blossom into a revolution, *but now*? Given what had happened in the tunnel, she was finally beginning to feel part of something bigger, and it felt real. And for the first time, it gave Ashton purpose.

"Mind if I join you? As you said in the tunnel, I could use the practice and from what I just saw, you know what you're doing," Blondie joked and Ashton smiled. "Of course."

Before long, several others gathered around them. Ashton began showcasing the basics of how to wield a knife, hold a gun, and run and point a weapon. They spent hours running through different scenarios and every time she turned around, another UnSuited joined them.

"If it's a Suit, go for the head or neck; that's where they're most vulnerable."

"Is that how you gutted one? I heard it was with your bare hands!" shouted someone from the growing crowd.

"Okay, a bit barbaric and no, it was an axe, and I got lucky. But it did prove they aren't invincible. You need to strike where it counts and that's the neck."

Ashton watched their progress in awe. As the hours passed and the impending threat grew, here they were calm and learning from each other—working together as a united front.

Night came too quickly and before long they were heading to the center Viking camp to eat—Bez had mentioned they had food supplies for at least three weeks. The day's training had taken Ashton's mind from Warren's plan and brought her closer to the workers of Augland 54, who joked and rallied beside her.

As they made their way to the Viking camp central hub, Ashton could see it was buzzing with activity—some workers were eating while others were nursing bruises or sore muscles. It wasn't hard to find Wolfe, who had several men and women surrounding him as he talked strategy, pointing to several exposed areas of Land of Legends hologram. Wolfe must have selected lead workers who would support different stations around Land of Legends.

His eyebrows were knitted together, showing his intense concentration, and his eyes scanned the now-enlarged hologram of Land of Legends while his brain catalogued and shifted through every detail. This was where Wolfe was at his peak, something he understood and could control. Ashton couldn't hear what he said, but glances around to his people and their return head nods had her guessing he had figured out their war plans down to specific orders.

"You coming?" Blondie said beside her.

"Soon. Save me a spot?" Blondie nodded in response.

Like he could feel her eyes on him, Wolfe glanced from the small crowd of workers to meet her gaze, and she smiled. Wolfe then excused and dismissed them and she walked along the perimeter of the camp to meet him.

His smile was infectious. "You looked good out there."

Ashton's brows went up in silent response.

"Before you say anything flirtatious, I'm saying that in all serious-ness. If you're going to be leading at the front lines you have to be able to shoot with precision, and your shot has surprisingly improved in just a day." Wolfe leaned against one of the pillars, looking out at the hundreds of workers in the dining camp. "I also noticed a group of workers that came to learn from you."

"I didn't expect that but can't say it wasn't nice to feel like I have a part in all of this. You and Joao, I mean, it feels like this is where you belong. Developing strategies and war . . . stuff."

"War stuff?" Wolfe laughed.

"You know what I mean. . . ."

Wolfe shrugged. "You'd be surprised how well this suits you. How well you fit in with worker rebels. Leading looks good on you." Reuben had said something similar to her.

There was a long pause while she internalized his words. She knew Wolfe cared, loved her, but to think of her so highly? Was she truly what he said?

"So, does that mean you're fine with me leading? If they want to follow me, that is." Wolfe looked away for a moment like his next thought was painful. "I know you're exactly what they need to feel inspired to fight against Augland. They believe it's possible because of you and frankly, I tend to agree. You've prevailed, and you've put them above yourself at every turn. If I was a worker in Augland, I wouldn't follow an ex-Head of Security or the son of the CEO, I'd follow the person who knows what I go through every day and is willing to sacri-fice herself for a better life."

Ashton was speechless as she hung on his words. Wolfe continued, "I'd hate myself if I prevented you from being exactly what you are just because I'm afraid I'll lose you. It's selfish of me. " She stopped him from going on and wrapped her arms around him, bringing him close to her.

"Thank you," she said in a muffled voice. Wolfe kissed the top of her head and then surprised her with his next message.

"You should go up there and let the UnSuited know the plan . . . I think it's time we unite everyone and prepare them for tomorrow—and you should be the one to deliver it." Ashton froze next to him.

"Wolfe I don't—"

"You can do this; speak from the heart." Wolfe unwrapped himself from her, tugging away and toward the center of the camp's spacious room. Ashton only nodded as she took a deep breath, mentally preparing herself.

"Can I get your attention, please!" he shouted. Ashton's heart skipped a beat. "Attention!" His voice boomed and the crowd silenced. "I'd like to introduce Ashton, JR105. Some of you know her by various aliases, but today she is Ashton, leader of the UnSuited revolution." Wolfe turned to Ashton, motioning for her to come forward.

She did. Her footsteps felt heavy, and she thought she'd faint. After so many speeches, she should be used to this, but those were memorized and drafted for her. Wolfe wanted something from the heart. Something that would inspire them. Ashton's palms were sweating profusely as she stepped closer to Wolfe, who gave her a reassuring smile before stepping behind her and giving her center stage. He was close enough to let her know he was there, but far enough to give her the podium. The room went quiet as the buzzing died down and all eyes remained focused on her.

Ashton cleared her throat. "Hello." She started, and took a deep breath. "You may not know me, but like Wolfe said, I am Ashton, worker number JR105. No last name, like you, just a number born and raised to be just that . . . a disposable worker. And for some time, I actually thought I was okay with it. In my own world at Maya Bay, working at The Hook with my childhood friend Niall, life could have stayed that way. But I was forced to leave, and my journey took me here, actually— Land of Legends, a new customer amusement park that showed me the darkest side of this industry. Out there, they killed innocent people on that battleground—for sport. Young, old, crippled . . . it didn't matter because we don't matter." Images of Sheva and Jagatha popped into her head as she continued on.

"But we do matter. And I realized that after I saw my friend Sheva, defenseless, waiting for a Suit to strike her down and take her life on this very battlefield. And instead of standing by, I decided I wouldn't let them take her from me. I wouldn't allow them to deem her life worthless and expendable.

"After that moment, I began to see the depths of Augland 54's cruel and vicious underbelly—CEO Warren's cages, his underground sweatshop, and his Customer Service Initiative." Ashton emphasized each word as if she tasted filth in her mouth. "Warren, Auglands, will never change and we will never be safe while he rules, which is why we are left with no choice but to fight. And we are fighting not just for us, but for all Augland workers."

"I've seen them—I've spoken with them across all Augnation. We want change—all of us, thousands of us. We want freedom, and we won't be silenced or cast out. But that means sacrifices will be made, and I won't lie to you. You've been lied to enough. They'll come tomorrow and President Warren will strike hard because he thinks he can break us. But he can't, and he won't because we will be ready."

Voices from the crowd began to rise as the people felt the same. She wasn't just speaking her story; she spoke theirs. The energy within the room changed. Smiles faded, but not because they were scared, but because they were ready. They were ready for revolution.

"Tomorrow, Warren will know one way or another. That workers of Augland 54, the UnSuited, will not be caged! We *will* be free." Claps erupted around her and workers jumped out of their seats, stood on chairs and tables, shouted and chanted. Ashton smiled as Wolfe stood beside her, a grin matching hers as he too began to join them.

"Freedom! Freedom! Freedom!"

"And tomorrow, we fight for that freedom!"

When the sun rose, their lives would change as it would be the beginning to the end; they just weren't sure which end would prevail.

CHAPTER 49

Ashton

LAND OF LEGENDS, AUGLAND 54

Ending the night on such a high note would have been perfect. Ashton's off-the-cuff speech was just what they all needed and injected more hope and inspiration than even Wolfe could have hoped for.

But then Bez and Joao showed up.

As soon as the excitement had peaked within the four walls of the Viking camp, Joao had hurried both Ashton and Wolfe out of the dining room and into the chilled, starry Land of Legends night.

"What is it?" Ashton asked.

"We finally got ahold of Rye. It took us awhile, but he finally got back to us." Joao avoided eye contact, which was a sure sign that something was wrong

"And?" Wolfe asked.

"He's backing out. Says Warren reached out with a deal he couldn't pass up." Joao shifted his feet uneasily, his words bitter with anger dripping from each word he spoke. They had all worked and sacrificed too much to get to this point and protect the STEMP from this kind of betrayal.

"A deal? And he trusts *that* man to keep his word?" Ashton referred to Warren, astonished that Rye could be so gullible.

"I guess so. Trust me, I had that and more to say to him, but he's adamant. Something about thinking of his people and what they went through last month under house arrest and the others who had to flee to the Colony. Warren apparently threatened to do much worse to NeuroEnergy if they even thought about supporting our rebellion," Joao continued.

Wolfe spun away from the group, shielding them from his untamable rage.

Ashton's mind reeled from the realization and betrayal. *How could he do this to them?*

Bez and Joao could only stare back at them, wordless, even though they both were perplexed by how Rye could switch his alliance.

"Warren hopes we surrender. He's backing us into a corner. He thinks that by breaking up our NeuroEnergy alliance and stopping STEMP, that will ensure a greater loss of our numbers . . ." Wolfe foreshadowed.

"Would he even save their lives if we surrendered?" Bez asked.

"Not a chance." Wolfe answered.

"Then, it's not even a question. We've always known Warren had the upper hand. But without STEMP, it makes things—"

"Impossible," Bez completed.

"More difficult," Wolfe corrected. "Suits aren't indestructible."

"But they are a weapon, and one that leaves no casualties and can keep attacking until we are all dead," Bez argued.

"There are more ways to win a battle than just manpower," Wolfe countered.

"So, what do we do now?" Ashton asked worriedly.

"We fight as hard as we can and pray we live to see another day. Then, we plan the next battle in this war," Joao said, siding with Wolfe.

Losing STEMP was a gut punch to Wolfe's strategy and Ashton's morale, but they couldn't act defeated, for the sake of the workers, they needed to move forward, display a united front and support them as they would be facing the opposition soon.

As night passed, the hype settled with the darkening of the Legend's sky. And as the sun rose the next day, so did the realization of what was about to happen. Joao and Bez had left hours earlier to get some much-needed shut eye before the day's events.

Neither Wolfe nor Ashton could sleep. The sun, obscured by a grey fog, hovered over the rolling, grassy hills. The day was quiet except for the whistling chirp of birds. Synthetic fog blanketed the space between grass and air, separating the Viking camp and the towering castle. In any other circumstance, this would be peaceful.

Ashton laid her head against Wolfe. "Be careful today. It's admirable to lead but don't be foolish," Wolfe said. Ashton agreed by a nod of her head. Just because she wasn't afraid to die didn't mean she didn't want to survive.

As if Warren himself could sense the peaceful nature of Legends and his goal in the world to disturb and disrupt, the moment came.

"Wolfe." Joao spoke over Wolfe's interconnect. "Augland security has been dispatched through the tunnel system. It looks like that is their plan of attack."

"Still, let's keep eyes on the engineering doors in case Warren splits his efforts," Wolfe replied. Joao was to lead the secondary attack while Wolfe led the first wave of infantry.

Wolfe looked at Ashton. "You ready?"

Was she? Ashton had never seen true battle before. Vikings versus the Saxons was staged and who knew if it was real or not. Ashton nodded.

"We should awaken the leads and prepare the workers to attack."

Wolfe scrounged for heavier clothes than he'd worn the previous day. While his clothing wouldn't help against a photon wound, they could give some protection against an attack from a knife. Ashton wore black clothing like the other workers, her hair was bundled up into a red bun, and her photon gun adjusted snugly across her body. Ashton slipped away to the bathroom for a moment of privacy while the others readied for battle. She glanced in the mirror to see that her eyes were sunken, most likely due to lack of sleep which made her faint freckles more prominent and her blue eyes popped against her ruby red hair.

Three photon fires sounded. Wolfe had said that would indicate when the first notice of Warren's men were near their barricade at the train station entrance. Ashton rushed from the room, running out onto the grassy meadow and toward hundreds of workers who had assembled. Against the green of the grass, they looked like a swarm of ants in their all-black worker uniform. No doubt Wolfe was already there, helping the squad leaders find their way through the plan of attack Wolfe had created.

As she approached the mass of workers, she walked from the back of the crowd, making her way to the front. Workers around her separated to make way for her. It was silent, completely different than the cheering chatter of the previous night's battle cries and comradery.

Ashton's grip tightened on her weapon. Her palms were sweaty. Her heart was pounding in anticipation. But what she didn't feel was fear. She had let go of that fear of death a long time ago.

She made it to the front. The group stationed there was a colorful combination of workers of different size and battle gear. Presumably, these workers had volunteered to be the front line. Ashton turned her gaze to each one. They showed no fear as their eyes met, and their mutual respect would bind them together, forever. Wolfe walked along the line of workers, stopping next to Ashton.

Boom!

The stack of chairs, table, and debris shook as Augland attempted their first strike at the barricade from the side of the train station exit.

"Get ready!" Wolfe shouted as Ashton readied her weapon.

Boom! Closer. This time, dust flew and debris tumbled from the wall of furniture, creating a gaping hole in the fifteen-foot barricade.

Wolfe glanced at Ashton and for a moment their eyes met. They both refused to say goodbye, and even dared the other to try and die.

Boom! Ashton nearly flew back this time as the push from the explosives nearly toppled a few of them. As the dust settled, so did the visualization of the gaping hole Augland explosives had created.

Within minutes the enemy began to walk in, like they didn't fear the UnSuited. Augland security, dressed in tailored dark green suits with the number 54 and with protective helmets began their advance. There was no way to tell if they were human or machine because they all looked the same. Wolfe's brow furrowed as he surveyed the enemy.

Seconds passed as they were paralyzed by the size and depth of the Augland army, but as they marched through, Ashton's instincts took over and she raised her gun in line with the enemy in sight.

Bang! She shot right for the heads of the leading enemy. The faceless man or Suit. He recoiled back and she stepped forward and shot again, and again, and then another time until the man—or Suit's—knees buckled, and he collapsed to the ground. Ashton breathed heavily, waiting for the thing to get up and fight, but nothing. Her eyes rose to the hundreds that now headed through the barricade's gaping hole.

Silence hung in the air for only a moment until photon fire erupted like wildfire around her. Ashton could feel rounds pass her in all directions. The Augland guards did the same and the fire across the grass ensued. Ashton brought her weapon back up, pointing and shooting, pointing and shooting, as she took small steps and the UnSuited rallied around her, doing the same. Their objective—allow no enemy through.

A nearby scream tore Ashton's attention away from her shooting. Looking to her left she saw a few members of the UnSuited down, bleeding from photon wounds. Looking right, she saw the same, and spotted Wolfe shooting one guard before taking his fists and hitting another that got too close. The guards and UnSuited fighting in close proximity now. There were too many of them. Ashton fired again, taking a step back now because the wall of green Suits were advancing on them.

Ashton shot, and shot again, and kept shooting but it seemed to do little good against the Augland army. Security guards were advancing more than they were falling and eventually they would run through the UnSuited rebellion.

We have to slow them down . . . they're coming in too quickly. The hole in the train station was ten feet wide, but what the guards hadn't touched was five to ten feet of debris still wedged together. If there was a way for her to help the remaining debris fall and close the hole, Augland forces would be forced to climb over the wall, giving the UnSuited time to target them one by one.

Ashton ran, her feet taking her before forward her mind could fully catch up with her plan. She had always been good at weaving around people, her small size giving her that advantage. Behind her, she could have sworn she heard Wolfe calling her name, but she didn't turn to see. She had one mission and that was to slow the attack on the UnSuited or they wouldn't last the hour. Ashton stood at the barricade, twisting her gun so it hung across her back and began to climb, placing her hand on the remaining chairs, tables, and steel beams of the train station opening.

Smoke from the photon fire rose and hovered near the top of the barricade wall, providing some cover for what she intended to do. From her vantage point, she could see that Augland 54 was beginning to overtake the UnSuited. The number of people she saw sprawled on the ground reminded her too much of the times she'd played Freya and acted out the battle between Vikings and Saxons, a memory she quickly banished from her thoughts. She had to keep going, she had to do this.

She moved quickly, all the way up, five feet, seven feet, ten feet, now fifteen feet until she was right above where Augland 54 troops were passing through. She looked at the remnants of the barricade still intact: piping, twin bunk beds, mattresses, chairs, and tables, all jammed together and resting against the steel beam outline of the train station opening. Ashton wedged herself between the furniture and the opening. With all her strength, she pushed against the debris, using her legs, but it nothing moved.

Refusing to give up, Ashton rotated her photon gun from her back and brought the butt of the gun down deep in between holes within the barricade makeshift wall. Positioning her back against the steel frame and the wall, again she pushed her legs against the debris and pulled as her weapon to loosen the debris in hopes that it would fall forward. The wall moved an inch but came back into its place.

Ashton inhaled, her muscles shaking at the effort it took. *Again!* she told herself. She did, and she screamed. An inch of movement, then another, and another before Ashton finally felt the debris at the top of the wall begin to wobble and fall. Her efforts were paying off as she grabbed for the steel frame and slipped down, now hanging from the opening as the debris fell and hit its mark, crashing down on Augland security and creating a five-foot partition for the guards to climb up and over the barrier. Ashton smiled as she saw the hemorrhage stop and the UnSuited begin formation again.

Ashton was brought back to her own predicament. Fifteen feet up and this drop could break bones. Her hands began to slip as she began shimmying to her right in hopes of getting closer to the steel frame where she could slide down.

"Ash!" She could have sworn Wolfe screamed her name.

Her hands began to sweat, and Ashton looked down, realizing that she wouldn't be able to make it. *It might not hurt so bad; it won't kill me, at least.*

"Surround the wall! Don't let them get over!" Wolfe shouted from below. "Hold on, Ash!" he yelled. Fear induced screams began then, *BOOM!*

Ashton's ears rang while piles of dirt and grass rained down on the UnSuited workers. "Grenades! Fall back! Fall back!" Wolfe shouted.

That was it, she couldn't hold on any longer. Ashton held her breath as the last strength she had to hold on slipped and she began to free fall. With her eyes were glued where her hands just were, she attempted to reach for the frame, even though she knew it was too late. She dropped and continued to fall.

Ashton braced herself for the impact she was sure wouldn't feel pleasant. And the anticipation she likely would be surrounded by Augland security.

BOOM!

BOOM!

Her back hit an Augland security guard now behind the wall she had just created—on the wrong side. The guard broke Ashton's fall and she rolled off of him as he lay motionless, clearly stunned by her falling on him. The wind was knocked out of her, and as she was catching her breath, another explosion followed by another . . .

Ashton scrambled to hide; her body hurt as she attempted to find cover from the enemy. She made it to the tunnel wall, where she could hide while dark green Suits began to back away from the front as a man shouted, "Send two more grenades and then cease fire!" Ashton didn't understand. Were they bombing and retreating?

BOOM! BOOM!

"Fall back!"

They did just that. Guards began retreating down the tunnel and disappearing into the darkness. Ashton was stunned, unsure of what to make of this. They weren't losing, especially after the bombs they had deployed, so why retreat? Did iHumanist, or Reuben, send help?

Ashton didn't hesitate; she limped up to a standing position and began climbing over the wall to the Land of Legends side, raising her arms up to show she wasn't the enemy. Ashton looked around at the damage, and there was *damage.* Limbs and blood everywhere and cries of desperation.

"Wolfe!" Ashton cried despite the ringing in her ears.

"Wolfe!" She shouted again. Ashton could see that like the grey fog from this morning, the Augland guards had disappeared.

"Ash!" Wolfe said, approaching her. "What's happening?"

He looked just as confused as Ashton felt.

He brought his interconnect closer to him as they both heard, "Wolfe! We are under attack! Behind the castle grounds, a second engineer door blown to bits! There's too many of them!" Wolfe's eyes widened as Joao reiterated what had happened at his location.

CHAPTER 50

Ashton

LAND OF LEGENDS, AUGLAND 54

Ashton's legs cramped as she ran full speed with Wolfe who was a few lengths ahead of her. The right side of her body ached from the fall at the barricade, but right now Joao and Bez needed help behind the castle grounds.

Ashton could hear Wolfe screaming into his interconnect, "Joao, answer me!" His tone became more worrisome at the continued silence.

Behind them, a quarter of the surviving workers, uninjured, trailed closely and were ready to fight. Some stayed back to protect the opening of the train station in case the Augland returned. They had just finished climbing a rolling hill when the castle came into view. Ashton's heart dropped as she surveyed the scene: flames, crumbled stone, and many dead UnSuited bodies.

She would have presumed the battle was over if it weren't for the sparks of photon fire on the other side of the castle near the forest perimeter wall. Wolfe and Ashton had the same idea, bolting for the north side of the castle to help the remaining UnSuited.

On the north side: screams, fire, and smoke created a layer of chaos that confused everyone. A group of Augland guards were firing weapons, forcing Wolfe to target them. Ashton followed.

Joao shouted and caught Ashton's attention. He was directing several workers to hold off the enemy near the castle. Shot after shot. Wolfe instructed his UnSuited to follow Joao's orders and surround the Augland security near the forest entrance.

Ashton pointed her rifle and shot, then shot again. Anger rose deep within her because with each flash of her photon gun, the bodies of the dead UnSuited were illuminated on the battlefield. It was all so horrifying, destructive, and senseless. She had felt hate and anger like this before—often with Warren as he sought total domination and control. Ashton couldn't take it anymore. She wouldn't let him win *this* game—not against innocent people.

She moved closer to the edge of the forest without realizing it. She wanted Augland to hurt, to spill as much blood as they had bled from the UnSuited.

"Ashton, what are you doing, get back!" Wolfe yelled, but she wouldn't listen. She was slowly treading closer and closer, pointing and shooting. Pointing and shooting.

Wolfe caved, seeing that even the other UnSuited followed, forcing Warren's men to retreat. "Attack! Push them back into the forest!" Wolfe shouted.

The battle had turned from a mosh pit of guards versus UnSuited to a sick game of hide and seek, with the foliage of thick trees to hide behind.

Ashton's pace slowed as she scanned the area around her and walked carefully on the forest ground. Smoke surrounded her. Photon shots and screams in the distance were a constant reminder that danger was still lurking, so she stayed alert. The Augland guards had spread out, as did the UnSuited army. Before long, Ashton was alone.

Minutes passed and the further she moved away from the castle grounds and into enemy territory, the more Augland guards she took down. She stepped from behind a tree to see a green-suited guard dart away. It felt just like hunting in the Olympics with Wolfe.

She shot, hit.

It was strange how the need to survive and support the UnSuited had changed her outlook so quickly. She had felt such guilt when she had accidently killed a guard during her tunnel escape, but this was life or death—her people or Warren's. That alone caused her to react outside of her moral compass. Or, maybe when the sun disappeared and the battle was over, she would hate herself for taking lives with such abandon.

"Drop it." *Click.* Ashton stilled her movements immediately, knowing the threat that corresponded with his tone. She glanced to the side where the voice came from and a guard in dark green walked out from behind a tree.

She quickly shifted positions, raising her own rifle and pointing at her enemy.

He paused before lifting his helmet from his head, exposing his identity. Ashton's eyes went wide. She recognized him instantly. The green-eyed guard from the tunnels. The one who had followed Warren's orders and commanded the deaths of workers seeking refuge.

Her expression must have given away her thoughts as his emerald-green eyes brightened in mutual recognition. He would relish the chance to exact revenge for her making his mission fail. "So, you remember me."

Her grip on her weapon tightened and she shot, but Green Eyes ducked behind a tree.

"Yeah, I remember," Ashton spat.

He then appeared with, gun raised, but Ashton quickly sidestepped behind her nearest tree trunk before his fire could hit its mark. "Warren was livid when you got away and killed fifteen of my men. I nearly lost my status as a security guard commander."

Ashton remained quiet, she could care less about how Warren felt or how it impacted this man. "And what will he think when you lose a battle against the UnSuited rebels? He may need to reconsider the qualifications of the people he puts in charge." She took a chance to fire at the commander—*miss.*

Green Eyes laughed out loud. "Have you and I been fighting in the same battle? If you can even call it that. Your workers fell so easily to just a few Augland units at the outside entrance to Legends. If you think that little skirmish was rough, wait till you see what Warren has planned next! It's going to bring your rag-tag gang of misfits to their knees. Although, I will say, I'm not sure how you knocked out our comms, even if only temporarily." The man shot at the tree Ashton still hid behind. *That was definitely Reuben.* "You know, I bet I'd be in Warren's good graces again if I brought you back—you or his son."

She swore she heard the rustling of tree branches, so Ashton came out from her tree pointing her gun and ready to fire, but the green-eyed guard was gone. She took a step forward, then another. But she couldn't hear anything except the distant sounds of photon fire.

Ashton's breath quickened. This didn't feel right; she could sense he was near. Something told her to turn and run. Ignoring her instincts, Ashton took another step and another. Then, a gun suddenly rested against her temple, making her freeze.

"Gotcha . . . now drop your weapon."

Ashton didn't have a choice. She put her rifle down, thinking of ways she could get out of this one. He was quick, but so was she.

"Kneel, down on the ground."

Ashton did as she was instructed.

"Dead's easier than alive. Say goodbye, Ashton JR105."

She didn't feel anything. She mostly felt numb, except for feeling regret that she hadn't said goodbye to Wolfe when she had the chance. Ashton closed her eyes, ready for her fate and praying that the UnSuited would prevail against the odds.

She heard footsteps, followed by a grunt and then a shot. Ashton kept her eyes shut as she sensed more guards had surrounded her, their shout drowning out all other sounds. She opened her eyes and again, found that fate had chosen a different path for her.

With a sudden stream of nearby gunfire, Ashton instinctively ducked down. Augland guards materialized from the woods, retrieving Green Eyes who no longer held a gun to her head. She stood up and was passed a photon rifle by an UnSuited rebel who had appeared. Though covered in blood from a fresh photon wound, she was down but not out of the fight.

Fate had turned her situation in a matter of seconds and the Augland guards retreated behind them with Green Eyes scowling.

Silence filled the air as the threat of an attack was gone. Ashton could breathe again. She inhaled as relief set in. Ashton had thought she was going to die. "Thank you . . . you saved my life." The UnSuited worker replied, "Thank Joao, he's one that found you."

A look of surprise on Ashton's face couldn't be hidden. She looked around for the towering ex-security officer turned close friend. But, no Joao. Ashton then noticed three UnSuited who hovered nearby. "Joao?" Ashton whispered.

Someone had brought down the green-eyed guard moments before Augland guards had carted him away. There was a shot fired by their commander that was meant for her . . . the realization hit, and her eyes discovered what her mind would beg her to unwind and re-do. Ashton pushed forward through the three UnSuited. Lying face down two paces in front of her—she couldn't believe it.

Her knees buckled and she crawled toward the body. Tears came without warning as she carefully rolled him over so his back rested on the forest ground. Despite blood and dirt smearing his features, she could see that it was still Joao. Ashton placed her hand on his chest where the photon wound bled, directly over his heart. Ashton's eyes shut, not attempting to control her sobs.

"Oh, Joao, no . . . please no," she said through jagged sobs, but she knew it was too late. She knew he was gone.

"Joao, where are you? Looks like they've retreated. Confirm on your end." She could hear Wolfe's muffled voice over the interconnect that was attached to Joao's belt. A second wave of pain rippled through her as she thought of Wolfe—his best friend now dead, after saving *her* life.

Time stood still as she grabbed Joao's hand, placing it in hers. "I'm so sorry, Joao. I'm so very sorry." She spoke like he could hear her, desperate for him to tell her that everything was okay.

"What should we do?" an UnSuited man behind Ashton asked. Ashton wiped the tears from her face, unable to look at him because she was barely holding herself together.

"Let's take him back to camp." She wouldn't leave him here, he deserved better than that. Ashton took his interconnect and let the UnSuited pick up her friend and carry him out of the woods. There was only silence as they made their way back to UnSuited territory.

In the woods, it was quiet and surreal. Back between the castle and Viking camp, destruction was everywhere. Fires had burned the pristine grass, now full of craters created by a barrage of grenades. The entire south side of the castle had collapsed. Ashton walked behind the men who carried Joao. Her hands trembled as they drew closer to the Viking camp. She thought of Bez, her best friend, and how much this would devastate her. The two people she loved most in this world would be destroyed once they learned of Joao's death—and that chipped away a piece of Ashton.

"Where are you?" Ashton's voice cracked over the interconnect, speaking to Wolfe.

"Ash? Oh, thank God you're okay." Relief filled his voice—a feeling she knew would be short-lived once he realized why she had Joao's interconnect. "Are you with Joao?"

Ashton didn't want to answer, "Wolfe, I—Joao didn't make it." Her words were painful to even speak and the silence on the other end, telling.

Day turned to night and the UnSuited picked up the raggedy pieces of their failed first attempt at a revolution. There were hundreds dead and the realization that they likely couldn't take another hit was debilitating to their morale. Solemn faces smeared with ash from the Augland bombs huddled around fire pits and inside tents. It was a vast difference from the previous night when they had hope and determination. Ashton diverted her eyes. One minute she had a gun against her temple, feeling numb and now she couldn't silence the typhoon of emotional devastation she was feeling—the loss of Joao's life.

All the dead were brought to a designated area near the Viking camp—Joao among them as Wolfe, Ashton, and Bez would not leave his side. Bez hadn't said a word since finding out. Her eyes were bloodshot from crying. Neither Wolfe nor Bez had asked how it happened. It would destroy Ashton to expose the truth because the guilt alone was hard to bear.

Wolfe's hand glided down to Ashton's, the only sign that he, too, needed comfort. He hadn't cried or screamed. He was silent and Ashton wasn't sure which was worse. Joao was his lifelong friend and the only person he trusted, besides her.

This broke him. His soul could handle only so much, and she knew exactly what this loss felt like.

She squeezed his hand as tears rolled down her cheeks as a large trench was dug for those lives lost.

Wolfe's interconnect dinged and Wolfe's eyes became glued to its message.

Without saying a word, he handed it to Ashton, displaying a message from Warren, as he looked back up toward the mass burial.

That was just a taste of what you can expect . . . so, graciously, I'm giving you a choice. Surrender and this all goes away. Continue, and you all die—and for what?

To be continued . . .

ACKNOWLEDGMENTS

First, I must thank my family for all the support they provide. I don't think I'd have the strength to put myself—or my work—out there without your relentless positivity.

My father, who has been my sounding board for all things Augland since day one of world building. I know you won't believe it, but this book wouldn't be the same without our think tanks, technology conversations, and overall storyline conversations. I come up with my best plot developments during those calls.

My husband: thank you for always believing in me, uplifting me during times of doubt or struggle, and dreaming alongside of me during this endeavor.

My son, my sisters, my mom, nieces, and nephews, and all the Reikows: thank you for always being my number one fans.

My editors: Elisabeth, Emma, and Arlyn and Chelsea at Inspira Lit, you all make Augland what it is today. There aren't words to express my gratitude for the love and care you put into each chapter, character, and Augland.

Finally, the readers who have fallen in love with the story of Ashton and Wolfe, nearly as much as I have, and have encouraged me to continue building the Augland story. I wouldn't have done this without you.

ABOUT THE AUTHOR

Erin Carrougher is a Pacific Northwest-based author whose dystopian novel series, *Augland*, is set in Seattle's technology focused future. This is her third book in the *Augland* series, and undoubtedly will not be her last. By day, Erin is a Sales Manager at an Information Technology company and by night, a dystopian fanatic. When she's not fantasizing about futuristic corporate takeovers using artificial intelligence, you'll find her spending precious time with her husband Joe, son Tobias, family, and friends. In her spare time, she enjoys reading fiction, cooking, and binge-watching reality television.

www.ingramcontent.com/pod-product-compliance
Lightning Source LLC
Chambersburg PA
CBHW061537190726
48289CB00004B/1080